Hear No Evil

The Book of Axel

The Brother Disciples

(Them Kentucky Boys)

Written by Tiana Laveen
Edited by Natalie G. Owens
Cover Layout by Travis Pennington

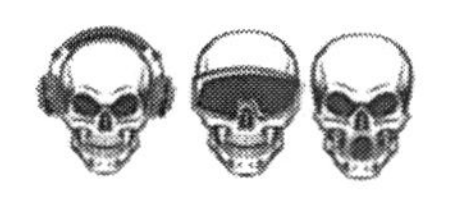

The Brother Disciples Series

Hear No Evil—The Book of Axel – 1

See No Evil—The Book of Legend – 2

Speak No Evil—The Book of Caspian – 3

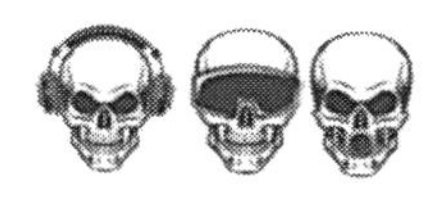

Three best friends—Axel, Legend, and Caspian, 'The Brother Disciples'—embark on a journey to find their karma and wrestle it to the ground. Each has been tasked to make good on a promise, and in that process, all heaven and hell breaks loose.

Book One:
The Brother Disciples – Hear No Evil

The Book of Axel

(Run up, and get done up.)

"What you think of me is pointless.

How you experience me is poignant…"

– Axel Hendrix

BLURB

Axel Hendrix is six feet, three inches of lean muscle and mischief. Born and bred in Portland, Kentucky, he is a sight to behold, covered from his neck to his ankles in tattoos and scars—both on the inside and outside. Industrious and quick-thinking, he eagerly works a grisly job that requires a stomach for the morbid and macabre: a crime scene cleaning business.

But now, Axel has attracted trouble with a capital 'T' by witnessing something he cannot unsee and drawing a target on his back. In over his head, he attempts to fulfill a promise, make peace with his inner demons, and get his life in order by eliminating the threat looming over him. But even a stone-hearted man like him has his krypton-ite…

Enter English Price.

English is already aware of Axel's reputation. Seeing him in the flesh sends unexpected chills and thrills up and down her spine. In spite of the instant chemistry, she refuses to give in to his lure. Besides, bad boys are bad news, and she's had enough unsavory situations in her life to write a book. The brief chapter of rough neck men is closed, never to be re-read again.

But from the moment they meet, a chain of events is set in motion, and the attraction cannot be denied. Their future is already written in stone.

Come along on a dark, twisted ride chock full of pain, payback, and passion. Axel has three assignments, and he plans to pass them with flying colors…

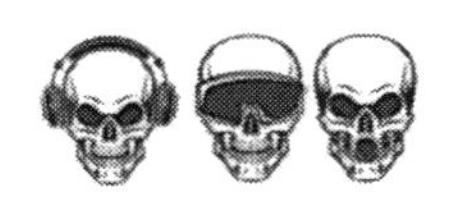

Hear No Evil -

The Book of Axel

COPYRIGHT

This book is rated:

BDE

BIG DICK ENERGY

This novel is sponsored by – (FAFOF)

The Fuck Around and Find Out Foundation

(Changing lives, one blast to the ass at a time)

This book is intended for mature readers only.

A part of me loathes providing these warnings, and some may deem them unnecessary, but at the end of the day, they are a courtesy to those not familiar with my work. The last thing I want to do is contribute to someone being blindsided or triggered by any material on these pages. I cannot predict or control a reader's personal experience, interpretation, or level of enjoyment of this book, but I can alert you of possible jarring subject matters. So, if the content doesn't bother you, that's awesome, let's ride, but just in case it may, here ya go:

This novel includes:

1. Profanity, and lots of it

2. Discussions of domestic violence

3. Graphic sexual encounters

4. Descriptions of death (Some explicit)

5. Alcohol, nicotine, and illegal drug consumption and sales

6. Violence. Brutality. Serious ass kickin'.

7. Depictions of poverty and illness

8. Dialogue that depicts character(s) discussing abuse as minors

9. Racial conversations, and occasional racial slurs

Oh, one more thing: For those unfamiliar with my work, I purposefully write 'goddamn' as 'gotdamn.' It's an intentional spelling error. Just personal preference.

Let's continue…

TABLE OF CONTENTS

DEDICATION

My bestselling book that preceded this one, 'Black Ice,' dealt with many topics and characters, but one non-speaking yet important character in that novel was Diesel, a black wolf the hero profoundly connected with.

Some may think it's unrealistic to have a pet wolf, even in remote areas of the country, but that isn't true. In fact, I had a pet wolf from the age of eight, until I was a sophomore in college. My father received him as a puppy from a member of our family and brought him home to me.

I debated on dedicating 'Black Ice' to him, but I was happy with my original dedication in that book, and wanted to leave it as it was. Yet, I promised my own pet wolf, Monster, the dedication in *this* book, regardless of him crossing over the rainbow bridge so long ago.

Though this book in the Brother Disciples series, 'The Book of Axel – *Hear No Evil*,' doesn't depict a wolf as a character, it still applies, because Monster was like a brother to me, when I was an introverted child. He was a goofball, affectionate, protective. Greedy and lovable. With a jet-black coat, he had glowing golden eyes—so striking. At times, he was my only friend. He was a wonderful companion, and never hurt me. I do want to apologize to the neighborhood children, my peers at the time, who he terrorized by chasing them up the street, then breaking into a U-turn, for he saw it as a game of sorts, despite their screams of sheer terror.

Monster, I miss you terribly, and just like I promised, this book is dedicated to YOU.

Love Letter to My Readers

Greetings, readers. I am elated that you've selected to purchase this book and embark on another excursion with me. As stated on the product description page, as well as the beginning of this book, this is a three-part series. However, each is a standalone novel and can be read independently, although they flow better if read together, in chronological order. I have never considered myself a series writer, per se. I wrote the Saint series, for instance, by mere accident. I wrote the first book, and a second book sprang instantaneously from me, without much forethought, then, before I knew it, I was producing a seven-book series, half of those double novels.

I typically lean more towards double novels, consisting of one story divided into Part 1 and Part 2 for easier printing and readability due to length. I have done other series but find that it takes a certain writing mindset and for me, at least, it has to feel natural. That's why I have sometimes gone into series with five or six books in mind, and stop at three instead—not because I grew bored or tired of the series, but because it would have felt forced, or wasn't a practical business decision. This time, things aligned just right.

The idea for this series came to me and I had to run with it. The Brother Disciples series was a unique idea that revolved around three men with different lives, who knew each other since childhood, drawn together through personal challenges and tragedy, united by a central figure who helped guide and mold them—their saving grace. The purpose of this series is to show that grace and understanding can help cultivate awareness, as well as be a guiding light during struggles, encouraging healing and becoming the catalyst to a passionate romance.

All three men embark on different voyages that overlap one another. Book 1 features Axel Hendrix. Axel has a strong personality, natural leadership skills, and not much can get under his skin. He is used to life being difficult and ugly, and strong women in his life as well, such as his mother and sister, among others. So when he meets an incredible and beautiful woman possessing a quick wit and determination, he can't resist.

English Price is a sarcastic, feisty, lovable nerd. A Black woman keenly aware of her differences from many of her peers. She meets Axel at a time in her life when things in her life were challenging to say the least, and though their initial time together is brief, he leaves an indelible mark on her. As Axel tries to get through a series of strange and, at times, life threatening events, he has to lean increasingly on faith. Though the two seem at times an unlikely pair, they are perfectly suited, and Axel falls hard for her. English proves quickly that she isn't afraid of Axel, or his darkness. Rather, she bathes him in light.

She herself is not without her own challenges, and finds solace in Axel, who is the shoulder she never knew she needed. The two of them make something beautiful out of the ugliness and heartbreak they've endured in life, creating shadows from their contrasts, on the wall of love. Axel becomes her muse, and she becomes his obsession, their love being tested through it all.

This is a gritty love story that takes place in the beautiful state of Kentucky, where the grass is called blue, the bourbon is strong, and the horses of the renowned Kentucky Derby run faster than the speed of light. Curl up and get comfortable. There's plenty of whiskey and mint julep to go around. It's time you hear the tale of Axel and English, and before it's all said and done, this brother disciple may have you speaking in tongues…

Prologue

GLINTS OF SHATTERED light stretched across the serrated blade of the gleaming knife in my hand as I rotated it against my inner palm. The house floorboards repeated uneven crackles and truncated creaks from the prowler's weight crushing them.

I listened in the darkness of the small room that smelled of time gone by, and mothballs. I closed my eyes, my senses heightened. I could hear every breath, every step, and every thought in his fucking brain. A small, crooked fan blew in the corner of the bedroom, oscillating from side to side, forcefully flipping the pages of a nearby magazine to and fro, as if handled by a ghost frantically reading an article about the local graveyard. Everything was now acute. My life was on the line. Again.

Between the exhalations of the broken, rusty swing in the backyard swaying in the night wind, and the crickets in the overgrown blades of grass, there, in the chorus of the country nightfall, were the bastard's irregular sighs and pants between heavy breaths—the pointed exhales and inhales of a man afraid to do what he'd come to do. Kill me dead. He was in the life. Not me. I'd never spent a day in prison. Although I was far from being an angel—some joked I was an abomination, in fact. Yet here I was, pretending to be a sitting duck. How ironic. Shouldn't the vessel of fear be the prey?

Another chicken shit afraid of his own shadow…

I sat there. Waiting. Growing impatient. Picking up my cigarette, I studied the orange glow of the embers, then brought it to my lips. The smoke soon surrounded me like a pair of foggy feminine thighs, strangling me with their supple beauty and the promise of a killer good time. Placing the cigarette down, I listened…

The motherfucker tried to quiet his breathing. I knew it because I heard him swallowing and pausing, too. He opened one of the bedroom doors down the way, the one with all the junk in it. Minutes later, he withdrew from that unoccupied room, coming farther down the hall towards me. I heard his gun click. Now I had to reassess my options.

I could get up, go out into the hall, and rush him. I could kill him fast, and make the call to the cops slow. But I decided to just wait. To sit there. To meet him eye to eye. This was my fate. My fortune. It was either him or me. One of us had to go, and as far as I was concerned, I was too sinful to die so young. The flooring lent way to his bulk once again, groaning with each timed step.

He wasn't close, but he wasn't far. I looked around me, listening to him open more doors and creep around like some stinkin' roach in search of crumbs. The bedroom I sat in was pitch black, just as I liked it when I placed my head on this old, smashed pillow that smelled of mold. I took a toke of my cigarette again, listening to the breeze flow through the trees just beyond the window, and a dog bark in the vastness of the night. Placing the stub in the ashtray beside the mattress on the floor, I waited as he stepped toward me, slowing down as if to think things through.

Maybe he figured he was too loud and he needed to pace himself, thinking of me in here sound asleep. A sure advantage for him, so he could pump me full of bullets while I dreamt of Hell and wished for Heaven. This was my life—where my bad choices had brought me. I didn't ask for this, but they'd caught up to me. They *always* catch up with us…

It was perhaps providence, for all the harm I'd caused in the world. I had a business nobody else wanted to mess with, and I was making money hand over fist, a killin', as the head honcho. But just my luck, as soon as my life was getting better, the one thing I'd never want to happen in my line of work did happen.

I walked in on the wrong thing, at the wrong time. And then, I had to handle it right away. A door closed a bit too hard—the small closet by the bathroom—jarring me from my thoughts. My heart beat harder, faster, pounding in my chest like woofer speakers from the hillbilly dope boys that caroused the streets in their souped-up cars late at night, blasting the sounds of Yelawolf.

And then, things went quiet.

I swallowed an acrid taste of resentment the moment I'd heard the son of a bitch break the glass window minutes ago, and now, that horrid flavor burned my throat once again. Destiny wanted to party. I gave her a fake address, but she found me anyway, came over uninvited, and she'd brought along her bitch of a twin sister: Karma.

I could fuck them both at once.

The bastard stood right outside my door. The planks moaned beneath his frame as he became a fortress. Stiff. Unmoved. I imagined he was sweating. Wondering if I was awake. If I would make this easy, or hard.

I sat there thinking, too, full of hate and regret. I'd been careful, despite not being in my right mind at the time it all went down.

Due to being half out of my head on pain killers the last few days, the fucker trailed me home after I'd been discharged from the hospital. The bullet was removed from my arm, but the trouble was just getting started. I was pissed when I realized the same white car was driving past my house several times a day. Casing me. I checked my cameras and noted a big man with a mop of brown hair as the driver. I'd stepped into a hornet's nest, and now, the worker bees were coming out to play. I hadn't been out of the hospital for five damn days before I'd have to kill again.

Damn it.

Suddenly, he backed away from the door and made his way down the hall, the same direction from which he'd originally come. I wasn't falling for that shit... He wanted to lure me out. In all of my thirty-four years on this planet,

I ain't been stupid in even one of them.

There was only one way to get out of things such as this, and that was to be smarter and faster—beat them at their own game. So I made a few dubious social media posts about clearing out a spot in need of repairs. An old rundown house I was renovating. My side gig. This was that house.

I made it clear I was going to be alone, working for days on end. People told me to take it easy, to rest. What happened to me had been on the news after all, and my family and friends were concerned about me laying carpet, painting, and tearing down walls so soon after being shot. It was all horseshit. This big fish took the bait. Here, there were no cameras, no neighbors, no gas stations, and the electricity was shoddy at best. The perfect spot to take someone out. Out in the middle of nowhere.

Now, here he was. In the house. Stalking about, with one mission, and one mission only: to kill me on sight.

Trouble had come knocking, and I braced myself for it, dressed in a suit of perspiration and ire. The stale odor of spilled beer filled the air, and my body was soaked in liquid adrenaline. Thoughts of my crazy life flashed through my mind, making me spiral out of control.

He padded toward the door once again. The knob of the bedroom door rattled but couldn't completely turn as it was locked. I watched it jiggle a few times, with increasing pressure. I heard the deep breaths of frustration, and the exasperation spewing forth from the man with each passing moment. This was it. Someone was going to die tonight.

I counted in my head…

5…

4…

3…

2…

1.

BOOM!

The door burst open and there stood a hulking man, his silhouette black as the darkest of nights. He stood there for a second, as if expecting me to do something, and then, he charged me, gun in hand, firing away.

But it was too late.

"AHHHH!"

I ducked down as he tripped over the clear fishing wire I'd tied and secured from one end of the room to the other. He fell hard, hitting the floor like waves of thunder. Leaping off of the mattress like a jackrabbit with wings, I crashed down on him, jamming my knife into his neck, over and over, until my hand grew tired. He struggled to get up and wailed and screamed each time I sank that blade into his thick skin. His voice vibrated through me like an airplane taking off the runway. He could kiss the smooth landing goodbye.

Spurts of blood pumped from his throat in a fast, delirious stream. I pulled the string on an old marmalade-colored lamp, then stood over him. His small eyes began to roll in the back of his head, and that crimson puddle of blood turned into a lake, then a ruby red river right before my eyes. He shuddered as his body went into shock. I calmly stepped away, placed the knife down on the mattress, and grabbed my cigarette. Wasn't much left.

I sat back down on that mattress, grabbed my now warm beer, and sipped it, savoring it like a fine wine. I smiled at him as he lay there shaking, dying, his blood all over my denim shirt, my fingers dripping with his essence.

"You shouldn't uh come here. I suppose that's crystal clear to you right now." I sucked my teeth, shook my head, then gulped the rest of that beer down before tossing the bottle aside. "I'm supposed to be at home, resting, but instead, I'm playing a game of cat and mouse with *you*. I was just doing my job, man." I shrugged. "I wasn't there for none of the shit y'all were into. Try to turn a new leaf, and someone throws a whole gotdamn tree at ya."

The piece of shit just kept gurgling, trying to reach for his neck to stop the overflowing blood, but couldn't gather the strength. "Your friend pulled a gun on me, man, and I pulled one on him." I shrugged. "Simple as that. Ain't my fault I shoot faster, and he shoots like a blind bullfrog."

There was a helpless groan from the mound of dying pulp. "No need in you exerting yourself like that. You're a water sprinkler at this point. You've got penetrating neck trauma." I took a small drag from my cigarette and tapped the ashes on the floor. "Pharynx damage. I bet there's some vascular troubles, larynx disruption… maybe even trachea and esophagus hemorrhaging, too. I got you pretty good if I say so myself, but it'll take a full exam to be sure. I should've been a doctor. Don't you think so, too?"

I laughed as he lied there, desperately trying to live,

grasping for his last breaths.

"If another one of you shows up, and I 'spose one, two, or three will, I'll deal with them, too. Y'all think you can come here and get one over. Think a country boy like me is going to be ill-equipped or run scared. I ain't running from shit. This is *my* turf." I casually glanced at my watch, then reached for a tiny bottle of whiskey—one of those cheap ones from the liquor store that fill a big bourbon barrel next to a display of loosies and no-name cigars. Cracking the tin cap, I tossed it aside and chugged it down. When I was finished, he wasn't moving anymore.

His eyes were fixed on me, and mine on him. His fingers no longer trembled and twitched, and his mouth was ajar. Spit and blood poured from between his lips, blending with the blood all around him. I sat on that mattress for at least another twenty minutes, stroking my beard and yawning before reaching for my phone and making that call.

"This is 911, how may I help you?"

"Howdy, ma'am. My name is Axel Hendrix. I got a property over here I'm fixin' up on 1872 Banks Street. An intruder entered this home tonight, so I sent him home, too. To meet his maker. Please send the police when ya can. Thank you, kindly…"

Chapter One

"I DON'T NEED it." Axel snuffed out his cigarette in the black plastic ashtray, hacked, then sat back down in his brown leather recliner. Grabbing the remote control, he scrolled the channels until he found the basketball game he wanted to watch. His nostrils flared as he inhaled hard. The room smelled of smoke and freshly brewed Colombian coffee. It felt nice to settle down in the living room of the house he'd worked so hard to obtain. It was a modest sized dwelling, newly built on a large plot of land. Now, his peace had been interrupted. Mama was on the warpath.

"Axel, you call to see if they have that prescription ready right now! You're fixin' to send me to an early grave. I thought you'd outgrown this crap. First you had that situation with that man at your job, now *this*."

"I'm not about to stand there and just take a bullet, Mama. What d'you expect me to do? Try to dodge it like I'm Neo from the Matrix?"'

"That's not what I mean, and you know it."

"Well, it sure sounds like it."

"I thought that Keno Wreath guy's name was Nemo in that movie?"

"Naw. Nemo is a cartoon fish. And it's Keanu Reeves…What other options did I have though, Mama? Got nothin' to do with outgrowing anything. It's about survival."

He untied his long, dirty blond tresses from the low bun, tossing them over one shoulder. His hair came down to the bottom of his back and required more shampoo than he cared to admit.

"I wish you didn't have this company, Axel. It's attracting the wrong folks. I'm proud of ya, don't get me wrong… you went 'nd got training, and started your own company, made somethin' of yourself. But it's a gruesome profession that wears you down. All that death. It's not natural."

"Mama, ain't nothin' more natural than births and deaths. It's part of life." He shrugged. "You get used to it." He looked at the television but didn't focus on the screen.

"You should *never* get used to a thing like that. Just like when your Uncle Ronnie came back from the war in Iraq. He was never the same." He smacked his lips and closed his eyes. "If you think about it, you got the same thing going on, only you ain't out in a foreign country, honey. It's in your own backyard." *Here she goes being dramatic…* "Things was bad enough when you were growin' up, and now, you get calls all times of the day to go trouncing around the 'Ville, cleaning up blood and guts. That has to wear on you."

He opened his eyes and adjusted himself.

"Not really." Lighting a fresh cigarette, he blew rings of smoke in the air and thought about taking a good snooze soon. He rarely had the pleasure of taking mid-afternoon naps. He couldn't recall the last time he'd enjoyed one.

"I don't believe that. I don't believe that one bit. I think you tune things out, find the 'OFF' switch, and twist it… just like when you were little. I'm worried about these folks trying to hurt my child, and I'm worried about you in this line of work, because that's what started it all."

"Been doing it for seven years. Damn good at it, too." He'd ditched the low paying construction gigs and seasonal handyman jobs, and decided to get into a trade. It also afforded him the opportunity to buy property and flip it. His life changed in ways he'd only previously dreamed of.

"Well, you can do other things, Axel, and be good at them, too. You're real good at fixin' stuff. How about you—"

"Mama, this *is* me fixin' stuff." He leaned forward and peered out his living room window. His neighbor, Henry McGromer, an older White guy with dull gray hair and thick-rimmed glasses who lived across the street, was pulling grocery bags out of his trunk and heading to his front door. There seemed to be a whole lot of beer. Either Henry was planning on getting smashed, or he was going to be having an epic party. Axel bet on choice #1. The man's wife had recently left him. Despite barely knowing him, Henry had told him the whole sordid story while in a drunken stupor one night, as he was outside fixing his motorcycle.

"Don't you get sick and tired of the police snubbin' you? You told me what happened that one time. They treat you like some janitor."

"That's not a constant thing. I don't just get calls from the police, OSHA, and the EPA, I get called to just regular ol' houses, too. People who have died in their beds and the family wants to get some closure."

"Closure? I think the death is closure enough if you ask me. You can't get more final than that."

"No, death is just the beginning. Mama, when I get the calls from families, it gets more personal. This isn't no owner of a big high-rise, or the cops at the scene of a head-on collision with fatalities. This is someone's home. A family. They want the smell of death out of the livin' room so the kids can stop crying. Once you smell that odor, you never forget it, and you're in constant mourning. The memories lock together, wearing on folks' psyche. They want it gone, so they can pretend for a lil' while, be in denial that their loved one is really gone. Take it away… all of it.

"The indentation removed from the cushion where their aunt, uncle, mother or father died. The blood splatter off the walls if they blew their brains out when the walls of life caved in on 'em. The piss, shit, and vomit obliterated if they were bedridden or sick. I come in and try to make it like it was before all the bad stuff happened. Probably better. I'm a human magic eraser, Mama. I've got a six-man crew that I trained myself. My standards are high, and that's why I'm the top rated in the entire state of Kentucky. Can't no maid, professional housekeeping service, or fancy carpet cleaning machine do what I do even if they tried. I think what I do is a form of fixing things, too. Just like I said. It doesn't have screws, bolts, chains, engines and gears, but it's still a repair. It makes a difference, and I'm the man for the job."

Mama was real quiet on the other end for quite some time. He imagined the wheels in her head were spinning hard. She'd been disgruntled about his profession since he'd started his company: *'Clean Start Cleaning Crew.'* Many probably wouldn't like the notion of it, which tended to make people feel queasy and uneasy. Hazmat suits, special disinfecting solutions, goggles, masks and gloves… He did play down to her just how grueling it could get sometimes, but it was necessary. Just like air to breathe.

"I know you told me before, but I still can't understand it completely, Axel. How in the world did this all get started? I'm asking because I want you protected. I'm mighty worried."

A commercial came on, and he turned the channel. He paused on a station showing a trailer for some action movie starring Dwayne Johnson. There was no reason for Mama to hear this story again. She'd had him tell her a million times, and he told her the same things, in the same way he would have explained to the police. Mama likened herself to a detective of sorts. Perhaps she was genuinely interested, or more likely, trying to find plot holes and accuse him of holding onto pertinent information.

"Just like I told you before, Mama, it all started when I was called to a scene to clean, over there on 32ND Street. When I got inside, there was a man in a business suit. Never seen him before in my life. He was holdin' a bottle of bleach and I could already smell it in the air. He'd been pouring it all over. He looked at me in my hazmat suit, flashed a smile, and pulled out his gun to shoot. Without a moment's hesitation, I grabbed my pistol and aimed for his forehead. Perfect shot." A flash of the clean hole in the middle of the guy's dome entered his mind. He wasn't happy about what he'd had to do, but wasn't exactly sad about it, either. "I'm just glad I was alone, and nobody else got dragged into this shit."

"Why in the world would you have a gun with your hazmat suit?"

"Mama, I don't go anywhere without the hammer. Heat stays on me like hot sun on a metal slide." He heard her utter a long exhale, then groan. "Anyway, I had no idea who I'd killed until it was all said and done."

"Well, I didn't appreciate finding out about all of this on the news! They say he was a dangerous person!"

"Yeah? Who is they?" He turned back to the game.

"The reporter! Some sort of drug smuggler. Lord, Jesus."

"Aren't we all dangerous under the right circumstances, Mama?"

"I'm not in the mood for any of your mind games today, boy. What did the police say that man's name was again?"

"Chase Evanston, and he isn't even from around here.

Come from Texas. Houston, I believe. He sold cocaine and fentanyl. Lots of it. He was a big player from my understanding. Too big to not be missed." He glanced at his pain pills. Only a few were left, but he refused to take them, much to his mother's dismay. He turned back towards the television.

"Who called you to do that job? The landlord of the building?"

"No. The police called me after their investigation to get the brain matter and blood out of the place. They finished their investigation."

"I watched the news and didn't remember seeing any guy like him around here, Axel."

"Who? Chase? I said he was from Texas."

"No, the one you were sent to clean up after. Not the one you shot, but the other one. The reason you were there in that building in the first place." Mama started coughing, then drank her coffee.

"Guy named Paul Hudson. Ruled initially a suicide. I was called to do a job. Just another day in my work life, or so I thought."

I'd taken down a shark in a small pond. Disrupted the feeding frenzy. Now, I've upset some folks I don't even know. He had something to hide, tried to clean it up, but he didn't seem to know he was too late, and he had no business being there in the first place. You pull a weapon out on me, you better use it and not miss. I could not give a flying squirrel fuck who you are.

"I called you so many times after that! I was worried sick, especially when I couldn't get a hold of you. Found out you were in surgery to get that bullet out your arm.

The doctor said you didn't want to be heavily sedated. I swear you some sort of sadist."

I tuned out the noise and did what I had to do. I hear no evil…

"You know how I feel about medication 'nd such. The whole reason we've been arguing today. Prescription refill…" *They can shove those pills right up their buttholes. I can't be doped up all damn day. I have work to do.* He yawned.

"I'm glad the police didn't give you any trouble, Axel. You've come a long way, and I didn't want them thinking my boy was involved in this. Drugs 'nd such." He could hear Mama sucking her teeth, and could just picture her shaking her head the way she often did when distressed. His mouth tightened as he grinned, imagining her holding her old cellphone that barely held a charge, and yet she refused to upgrade it to a newer model, even when he offered to pay for it. He figured her hair was as it typically was, parted down the middle, with gray and blond straight strands that hit her shoulders. Mama wore thin framed blue reading glasses most of the day that accentuated her bright sapphire eyes. There was a permanent gash on the side of her head from when her father had thrown a flowerpot at her during one of his manic rages when she was seventeen.

Mama had daddy issues, she said so herself, and she always chose bad men—his father being among them. Nevertheless, she got rid of them fast, too, never letting the milk get rancid once it turned sour. Refused to be a mistress. Refused to be used and lied to and be a punching bag. He respected the hell out of her, despite their occasional bumping of heads. That was his mama, and he loved her with all his heart and soul.

"They better not turn around and try to arrest you, Axel." She blurted the words as if the notion had been keeping her up all night.

"My situation was ruled a self-defense killing, but see, these folks this guy ran with are upset not just because I shot him, but 'cause now the police know this was no suicide after all. He'd killed him."

"Axel, they need to put you in witness protection! You're my only son! Oh God, I swear if you'd just—"

"Mama, I'm not scared of these people. He tried to destroy evidence, including me, since I became a witness. I've seen far worse in my lifetime than him and his little druggie squad. He's a dime a dozen. Hell, I've got friends that work in his 'industry,' and they'd put him to shame."

It was a bunch of bullshit. Instantly, my name was wrapped up in this crap like a burrito. I'd never sold narcotics a day in my damn life, and I'm no drug user, either. Never been convicted of a felony, either. I've done enough unscrupulous things in my life to understand how these things work, though. Definitely not an angel, but I know right from wrong. The police looked at me sideways after the second murder. Again, self-defense, as if I had anything to do with this shit. I was minding my business. Had to kill the drug dealer, and the guy sent to kill me, too. Wasn't about to wait around after a call to 911.

The police had the boldness to say to me, 'Well, Axel, you don't seem too shook up about it.'

You motherfucker… I clean up gore for a gotdamn living! Why in the hell would I be moved by this?! I see death on a daily basis, for God's sake. Don't bring no slow drawin' water gun to the O.K.

Corral. Knuck if you buck.

"Axel, what if they're not done?" Mama's voice trembled, interrupting his thoughts.

"I'll handle it. We've all got enemies. Some just fall off the rails faster than others."

"I wish you'd listen to your doctor, if not to me, Axel. You're moving around like nothing happened. Take those pills!"

"Not this again… Mama, I can't just ball up somewhere in a corner feeling sorry for myself, and not move another muscle. Bills still need to be paid, and I have employees. They have families. They gotta eat."

"Axel," Mama's voice got shrill, "if you don't stop boppin' around everywhere, you're going to land yourself right back in the hospital. The doctor said that arm of yours needs to be still. You had to defend yourself against an attacker, again, and if bad luck was a lady, you'd be three-times divorced, and engaged to another. Now you're off the pain pills, which is against doctor's orders. I understand you were concerned about getting addicted to them, son, but I could tell you were hurtin' when I came by yesterday. You have refills. Get them. That's all I'm saying."

"No pain, no gain. Mama, I appreciate your concern, but I'm just fine. You can stop your worrying. That goes for Dallas, too. Your partner in crime."

"Ohhh, don't you start! You should feel blessed you've got a sister who cares about you like she does! 'Specially after how you did her when you two were little!"

"She come calling here this morning, waking me out

of a sound sleep." He reclined in his seat, praying the conversation would end soon. He hated talking on the phone, especially to his mother. More times than not, she was worried about something he said or did, and trying to force him to make promises he couldn't and wouldn't keep.

"She's your sister, and she's worried about you, Axel. We all are."

"I appreciate your concern, Dallas' too, but it doesn't change nothin'."

"Axel, everybody needs help from time to time. I don't know why you act like you're the exception."

"Show me one time in history, Mama, when worrying solved a problem?"

Mama sighed, frustration shining through. "I'll let you go, but I'm coming by tomorrow anyhow, whether you like it or not." She chuckled.

He could hear her draw on her cigarette, then sip her coffee once again. It gave him a sense of comfort knowing that she was okay, and despite the conversation, in her happy place.

"Love you, Mama. I'll talk to you later."

"Bye. Love you, too." She disconnected the call.

He sat there, minute after minute, enduring a forced day off. Doctor's orders. He asked Alexa to play a some of his music, and mndsgn's, 'Rare Pleasure' started to play on low volume. He raised his arm and rotated it, working out the kinks. It hurt a lot less today. Picking up the remote, he channel-surfed. There was 'Money Heist,' on Netflix, but he feared being sucked in, unable to relax.

I need to watch something I don't care about. He kept changing the channels until he landed on an old black and white film, 'A Streetcar named Desire,' featuring Marlon Brando. Indulging another yawn, he rolled over to his side and pulled a thick white blanket over his body. It couldn't have been more than five minutes before he was sound asleep.

Chapter Two

IT HAD BEEN a restless night. What began as a slow ease into slumber soon turned tumultuous and strange. The constant tossing and turning, the awkwardly bent limbs that became dumb and prickly, and the sporadic gasping for air had gotten far out of hand.

"Damn it." He sat up in his chair. Angry. Weary. Tired. Even his eyelashes felt exhausted. He wiped the sweat off his forehead.

Finally get a day off, even though it's forced and through no choice of my own, and can't even manage any damn sleep.

He'd wanted to use this day to recoup, but his body and mind would not release him from exhaustion. Rising from the chair in a huff, he made his way to the bathroom near his home office, relieved himself, then splashed water onto his face. He looked into the toothpaste splattered mirror for a long while, still in a bit of a daze. He debated on returning to the comfortable chair and trying to rest once again, but decided against it, just in case it was the cause of the problem. So, he went to his bedroom.

The faint odor of leather from his new black jacket, sneakers, and boots greeted him. Boy, did he love it. Removing his shirt and tossing it on a black chair with a burnt orange blanket draped across it, he snuggled up under the dark gray sheets and thick black blanket that smelled of Gain fabric softener. The alarm clock said 9:42PM.

Axel's body felt as if it were floating. Half-conscious, he could feel himself dropping lower and lower into the upside-down clouds of inertia, and had no true control. Keenly aware he was sleeping, but also unable to wake himself, his extremities went from cool to hot, so he flung the blanket off his body. His muscles strained as he heeded an all-too-familiar voice.

His ears burned from the memory, singed with words of a time gone by.

"Axel. We've got some talkin' to do." He pulled at the edge of his pillow, brought it over his face to drown out the ruckus of his thoughts as his heart galloped. "Boy, I know you hear me. Listen to me…"

He fell deeper into the dream, a captive of his own subconscious. In a cloud of mist, a Black woman with a thick, kinky mane of dark brown tightly wound curls, pulled back with a light blue satin headband, regarded him. She sat up high on a golden and ivory chair so enormous, she looked like a doll in it. Her carob skin was smooth, wrinkle-free like a baby's, even though she had to be at least sixty years of age. Just how he remembered her…

Ms. Florence…

Wearing a pink smock dress, her legs reminded him of tree trunks as they hung over the chair, and her wrists were adorned with gold, silver and colorful bangles that clinked together every time she moved. Her bejeweled fingers sported all the colors of the rainbow. Large gold and diamond hoops hung from her lobes, and her broad mouth was painted bright red. When her lips parted, she showcased sparkling white teeth, most of them with gaps. He could smell her perfume—sweet and old fashioned, but pleasant, with a hint of spice.

His heart fluttered as she pointed at him with her long red fingernail. Talons that curled under, just as he recalled from so long ago.

"Axel, I'm talkin' to you. Do you hear me, boy?"

"Yes..."

"Good. Nap time is over."

But I haven't slept for more than ten minutes...

"You're a workaholic so no sleep to you shouldn't mean a hill of beans! This is important. Do you know why I'm here?"

"Because you're a hallucination, and I'm still apparently loopy and drugged up from that quack psychedelic medicine..."

"You can stop saying all of that foolishness. I see nothing has changed... still got that smart mouth of yours."

"But I'm not talking. These are just my thoughts. I'm dreaming. My lips aren't moving."

"Keep on, ya hear?! Be quiet! No, it's got nothing to do with any medicine, the one you refuse to take because you're too proud to admit you're hurting in the worst way.

And not just physically. I am here, Axel, because you've left me no choice. This is a prime time to speak to you. Things have gotten completely out of hand, and I want to help you before it's too late."

"I'm fine. Help me with what?"

"Fine? Axel, if you havin' to shoot and kill two men within a month's time is fine, then I'd hate to see what 'not so fine' is for you." Scowling, she began to fan herself with a large cluster of sparkling white feathers. "You and I spoke about many things over the years, and though I'm proud of your professional success, you have turned your back on other things, *important* things, and acted as if you don't care at all."

"I have no idea what you're talking about, Ms. Florence."

"Well then, let me jog your memory now that it's clear of alcohol," she chastised. "I'm talking about listening and hearing a good word. You don't hear nobody, Axel, because you don't trust nobody. You feel like you've been lied to so much, what's the use? You can't live this way."

"I'm not going to sit around and listen to a bunch of bull, if that's what you mean, Ms. Florence. People make excuses and tell tall tales all the time."

"Not everyone is out to get you, or pull a fast one. My advice to you went in one ear, and out the other. You told me you would do the heavy liftin' and work on that. Lies! Now who's tellin' tall tales? Look, boy, you better give me what you owe me. You, Legend and Caspian, too! I'm so disappointed in you boys, I could spit!" She waved those feathers faster and faster until he could have sworn he could feel a breeze from that direction.

"This can't be happening. No, this is a dream… It has to be."

He was trapped in his own mind. He fixed his gaze on her, trying to see if she was somehow going to vanish in a puff of smoke, or better yet, attempting to will himself awake. No such luck. She looked so alive, and yet, she was almost transparent.

This can't be real…

"It's real!" she yelled, reading his subconscious mind again. "You're dreaming, but it's definitely real. Make sure you tell your friends about this. I called y'all the brother disciples… my three sons. Not by blood, but by sweat and tears. None of y'all kept your word to me. This recent mess with you is the last straw. If it wasn't for me and your mama, you'd be dead or in prison. You have no idea how many prayers I sent on your behalf. I know God was sick and tired of hearing me call out your name."

"You say prayers in Heaven?"

"Yes, and I did it when I was still amongst the living, too. You were hardheaded as a teenager, and still are as a grown man. People said you always did your own thing. You didn't take any orders from anyone, sometimes to your own detriment. Bucked authority. It was like you were deaf… but I knew deep down that all the back talkin', fightin', rebellion and anger was actually a cover for hurt and sadness. You kept many bad habits into adulthood, too." She smiled and winked at him. "But then, your conscience started eating at you, didn't it?"

His stomach knotted and panged as if he hadn't eaten in days. Her words were gnawing at him, opening old wounds, causing emotions he'd squirreled away behind lock and key to come pounding, demanding a way out.

"You remembered what I told you. I can feel it… I saw you praying when your mama got sick some years ago. I think that's the only time you've cried as a grown man. You turned yourself around… and then *this* happened…"

He tried to speak, to respond to her several times, but couldn't. This dream was hearty, robust, and textured. Excruciating and layered. He could still smell her perfume, hear her voice so clearly, and see her as if she were truly standing before him. Yet, there were no walls, no floor, no ceiling. It was him and her, as well as something far more powerful than either of them, too. God?

"You're still struggling. All of this success, the nice house, the flourishing business, the fancy cars, motorcycles, material goods… and look at you? Tall. Smart. Strong. Handsome. Don't make no difference, now do it? You're still broken. You went from a poor little boy to being financially secure, but it didn't heal the pain. Gold and diamonds never do. They just make the ugly mess shine brighter. Soft, pretty music playin' in a nightmare don't mean you can relax, and suddenly hear the angels whispering the chorus, now do it? You still toe the line. It's bothering you because you know you ain't doin' right, Axel. In the past, you've stolen, attacked, coveted, beaten, and now, you've killed."

You think I wanted to shoot those men? I had no choice!

"Baby, you don't understand." She shook her head as if she pitied him. "You can hear me, but you're not listening. I know you didn't mean any malice, Axel. And yes, a man has to do what a man's gotta do! You had to save yourself, but Axel, this is more than you bein' at the wrong place at the wrong time. This is your past sins coming back to haunt you. Your past will return to haunt you over and over again, until you cut off the snake's head. To stop a speedin' train, you don't grab the caboose. You pull the brakes in the front. You owe not only me, to do good on your promise to finally hear what your heart has been saying to you, but you especially owe yourself. Here you are, thirty-four years old, and still stuck. You have to *listen* to your pain. HUSH… it's trying to tell you somethin', boy. LISTEN! LISTEN! LISTEN! Hear Me!!!"

Her voice vibrating through him, blew him back. His hair wafted in the air and a cool breeze came over him, from head to toe, freezing him to the bone. He could feel the sheets move from his body onto the floor. Chills ran up and down in his spine, and goosebumps formed along his arms.

"I don't know what you want from me! I didn't understand back then when you died, and I don't understand now!"

"And if we know that he hears us—whatever we ask—we know that we have what we asked of him. 1 John 5:15.' The answer is inside you, where it's always been. You gotta listen, Axel. God is tryna tell you something…"

And then, she was gone. Opening his eyes, he looked around, a sense of emptiness filling him—as if he'd won the lottery, had it all, and then, just like that, it was all gone, in the blink of an eye.

Axel sat up in the bed, his thoughts racing. He looked

at the ceiling, at a large stained-glass window he'd taken from a rundown, abandoned church and used in his own home. His heart beat painfully fast as he noticed the sheets on the floor. With a sigh, he got to his feet.

I must've flung the sheets off the bed during that crazy vision. Ms. Florence… my old teacher. Wow. That was wild. I've had a tripped-out dream. Real crazy.

He laughed mirthlessly as he maneuvered around, trying to catch his breath and steady his racing heart. He made his way to the kitchen, brushing his long hair out of his face with slightly trembling fingers. Taking a glass from a cabinet, he placed it on the black island, then reached into the refrigerator and poured himself a glass of water. He stood there for a long while, mulling things.

What if it wasn't a dream?

That's stupid. Of course it was. I don't believe in shit like this. When we die, we die. Ain't no coming back. I see death every day… never seen no ghosts while I'm cleaning up after dead folks. I've heard the stories though. Plenty of 'em. Some almost believable…

He drained his glass, the cool liquid reviving him a little. His eyes dampened as the aroma of that woman's perfume seemed to fill every inch of the house. He closed his eyes and inhaled, feeling his nostrils flare and clenching his jaws.

Okay…Okay…She's waiting for me to do some things, right? Ms. Florence said for me to tell my friends. Tell them what? That I saw her?

He placed the glass down on the counter and crossed his arms as he looked out the kitchen window. Plenty of stars in the pitch-black sky.

I'm sure she meant Legend and Caspian. She called us the Brother Disciples. All three of us got close to her. They're the only two friends I trusted. Legend had some crazy shit happen to him after all of these years. He's been in and out of jail. Hell, he might be in there right now for all I know. I haven't spoken to him in like two years… And Caspian moved away. He never returns my calls. I stopped trying 'bout a year or so ago. We used to be so damn close… We were like brothers. Better than brothers…

The three of them used to be the three amigos. Thick as thieves. Family. They met in elementary school, then went to the same high school. Their history teacher, Miss Rhonda Florence was a widowed woman who wore colorful clothing, and sported a calm demeanor. She was real smart, too. Not just about history, but life in general. The only Black woman in the entire school, in a sea of White staff and children who at times, he imagined, made her life a living hell. That lady had a special way of breaking down boring material, and making it seem as exciting as the 4th of July. He loved math, but hated English and History class, until Miss Florence showed up.

They'd talked about so much more than just history. She took an unlikely interest in him and some of the other kids—perhaps the children the world had written off. The ones that would grow up and be considered no good. Their bond grew, and right before she died, he made her a promise.

Oh, yeah. THAT promise. I remember now…

It dawned on him then that all three of them had made a promise to her individually. He'd never discussed it with Legend and Caspian, nor did they disclose what they'd told her.

He poured a little more water and drank that while he was submerged in an ocean of begrudging remembrance. Taking a deep breath, he shook his head in disbelief, then finished his drink, placing the empty glass in the sink. Returning to the bedroom, he found his cellphone and stared at it for a long while.

Just do it…

He dialed the number he had for Legend, not even certain if it was the right one anymore. It rang and rang, then went to a generic automated voicemail.

"I hope this is you. Motherfucker, it's Axel… Look, Legend, if this is your number, and you get this voicemail, call me back when you get a chance. It's been a long time, man." He pinched the skin between his eyes when a budding headache made itself known. "We need to talk."

After that, he called Caspian and got another voicemail: "Hello, you've reached Caspian St. James. Please leave a message, and I'll return your call at my earliest convenience."

"Caspian, it's Axel Hendrix. You seemed to have dropped off the face of the Earth." He chortled, biting his tongue, wanting to say something else, to tell him what a snooty piece of shit he was. He'd have liked to say how Caspian seemed to think he was better than everyone else now—he'd forgotten where he came from. He could remind him that he ate mud pies as a kid, just like the rest of 'em, and wore the same dirty ass clothes for days on end.

Now he's some big-time journalist I hear… Too good to talk to anyone from back here in ol' Portland, Kentucky. The 'Ville. Stuck-up fucker. "I'm sure you're livin' it up in Atlanta, huh? Doin' your thing down there in Georgia. That's good... Just, uh, call me back, man. It's kind of important. Thanks."

He quickly ended the call, and poured himself yet another drink, but this time, something strong: Woodford Reserve Kentucky bourbon. He checked some emails, mostly business related, trying to clear his mind of the disturbing dream that still filled him with unease. An hour or two passed, and he couldn't clear his mind after all.

Why in the hell did I call them? This is senseless. That dream has completely messed my head up... has me calling my friends that I haven't spoken to in forever, like they're even going to believe that shit. They'll probably try and have me committed to some mental hospital if I tell 'em the truth. I'll have to figure this out.

He started to pace and run his fingers through his hair, moving it out of his eyes once again. Tonight, it seemed to have a mind of its own. *This is crazy, and I'm crazy for thinking it was real. I'm going to the bar. I gotta get out of this house...*

He ran to his master suite bathroom, then paused. There, on the floor, was a small white feather. Bending down, he retrieved it, turning it back and forth between his forefinger and thumb. He placed it on his nightstand, now more determined to make this whole damn thing go away, and took a hot shower. After splashing on some cologne, he combed his hair back, threw on a pair of blue jeans, cowboy boots, and a long-sleeved black shirt. Then, he slipped on his black leather jacket, grabbed his car keys, and headed to his white Chevrolet Silverado in the garage.

Time to listen to some ear-bleeding music and get wasted. Now *that* would be a dream come true.

CAVALIERS INN, ON Main Street, was bopping with country tunes, B-side 80s punk rock, and classic rock music, filled from wall to wall with inebriated, dart-throwing and greasy-food-scarfing people. English sat at the bar, still in her work attire—a burgundy pant suit with an ivory, satin blouse beneath the blazer that stretched to its limit across her heaving breasts, confined in a new push-up bra.

She blinked a few times from the thick smoke in the place and cursed out people in her mind that walked about acting like fools. Meanwhile, she nursed a glass of merlot as she spilled her problems onto her friend, Melanie, one of the bartenders at the establishment.

She glanced up at the television and noticed a car commercial coming on, interrupting some basketball game she was barely paying attention to.

"…And then I told him he could stay the night." She didn't dare make eye contact with the lady, for she knew what was to come. The hammer of judgment.

"Eeeeeenglish!" Melanie shook her head, as if to say, *'Shame! Shame!'*

"I know, I know!" English dropped her eyes and peered into her glass, both hands wrapped around the stem as if that somehow gave her a bit more strength to speak her disgraceful truth. She could see her reflection in the dark red concoction. All watery and warped. She smiled at herself, yet she battled with a surge of sadness, too. "He just had such a hold on me for so long, Melanie. I mean, yeah, I initiated the breakup, and I don't regret it, but I missed… you know, being a couple. Like when things were good between Willis and me."

"No, you just missed the sex. That damn devil dick of his is a demon." The woman rolled her eyes as she grabbed an empty glass from a rack behind her and filled it with booze. "Dick is a dime a dozen, girl. Trust me, I know. I've been dick-stroyed one too many times myself. I'm worried about you, English. It's usually me that does the backsliding." She grinned at her, eliciting a smile. "I'm serious though. I don't want you hurt."

"You're right about the sexual pull, but this had nothing to do with sex this time around. In fact, we didn't have to screw at all. I just wanted the company." She shrugged. "In the morning, things were awkward."

"Why? Because he wanted to fuck and you said no?"

"That, and the fact it kind of seems like we both have unresolved business, and we just have to leave it that way. There was no real closure."

"The closure was when he neglected the relationship for two years, wouldn't keep a job half the time, and expected you to help pay his back child support on a kid you didn't even know he had until the final hour! The hell?! I can't believe the words coming out of your mouth right now. Someone must've body snatched you, because the English I know wouldn't be caught dead with that idiot again. This some low vibrational shit, and you out here lickin' your wounds over a Pookie."

"No, I'm not. Like I said, he caught me at a weak moment… I'm human." She hated how silly she sounded. If she were Melanie at that moment, she'd want to slap her across the room. "I'd had a rough week at work, and he just happened to call that day. I had been doing well ignoring him, too."

She looked optimistically at the woman. Perhaps she'd earned some redeeming score? Extra credit? A few brownie points for effort. Melanie looked even more perturbed though, so no such luck. "He'd been calling and texting for a while, but I never responded, until then. Anyway…" She sighed, then took a taste of her wine. The warm, rich alcohol tasted so good going down. "I haven't spoken to him since. That was over two weeks ago. The breakup happened almost eight months ago, but when I saw him… when he came over… Oh God, Mel, those old feelings rushed me. He looked so good… All that chocolatey skin, black shiny waves on his head, trimmed goatee, smelling so damn good…I hated myself for it. You know I did."

"I'm sure you did, because you know deep down, he has nothing to offer you but STIs and the broken fragments of your heart." The woman aggressively pushed a cloth back and forth along the counter, cleaning up a small spill. "You've given me the same advice when I doubled back and messed with Desmond, who also possessed a demon dick, and knows how to use it. I knew better…knowing it was like opening up Davy Jones' locker. I wish Desmond's ass would lay at the bottom of the damn sea, I tell you that much. Never mind. Scratch that. My ex-husband would just try to screw the starfish and mermaids." She snorted. "Hopefully, a shark would come and gobble him up before he got the chance to fuck Starfish-Keisha tuna and the sardine-ettes. Save everyone the aggravation. Better yet, maybe his devil dick would be mistaken as a worm? You know the rest of that fish fantasy… Bon Appetit, mothafucka. You a eunuch, now. Magical powers finally destroyed."

English cracked a smile, then burst out laughing at that. After all, her friend was as much funny as she was right.

"Jokes aside, don't question yourself, English. You did the right thing by calling it off with him. Willis wasn't any good, and he didn't deserve you." Melanie's bright hazel eyes turned to slits as she scooted closer to her, leaned over the counter, and whispered so the other patrons wouldn't hear, "Just like most of the guys here in Louisville. Girl, it doesn't matter their age, how much money they have, their race, or how good they look. I've tried them all. Even the ugly ones with a piece of a job have the audacity to run game on me.

"Talking about they're high value men, and questioning what we bring to the damn table. They're high, and that's about it! Bring to the table? That table is in their mama's musty ass basement." English tried to not laugh at her friend's absurdity, but resistance was futile. "Most of 'em are bums, too. Cheaters. Druggies. Narcissists. Neither one of us is still twenty-one and gullible, Barb the Builder, or Captain Save a Bro. Come correct or don't come at all. English, Willis didn't deserve you, and I was the only one bold enough to tell you so. He was charming, sly, and good looking. That's it. You're smart, funny, educated, and ya look good, too, with your sexy self!"

English tried to lighten her mood but she felt too tense, especially when her friend's smile quickly faded. Melanie's own anguish was hemorrhaging, bleeding onto the words she spoke, as if a razor blade had sliced across her thoughts before tumbling out of her mouth.

"I'm serious, English, and you know it. I guess I'm too bitter to give a shit anymore. But you? Nah, you're just getting started." The woman blinked fast, as if to wash away angry tears. She tossed on another smile, but English wasn't fooled. "The dating world is your oyster, baby. Find you somebody new. When you take out the trash, leave it on the curb. Second chances are exclusive to children—or to our own selves. Everyone else gets put in a Glad bag."

English crossed her legs and held her head up high. She had no intentions of diving into the swamp of temptation, only to drown a slow, agonizing death while gripping the memories of 'what once was' firmly to her chest as she descended into her watery grave. *It was a simple mistake. An error in judgment.*

"I'm done with it. I'm done with *him*. Trust me."

"Good. I have to serve these beers."

English nodded in understanding as her friend maneuvered around the bar counter with a tray of cocktails and pints. Melanie had had a hard life, but to many in town, she was simply a good-looking woman, tall with a small waist and wide hips. Beautiful dimples, full lips, high cheekbones, slanted eyes, smooth sand-colored skin and thick, wavy dark brown hair she deemed unmanageable and threatened to cut off come every summer. They'd met several years ago when English moved to Louisville from Dry Ridge Kentucky for a job offer. She'd stopped in the bar one evening with a couple of co-workers, and the two had been inseparable ever since.

The rock tunes morphed into rap and Hip-Hop music as the crowd thickened. Melanie was in high demand, making abundant tips, and got far more chipper as the night wore on. Just as English decided she'd had enough to drink, watching people toss darts, as well as swatting away a few overly eager men who attempted to pay for her pussy with a cocktail, she looked up from the bar, and her heart stopped at the sight that greeted her.

Well, shit…

In walked a tall son of a gun with long, dark blond hair flowing down his back like some golden cape, piercing green eyes, and a dense brown beard. He looked vaguely familiar, but she couldn't place his face. Her eyes burned into him, as did others, for he was the sort of man who commanded attention. He slapped hands with a few people, smiling and enjoying the welcome. A gun sat in a holster on the side of his hip, and he moved with purpose, as if he had one damn thing on his mind, and he was there tonight to take care of it, once and for all.

Maybe I'll sit here a little bit longer after all. There's nothing wrong with sucking on a bit of eye candy. Besides, I've got an insatiable sweet tooth, and I've stuck to my diet for a mighty long time. Time for a tasty reward. This sweet treat is wrapped in black leather and sounds like revving motorcycles and a barrel of bourbon covered trouble. He's a sucker in need of a good lick, a drop desperate to be swallowed…

I'm not thirsty, but there's no shame in tasting the samples. I'll take seconds, and thirds, thank you very much.

Chapter Three

S*EEMS TO ME, the more knowledge some people are given, the stupider they become. Some people though become sexier the more they learn, and that makes them so damn irresistible…*

Axel walked into Cavaliers Inn and immediately heard his name being yelled and slurred from various usual suspects.

"Axxxel!"

"Hey, Axe-man!"

He nodded at a couple of acquaintances from the neighborhood, then locked hands with Magoo, an old head who did car repairs and a guy he'd known most of his life, like so many others in town. He strolled on to the beat of 'Bloody Valentine,' by Machine Gun Kelly, eager to make it to the bar. He looked behind the counter, his eyes resting on one of the mixologists. *Melanie.*

"Mel," he raised his arm and wiggled his fingers a bit before slumping down onto the stool, "long time, no see, honey."

"Heeeey, handsome! I haven't seen you in forever,

Axe. How've you been?"

The lady's cat-eyes narrowed on him with a mischievous gleam.

He shrugged, pulling out a lighter from his leather jacket pocket, then his pack of cigarettes.

"I can't complain." He lit up, sweeping the place with a quick gaze.

"Hmph." She smirked as she dried a glass beer mug. "That's not what the news stations been sayin'."

"You can't believe everything you hear."

"I'm a bartender. I hear it all. I can weed out truth from fiction."

"The reporters and coroners aren't drunk. Just corrupt. There's a difference."

She shook her head, then burst out laughing. "At least I see you're still good with a gun. Damn, boy. You handled your business, that's for sure."

"Mmm hmm." He blew smoke out the side of his mouth. "I'd like nothin' more though, than for things to go back to normal."

"Well, let me help you forget your troubles. What can I get you?"

"Let me have a snake in a barrel." Right at that moment, he could feel eyes boring into him, as if someone were rummaging right into the pit of his soul. He turned to his left, and two seats down the way sat a dainty brown satin doll with big doe eyes. Considering her posture, clothing and jewelry, she possessed a certain sophistication that definitely didn't match this place.

She must've gotten lost.

He laughed to himself, then turned back towards Melanie, taking the drink from her grasp. "Thank you."

"Oh, I'm so rude." Melanie rolled her eyes in a dramatic sort of way, then pointed at the very woman who was sitting there nursing a glass of red wine. "This is English. English, this is Axel. Known this man for practically my whole life."

The woman in question sat a bit straighter, and her lips curled like a cat's after it finally found a stash of hidden delicacies. Both women were now ogling him, speaking in some language he couldn't understand as they bounced glances and silly grins at one another. He hated when chicks did that.

"Nice to meet you, Axel." English placed her glass down and stretched out her arm, dangling her hand. He looked down at it. The long fingers. Perfectly manicured nails and the slight sheen on her flesh, as if it had been lubed up with liquid gold and diamond infused baby oil. He stood from his seat, holding his drink, and made the two second trek in her direction to take her hand and shake it.

So soft. *Ridiculously* soft, as if she'd never lifted a finger a day in her life. *She must've been born with a silver spoon. How does Mel know this lady? Is she her probation officer or something?*

"I'll let you two talk for a while. I've got work to do and these tips have to be earned by more than just a smile." Melanie moseyed away, but not before winking in her friend's direction. It was crystal clear now—the woman was trying to hook them up.

"So, let's talk, Axel. Have a seat." English removed her

purse from the chair next to her and placed it on the bar counter. Sliding onto the seat, he studied her, smoking and taking sips of his drink. "What do you do?" she asked, lifting her glass of wine to her lips.

"What do I do?" Since he hated that question, particularly if it was the first thing to roll out of a woman's mouth, he decided to mess with her a bit. "I work."

He exhaled a few rings of smoke and watched them dissolve on the way up to the ceiling as Moneybagg Yo' rapped on with, 'See Wat I'm Sayin'."

"What do you actually do for work, smartass?" she said with a twang and a smile, then waved at a white guy behind the bar who was pouring drinks.

"Oh, you're one of those." He grinned, clicked his tongue against his lower teeth, and sat a bit straighter.

"I'm not going to fall into your trap and ask what that's supposed to mean. If by chance though, you mean someone who—Hold on." The bartender approached and she pointed to her now empty wine glass. "I don't want any more alcohol, but I would like a glass of water, please."

"You got it." The man took her glass and meandered to the other side of the counter.

"As I was saying…" She crossed her legs and looked him directly in the eye. "If you meant to say I'm someone who asks direct questions and expects an honest answer, then yes, I'm one of *those*."

He nodded, took a swig of his beverage, and stood to his feet. Then belched. Her look of disgust didn't get wasted on him. He responded to her expression with a proud smile, happy to have brought her down a peg or two into the land of reality.

"Lady, you asked me to come 'round here and sit down." He pointed to the stool. "I wasn't payin' you any attention. Second, it's rude to ask someone what they do for a livin' within thirty seconds of knowin' them. You could've asked me all sorts of things, but you went straight to the wallet."

Her eyes had the nerve to get big. She was utterly shocked at his response.

"Well, I don't mind telling you what I do for a living," she stated, resting her hand across where invisible pearls would lie, ready for her to clutch.

"I didn't ask, and I don't too much care."

"I didn't think it was rude to ask you that. It's just a question to get to know someone. You're defensive."

"If you say so." He yawned as he checked his wallet to ensure he'd placed his I.D. back inside of it, then slipped it back in his pocket.

"Do you take recreational drugs?" She burst out laughing, as if that were somehow amusing. "You seem a bit high strung is all. Are you okay? Should I call for help?" She took the water from the bartender and smiled smugly. "Thank you."

I don't give a shit how pretty she is. I don't care if her head game is otherworldly, or how wet and tight the pussy might be. I didn't even come up in here to find someone to smash. I get that opportunity wherever I go, but I'm not even in the mood. It's been a messed-up week, and a messed-up day. I'm trying to clear my mind… I don't have time for this shit.

He swallowed down the things he really wanted to say. The cruel, verbally violent words he was known to toss into the ring of fire and force his adversaries to choke on the smoke. Deciding she wasn't worth any more of his time or energy, he waved goodbye to the woman, then made his way to the small area where people were dancing and laughing, having a good time. He saw more familiar faces and yelled over the music, trying to catch up with folks but not get caught up in conversations about his recent cameo appearances on the evening news.

Jack Harlow's, 'Churchill Downs,' featuring Drake started to play through the blasting speakers. Everyone got hyped up at that point. Jack Harlow was a skyrocketing rapper out of Kentucky—the 'Ville, to be exact. He was their very own home-grown sensation.

"Louisville in tha house! Louisville in tha house!" People began to chant the lyrics to the song. He started to sway to the music, arms up, lost in the rhythm and happy as the crowd got thicker. A woman approached him, stars dancing in her lustful eyes. Her dark brown hair hung to her shoulders, and her lips were unusually juicy and big, reminding him of one of the Kardashians. Her breasts were practically spilling out of her tight white shirt, and her jeans hugged her curves like a vehicle on an old country road. Getting close, she began whispering in his ear, something about taking her home…

Out of the corner of his eye, he spotted English dancing with some guy. She'd taken her jacket off, and a tiny shred of something green and awkward, a kernel of jealousy, sprouted from his inner Earth. He could see her shape better now… and damn did she look good. *All of that was hidden under that coat? Damn, baby.*

She was laughing and swaying her body in a sexy way while the goofball she was draped around looked desperate and thirsty, but not for beer or the sauce off the chicken wings. Axel scanned her body real slow, from her head to her heels, then back up again. That was when she swung her head fast in his direction, stuck out her tongue, and winked.

Busted.

He quickly turned away, laughing. He'd been set up and had. She knew he'd been looking the whole time, acting interested, despite the words they'd exchanged. Something about her got his engine revving. She was annoying and intriguing all at once. A beautiful woman with brains turned him into a puddle. He was used to smart women, and he craved to be able to not only seduce and fuck a woman he desired, but also to have meaningful conversations with her. He had a feeling she was far from a dingbat, who couldn't teach him shit. Such a woman would only be good for one night. But a woman that could hold her own and was intelligent… well, she could last a lifetime.

When he came back to reality, the one with the Kardashian lips was glaring at him with her arms crossed. Rolling her eyes, she then stormed off. *I guess it was obvious my attention was elsewhere…* He tossed up his hands and continued to enjoy the music for a while, then, feeling thirsty, returned to the bar and knocked back two more beers. He followed that with a game of darts with his buddy Greek—a nickname given to him because his last name was Papadopoulos, even though he swore up and down he wasn't from that country.

"He had the whole year to turn it around!" Greek yelled, going off about one of the Cincinnati Bearcats.

He felt a tap on his shoulder and spun around to see Melanie standing there, her hand on her hip.

"Did you and English get a chance to talk?"

"How long is happy hour?"

"Stop playing with me, Axel." She chortled. "You didn't arrive in time for happy hour, and you know it, but that answers my question. Why don't you like her? I think y'all would be a cute couple! Oh wait… are you with someone? Jackie said you and Tonya broke up, so I thought—"

"What are you, a secret service bar detective and tavern Cupid? No, I'm not dating anyone, but I'm still not trying to get to know your friend. By the way, your brother has been dodging me like a bill collector. Where the hell is Legend?"

Melanie rolled her eyes. "Axel, he just got out of prison a few months ago."

"What for?"

She grimaced and crossed her arms. "You know what for. What it's *always* for… Anyway, Mama is all upset about it. Last time I spoke to him, I told him he needed to get his shit together, and that getting involved with all of these crazy people he hangs with is going to ensure he ends up dead. You know he doesn't like people telling him what to do. He's hardheaded."

He couldn't disagree with that. "So, your guess is as good as mine as to where the hell he is. Legend is not talking to me and mama, either." She shrugged. "I wish he would talk to you, though. You and Caspian were his best friends… he listened to you. He respected you, and Legend respects few." An expression of sadness washed over her. "Back to English."

"Naw, not back to Spanish, Italian, or English."

She cracked up at that, but he was serious.

"Come on, Axel! As soon as you walked in, all eyes were on you, and she was one of the pairs! I know you've been going through some mess, too. Everyone needs someone to lean on. I don't know why I want y'all to go out so bad, but I just do. It's a gut instinct."

…And my gut tells me that you're full of shit. You're up to something, Mel.

He looked across the room and saw English still speaking to the same dude.

He thinks he's taking her home tonight… What an idiot. She's not going any-damn where with him, and definitely not letting him hit it. I know her type. She's just using him for a little conversation since she's finished with drinks. She wants to set it up so she can use him later in the week or month when she's lonely and wants someone to take her to a fancy restaurant, or out shopping so she can run up their credit card.

"She's just talking to him to pass the time. She really wants to talk to you," Melanie interrupted his thoughts.

"So what? Look, Mel, I can see you're a caring friend, but I'm a grown ass man and this is all very childish to me. I don't need to be hooked up like we're in high school.

She's not my type, and that's all right. It's not even that serious." He shrugged. "What's on sale tonight? Any drafts half off?"

"She's a really amazing woman, Axel. I saw how you looked at her, too. You think she's beautiful, don't you?" He refused to answer. Besides, that wasn't the point. "She had a bad break up and is still—"

"Triple nope."

"What? Why?!"

"That sounds like a headache. So not only is she irritating, but she also has baggage. One way airplane ride to drama-ville. I'm not catchin' any flights or feelings for a nutjob. I'm good." He turned back around and picked up his cigarette out of a nearby ashtray. Laughing, Melanie jerked on his arm, forcing him to face her.

"I'm going to text you her number. Is it the same as it was?"

"Don't waste your time. I'm not calling it."

"You'll call. I think you two just got off on the wrong foot. Not your type?" She rolled her eyes. "She's *exactly* your type. Anyway, I just want to tell you that I'm so proud of you, what you've made of yourself. You stepped in and helped me when Legend couldn't. Our daddy wasn't in our life much, Light bill. Paid. Even when you barely had money yourself. You fixed my doors in my apartment after the break in, when that good for nothin' landlord wouldn't help me. I've watched you over the years. People look up to you. You're a born leader, and… I want you to be happy. If anyone in this whole place deserves happiness, it's you and English."

"All these compliments tryna butter me up. You're up to something."

"I *might* be, but I'm right about her being your type. She's your type. Say it with me."

"You don't know my type. You're my friend's little sister, Mel."

"What are you talking about? I was around y'all all the time."

"You barely saw us because we were always out in the street or over someone else's house. Now you're in here trying to boss me around and treat me like a Tinder app," he teased while a new dart game was being set up. "Don't you have work to do? Some drinks to make and serve?"

"I was around y'all and you know it. Besides, this town isn't big enough for me not to know your business."

"I 'spose you're right about that."

"I *can* tell you what you like. I'm observant."

"You're more irritating than my real-life little sister, Dallas. In fact, you're worse, Mel."

"Dallas is good people. Stop talkin' about her like that. She and I were in high school choir together. Nice voice." She grinned. "You like smart women." She began to count off her fingers. "Ambitious women. Kind women. Strong women. You like—"

"Just stop. Why are you being so pushy about this? I know you've got plenty of other friends you could hook me up with if you wanted to, but I don't want a hook up in the first place. I'm cool."

He turned back towards the dart game. The truth of the matter was that affairs of the heart were tiresome.

Women were stressful, no matter how nice they first appeared. There was always some bullshit later down the line. Jealousy. Accusations of cheating, even when he wasn't. Emotional outbursts. Things had gotten significantly worse when he finally got some money under his belt. The gold diggers came out in droves, pressuring to get married. One lady had even poked holes in his condoms.

It was just too much. He'd put a pause on courting. Not pussy, but definitely dating. English was the type of lady where you weren't going to hit and quit it. He realized that within ten seconds of looking at her, so there was no need to even try to use her for a mere one-night stand. Besides, women tended to lose their shit if he took them to bed. They'd become clingy and possessive, regardless of him saying right off the bat that he didn't want anything serious. He was just that good. This wasn't arrogance. He just had solid knowledge of the female body, sexual confidence, endurance, stamina, and a big dick and long tongue definitely didn't hurt.

"You're a good man, Axel, and after hearing my friend pour out her heart to me tonight, I just… I just thought that maybe y'all could at least be friends. I didn't ask you to marry her or anything. Damn. A conversation and a cup of coffee never hurt nobody." And with that, she walked back towards the bar.

Axel played a game of darts, and debated getting another beer, but thought better of it. The crowd began to thin out as closing time approached, and the last call for alcohol was made. He caught sight of Melanie speaking to another bartender. Money was going between their hands. Initially, he thought they were settling the tips, but then they both shot him a glance, and they went back to counting.

Melanie, you're a real piece of work. Think you're slick. You and Legend stay on some shady shit. I still love ya, though.

His gaze then traveled to the woman who'd gotten under his skin within a matter of seconds.

English was now messing around on her phone, and the goofy nerd man was nowhere in sight. More than likely licking his rejected wounds behind the wheel of his Thunderbird, or perhaps, jacking off to release some tension in the men's room. He watched from a distance, as she slid her blazer back on, then talked to Melanie for a bit. After a while, the two of them hugged from across the bar counter. She grabbed her purse and made her way towards the exit. Meanwhile, Greek was still going off about another college basketball team that had let him down.

Just then, his phone vibrated in his pocket.

He'd been ignoring calls, texts and emails since he'd arrived at the bar, wishing to be left alone, but he shot a look at Mel, figuring she was texting him English's number, just as she'd vowed to. She in fact had her phone in her hand, but he didn't bother to check. Instead, he followed English out of the bar. The scent of her perfume lingered in the air as he walked past the door.

He could hear what sounded like keys dangling in her hand as she approached a white Lexus with matching leather interior. Oddly enough, it was parked right next to his truck.

"Hey, English."

She paused and turned in his direction.

"Yes?"

"Do you mind if I call you sometime?"

"I *do* mind." She chortled, then turned around and kept walking.

"Well, Melanie bet someone some money that I'd call you, so we may as well let her get a little extra cash."

She paused once again and spun to face him.

"And just so we're clear, I wasn't in on the deal. I was a victim of her scheme as much as you."

"She wouldn't do something like that."

"Look, I've known that woman since she was barely out of diapers. I don't know how long you've known her, but she's a chameleon. She's been through a lot of shit, and it shows. Melanie is a sweet girl, but she's always in survival mode. You can be her best friend in the world, and she'll still make a buck off you, if she can, all while helping you stand up straight for auction."

English stood there in that parking lot with the muted sounds of Jack Harlow's, 'Like A Blade Of Grass,' playing in the background. Hands in his pockets, he walked toward her, closing the distance between them. He stood so close to her now, he was staring down at her like a beacon of shadows competing with the light in her eyes.

"Mmmm. You smell good…" he complimented her. Her scent was driving him crazy. It was robust. Rich. Sexy.

"Thank you."

"What is that?"

"El Musty. It's French. I didn't shower after I worked out at the gym."

They looked at one another and burst out laughing.

"I own a cleaning company," he said, sliding his hands out of his pockets and folding his arms. Something about her eyes drew him in to a place he just didn't wish to leave. He was roaming inside her mind, trying to figure her out. Trying to see beyond the killer body, gorgeous face, and dark, pure eyes that made him captive to her charms.

"Oh, a cleaning service. That's great. I bet you're a beast with mirrors and carpet."

"No, not that type of cleaning service. Biohazard remediation, and forensic cleanup."

"Oh. OHHHH…" Her eyes grew big once again as the reality of the situation set in, and her complexion deepened. "I'm astounded."

"Why?"

"You don't meet someone who works in your field every day. That has to be tough."

He shrugged. "You get used to it."

"What made you, uh, go into that profession?"

"You know that little sensor inside most people that tells you when something is gross, uncomfortable, or disturbing? So much so, that you feel mighty sick, lighthearted, or want to vomit or even pass out?"

"Yeah?"

"Mine is severely under-developed. It's barely there. I have a strong sense of smell, but I got past that, too. It takes a lot to get me to respond to things that make most people nauseous. I've always been that way. Gory horror movies have never made me uneasy. Bad car accidents, I barely bat an eye. People would start puking at some things, and I would just be standing there."

She smiled at his words.

"What was your training or first experiences in your line of work?"

"I had a friend back in the day who worked for a company that did the same thing I do. I used to work in construction and that's not always consistent, so they were hiring, and he got me on board. After a few years, I realized I was so good at it, I could start my own thing. I've got a good business mind, so I went to Jefferson Community College and got a business and accounting degree while I kept workin'. I started my own company soon after I graduated. Got my own employees now, too, and it's been good ever since."

"Good for you! Someone has to do it. Might as well be you, right?"

"Yeah. I feel that way for sure. What about you?"

"Have we passed the thirty second mark yet? Wouldn't want to accuse you of being rude after asking about my occupation," She teased. "I'm a book conservator."

"What's that?"

"You mean you don't know? I thought everyone knew what that was! It should be obvious!" She looked at him seriously, then burst out laughing. "I'm teasing you, Axel. I mean, not about being a book conservator, but about everyone knowing what it is."

"Oh. I don't know you, so I am not familiar with your

sense of humor or how you like to joke around."

"Okay, well, I'll tell you off the bat that I'm pretty sarcastic."

"So am I."

"I can see that… Good. We have something in common. Let's see, well, I have a Masters in Conservatorship, emphasis on library science, and a PhD in historic preservation."

I fucking knew it. She's drippin' with big brain vibes. Smart women with sexy bodies are usually crazy. And yet here I am…

"Went to University of Kentucky for undergrad. Bachelors in History."

"So, how do you use these degrees for conservatorship? What are you doing with them right now?"

"I work with books, periodicals, and texts from historic African American essayists, playwrights, authors, songwriters, journalists, and activists such as those involved in the 1950s and '60s Civil Rights era, and even pre-civil war documents. If it's written down and published by an African American and has any ties to historical references, decrees or laws that were based around discrimination, abuse of power, race connections to criminality discrepancies, or social injustices, then chances are high I've seen it, or will see it. I have also helped assess the value of certain vintage books and journals from the Jim Crow era. I'm often called upon to help gauge authenticity of tomes from old estate auctions, pawn shops, museums, things of that nature. Occasionally I assist with fiction books, too, but I have an ongoing contract with the Roots 101 on 1st Street, and the Kentucky Center for African American Heritage."

"I know where Roots 101 is. Never been inside. Guess I need to check it out."

"I'd urge you to do so if you're open-minded, and truly willing to learn. It's really amazing. I also teach a monthly class that focuses on African American history, particularly in Kentucky, Indiana, Illinois, and Ohio at a couple of the local libraries. I am now on a committee to help fight against the removal of important books in schools that have been dubbed racially charged."

"I heard somethin' about that a few weeks ago. Like, 'To Kill a Mockingbird.' I read that in school. That's crazy to me. This censorship is going too far."

"It is. That's just one of hundreds of books on the chopping block. Who in the hell tries to remove 'The Catcher in the Rye,' and 'A Raisin in the Sun,' from the school library?"

"You ever heard of 'Maus'?"

"Of course. It's about the Holocaust. Written by Art Spiegelman in 1980. It, too, has been on the chopping block several times over the last two decades."

"I read that cover to cover."

"You like to read?"

"Sometimes. My favorite teacher was a history teacher. She got me interested." He suddenly felt a rush of warmth flood him. The conversation almost felt like déjà vu—or as if he was supposed to be there, right then, with her. He'd run away from his house, run from history, and now, he'd found it again.

The woman was truly in her element now, rambling on

about various books that should be kept in the schools. Many of the titles he'd at least heard of. Impressive.

Funny how memory stores this stuff away. I had forgotten about some of these books. She's really into this conversation, too... Look how she's moving her body, all excited as she talks about it. Smart people can be annoying though. They think they know every damn thing. Hell, I've been accused of bein' that way, too. A know-it-all. She's kind of funny, too. Definitely easy on the eye... Me and this woman may have some things in common after all. Damn if Melanie's sneaky ass wasn't right...

"Sounds boring, huh?" She chuckled, dragging him from his deliberations.

"Nope. Sounds exciting, actually. I don't know much about what you do. This is a good start, but I'd like to hear more about it when my head isn't swimming in beer, and you're not in a stiff suit and looking down and dejected."

"Did Melanie tell you my business?" She huffed, visibly miffed.

"Nah, she didn't do that. You looked like you had a lot on your mind tonight is all." She leaned against her car, and he followed suit, both hooked on each other's gazes. After a while, she placed her fingers along his arm, trailing them across the leather of his jacket. He wanted to kiss her but decided to practice restraint. This wasn't the time.

"You smell good, too, Axel. Like good quality cologne, leather and earth. I like your hair."

"Yeah? I'm glad you like it." He reached for her cheek and caressed it gently with his thumb. She leaned into his touch. It felt natural. Fluid. Normal. "I gotta get ready to go, but I want to take you out sometime soon." He cocked his head to the side, and she smiled back at him, her cheeks deepening in color.

"Okay. I guess we should exchange numbers. I have... Wait. Oh my God!"

"What?"

"I know where I've seen your face!" She jumped about, waving her finger in his face. "On TV! You had to shoot some guy, right?" Her eyes did that thing they did when she was surprised, or speechless—got big and glassy.

"Yeah. I figured you already overheard that when I came in and Melanie was talking about it."

"To be honest, I was only half listening. I was too busy thinking how sexy you were. What a time to zone out..."

"It was self-defense."

"I remember you explaining that on that television."

"So, does that change anything?"

She looked at him for a long while, as if deliberating it.

"No. A person has the right to defend themselves, their life. I'm sorry all of that happened to you. Are you all right now?"

"Yeah, I'm fine." He slipped his phone out of his pocket and noticed Melanie had in fact texted her number. He asked English to send it anyway, and he did the same for her. When she got into her car, he closed the door for her. The parking lot was becoming bare, and a slight chill hung in the air.

"Drive safe. I'll be callin' you soon," he said as he backed up from her ride.

"Okay. It was nice meeting and talking with you tonight, Axel. See you later."

"Yeah. See you." He waved as she pulled out of her space, then drove away. After she entered the stream of traffic onto the street, he pulled his phone back out and texted Melanie.

Any friend of yours has to be fucking nuts. I'm going to play squirrel and see what's up with her anyway. How much money did you get off me?

Melanie: *She's different and fun, isn't she? I knew you'd love her!*

Axel: *How much, Mel?*

Melanie: *$35.00. How'd you know?*

Axel: *Because I'm not fucking stupid.*

He made his way to his truck, got inside, and sat there with only the glow of his phone and the thumping music drifting from the bar, probably the last song of the night.

Melanie: *We make bets on couples all night to see who is going to link up. Don't tell her. She wouldn't understand.*

He started up the truck.

Axel: *Too late. I want free beer next time I come in here. I want it for an entire month if she turns out to be some Aileen Wuornos type lady.*

He placed his phone down, lit a cigarette, turned up his stereo, and drove away to the sounds of 'Rodeo,' by Juvenile.

Chapter Four

I'M A MENTAL case and a fraud, and you know what? In the right circumstances, I'm okay with that. I avoid bad boys as a rule, tending to go for the educated lames, but I was never happy traveling that predictable journey. Come to find out, the educated lames are sometimes just as bad as the thugs and bad boys, if not worse. Make it make sense. I'm also sickeningly attracted to White boys with long hair and tattoos. I don't know what it is, but it's beautifully strange, just how I like it. I like my men either Black as night in a starless city, or some tall glass of melanin-deficient son of a bitch who acts like he owns the damn place.

I look nothing like how I behave, and I'm more than fine with that. Only a few people know the real me, and those folks always ask me the same question that demands a complicated answer: How could someone with so much education, common sense, and a good family such as my own be so dark inside? I don't know how to respond to this, but that is how I am, and it's mine to keep.

I called myself a fraud. I am. It's not a common occurrence, but a tool I use when necessary. Why am I a con artist, you may ask? I'll tell you… I was acting my behind off at the bar tonight.

Of course, I knew who the hell Axel Hendrix was within five seconds of him entering the pub. I never forget a face, and this photographic memory of mine has served me well in my thirty-two years on this planet. Melanie began speaking fast, giving me his resume, and she seemed in shock—something about not seeing him for years, and that he'd been her brother's best friend. Meanwhile, I watched him interacting with people and knew then, I wouldn't need any introductions. After all, how could anyone forget that rumbling, rusty voice, and the long, dark blond hair that at times hung almost perfectly over one eye, so he'd gently flip the strands over his shoulder.

And good God… that face. Imagine Josh Holloway with a thick beard, but not too thick, and long ass hair. Yeah, now you understand.

Axel's features were striking, something you'd pause for and give a double take, Then he had all of those tattoos… Whew. Angel wings and classic symbols that let me know that he enjoyed history, too. I noted the Neptune, Venus, and Mars on his body, all the Roman deities. Seeing him in the flesh was an unexpected treat.

Several weeks ago, I was home, stuffing my face with Pamprin for some monster menstrual cramps, hugged up with a pint of Rocky Road ice-cream, Kleenex in my hand while I cried about a story on Instagram, and just lying across my bed in a dramatic way no doubt, hot water bottle on my bloated abdomen, and then I heard the news come on. I looked away from my phone towards my bedroom television and literally said… DAMN.

There was something sexy and sinister about a man who could shoot someone without a second thought, and something noble about him making it clear he was no killer, but he'd rest easy knowing he did what he had to do. He gave no fucks or apologies, but he wasn't bragging either. I liked that. He stood there with that reporter, smoking a hand-rolled cigarette that looked more like a joint, and calmly discussed how he blew a hole in a man. It was obvious he didn't want the media attention—he was looking everywhere but at the damn camera—but still, his confidence and persona exuded from the screen. Now, I've met him. I have his number, but will I call him? He's yet to call me. Maybe it's for the best…

English sat at the sterile white desk in her office and snatched off her reading glasses. She had a mundane, monotonous job at times, but she loved it all the same. She closed her eyes and massaged her forehead, praying that the up-and-coming headache would take a back seat. It had only been a few hours into her morning, but it felt as if she'd been working for an eternity. Taking a sip of her lukewarm coffee, she sat it back down as '*Another One Bites the Dust*,' by Queen blasted at top volume from a car passing by outside. She grabbed a book from a stack on her desk, and studied the cover:

> 'Our Nig,' by Harriet E. Wilson, first published in 1859. She opened it carefully, noting that even though it was a nice piece to have in one's collection, it wasn't considered collectable by any stretch of the imagination, due to it being one of the republished versions from 1981, proof of such was the introduction by Henry Louis Gates Jr. However, one thing stood out to her: the initials, *L.J.*

There was also a stamped cluster of grapes in faded red ink on the dedication page. Those stamps were often used in 1982 to mimic a popular postage stamp at the time. Perhaps, Henry Louis Gates had signed this copy himself, and LJ was for Louis Jr.? Suddenly, her cellphone hummed, drawing her out of her pondering. She glanced at her computer screen, seeing over fifteen unread emails, shook her head, and answered.

"You have some nerve." She cradled her phone closer to her ear. "Stick to betting on the derby, Melanie."

"Look, I was sincere, regardless of my ulterior motives." Melanie laughed on the other end. "He's a catch. I think y'all would be good together."

"Don't start..."

"I'm for real. I hadn't seen Axel in forever, English, or I would have brought him up sooner. You know I've been trying to hook you up with someone for weeks. Anyway, there's a comedy show down here at the bar next weekend, and I wanted to invite you. Feel free to bring others. Tickets are ten dollars in advance, fifteen at the door."

"I don't know... I have a lot of work to catch up on, and besides, you may decide to try and hook me up with someone else and place another bet on me, too. Like I'm some horse."

"You aren't kidding! Oh my God. You are actually *really* mad about that, English?"

She couldn't believe the gall of her friend. "I'm not mad, just disappointed in you."

"You sound like my mama."

"Melanie, I knew you were a whole scam artist, but I thought, or I should say, I *hoped*, I would be exempt from your sidewinder ways. All of these years we've known each other, been cool, and then you turn an evening where I'm feeling sorry for myself and vulnerable, into an opportunity. All I was doing was speaking my truth, and then you used it for your benefit. You know you were dead wrong."

"Why should everyone suffer just because you were? It's best at least one of us got lucky off your misery!"

"Shut up." She stifled a laugh.

"You know I'm just playing with you." Melanie cackled. "Come on, I thought it was harmless. Have you two spoken again? If you have, I got another five bucks coming."

"I'm not telling you anything, but I will say this: You should know me well enough to understand I wouldn't like somethin' like that. You could've just told me, like, 'Look, English. I want you to go out with Axel, and I have some money riding on y'all exchanging numbers.'"

"If I did that though, I would've been disqualified and lost the bet. That's like giving a horse a steroid shot right before the Derby. We bet on a few people that night. I came out victorious. What can I say? Lady Luck was on my side. Now I don't have to start an Only Fans to support my plans to burn this city down. Don't nobody wanna see my flapjack titties no damn way."

English rolled her eyes when she heard her friend laughing on the other end, amused with herself.

"I feel like I'm on the phone with a pimp."

Melanie began to sing the old 50 Cent song, "P.I.M.P.!"

"If the shoe were on the other foot, you charlatan, you'd be mad."

"No, I wouldn't. Bartenders do this all the time. If the roles were reversed, I would just ask for my cut, English. I'm not new to this, I'm true to this."

"Oh, trust and believe, you owe me, and I will be getting payback. You've been watching too many Blaxploitation movies I see. How much did you make off me, you sneaky ass weasel?"

"I prefer to be called a sly fox. Only twenty."

"Liar."

"A P.I.M.P. never discusses money matters with her employees. So is this why you've not been returning my calls? That's so petty, English! You can hold a grudge." She laughed.

"That, and I'm genuinely busy, girl. It's been crazy." She went on to explain about the shipment of books sent to her two days ago, some of which were in horrific condition. She'd been given a tight deadline to go through them and help prepare them for a local exhibition.

"Damn, okay. Try and come through, anyway, even if only for an hour or two. It would be a good time. I'm going back to sleep. Have to work tonight, but I'll be talking with you soon. Enjoy your day, sis."

"Okay, talk to you later." English disconnected the call and picked up the book once again. She flipped through it with gentle fingers, then placed it back down, and surveyed some others. A couple of hours later, she found herself with full body and mind fatigue. *I've been sitting in that same position too long… Time to stretch.*

Making her way to the break room in the employee area of the museum, she greeted a few coworkers, then grabbed a bag of chips from a vending machine. *I've got to work through lunch if I want to get out of here anytime soon.* As she headed back down the hall got on the elevator, her cellphone buzzed. She slipped it out of her pocket, and her insides dropped, as if she'd been jerked about on a roller coaster.

Clutching her bag of Doritos, she got off on her floor and returned to her office, sporting a stiff smile as she passed by a number of people, feigning calm. She entered and softly closed and locked the door, then went to sit at her desk, placing the unopened bag of chips down. Suddenly, her appetite was gone.

On a deep breath, she reached for her phone and looked at the ID. His number was the same. She had it etched in her memory. How had he gotten her new number? Well, it wasn't his first time he'd traced her, and she highly doubted it would be his last. Sliding her fingertip along the screen, she braced herself, and listened to the voicemail. Her back slumped and a sticky warmth consumed her.

"I don't have to do an introduction. You know who the fuck dis is. I know you see that I've called you twice now, English. Goin' by that government name again, I see. Your name is *still* Shira in my eyes. *I* named you Shira, your *real* family, and that's what it'll always be. Call me. Don't make me have to call you again. I mean it."

She played the message again. Why did she do that? Wasn't one time enough? Those words made her insides freeze and her skull throb.

And then, the wave of shame came forth. The humiliation from that time in her life many years ago, one she'd wished to be rid of. There was no way to erase the past, no antidote, no way to drown it out and make it go away. There weren't enough bottles of wine, mind-altering pills, sugary snacks, or syringes full of death that could give her a reprieve or cure her disgrace.

I knew he'd be back—all of them. I knew this was coming. They always come back.

She placed her phone down on her desk, turned some music on, and took hold of the first book once again. Her YouTube playlist, starting with 'Let 'Em In' by Paul McCartney, started to play. She was in the mood for something relaxing, versus her typical R&B, upbeat jazz, Trap or Rap music selections which were her guilty pleasure. She brought the book to her nose, smelled the time-worn pages, and smiled. She opened it to read a few passages. Certainly, this book could take her away from this place for a moment, trick her mind into thinking everything was okay, one page at a time.

Books had a way of doing that, transporting those who needed a journey. Worlds within words, especially when reality became too much and stood outside one's door, knocking. She refused to hear any evil, but it was pointless. That book had a final page, and she'd read 'The End' far sooner than she'd wished. All that mess she'd buried and covered in sand like some cat in a litter box would be waiting for her. Stinking. And all that pain within would seep through the cracks of her firm exterior.

Then her heart would cry out, demanding to be heard.

THE HOLLIES' 'LONG Cool Woman' played as Dad sat on his old, rickety porch with a beer in one hand. A soiled blue bandana was wrapped around his head, and his thin, straggly dark brown hair flowed in greasy threads over his bony shoulders. Tall and rail thin, the outline of his skull was practically visible beneath a thin veneer of sun-bathed skin. Faded prison tattoos covered his exposed limbs as he peered at him with bright blue eyes, surrounded by crow's feet. When he smiled, a missing side tooth made its appearance.

The house was filthy, in need of a good power wash, but the land it was on was blessed with beautiful, lush grass and mature trees.

"Axel! My boy!" The older man laughed when he got out of his truck and closed the door. Dad went to scratch his knee over his jeans that were far too big for his frame. He went at himself like a host of fleas were performing for some circus on him. From the looks of the man, Dad was drinking himself to death—again.

They'd been down this road before.

Axel reached for a beer can that sat in a cooler beside his father. He glanced at the screen door and could smell food cooking. Dad's longtime girlfriend, Tammy, had to be in there whipping something up. Probably pork chops.

"I thought you said you were trying to get sober." *Lyin' son of a bitch…*

"And I thought what I do is none of yer beeswax." Dad removed a can of snuff from the front pocket of his red and black checkered tank top, stared at it as if he needed assurance it was still there, then put it right back.

"You done come down wit' cancer a few years ago, barely made it, and the doctor said you needed to lay off that booze, and whatever else you like to toss down your throat and shoot in your veins."

"Well, aren't you self-righteous? You told me just a few months ago to go fuck myself. Think you're the big man in town 'cause you been on the fuckin' news. You prick." The man laughed, but Axel knew Tommy didn't find a damn thing funny.

"I'm not here to fiddle and fuss with you. Your mail came to my house again." He removed the wad of folded letters, mostly bills and what not, and waved them before his father. "Just droppin' it off."

"Did Dallas tell ya that I won the lottery?"

Axel tossed the mail down on a nearby swing that was barely hanging on. It landed flat against a grimy yellow pillow with the words, 'Sunshine Fine,' sewn across it.

"What lottery, Dad? The one in your head? Bunch of balls rollin' around in there stuffed with cotton from the land of make-believe?"

His father's eyes narrowed on him, and he balled his fists up real tight. Suddenly, the screen door slammed open, and there stood Tammy in a frilly pink and white sundress, the woman who waited on his father, hand and foot. A fairly big woman with light brown hair and smiling hazel eyes, she worked at a nursing home giving baths and helping to serve meals. Just taking a few steps had her breathing hard—she had to sleep with one of those machines at night.

Tammy was one of the kindest ladies Axel had ever known. Shame that she'd gotten wrapped up with the likes of Dad. She certainly deserved better.

"Hey, Axel. Nice to see you! You stayin' for dinner, honey? I've got plenty." She pointed back towards the kitchen.

"Naw, I just came by to—"

"Come on and have a visit, Axel! Stay and eat. You know you should, or Tammy'll eat it all. Ain't no food safe around this lady!" He chortled. Axel shot a look at the woman, who even laughed at his father's tactless words, but a deep pain shone in her eyes now, and her cheeks had darkened undoubtedly from embarrassment. "Have a seat by me, Junior," his father urged, pointing to the broken-down chair beside him.

"I'm not a Junior."

"You were!"

"No, I wasn't."

He hated when the man pulled this shit. Lie after lie after damn lie. It was like a game of Jinga. Blocks of falsehoods, deceptions, and fabrications. It drove Axel nearly insane. He couldn't recall one time he'd ever been with his father, in his youth or as an adult, when the man wasn't exaggerating about something that happened, turning a fallacious story into a reason to brag about himself with false bravado, or outright lying. He'd lied about so much, there was no way he could keep up with it all. Perhaps a spreadsheet would help.

"Your middle name was my first name," Dad continued, refusing to let the matter go.

"That's not a Junior. And that's not what Mama said."

"Your mama's word doesn't mean a damn thing."

"And your word is about as good as a promissory note written in pissy letters from a rabid dog's cock sprayed out onto the snow."

Tammy left in a hurry, softly closing the door behind her.

"Summa uh bitch. You're not too grown tuh get the fuck smacked out cha." *I dare you. You'll be eating a dirt sandwich you lay a finger on me.* "When you were first born, *Junior*, you—"

"Your name is Tommy. Stop calling me Junior. I'm not nobody's junior, and I'm not gonna stand here while you disrespect Mama the way you like to do when you've had one too many."

"I'm still your papa, and you ain't got no right to talk to me like this, Axel."

"You got what you signed up for. Respect is given when it is earned. I always pay on time when it's due."

"And it's due to me, because without *me*, there would be no YOU." Tommy Theodore Hendrix II's voice quaked as he yelled and waved a finger at him.

The old man knew such shit got on his nerves. It was a pet peeve. *Why in the hell would I want to be a junior to someone as foul as you? Lying down and fuckin' don't make you no daddy. You popped up when it suited you.*

"Your name was Tommy when you were born. Your mean, rotten mama went and changed it after I had had enough of her shit and left her." The old man spat a wad of saliva on the ground, full of foamy venom. That evil inside of him was raw and youthful, despite his obviously weakened and inebriated state.

Dad was lying again, as usual. He lied about everything. He even lied on his lies. He didn't leave. Mama kicked his drunk ass out and filed for divorce after finding out he'd had yet another affair. Dad was going on another mendacious tangent, then, he saw Tammy's face in the window. She offered him a smile behind a sheer white curtain—sad and soft. Maybe she wanted the company? It sure looked like a pleading invitation to him. Dad offered nothing but insults and liabilities. She disappeared again, leaving them alone once more.

Axel cracked the can open, took a hard gulp, and plopped down beside him.

They were quiet for a while, during which Temple Of The Dog's, 'Hunger Strike' played from the television inside.

"I did win the lottery, Axel." He took a sip of his beer. "One of those scratch offs. Five hundred dollars."

"Congratulations," he stated flatly before taking another gulp.

"You want a hundred of it?"

"Nope. Every time you give me something, it's got strings attached. Thankfully, I'm not in a position where I need to borrow from anyone, anyhow."

"I know you don't. Got that nice house… the cars 'nd such…" The music kept playing and another song began.

"Taaaaa-mmmmy! Is that grub done?"

"Almost, honey!"

"She slow *and* fat now. Jesus Christ. When I first got with her, you remember I'm sure, she wasn't that big. Nice lookin', just a bit chubby. I can handle that. Now?" He shook his head as if repulsed. "I can barely fuck her. Can't find 'er pussy between all them rolls. If she got on top I'd probably fall right down through the floor and be in the basement." Dad laughed, as if he'd said something real nifty and hilarious.

Axel calmly lit a cigarette and shook his head in disgust. He looked out into the open yard. No neighbors or other homes in sight, just the two of them in the middle of nowhere with traces of cigarette smolder, greasy fried pork chops, and misery filling the air.

"That's supposed to be your ol' lady."

"She is."

"Look how you talk about her. She took care of your diseased, stinkin' ass when you were sick."

Dad rolled his eyes. "You're a mama's boy, Axel. Always taking the woman's side. Tammy knows I love 'er. It's just a joke. Lighten up."

Not once had Dad asked how he was doing after he'd had to shoot and kill two men. He knew he'd been hurt in one of the altercations. Not once had he asked about his business in the last year, or what he was up to. His goals. His life in general. It was always about Dad… about what *he* needed. What *he* felt. What *he* believed was funny and necessary. His selfishness ran deep.

"You're just like me, Axel. Got your own mind. Say things how you feel." The old man's voice was low and gravelly, covered in wickedness like gravy.

"I'd never talk about my ol' lady the way you talk about yours, after all she did for you."

"All she did for me?" Dad rolled his eyes and laughed mirthlessly. "I think she's fuckin' around on me with one of those male nurses at her job."

"What kind of garbage is that?"

"I'm serious. Come home smellin' funny sometimes, and for your information, it's my social security money that pays the bills 'round here! She doesn't keep a clean house, either, and if you so gotdamn worried about her, why don't you go up in there and help her get her shit together?! Show 'er where the bucket and mop is?!"

Axel flicked ashes onto the porch, and smirked.

"She should take that pot of mashed potatoes she got on that there stove, come on out here with it, and drown your ass in it. She bet not offer you no life jacket, either. Not even in damn Cheerio."

"Lord… You hate me that much, Axel?" The bastard had the nerve to sound wounded. His father's eyes were sad now, drooping a bit. The spunk was out of him, all of that fire he'd been blasting fizzled out.

Axel shrugged.

He didn't want to do this… *couldn't* do this. He quickly finished his beer, crushed the can in his bare hands, and tossed it in a cardboard box on the porch before standing and walking towards his truck.

"Axel!" his father hollered out, getting to his feet.

Axel got in his truck, started the engine, and pulled away from the unpaved driveway, dirt and dust kicking up as his wheels peeled out. After a few minutes, he was on a main drag, his breathing even and his temper calmed. A song came on the radio as he reached a red light—one that had been playing at the bar the other night when he was speaking to English.

He smiled when he thought about her but had decided he wasn't going to call her. He didn't want to date anyone who might have expectations. So many things he had to do, and dealing with a woman like that was work, and emotionally exhausting. He hadn't been in a serious relationship in a long while, strictly by choice. He figured one day he'd be ready to settle down again, but he worked a lot, too, and it would be difficult. English was no ordinary lady. He could tell after speaking to her that evening.

He kept driving, and that song kept playing, until he couldn't take it anymore.

When he got on the highway, he grabbed his cellphone off the dash and called her, placing it back in the holder as it began to ring.

"Hello?"

"Hey, English. It's me, Axel Hendrix. I met you at Cavaliers Inn the other night."

"Ahhh, yes. Hi, how are you?"

"I'm doing good. Real good… Are you in the mood for some Chinese food? I know a spot. I'd love to see you tonight…"

Chapter Five

DOUBLE DRAGON, FROM outward appearances, wasn't much to brag about. It was a little spot in a desolate strip mall alongside several shut-down businesses and vacated storefronts, most of which had seen better days.

The typical red neon letters blinked and buzzed, spelling out the name of the place, and a sun-faded menu with washed-out pictures of the culinary fare was taped to a window, the glass foggy and dotted with children's handprints. To add to the already questionable location, the staff in the restaurant seemed irritated as they spoke sharply in Chinese, shouting back and forth as people waited for meals, or to place a takeout order.

Nevertheless, English stood there with a stiff upper lip. The food smelled amazing, and she could see two cooks in the back, shiny faced Chinese men sweating from the heat of their fiery stoves, their expressions serious as they handled huge steel woks. It was almost artful the way they dumped seasonings into broth, and stirred in vibrant vegetables, or cracked multiple eggs in rice.

"*Kuàidiǎn!*" the lady at the register yelled to the chefs, her lips twisted like grapevines. When she turned back to the crowd, she made quick work of re-organizing the large takeout bags with their logo on the front on the counter, each with receipts stapled to it like a badge of honor. A pencil rested along the back of her ear, and her straight black hair, streaked with a little gray in the front, was bobby-pinned on the sides in a makeshift fashion.

So, this is where he takes me… Okay.

English stood there trying to make heads or tails of the situation. She had no idea that when Axel called and they'd arranged a dinner date, he'd be taking her to a carryout spot, an Asian greasy spoon.

I took all of that time getting pretty just for this lady to yell and scream and give everyone in here the evil eye, as if our existence bothers her soul deeply… My word. I wish I knew Chinese so I could understand what she was saying. I learned Spanish, French, Italian, and Swahili while in high school and college, but decided to not take it when I had the chance. Regrets.

She glanced at the front door and noticed it was almost dark now. Shadowy, ashen clouds and shades of navy blue blended together, creating enchanting hues. The spellbinding moment of dusk was almost gone, and the night had spread her dark wings to clock in for the third shift. The door chimed when another person entered the place—an older guy wearing a beat-up ballcap, holding his cellphone to his ear. English felt like a fish out of water as they drew closer to the register to place their orders. Two people were waiting in front of them. It wouldn't be long now.

Look at my clothes. Damn!

She'd carefully chosen a light periwinkle button-down sweater with faux diamond buttons, flared black pants, and simple black three-inch heels. Her hair was parted on the side and combed back, and she'd spent far too long on her makeup, trying to get her cat eyeliner on hooded lids just right. Everyone else was dressed down in ripped jeans and sleeveless shirts, smelling of sweat, sawdust, and the outdoors. Huge tattoos stood out, as well as tight leggings jammed in various ass cracks, paired with halter tops that barely covered some of the oversized melons on display.

See? This is my fault. I always look before I leap, but I was so happy to hear from him today, I didn't even think about it. I should've asked more questions.

Here she was in her favorite pair of sparkling teardrop earrings which finished her look, making her look like some queen amongst worker bees that may turn on her and sting out of pure entertainment. It would come as no surprise if he could read her mind. She already knew what he thought of her from the way he'd sized her up at the bar when they first met. It wasn't the first time she'd heard it anyway—people thinking she felt superior to others.

I guess I'm proving him right by looking down on this restaurant and the people in it. I'm trying to be good. But hold up, are those clumps of hair on the floor?

Her eyes narrowed on a dark, strange shape in the corner of the restaurant, where lighting was poor, and God only knew what grew there.

Oh my God. Who lost their weave tracks? Oh… I think it's just dirt.

She sucked her teeth and almost laughed at herself. *I'm not stuck up, but I can be picky, and I'm not even trying to hold you because I'm not apologizing for having standards. I mean, a first date is usually people trying to put their best foot forward. Hell, this might be his best foot for all I know. Next time, if there is a next time, he could be taking me to Burger King, and using coupons for it, too. Let me stop. Now I really am being stuck up. It's cool. As long as the food is good, that's really all that matters. God, please don't let me get sick, though.*

She briefly closed her eyes and clasped her hands together in prayer.

The kitchen looks like it could use a good wash down. With a power washer and 100 gallons of bleach. Holy Hygiene and Saint Sanitation, please be on my side.

Her stomach roiled, a fluttering of flirtatious lust knotting within her when he suddenly leaned into her, tearing her away from her deliberations. He bumped against her ever so slightly, perhaps by accident, but just enough for her to be titillated by his touch. Looking up at him from over her shoulder, she watched his striking green eyes scan the menu on the back wall. His shiny, long hair was pulled into a ponytail, and a pair of sunglasses sat atop his head. Axel was wearing a short-sleeved army green shirt and jeans—nothing fancy, but it suited him for sure. His muscular arms, covered in tattoos, were in full view. She suddenly sensed *he* knew she was looking, so she begrudgingly turned away before things became more awkward.

He smells like Irish Spring soap and cologne. So good…

The Chinese woman regarded Axel, then her.

"May I take your order?" she asked abruptly.

"Yeah. Two Sweet and sour chickens with fried rice, and 1 pork egg roll. 1 beef Lo Mein, order of boneless spareribs. One bourbon chicken."

"Ten extra minute on bourbon chicken!" the woman barked, though she sported a slight smile. Strange. Perhaps that was just how she always spoke, and meant nothing by it at all.

"That's fine." His eyes tapered as he looked at the menu once again, rubbing his hands together like some fly about to land on a pile of hot shit. "I also want an order of your Crab Rangoons. A Coke, too. Light ice. Don't give me none of that Dr. Pips pop, or Walmart cola—the grocery store brand y'all stockpile in the back and then charge full price for. I want the name brand."

Oh, so not only is he demanding with the staff and calling them out on their mess, he also ordered for me too, instead of asking what I wanted? I don't want no damn short ribs and bourbon chicken. I'm hungry. Shit. She stood there and stewed. *I'm about to order what I want anyway, and he can just stand there looking silly. He might be trying to control how much he spends. He should have never asked me out then, and from the truck he drives, and me being nosy looking him up online, he isn't struggling. What with him owning his own company and all. I make good money, but HE is the one who asked ME out. He damn sure should be able to afford some takeout. Yeah, there won't be a second date.*

"They're waiting. What do you want?" he asked, knocking down her theories like a bulldozer crashing into a ton of bricks.

"What? Wait a minute. All of that food was just for *you*?" she asked in shock.

He nodded, seeming genuinely confused as to why she'd ask such a thing.

"Uh, okay. I'd like the—"

"Oh, and this is all on one bill. Ring her shit up, I mean, her stuff, too, with mine."

She placed her hand over her mouth, curtailing an urge to laugh at this whole situation. *I'm so glad I have enough good sense to keep my thoughts to myself when I get like this. I was wrong about him a million times over. Thank God.*

"Hurry and order, lady." The woman frowned, her look almost menacing now.

You rude ass heffa…

"I am, *lady*. Can you give me a second to speak?"

"You holdin' up line!" The lady waved her arm about.

"You act like this place is going to implode if I don't speak at a hundred miles a minute. If you spent as much time putting some soap and water on these dirty floors and counters as you do running your mouth, you'd win the Mr. Clean Award of Louisville." The woman tried to talk over her but got shut down fast like a raid on an illegal dog fighting ring. "This isn't a James Bond movie. There's no bomb about to go off if I don't speak within three seconds! You talk to the cooks like trash. I don't need to understand what you're saying to know that—tone is universal—and you talk to these hardworking people in here, who are spending their money to get something to eat, as if you are doing *them* a favor by your mere existence. That's *Dr.* Lady to you, and you've got me messed up. Please don't let the attire fool you, sweetheart. I can get just as ig'nant as you in one second flat. I might be slow on the draw, but I'm fast on the blast. Good grief!"

Some people waiting in line burst out laughing, including Axel who was bent over at the waist, barely catching a breath and his eyes watering. However, English was dead serious, and she wasn't going to be disrespected, especially in front of all these folks. Rudeness was a pet peeve of hers, and it riled her up to a fast rage. The woman, obviously annoyed by her response, began to mumble under her breath in Chinese.

"Now, I'd like the Moo Goo Gai Pan and a vegetable egg roll, please." English grimaced and crossed her arms.

"That all?"

"...Yes."

The woman rang everything up, and Axel pulled out his wallet and paid for their dinner. They got out of line and took a seat at one of the small wooden tables. The chairs rocked and wobbled like some amusement park ride. Sitting wide-legged across from her, he looked about as he tapped his fingers along the table.

Damn, he looks good... What is wrong with me? A pussy drought. That's what's wrong with me.

"You let Tao have it," he said with a grin.

"Oh, you and she are on a first name basis?" She crossed her legs and smirked.

He nodded, then got up and grabbed his soda when called. Back at the table, he unwrapped his straw.

"I come in here at least once a week for lunch. Real

good food. Big portions, too."

"Is she always like that?"

"Grumpy? Mmm hmm." He took a long draw from his drink, then shook the cup. "You want some?"

"No, I'm fine. Where are we going to eat the food? There are only two tables in here, and I figured we must be going someplace else to eat it."

"My house."

"Uh, I don't think so, Axel." She pressed her thighs together at the mere thought of it.

"Why not?" His brow rose, that same curious and confused expression on his face as earlier, when she'd asked about all the food he'd ordered for himself.

"Because I don't know you like that. I don't go to men's houses that soon."

"Men's houses that soon?" He threw up his hand and looked taken aback. "I didn't say we were eating in my bedroom, and then eating each other right afterwards." He chuckled. "It would be relaxed and chill."

"Uh huh… like Netflix and chill. Everyone knows where that leads." She rolled her eyes.

"We'd eat in my living or dining room. The kitchen. Wherever you felt comfortable. I even have a balcony and patio if you want to sit outside. I could light the fire pit."

"No, that's okay." She grabbed her purse and rustled around in it for her phone. "I just don't think that's appropriate."

He rolled his eyes, laughed, and shook his head.

"Where should we go then, English, that would make you feel more at ease? A Catholic church? Ask to eat in the convent lunchroom?"

She ignored his little jab. "Maybe we can eat in your truck at a park?"

He stared at her with a mixture of irritation and amusement.

"Fine," he finally said with a shrug.

After a few minutes of small talk, their order was called. Axel shot up like a rocket, gathered the bags from the counter, and they made their way out the door. The burst of cool air felt good against her skin, and moments later she was in the passenger's seat, the warm food on her lap as they made their way out of the strip mall parking lot.

He turned on the music, and Weezer's version of Metallica's, 'Enter Sandman' played as he explained that he was taking her to Cherokee Park. She'd never been, but he said it was nice. He then turned the volume up to an ear-splitting level, and the hard rock song vibrated through the entire truck. Axel was vibing to it, beating the steering wheel in rhythm. WAP! WAP! WAP! The music filled her core and flooded out, making her nerves jump, her ears ring … and the song? She liked it. He began to sing the lyrics at the top of his lungs, and she burst out laughing because he sounded so good.

"It's a good song, right?!" he screamed over the roar of the music. He removed his sunglasses off his head and tossed them down, brandishing a toothy grin.

"Yes!" she screamed back, loving how his hair was now coming undone from the ponytail each time he rocked in his seat, flying back and forth like flaxen whips.

She had no idea how he could see as he drove, but he seemed to be navigating the road just fine.

When they arrived at the park, which truly was beautiful and aglow with pole lights, he found a rather secluded parking space and turned the music down to a low roar. She reached into the bag, handed him a fistful of napkins and sauces, then they got settled with forks and chopsticks… music… crickets.

They talked a good while, and then, the conversation drew to more interesting concepts and ideas. Something she could sink her teeth into.

"Well, I must say, it was worth her terrible attitude. This is honestly some of the best Chinese food I've ever had, and that says a lot because I've traveled practically this whole country."

"See?" His eyes lit up, proud of himself. It was actually really nice to see that he cared about her being satisfied. "I told you it was good."

"Axel, let me ask you something."

"Yeah," he said around a mouthful of food, which he washed down with a long gulp from his drink. She now regretted not ordering a beverage, too. "What is it?"

"What made you decide to talk to me after you all but told me you weren't interested."

He looked straight ahead, as if mulling his answer.

"Well, that weirdo you were dancin' with and talking to, I peeped him staring at you when you were roundin' up to leave. I thought he'd left, but he hadn't, and I didn't like how he was looking at you. He was up to no good. I knew he was going to try 'nd follow you out, and sure enough, he started doing just that, so I made sure I walked you to your car and stayed put until I saw him give up and leave. And that got him off your trail."

Her face heated as she stared into Axel's eyes. She had no idea that man at the club had been eyeballing her, looming in the darkness. She did remember him getting a little too touchy feely, and she had to tell him to buzz off when he kept pushing his luck, then had the audacity to try and slip his hand between her thighs. She'd cussed him out then, and he moved along. Or so she'd thought.

"Oh. So you were being protective. Well, thank you."

"Yeah, but that situation made me come and talk to you outside, so he'd go away before I had to do somethin' to him… and I found myself liking how you were expressing yourself then. 'Bout your job, things like that. Honestly, English, I was attracted to you as soon as Melanie introduced us. I mean, hell, you were the best-lookin' woman in there that night." She was certain she was blushing now. There'd been many pretty women in the place, but he'd singled her out. "I also wanted Mel to win her bet, as silly as that might sound, because she was right."

"Right about what?"

"You being my type."

She was definitely blushing now, for heat rushed to her face. Something about Axel made her feel like he was genuinely concerned about what she had to say, and not just trying to get in her pants—though she was certain the potential of her pants being down around her freaking ankles had something to do with his suave words. She wasn't that damn enamored with the man that she forgot he was, well, a man.

"...and uh, though your question about my job rubbed me the wrong way, I meant what I said to you. But there was just something about you as we were out there talkin' beside your car. That goofball gave me a chance, an opportunity if you will, to hit the rewind button. I was out there to make sure you got to your car okay, and that he didn't follow you, but then, more happened."

"And what was that?" She dipped a Rangoon he offered her in the sweet red sauce, and popped it into her mouth.

"You grabbed my attention is what happened. I wanted to give it another try in case I was wrong about you." He shrugged. "I'm usually not wrong about people though, to keep it uh buck wit' you, but I know that whatever I think I know, first impressions aren't always accurate, no matter how good I am at scoping bullshit. People get nervous, or might be in a bad mood and stumble over their words. 'Specially when alcohol is involved."

"Thank you. That's true, too." She smiled at him.

"You want some of this Coke? You probably need something to wash that down. They put a lot of salt in the food, sometimes too much. Makes ya thirsty."

The moonlight stroked his face, and his hair glowed around the softness in his gaze. Axel typically appeared hard. He spoke hard. He acted hard, and it didn't seem phony either, but in that moment, his smile seemed gentle. She liked it. She liked it a lot.

"Yeah, I'd like some."

He slipped the lid off his cup and handed it to her. *How thoughtful of him to remove the straw and such for me…* She took the cup and swallowed hard, only to have some of the liquid dribble down her chin onto her shirt.

"Shit."

She went for a clean napkin to dab at it. Axel immediately jumped into action, removed the cup from her hand, and started to do the honors.

"I got it," he offered.

He dabbed gently along her face with the papery brown napkin, then down her neck and collarbone. When he got down to her breast, he didn't hesitate, but she noticed the pressure of his hand was softer.

"There you go." He balled up the napkin and tossed it in a bag.

"Thank you."

"No problem."

"So," she picked up her fork and resumed eating. "You're from here? Louisville?"

"Yup. Born and raised in Portland, Kentucky. You said you were from Dry Ridge on the night we met, right?"

"Yes. Most of my family is there, too."

"I got some associates 'round that way. Not much going on out there is it?"

"No. It's fairly quiet. Peaceful." She paused. "I'd like to talk to you about your job. It seems so interesting. What kind of—"

"Naw." He burst out laughing, food in his mouth.

"Baby, you don't wanna talk about that while we're sittin' here tryna eat. I can talk about it just fine, but I've learned from experience that it's not what needs to happen when food is close by. Ain't nothin' pretty about what I do, and I ain't got nothing to hide, but that's not dinner conversation, sweetheart. Ask me some other time."

"You're right!" She laughed. "Never mind." She waved her hand about in surrender. "Point taken!"

"Let me ask you something though." He swiped his napkin across his mouth and turned her way, looking rather serious. "So, you study African American history, go through those old books and what not, and you seem like an activist, I guess you could say? Is that right?"

"I wouldn't call myself an activist per se, no, but I'm knowledgeable on the African American experience as documented in books, their growth and struggle from the time my ancestors' journey began non-consensually from the continent of Africa, ending with their arrival in the United States. Mainly, it was people from Gambia, Senegal, Mali and Guinea-Bissau and west-central Africa. My focus is on the post-slavery experience, particularly the 1920s when the music and poetry scene erupted and became a movement of its own. Also, the Great Depression of the 1930s, as well as the 1950s and '60s civil rights movement. Besides, I have studied texts written by the Black Panther organization founded by Huey P. Newton, as well as the Black Lives Matter movement."

"BLM... Didn't that founder lady trick that money off and she up in a big fifty-room mansion in California right about now?"

"Look, there's been some questionable behavior with BLM, I will admit that, but I'm not their spokesman. My focus is on historical texts. One day, they will have historical texts, too. I am still following current events like you and everyone else, but not studying them per se."

"I mean, I wasn't tryna get you off focus or nothing. I just thought maybe you knew. Isn't that a shame? She's a deceiver and a thief."

She didn't know if Axel was trying to poke the bear, or if he was serious. Perhaps he was trying to see if she co-signed with some of the dubious conduct, because that was her lane, and she was Black, too.

"You want to talk to me about Black Lives Matter, Axel? Is this how you wish for the night to end? Really?"

He shrugged and looked rather blasé while reaching for a toothpick and twiddling it in his mouth. *No home training.*

"Not really. I think it's pretty self-explanatory what happened with BLM. They're full of shit, and contrary to what people might think or assume about me, if you ask me, both parties of our government are full of shit. Straight, no chaser. They don't give a crap about the common man or woman. Voting don't make no damn difference. All of 'em are going to get in office and screw us over. We're pawns in their game."

"I think voting for *you* is different than voting is for me, because Axel, you and your people always had the right to do it. Especially White men. A White man born with privilege from your birthright alone. Now, riddle me this: if you are right, and if voting didn't matter, one party wouldn't be trying so damn hard to stop a certain people from voting, now would they, by having all of these hoops for folks to jump through, and making it harder to reach polling stations? This is happening especially in the Midwestern and Southern states where they know that vote swings harder in one direction than the other, due to the racial demographics, segregation, and disparity. If something doesn't work, people don't bother to try 'nd stop you, now do they?"

He regarded her not in confusion, but with an expression of admiration. That warmed her soul. Was he getting it?

"Although we could argue if that's really the motivation, I see your point. As far as the broader topic at hand, I know damn well racism is alive 'nd well, so let's get that out of the way. I got friends from all walks of life, and I've got some racist family members, too, so I've seen and heard it with my own eyes and ears my whole life. What the police did to Breonna Taylor was fucked up in a major way, right here in Kentucky. In our own backyard. Shameful." She nodded in agreement. "But back to BLM… they got greedy. Just like a lot of groups. Don't matter the race of the group, or how they start—the intentions might be pure at the beginning, but then, all that money comes rushing in fast, to people that ain't ever had that kind of money before, and evil takes hold. They're not above it. *Nobody* is." His eyes turned to slits. "Corruption happens all the time. Anyway, continue with what you were saying before we got into politics and all that other bullshit."

She agreed with a lot that he said—not all of it, but a nice majority. That was refreshing.

"Thank you for sharing your perspective with me. So, as I was saying, it's my job to know these things, including the touted critical race theory, which is a bunch of crap, amongst other things. This theory directly affects books. My job. Yes, I take pride in that, and I take pride in my work, my family, and my culture."

"Okay, so, with all that being said, you havin' pride 'nd all, what would make you agree to a date with me?"

"What do you mean?" She knew damn well what he meant, but she was a bit taken aback that he broached this topic right then in the middle of a serious conversation.

His lips curled in an all-knowing grin that made her feel a bit on the spot.

"Come on now, Dr. Price, you know what I'm talkin' about. I'm as White as they get. I'm a country boy from Portland, Kentucky, and here you are, this Black woman, into Black American culture—so much so, it's pretty much your job to breathe, eat and sleep with it." He moved his big hands around, involving them in his communication. "Seems it might be a conflict of interest."

He drank from his cup with a mischievous smirk. Maybe he had legit concerns, but he was also a king-sized shit starter. Either way, the question was on the table now, and she was going to deal with it.

"To be completely honest with you, Axel, when I was first approached by a man who wasn't Black many years ago, and he asked me out on a date, it made me uncomfortable."

"Uncomfortable? Why?" He unwrapped his eggroll from parchment paper, and began to chew on it. The filling of carrots and cabbage sprang out the fried outer shell.

"I declined to date him based pretty much on that alone."

"Him being White?"

"Yes. I know it sounds bad, but you asked, so there you go." What could she say?

"Naw, I always want the truth," he said, not seeming the least bit phased. "The truth doesn't hurt me none, but it's the lies that get ya. So then, what happened? What changed your mind?"

"Afterwards, I regretted it. Not because my relationships with mostly Black men didn't always go in the direction I wanted them to, but because I never gave him a chance. He had, at least on paper, all the things I'd want in a person to date. He was attractive, intelligent, and goal-oriented. He had a good career and was funny… a nice guy… but he was White. As I matured, I realized that I can have pride in my race, and fight for my people, love the books I help preserve and prepare for others to enjoy, and still love whoever I want to love. So, when the next non-Black man approached me, him being Korean, I went out with him. We had a good time. There was no chemistry, but he was cool, and we follow each other on Instagram."

He smiled at that.

"I had another opportunity, then another and another, and I was open. Great dates, interactions, even dated a

Colombian man, Arturo, for several months. But then, I met my ex-boyfriend, Willis, a Black man who happened to meet my criteria, or so I thought…" She paused and rolled her eyes. "We were together a while." She shrugged. "Now, I'm back in the dating arena so to speak, and again, the gate is open. I'm accepting applications, but I'm more careful now. Older. Whatever man is best for me, Axel. I'm not turning *anyone* down as long as they have the attributes that I consider non-negotiable."

The man put on a thoughtful expression. He just sat there, listening to the soft music, chewing and drinking. Had she said too much? She expected him to ask more about what she said, perhaps drill her a bit, but he didn't. *Maybe what I said was enough then?* She went back to eating her food, and though they'd gone on radio silence, she was enjoying the vibe—awkward beginnings at Chinese carryout places and all. She looked around, noticing the lush, vibrant trees. Soon, their colors would be changing. Autumn was definitely in the air.

"What about you?" she asked before tapping the side of her mouth with a napkin. He offered her a piece of succulent sweet and sour chicken from between two wooden chopsticks, and she accepted.

"What about me?" he asked while she rested, her belly full while she savored the tender meat and bits of pineapple.

"I know I'm not the first Black woman you've dated because you said I'm your type."

"It's not a race thing."

"Oh?" This sparked her interest. She leaned slightly

closer to him. "Then what is it?"

"It's a vibe. It's the body shape… the mind. The chemistry. I know it sounds like a line of bullshit, but I'm for real. I can't stand stupid people. Not like folks that are slow—that's not their fault. I'm talking about—"

"Willfully ignorant."

"Exactly. I like nerdy girls, but sexy nerdy girls."

She burst out laughing.

"I'm for real. Hope you're not offended."

"No." She shook her head, a bit taken aback, yet appreciative of his honesty. "I've been called that several times, and it's okay."

"You don't look like one. You're sexy, have beautiful eyes, but uh, you *act* like one, and that combination isn't easy to come by. So… Melanie knew what she was talkin' about. Like she said, she's known me a long time, and her brother and I are, well… we *were* close for most of our lives."

He looked away, running his knuckle along his nostril as if to cure an itch. "You ever meet Legend?" he asked while cleaning up their trash and stuffing it in one of the larger bags.

"No, I never met him. I've known Melanie for about five years, and he and I never crossed paths. I saw a picture of him, though." *The man is fine as fuck.* She could only imagine what young ladies would think, seeing Axel and Legend walking in places together like they owned them. They both had that… what was it called? Big dick energy. The pussies in those areas must've cried for days! Two rough, buff country bucks. Like when the Beatles would get on stage back in the day. Both of them were incredible eye candy, as they were both unusually good-looking. The type of good-looking where all you could do was stop and stare.

English herself had swooned a bit when she saw some short video clips and pictures of him years ago. A rugged, tall, muscular guy who also had a darkness in his eyes that rubbed her the wrong way. Besides, he was an ex-con, so that was a definite no-go for her.

"Axel, I have soooo many questions for you, but I don't want to bombard you all at once."

He shrugged. "You can ask me whatever. But it's not like we're not going to see each other again."

She smirked as he started up the engine. He too must've realized they'd been sitting there laughing and talking for hours. The park was now closed. "Oh, is that so?"

"Yeah, that's so." His teeth sank into his lower lip as he traveled the path toward the exit. *So hot.* "So, what do you think about Sunday? My work schedule is kinda crazy, but I can do Sunday afternoon."

"What are we going to do? Go to an Italian place where the mafia is sitting around with guns pointed at us?" she teased. "You might have a habit of taking me to good but dangerous places. That lady's mouth was reckless."

"And so was yours. You see she shut up."

She couldn't help but giggle at that. Perhaps she went in a little too hard on the woman, but oh, well.

"Sunday at what time?" She reached into her purse,

grabbed her lipstick, and reapplied.

"Maybe 'round five as long as I don't get a call from the police or anyone." She nodded in understanding. "And I don't know why you're putting on lipstick. I'm just gonna eat it off."

She shrieked when he yanked his truck over to the side of the road, parked it, and proceeded to suck out her soul when his lush mouth touched hers. She melted into the motherfucker, her body on fire. Then, when she had turned to jelly, he broke the kiss, put the truck in drive, and went on about his way, as though nothing had even happened. When he arrived at her condo, he helped her out of the truck and walked her up to her front door.

"I had a nice time, Axel. Thanks for dinner."

He nodded, then leaned in and kissed her cheek, heading back to his vehicle after he saw her open her door.

"Good night, sugar." His tone was wispy, low-pitched and sexy.

She watched him walk back to his truck, his footsteps hard, then get inside.

Tonight was more than just a good date. This was a solid connection…

They waved to each other once more, and she entered her home, locking the door behind her. She smelled like delicious greasy Chinese food, and his cologne. She didn't know the name of it, but she'd forever associate that scent with him. It became a part of her over the last few hours, just like the smile that took over her face.

Chapter Six

AXEL STOOD UNDER the roaring shower, shampoo in his hair. The water was almost too hot to bear, but he wanted a deep clean, so he kept it that way. Grime. Filth. Stench. Pain. *Be gone.*

In the basin of the shower enclosure, the once dirty water was now clear. He stared at his big feet, the suds collecting around them until they, too, were gone.

He'd been covered in proper protective attire from the top of his head to the bottom of his thick rubber boots, as he always was for his job, but he'd been called over to a hoarder's home, and that was a different animal altogether. Irrespective of the elaborate equipment—clothing layers, goggles, elbow length gloves—he still felt as if he was encrusted in dirt and dust after walking out of that place. He and his crew worked around the professional junk haulers transporting considerable piles of trash. It was a small two-bedroom, well-built house, on a nice tree-lined street, that was roach and vermin infested. Besides the critters, the old man had died alone.

He'd been there amid the countless stacks of garbage, papers, expired and rotten food, overflowing sewage from the non-functional toilet, moth-eaten magazines from the 1980s, and grocery sacks of soiled adult diapers in each and every room. According to the coroner, the man had been deceased for at least a week. Only the mailman noticed something was amiss, for the old man always retrieved his mail from the box, and said hello to him when they'd spot one another. But said mail had begun stacking up. Red flag. And then, there was the odor—far more pungent than usual. The mail carrier called the police for a wellness check once six days of no mail retrieval had passed.

Axel grabbed his bar of soap, lathered his fingers for the third time, and took great care in going over his nails and knuckles, and in between his digits, too. His mind kept drifting to the old man, no matter how he tried to hum songs and push the thought away. Perhaps due to his own trials and tribulations as of late, this case had yanked on the fact that no one is promised tomorrow. Life was so fragile.

Such cases were always a bit harder to deal with—elderly lonely people with no family or friends, left to literally rot. Just as bad, if not worse, were the cleanup jobs after children had passed away. Sometimes, it was due to violence or neglect, occasionally due to them being in hospice at home, facing death after enduring a lifelong pediatric illness. He could stomach the gruesome scenes, while so many others fell apart. He could tolerate the bilious smells. The crying and prying eyes of neighbors and fair-weather friends. The dried blood, piss-soaked sheets, feces and maggots.

But it was the grief that got him.

That raw, gnawing pain that most humans experienced at least once in their life, some more than others, changing them forever. He had to see it over and over again, in its ugliest, and most vulnerable form. He heard the stories behind how it all came to be. *That* was far more potent and important than the death of flesh and blood.

Axel rinsed his hair, wrung it dry with a few hard squeezes of his hands looped around the long, heavy tresses, then turned the water off. He stepped out of the shower, dried off, and wrapped a black towel around his waist.

Music was playing in his bedroom, and he could hear it better now that the shower was turned off: 'Goldlink,' by Crew, an extended version on the WBTF The Beat 107.9 FM. Making his way there, he never got over the beauty of the multi-colored lights. Several of the windows throughout his home were made of colorful stained glass. He'd installed them himself after obtaining them from an old Catholic church that had been doing renovations after being struck by lightning. He walked across the room, suffused in sunny streams of red, gold, and green filtering through. Opening his dresser, he grabbed a pair of boxer-briefs from the drawer.

Jesus with a halo was held by his mother, Mary, both looking down upon him, along with several saints, whose eyes seemed to focus on his movements. Thoughts of Ms. Florence came to mind.

Since the evening of that dream, he'd on occasion had trouble sleeping. He'd wake up abruptly with no sound reason as to why. Neither Legend nor Caspian had returned his calls.

I can't control that. I can't make 'em call me back. Is she angry with me about that?

He'd thought of a million justifications to categorize it all as a dream and nothing more, but that didn't explain the white feather on his floor, and the odd sensation he had when he first looked into English's eyes. When he realized she was a history buff, that drew him to her even more. Ms. Florence had also had a sophistication about her, despite her often-whimsical attire, as well as knowledge, intelligence, and the ability to attract others to her. He was coming to terms with something he'd never considered long enough to admit to himself, let alone anyone else.

He'd had a crush on Ms. Florence, and somehow, someway, this played on his future attraction to certain women. Hence, he got rock hard when in the presence of a gorgeous nerd. He shook the thoughts away and continued with his grooming. He bobbed his head to the music as he sprayed on deodorant and cologne, discarded the towel on his bed, and put on the rest of his clothing—a dark red long-sleeved shirt, jeans, and a pair of black and white Adidas. Grabbing the towel once more, he dried off his hair, then stood in front of his dresser mirror while running a fine-toothed comb through his beard. When he was done, he gathered his tresses and arranged them into a low, loose manbun.

He picked up his phone to check movie times at a local theater, planning to follow up with English and ask if she wanted to catch a flick. He was feeling her, enjoying their time together. They'd been out a couple more times, and he was definitely interested in Dr. English Price. His reservations about her were gone, and she was no doubt a viable candidate. There was just one problem…

She plays hard to get, and I'm tired of it. We're not kids… too many games. It's getting old. He still hadn't gotten invited inside her house, and she kept skirting around coming to his home. Still, although he was a little sexually frustrated, she was a bit of a tease, so it was just a matter of time before she caved in. The woman had enjoyed wearing tight and short clothing for their more recent dates, playing with him, kissing him all over his face, flirting, saying sexual suggestive things, letting him feel on her ass and suck on her neck. He had her practically drooling in his truck as he kissed and held her, but she still managed to gain her composure and wiggle away.

He knew she wanted him as much as he wanted her—there was no way she could keep this charade up much longer, as far as he was concerned.

As he got online, he noticed several missed calls from a number he didn't recognize, and someone had left a voicemail. He played the message, putting it on speaker as he gathered some clothing from the floor that he'd tossed there the night before.

"Hey, Axel, this is Gee. I'm callin' from work. The gas station. Look, some guy was around here asking about you. Wonderin' if I knew you and askin' where you hang out. Never seen him before, and neither had Henry. I told him I didn't know who he was talking about. I didn't like his vibe at all. Call me."

Axel placed the clothing in a hamper, grabbed his gun out of his closet as he always did, and put it inside his holster. He snatched his phone from off the bed and called Gee, an old friend of his, back.

"Circle K, Gee speaking."

"Gee, it's Axel. Got your message. What's up?"

"Yeah, man. Some short guy came up in here buying some beer, then asked if you lived 'round here. I asked why? And he got an attitude and acted like I was just supposed to—"

"Did he say his name or what he wanted?"

Axel leaned over his nightstand, pulled open the drawer, and grabbed a lighter, then a pack of his Marlboro cigarettes.

"He told me and Henry that his name was Len, but that was probably a lie. He ain't say what he wanted beyond where you like to hang, thangs like that."

"All right." He lit the cigarette. "If he comes by again, call or text me right away. Thanks for the heads up."

"No problem. We look out for each other 'round here. I know dem dudes from Texas ain't tryna catch no trouble with you after you showed 'em better than you can tell 'em. Catch you later."

Axel ended the call and sat quietly for a while, staring off into the distance. Picking up a bottle of water from the nightstand, he drained it, then smoked his cigarette for a few moments before checking out the cinema times on the website he pulled up on his phone. As with his job, Gee's call didn't cause him much alarm. It was the nature of the beast.

If you stay ready, you ain't got to get ready. Let me call this cutie. I want to see my Olde English 800 malt, tonight…

"What's up, Ms. Doctor?" He smiled as soon as she answered her phone.

"Nothing much! Did you get your new tattoo?"

He'd told her about his intention to get one of the Greek Gods, Hermes.

"Not yet. I had to work. Got a couple of calls. I'll probably get it next week. What are you doing right now?"

"Uh, just got home a few minutes ago, actually." He heard a door close. "Was about to make myself a little dinner, warm up these leftovers, and call my mama to see how she's doing. What are you up to, handsome?"

"You want to check out that new Tom Cruise movie?"

"Tonight?"

"Yeah."

"I have to take care of a lot of stuff tonight, Axel."

"You said you were going to warm up leftovers and call your mother."

"Yes, but after that, I need to go over this book that was given to me last minute today by the museum, and it's almost four hundred pages. The damn thing is falling apart. I'm going to try and see if any of it can be salvaged. It's only one of fifteen copies, and on top of that, there's water damage and—"

"Come on, baby. If it's raggedy today, it'll still be raggedy tomorrow. One more day won't change that. Nothin' you can do to save it right now, anyway."

"You're being selfish. You know that's not the point."

"You're being selfish by not jumping on this opportunity. You know how my schedule has been this last week, so whenever I have some time for myself, I try to make good use of it. Spendin' time with you *is* good use of it, if you ask me."

"Is that so?"

"Yeah. I'll swing by around seven-thirty?" He tapped the cigarette ashes into the ashtray. "It starts at eight-fifteen at Rave Cinemas. Let me come see you..."

"...Okay."

"I'll be there soon, beautiful." He disconnected the call, got to his feet, smashed his cigarette in the ashtray, then slipped his gun back out. He checked the chamber of his Glock 19. All fifteen rounds were ready and able.

No one is going to make me walk around my own hood in fear. These bastards aren't even from 'round here, trying to tell folks what to do and how to do it. You're not going to try and kill me twice, and then have the family jewels to wage some war against me because the police are investigating your asses for some bullshit YOU did. I've seen death too many times in my lifetime to be afraid of it, or to just lie back and let that shit happen to me, too. My life hasn't been sunshine and roses, but it's mine, and I will protect it—come rain, sleet, snow, or blood...

He grabbed his truck keys and headed out the door.

Chapter Seven

AXEL SMILED AT the screen, looking a bit like Josh Turner under the spell of the theater's ambiance. They'd both been fairly quiet during the film. Shared a few glances, and at one point, he winked at her and intertwined their fingers. As usual, he smelled good, looked practically delicious, and she didn't miss the big ass bulge in his pants when they'd first sat down, taking their seats. Something about the way his pants wrapped around his groin allowed her to see the full outline of his dick and balls, and if looks aren't deceiving, Axel was packin' like he was leaving on a midnight train to Georgia.

He was paying close attention to the movie, very much into it, while all she did was lust after him at various intervals, or pondering things, asking herself questions such as, *'How tall is Tom Cruise?'* and, *'Isn't he a bit too long in the tooth to be doing these stunts?'*

Axel's hands were covered in butter from the popcorn he'd scarfed down, but she didn't mind. He lit up the room with his booming laughter. She'd enjoyed hearing a full belly laugh from the man multiple times while seated next to him. It sounded like thunder and orchestra music, a perfect blend. He just dripped with sexiness, more so because he didn't even try. The theater exploded in applause when the final action scene played out. But her mind then drifted to work, her mounting to-do list, and other issues she could do absolutely nothing about. She slurped on her cherry Icee as the movie ended, then gathered her belongings when the end credits began to roll.

"That was good. Are you ready?" he asked. The lights came on and he put on his leather jacket.

"Yeah, I am."

Before she knew it, the bastard had snatched her Icee out of her hand and began noisily slurping on the straw, trying to garner anything that was left.

"Excuse me!"

"Mmm hmm," he hummed, looking anywhere but at her.

"Axel, that was so rude."

"You were just gonna leave it here!" He pointed to where it had been sitting during most of the movie, as if that somehow drove his point home.

"You don't know that. You could've asked." She rolled her eyes at him, pretending to really care. She actually found it hilarious, but this was far too entertaining for her to back down now.

"Shoulda, woulda, coulda. Do you want another one? I can buy you one if it means that much to you."

"No. You go on right ahead and knock yourself out."

He kept drinking, then got to his feet when he was good and satisfied. As they walked out, he tossed his hollow popcorn bucket and the now empty Icee cup into the trash receptacle.

"I need to make a stop in the restroom," she explained as they neared the exit.

"Okay. I'll wait over here."

He leaned against the wall, messing with his phone, while she went to the ladies' room.

He has butter on his hands. You'd think he'd want to wash them. I'm going to say something about that when I get out of here. Men are trifling.

She waited in a short line, and then when a stall was available, she went inside, taking small breaths of air through her mouth to prevent from smelling too much.

Damn! Somebody blew this stall up! It smelled like gorilla shit in that cubicle, combined with a million dead mice, and hot city garbage. *I'mma be sick!* All she wanted to do was take a pee and be on her way. As she layered the toilet with paper to protect her bare behind from the seat, she felt her phone vibrating. She sat down, rummaged in her purse as she urinated, and finally got a hold of her phone.

Her heart sank. It was a text message from Master.

I've waited too long for you to call me back. Shira, I'm done playing with you.

She placed the phone back into her purse, blinking back tears of anguish and frustration. Moments later, she was at the sink washing and drying her hands as some woman argued with her daughter on the phone. English regarded herself in the water-stained mirror and tended to herself—fixing her hair and reapplying her lipstick.

I look unbothered, don't I? Can I pass that off? I have to look okay. I'm not going to let this mess ruin my evening. I said I was going to take my life back, and that's what I did. I can't go through this again. This was supposed to be over.

She fixed her twisted bra strap and sprayed a bit more perfume behind her ears.

I should go to the police… but what if he does good on his threats from before? I don't want anyone else involved in this!

She went out into the lobby and screamed. Axel was standing there with a man in a half nelson, squeezing the life out of him. A vein bulged from the bastard's forehead, and he was turning a deep purple, his arms flailing loosely, and his knees giving out. What was heart stopping, and incredibly creepy, was how calm Axel looked while he administered this level of violence. As if it was just another night at the movies.

"Axel!"

She raced toward him, where a small crowd had gathered and a security guard stood somewhat nonchalantly, talking into a radio about needing backup.

"What's going on?" She brushed past someone. Was he crazy? Was this why he'd been on the news? Was he a loose cannon always popping off at the drop of a dime?

But she'd looked into him. Axel had no criminal record, with the exception of a few speeding tickets.

"He tried to come up on me and take my fuckin' phone," he told her.

"Sir, please let him go. We have the police on the way."

"I told you I'm not turnin' him loose until they're actually here. He'll just run off."

Axel's prisoner seemed to be losing consciousness at this point. Thankfully, two police officers appeared soon thereafter, making a beeline towards them. Axel turned in their direction and repeated his story.

"I was standing here waiting for my friend to come out of the bathroom. I was on my phone, and this son of a bitch raced up to me and tried to snatch my phone out of my hand and take off. He ran into the *right* one, tonight. I can promise ya that."

"Let him go," one of the officers demanded, sounding a bit perturbed.

Axel glared at the cop with an expression of challenge and then, with a forceful shove that landed the man on the ground, he released him.

"He did it! He tried to steal that man's phone!" an older White guy with a red ball cap on stated loudly, as if he wanted in on the attention in the worst way. "I saw him try 'nd take his phone, officer."

"He's lying!" the man on the ground said between coughs, while skulking about on his knees.

"Look at the tape. There's cameras all around here," Axel protested.

What started as a simple enough ending to a date night had turned into their own personal action adventure, but without Tom Cruise. So much so, she'd almost forgotten about her troubles. The police took several witness statements and jotted Axel's information down. The man who'd tried to steal the phone was ultimately arrested due to some outstanding warrants, and promptly removed from the premises. Apparently, he'd done similar crimes in the city, too.

"It's too late to get dessert now, right? They close soon," Axel asked as he walked her out to his truck. They'd planned to go to Graeter's Ice Cream after the movie, if time permitted.

"You just choked a man half to death, Axel, and you have the audacity to still be thinking about food?! I can't believe this..."

"Am I supposed to lose sleep over this? Who cares?" He shrugged. "I don't give a damn about that man. I'm out with you. Besides, it wasn't that serious."

"It wasn't that serious? Axel, take me home, please. I think we should skip dessert. I've had enough excitement for one night." She readjusted her purse along her shoulder, unnerved by his casual attitude. "We can get ice cream some other time," she added for good measure. *Damn. I really wanted that ice cream.*

"We can go tonight. Like I said. Why let someone like that have that sort of power over you to the point it changes your date plans?" He opened the truck door for her.

Some ice-cream does sound good, but I can't get over how this fool is acting, like he didn't do anything serious, or nothing severe happened. He didn't just have him on the ground, or something like that. No. He literally was choking him out. I wonder if he makes it a habit of yokin' people up? See? This is why bad boys are bad news. He's oblivious.

"What type of insane person are you?"

"Type? As in flavors? Is there a variety pack or something?" His brows rutted. He looked downright pissed.

She got into the passenger's seat, ignoring his sarcastic question, and he politely closed the door behind her.

Getting in the truck, he hit it in reverse, then kicked it into drive, out of the parking lot. He turned on the music, and Aesop Rock's, 'Long Legged Larry' began to blast out of the speakers. She could feel the bass and rhythm beating hard inside of her, vibrating her entire body like a cruise ship about to leave the port.

"Can you turn that down a little?"

"Huh?" he said, hands on the steering wheel, looking straight ahead.

"Can you turn the music down, please?"

"Huh?"

"AXEL! THE MUSIC IS TOO DAMN LOUD! TURN IT DOWN, PLEASE!"

"Huh?"

It was then that she saw the gleam in his eye, and the flash of a smirk, so fleeting it was almost undetectable.

"You heard me the first time! You're an ass!"

He burst out laughing, and she swung on him, pummeling his arm, but he only laughed harder. Mac Miller's, 'Good News' started to play. She fell back onto her seat, wanting to choke him like he did that man.

"Black raspberry chocolate chip, right?" His teeth sank into his lower lip, brow arched as he shot her a seductive glance. "That's your favorite, isn't it?"

"Don't make it seem like you solved some ancient riddle. That's most people's favorite from Graeter's."

"Black raspberry it is."

She shook her head, amused, hating how she loved every ridiculous thing about him. He was that good shit. That forbidden shit. That 'Take me as I am, I don't give a damn' shit. She felt safe and on edge with him at the same time. She wanted to open up with him, expose more of her folded petals—like one of her books, read him from cover to cover. But she had to practice patience. The best books needed to be savored and re-read a hundred times to be fully understood.

"Here we go." He pulled into the ice-cream shop, and it wasn't long before she was red in the face, laughing at his jokes. They sat outside at a small table, the air sweet and cool, like their dessert. People mingled about, talking and carrying on. Cars drove past, and life was good.

"Mmm!" She licked at her cone, tracing a dark purple drizzle of the delicious stuff.

His gaze was transfixed on the action. Focused on her tongue.

"You're coming over tonight," he said matter-of-factly as he gobbled up his ice-cream, the same flavor as hers. He seemed in a big hurry to finish.

"No I'm not." She took another satisfying lick.

"We'll see about that. You want some water?"

"I'm fine. Thanks." He offered her a few extra napkins to wrap around her cone. "Thank you." As she took them from his grasp, their gazes hooked, making her freeze. Swallowing, she waited as he leaned in to press his soft lips against hers. The warmth of his breath blended with the nip in the air, his arm wrapped around her waist, drawing her closer. She stiffened, then relaxed at the taste of his tongue entering her mouth. Slow and easy, he intensified the kiss, yet at a measured, controlled pace. When he pulled away, she was breathless.

And he went back to licking his ice cream, real slow…

Stay strong, English. Don't go home with this bastard tonight! I know your pussy wants him, but you must resist. Fight the power!

They resumed their lighthearted conversation, discussing everything from their favorite drink to the worst 90s TV show. She noticed quite a few people staring at them. One man, however, stood out. He'd just come out of the eatery, holding a three-scoop bowl of chocolate ice cream. It was the oddest thing. He just kept ogling them as if they were characters on a television screen.

"What are you looking at?" Axel glared back at the man who was shifting his gaze between the two of them like one would at a tennis match.

I should've known he'd noticed him, too.

"You. That's who. Disgusting. This is a good Christian neighborhood."

"Go on somewhere, man. Leave us the hell alone." Axel shooed the guy away, then flashed her a gorgeous smile. Perhaps the guy was drunk, but one rarely needed liquid courage to be a full-blown racist. An inflated sense of self-importance, paranoia, and hateful mantras were usually enough to fuel that fire.

"You should be ashamed of yourself!" the man yelled so loud, he garnered more attention. This was the second time in one night that things had gone from zero to ten.

"We're minding our business. I suggest you do the

same," English stated as she shook her head in aversion.

"Couldn't you find a Black man? Couldn't you find a White woman? What's wrong with you two?!"

"Sir, please don't do that. Just leave 'em alone. They ain't hurtin' nobody," someone spoke up, clearly irritated with the situation as well.

She looked down at her lap, her stomach sinking. She'd had to face such reactions before, but she felt cheated in the worst way. She was having a good time with Axel, and now, it was being ruined again, by yet another person who wanted something he wasn't supposed to have. First, it was a phone; now, their peace of mind. Anger and sadness boiled within her. *I can't ever have shit go right lately…*

"Your mama sure must be proud!"

Axel calmly placed his ice cream down in the paper bowl, scoop first, and slowly got to his feet.

"Motherfucker, you wanna go? Let's go."

"Axel, no! No!"

"I ain't scared of you, boy! Somebody needs to tell you the truth. If you don't like what I'm saying, you can leave."

"I'm not going any damn where, and neither is she."

"Axel…"

"I told you to come on over here. If you're feelin' froggy, jump," Axel continued, ignoring her pleas to disengage with this chump. "You wanna fuck around? You're about to find out!"

"I'm not about to fight with you. I'm just telling you we don't like that sort of thing, 'round here. I don't have no issue with colored people." He waved his hand around as if that somehow made everything okay. Cleared him from being a bigot. "But we ain't supposed to be race mixing. It's in the Bible. That's what's wrong with this country. Nobody has the courage to stand up for the Word of God, and what's right anymore! Gay marriage, and all this nonsense! In today's society, men want to be women. Get their manhood cut off and smear makeup all over their faces. Like that makes 'em a lady all of the sudden. Women want to be men. Walk around in work boots, grow beards, and cut their hair short as the fuzz on a fly's rear-end. Folks wanna freeload off my tax dollars instead of getting a job to earn an honest living, or smart-off at the police, run off, and be surprised when they're shot dead for breakin' the law. Do the crime, do the time."

"None of that shit you're ranting about has anything to do with me, this lady, and some fuckin' ice-cream."

"You're a traitor to your race. You're lookin' in the face of a *real* American."

"Come 'ere, let me see that real American face a bit closer. Make it all red, black and blue…" Axel curled his finger, motioning the jerk to come on by for a visit.

Oh God… he's going to jail tonight. He's definitely going to jail.

There were no Black people around besides herself. She was thankful that few seemed to be on this man's side.

"Couldn't you get a Black man, or you get a White woman?" he said again.

"I got who the hell I *wanted* to get, you piece of shit, and you're just mad that your sister finally stood up to you and told you, 'Not tonight, Bufford.'" Pockets of laughter rang all around.

"Well, aren't you funny?" The demon's eyes grew darker. His ice cream too was no doubt melting in that cup. Not from the temperature outside, but from his hellish heat. "You must be Quaker Oats, and this here is Aunt Jemima!" He cackled. Several people booed.

"Oh no, the hell this inbred bastard didn't just say this to us," she mumbled, her patience wearing thin.

"You want to talk about breakfast foods 'nd such? Well, I think it's time for you to get served."

The man's eyes shifted nervously as Axel stepped to him. The shop patrons were becoming nervous, but a few egged him on, encouraging Axel to kick his ass. English grabbed his arm, pulling him towards her.

"No. We're not doing this tonight. Enough!"

"Get out of here! You're out here starting shit, and there's kids around!" someone yelled in their defense. "We've heard enough!"

"You ain't no Christian! Jesus loves everybody," someone else piped up.

"If you don't like what cha see, you don't have to look!" yet another person said. A wave of relief washed over her as more and more people shooed the man away, barking and cursing at him. The guy looked stunned that so many had turned on him. He should've been counting his lucky stars—it was the only thing that seemed to slow Axel down.

"Leave 'em alone!" came another admonition.

Axel's jaw was clenched, and he no doubt itched to start a fight. But then, suddenly, he gave in to her and—very slowly—sat back down.

An employee exited the ice cream shop, looking rather perturbed. "I'm calling the police, sir, if you don't vacate the property. You're causing a disturbance. Please leave."

Oh, now you show up?

The guy got in his car and drove off at last, muttering to himself. Her gut was in knots, and her head throbbed. *Too much drama. When I wanted an exciting man, and asked for one in my prayers, this isn't what I meant… Gots tuh be mo'e careful.*

"I know what you're thinking," Axel said after things had quieted back down. He picked up his melting ice cream. "You're thinking, wherever I go, trouble follows."

"So you really *are* a mind reader. The ice-cream flavor guesstimate wasn't just a presumption. Let me start calling you psychic, Axel. Do you charge $9.99 a minute? That's out of my budget."

He smirked at that, then got to work once more on his ice cream.

"English, all of my life, I have defended myself, so this is second nature to me. I don't let people just say and do whatever they want to me. My mama always taught me that we teach people how to treat us."

"Yeah, but if we respond to every rude jerk, Axel, we'll be fighting every day, or end up in jail or dead."

"Who said I respond to every jerk?" He gave her a quizzical look. "I let a lot of things go all the time." He turned away. "I pick and choose wisely. I get disrespected sometimes by the police who try 'nd tell me how to do my job. I get my patience tried by my employees who've sometimes mistaken my kindness for weakness. I've had a lot of people in my own family push my buttons, try to get over, and I've had to burn some bridges so they'd understand once and for all, I'm not okay with that." He took a deep breath, then yawned.

"That's what life is sometimes, Axel. People testin' us."

"Testing us. You said it. And what are you supposed to do with a test? Pass it." His expression was earnest.

"Sometimes, tests aren't meant to pass or fail though. They're meant to learn from."

"Naw, that's called a lesson. You learn from lessons. Life experiences. You don't learn from tests. By the time the test rolls around, you're already supposed to know your stuff. Be proficient in it." What could she say? He was right. "You're not going to stick a gun in my face and then I don't try to save my own life. You're not going to lie on my mama, and I not speak up about it, even if you're my father. You're not going to jump my sister, and I not even the score. You're not going to take my phone, with all of my financial information on it, and run off scot free without a fight. You're not going to disrespect the woman I'm with tonight on a date, by callin' her something racist, and I just sit here and let it happen. See, that's the problem with the world right now, English. It isn't that American, fake Christianity stuff that guy was pretending to be… The problem is that there aren't enough real men around to take a stand. Everybody is running around scared, or saying and doing shit they can't back up. *Real* men protect themselves and the people they care about. Thank God for my pappy."

He shook his head in disappointment, letting her into his world. No mention of his father, just a grandfather he considered a male role model.

"I get what you're saying. I just don't want you to get hurt is all. No one is invincible. Even a superman like you." She ran her fingertips along his ear, then tucked a few wayward strands of his hair behind it. "I appreciate you standing up for my honor, though." She leaned in and kissed his cheek as he gave her a faint smile.

"I've watched too many people in my life get picked on and messed with, English, all because they didn't, or *couldn't*, set boundaries. I'm not that man. I'm sorry if you're disappointed in me, and I understand if you think I'm just too much. I gotta be me though. You may as well see the real me now, instead of later. No sense in bein' phony to try and impress you, or nothing like that. The truth always eventually comes out, anyway." He kept his eyes on the ice-cream and grabbed another napkin.

She was going to say something back, something without much thought, a witty reply, or perhaps something uplifting, but then, she thought better of it. Instead, she ran her hand along his broad back. She looked at him, but he didn't look at her. He just kept eating his ice cream—appearing neither angry nor happy. He was likely floating in that gray, fuzzy space in between.

They finished their dessert in silence. It wasn't long

before they were back in the truck, and when he turned on his music, he set it at a low volume. 'Bad Dream,' by Cool Heat, serenaded them.

"Can I talk to you about a date no-no?" she asked with a smile.

"A date no-no?" He shot her a glance as he got on the onramp. "What do you mean?"

"I want to tell you something, and in order to explain it well, I need to put it in context. That includes talking about my ex."

"Yeah, that's fine. I don't mind that."

"Okay, so, I had been with my ex for a long time. I thought we were going to get married. I got used to him. It was comfortable, even though I hadn't been happy in that relationship, way before it ended. Have you ever stayed with someone longer than you should've because you were comfortable?"

He cracked the window, taking his time to answer.

"No, not really. I mean, to me, it's kind of like walking down a long road, right? You keep walking and walking with that person, and y'all are bickering about the map, where to stop at and eat, and everything else in between. I'm not going to keep walking down that road with them just because I'm used to them being there by my side. Sooner or later, that road will run into a cliff. So, just because I've been with her so long, am I supposed to just go over the cliff? Drop off the face of the Earth because I kept on traveling with her? Ignore the warning signs, all because it's comfortable? Hell, no. There were too many chances to part ways or turn around. If I stay because I'm comfortable, it means I never understood what being uncomfortable really was. That's not comfort. That's laziness and fear."

"Well, damn!"

They both burst out laughing.

"I mean, baby, I'm not tryin' to make you feel bad or anything, but you asked me a question and I can't relate. Once I realize a relationship isn't going anywhere, I don't drag it out. When I'm sure it's a dead end, I let it be known that I'm done."

"Got it. You can't relate. That's more than evident. I get what you're saying though. I wish I had been more like you at the time." She sighed. "Because let me tell you, staying in that bad relationship changed me, and not completely for the better. He wasn't a great person, but he had some good qualities, and I wasn't perfect, either. We were more toxic together than apart. It's like we brought out the worst in one another. So, I brought that up because I learned some important things from that experience."

"Like what?"

"Like, I know exactly what I want in a relationship now. I know what I'm not going to put up with ever again, too."

He nodded in understanding.

"You want me to go home with you, I know. I brought this up for that reason, too."

"I don't need to talk about this with you, English. Either you want to, or you don't. Once people start having long discussions about it, it kills the mood anyway.

I tried to entice you a little, but you're not ready, so that's that." He shrugged.

"No, no, no, please let me explain. This isn't some long drawn-out discussion, it's just me trying to allow you to get to know me more, and understand my perspective. I was holding out for sex not because I've been reading a bunch of Steve Harvey books, or think it'll make the man appreciate me more. That's bogus, because I already know that nine times out of ten, if a man waits for sex from a woman, he's getting it from somewhere else in the interim. He'll lie and say, *'I been waiting so long for you, baby,'* knowing just two days ago Debbie from down the street was sucking his dick, and a week before that, Patty from work was riding him like a bronco. This is about me... for *me.*" She placed her hand across her chest.

"If that's what you want to believe, that's fine."

"It's not just what I want to believe. It's the truth. I've had my one-night stands and quickies—not going to sit here and try to pretend to be some prima donna, but you know what? More times than not, it was unfulfilling. I don't want to do that anymore. I really like you, Axel, and I don't want to move too fast and tear everything all up. Sex can complicate things sometimes."

"I like you, too."

"But you don't agree with me, do you? About the whole waiting to have sex thing?"

"I don't have to agree with you about this. You've got your own mind, and I have mine."

"I know, Axel, but do you agree with what I'm saying?"

"No."

"I want to get to know you, *really* know you, before I open myself up like that again."

"All right."

He seemed so cool and relaxed, it was almost unnerving.

"Why are you doing this?" She was halfway amused, and somewhat annoyed.

"Doing what?" He got off the exit.

"Never mind. We've been having a good time, and great conversations. I love your work ethic, your sense of fairness, and how chivalrous and just *real* you are. Let me ask you something else. When was your last relationship?"

He stopped at a red light and stroked his beard. "Real relationship? Where she was my actual girlfriend? 'Bout a year and a half ago. Tonya. I think I told you this last time we went out when you asked."

"You did, but I wanted to be sure I remembered correctly."

"Nah, you remembered. You've got a good memory, I noticed that early on. You wanted to see if I was going to be consistent or have a different answer… see if I'm a manipulator or a liar."

She burst out laughing. "Okay, you caught me. What we didn't discuss, though, is how long you two were together?"

"Let's see, Tonya and I were together for almost two years."

"Did you love her?"

He snuck her a glance. "Why are you asking these

questions?"

"Because I want to know more about how you handled your relationships in the past."

"Yeah… I loved her."

"Do y'all still keep in touch? Friends?"

"No. It ended on bad terms."

"Why?"

"Because I wasn't who she wanted me to be, and she wasn't what I needed."

"What did you need?"

He was about five minutes away from her house now, and it began to drizzle.

"Somebody like you…"

Chapter Eight

THE BUZZ OF the lawnmower finally stopped ringing in Axel's ears as he stood on his front porch, gulping down some ice-cold water and sweating something fierce. The ringing seemed to last forever, and his limbs felt rubbery and numb from pushing the machine for so long over the grass.

He'd mowed his entire yard, front and back, until the flawless lines he loved to create were picture-perfect. It was a long, drawn-out job. Not one he particularly loved, and he'd hire a professional service to do it most times, but he'd had a few hours to spare, and truth be told, it was a great stress buster.

Draining the bottle of water, he mulled the second—and pretty realistic—nightmare he'd just had featuring Ms. Florence, which left him angry as hell. Perhaps because it was just her eyes upon him. She said nothing but simply sat there, dressed in white, judging him.

Was it a fluke that she'd appeared the same evening he'd hung up on his father right before going to sleep? *Too much bad blood...* Ms. Florence had known of some of his issues with his father. How could she not? It was a part of him, as well as a big reason why he barely trusted a friend, let alone a stranger. Things had gotten out of control back then, and they weren't much better now, either.

He and Dad had an argument last night. One of many. Axel got a call from a friend who told him he'd seen his father's face plastered on camera, yammering about justice, fairness, and things of that nature. *Now, isn't that rich?* If Dad wasn't getting into it with someone for no reason, taking somebody to small claims court over some shit he did, lying to manipulate some poor soul out of their money, or flapping his gums to impress the world, he was calling some radio or news station with trumped-up allegations that were always salacious in nature, and more than likely, crammed with lies. This time, he'd gone too far.

Tommy had taken it upon himself to go to the news and talk about the drug element entering the city, destroying their town. All this little stunt did was put Axel's face back in the news as soon as things had died down. Now it was like starting from ground zero.

What right did he have to do that? Calling Channel 32 and talking about, "My son is a hero! He's doing the law's job. He wouldn't have gotten into an altercation in the first place if the Louisville police kept the drugs out of their hood instead of worrying about parking tickets and homeless people asking for a dime.' Dad was right, but that wasn't the point. Right message. Wrong messenger. That was in fact the thing about him.

Not only was he a big-time liar and opportunist, he

was also an attention seeking fiend. On birthdays, he had to do something outrageous so he could take centerstage. He'd done it to him and Dallas—ruining birthday parties. Thanksgiving. Christmas, too.

Axel slid his phone out of his pocket and noted a couple missed calls, his father being one of them. *Let me just get this over with.*

"What?" Axel asked, calling the old man back.

"You had no reason to be sore at me and hang up! I had a right to go to the news and tell the truth!"

"This ain't the sword you wanna die on, Tommy. I'm tellin' ya now, it ain't got nothing to do with truth or tall tales. It's got to do with the fact things were starting to die down, and then here you come! Squirming out the woodwork like some worm, kickin' up dust. All so you can be in the limelight off of my name. You put me in more danger!"

"Me telling people that the police aren't doing their job is not putting you in danger. I'm helping you! They still ain't found out who sent that man down here to mess wit' you… all the way from fuckin' Texas. So it *needs* to be in the limelight, don't you think? Not just for me, but for you, and the police ain't found out nothing to stop the harassment."

"People know where they came from. It's no great secret. I'm trying to keep my head above water, Dad, and then here you come, asking for a storm. Jesus! I sure as hell wish you'd sit down somewhere and be quiet."

"I ain't gonna be quiet, not as long as you have to look over your shoulder. Them phone calls you've been getting? I know all about them!" Axel shook his head. Someone had blabbed their mouth. "Yeah, that's right. I know all about it." He could picture his father with a big, sycophantic smile spread across his sunken face. "People talk 'round here and word travels fast. You got somebody callin' and threatening you, wishing death on my boy, and you expect me to just sit back and flow with it. Then they—"

"It's nothing I can't handle, but the messed-up part is you didn't do this for me, out of concern. You ain't do it for the city either, for brotherly love, or the betterment of mankind… tryna keep folks safe from the druggies and dealers like you're some advocate. What a crock of crap."

"Who'd I do it for then, Axel? You got all the damn answers, right? Mr. Smarty Pants. All them fumes from them damn chemicals you gotta use to clean up; guts, spit, and shit must be gettin' to your brain."

"Is that so? I know you're not talking about smarts and brain damage, of all people. If your brain was a stick of dynamite and exploded, it would only make your hair on the top of your head blow like it were in a summer breeze. Wouldn't make no difference."

"You fuckin' smart-mouthed pecker. Who'd I do this for then, Axel? Tell me! I did it for Winne tha fuckin' Pooh, huh? Is that who?"

"You did it for YOU. I gotta go."

He ended the call and looked about. The street was rather quiet. Typically, he could hear faint music, people laughing while lounging on their porches, or kids playing in their yards. To his left, an old gray Buick was coming down the street. He locked eyes with the driver, a guy with glasses and short blond hair, and a funny feeling came over him. He nodded at the man and shifted his position a little, allowing a clear view of the gun on his hip. The driver in the Buick kept sailing by.

Whatever Pandora's box he'd opened months ago by simply doing his job was far from over. He had to stay vigilant.

For all I know, they're lost and don't know where they're going, but I'm not taking any chances.

He went back in the house, freshened up, and thought about making himself a sandwich. Opening the refrigerator, he didn't see much to get this meal underway, and figured he'd need to go to the store soon. As he rummaged around for mustard, bread, and slices of ham and cheese, his phone rang.

He pulled the device out his pocket and cradled it between his shoulder and cheek.

"It's my favorite book lady."

"I'm the only book lady you know." She casually laughed.

"Since you're at work right now, can you do me a favor?"

"What kind of favor?"

"Research an old porno magazine from back in the day, called Forest Humps Adventures? There's a spread in there on Jeeeennny!" He said the name just like Forest Gump did in the famous movie. "I need you to bring it to me… shrimp gumbo… for research purposes only, of course…"

"Axel, shut up. You are crazy." They both laughed as he sat things on his kitchen counter and put her on speaker.

"Is there really a pornographic magazine called 'Forest Hump's Adventures'?"

"I don't know about a magazine, but there's a porno movie with that name, and other movie title spoofs like, 'Add Mama to the Train,' 'The Slutty Professor,' 'Pulp Friction,' and 'Bi-curious George.'"

"You are sick!" She cackled.

"How am *I* sick? You're the one laughin'." He got a plate out of a cabinet.

"You actually know the names of these movies."

"I know more than just the names. I starred in a few," he teased. 'Beverly Hills, 9021-Ho!'

"Pervert."

"And 'I Dream of Weenie'. What are you doing?" *Should I use this lettuce? It looks kind of wilted…*

"Working. You're weird."

"Yeah, but doing what exactly? 'Whorrey Potter and the Sorcerer's Balls'… I wore a black magician cape in that one, and nothin' underneath."

"STOP!" She laughed so hard this time, she began coughing.

He opened the bread, placed it on the plate, then grabbed a butter knife from the cutlery drawer. Meanwhile, he could hear 'I Love Rock and Roll' by Joan Jett playing from his neighbor's house.

"I'm waiting."

"Like you really want to know what I did at work today."

"I do!" He went back to the refrigerator, grabbed a two-liter of Mountain Dew, and poured himself a tall glass.

"I know this may sound boring to most people, so I won't get into the details, but earlier this morning I finished up a couple of memoirs. I had to take care of them in the sterile lab. I always wear gloves anyway, but these were so delicate that one wrong turn and the book could fall apart. They're handwritten, and beautiful. They were found in an estate in Indiana."

"Oh, okay."

"Like I said. Boring. But I am lovin' it."

"It's not boring to me." He took his sandwich and drink and sat down at the kitchen table, happy to get off his feet. "And I'm glad you're enjoying it because we really should like our jobs. We spend too much time doin' them not to."

"That's true. It's hard for me to wrap my brain around you liking your occupation, Axel, but I know you do. It's obvious you take great pride in your work. I salute you. I do. I know I couldn't do it, though. It's one thing to read about gruesome stuff in some of these books. Many times the details are true, and that's chilling enough. It's another to see it with your own eyes."

"Well, it's understandable to feel that way, but as we discussed, it doesn't disturb me the way it bothers most folks. At the end of the day, I'm makin' an honest living, and while doing it, I'm helping people. That's important to me."

"I love that about you… Not trying to darken the mood or anything, but I can't shake what you told me."

"What did I tell you?"

"That story you told me yesterday about that lady's fingers… Oh my God… made me sick! But I couldn't stop listening to you. You're a great storyteller, you know that? You should look into doing audiobook work. Your voice would be perfect for southern mysteries and suspense. It's deep. Baritone."

"I don't think I'd like that sort of gig, but what I told you was all true. One of my first times on the job, too. Can you imagine getting your cherry bust like that? They never did find her killer. That situation would have most people runnin' for the hills."

"I want you to tell me more stories about what you've seen and dealt with. I find it so fascinating. True crime is sort of a guilty pleasure of mine."

"You keep asking me for more and more stories. You're kind of sick, too," he teased.

"It's a morbid curiosity."

"Yeah… I get it."

She was quiet for a bit as he washed down his food with the pop. Something special was happening. A bonding. A friendship. That initial physical response to the long-legged, gorgeous woman had morphed into something deeper and more important. The shallow layers were pulled apart, revealing the loveliness of a brilliant mind. She understood and appreciated his sense of humor—laughed at his jokes. She kissed him back with the same desire he showed her. She was hard-working and took pride in her job, and from her words, she had a good mama, daddy, and homelife. He thought about her far more often than he'd ever admit. It was almost too good to be true.

"Thank you for not pressuring me to move faster than uh… than I want to, Axel. I know you're more than likely screwing someone else, because you're not my man or anything like that and you have needs, but—"

"Hold on, hold on." What the hell was she going on about? "I have to interrupt you. Let's get some stuff straight, okay?"

"…Okay."

"Now, you've said this more than once, so, I'm going to address it this time around. Just because a guy wouldn't mind having sex with you, that guy being me, and is sexually charmed by you doesn't mean he wants *easy* sex from every lady he meets. Some women you smash and forget. Some women you smash and maintain a loose friendship with for occasional benefits down the line. Some women you take a bit more time with. We make that determination on some shit you probably don't understand, because you're not a man, and it might sound chauvinistic, but we think differently than y'all, and that's just the bottom line. On top of that, English, I'm not screwin' anyone else right now, but I'd tell you if I was. Now, could I have sex with someone else tonight? Yes, because like you said, we have no commitment to one another.

"We're dating. Nothin' more, nothin' less. Lastly, contrary to whatever you think about me, with my high sex drive and all, because yeah, it's off the Richter scale, I'm not some wild animal out here humping everything in a skirt. I have self-control. I did all that runnin' around in my teens and twenties, and I'm over it. I use discretion with who I sleep with because my dick is just as important as your pussy, pardon my French. I'm not trying to get some lady I don't even like accidentally pregnant, so I'm careful nowadays. I got a little money… a few assets, things like that. I have a lot to lose if I hook my wagon to the wrong horse, but most of all, women get too damn attached to me after sex."

"Ohhhh, brother!" She burst out laughing. "Welcome to the planet of Ego, where Axel Hendrix is not only a client, but the president!"

"I'm serious! Everything I want to achieve, and that includes bedroom activities and proclivities, I put my whole heart into." *We spend more time talking about the shit, than doing anything about it. She's always bringing this up. But whatever.* "Yeah, I want to have sex with you, that's a given, but it's not consuming my mind." *But it sure is consuming yours, English.* "And for the record, because this really pissed me off about you, I wasn't going to try anything on our first date by inviting you to my home, regardless of what you believed."

"I *don't* believe you, but damn, are you smooth. You could talk the skin off a snake."

"Naw, I'm just a real motherfucker, English. You're not used to guys like me because we're rare, so you don't know how to respond. I'm not pullin' your leg, or playing games. Every ex-girlfriend of mine can say plenty of shit about me, but one thing they can't say is that I pretended to be somebody I wasn't. I'd rather eat crumbs with bums, than steaks with snakes. I can see through people. I can tell who's real and who's fake. That's why I'm still talking to you… because we've got some things in common, and I can tell that you're a good person, and you're just tryna live a good life."

"I am… Maybe you're right. I haven't met anyone like you. Time will tell."

"Time always brings out the truth. I don't like fake clothes. Fake jewelry. Especially not fake people, including the women I date. I don't surround myself with bullshit. I don't talk bullshit in serious situations, either. If I tell you I'm going to help you, I am. If I tell you I'm going to fuck you up and make your life a living hell, I'm going to do that, too. I don't do things that amount to a bunch of bull. Life is too short to waste pussyfootin' around, being a great pretender. So, here's my resume. Plain and simple."

"Why would you need to show me your resume if we're just dating? I know you're speaking figuratively, but—"

"Because continuous dating with no plan in place is a waste of my time. I don't casually date. I deal with women who I think I might be able to get serious with down the road. Now, you ain't gotta to tell me no more horror stories about exes. I can see through it. I'm sure you weren't no angel all the time, either. Smart people do the most shit because y'all can get away with it." The woman burst out laughing and he smiled. "You're laughing 'cause it's true. I'm smart, too, and I know the things we do."

"I was never a cheater, if that's what you're implying."

"Not at all. I'm talking about being manipulative before we grow up and mature to get our way. Creating confusion so we can hide our dirty work. I played games like that when I was younger. Smart people have all kinds of tools of the trade. When you can fool so many, you can use it to cause harm, and I'm guilty of that, too. Just like I said. I ain't perfect, honey. I can sometimes have a hell of a temper. Been told I am too jealous when in a relationship and micromanage folks at work. I got a mean streak for folks that cross me."

"Well? Is that true? Are you jealous? Do you micromanage? Do you have a mean streak?"

"I got my crosses to bear. I grew up with that sort of thing, lying and fakeness, and I hated it."

"Your mother wasn't her authentic self?"

"Oh, no." He laughed mirthlessly. "My mother is as real as they come. It was my dad. My father isn't a decent human being, English. He caused a lot of trouble in my life, and my mama's, too. I got in some jams on account of him. Anyway, whatever. This ain't about him. The point is, I don't roll like that."

"Can I admit something to you?"

"Yeah. What is it?"

"I would have been jealous if I knew for a fact that you were sleeping with someone else. I don't know if I believe you, but I—"

"Well, you don't have—"

"Well, butter my butt and call me a biscuit!" Dallas yelled as the front door opened and slammed behind her.

"Huh?" English questioned, hearing the commotion.

"My sister just barged in here," he muttered, getting up from his chair and pissed that his privacy had been violated. "I told you to stop showing up here without calling ahead, and to give me my keys back!"

"You don't never answer your damn phone, Axel, and as for the keys, I did," She smiled all big and wide. "I made a copy, though. You ain't say nothin' 'bout making no copy. Why is there dirt all over your face? The last time I saw something that looked like you, I flushed it."

"…I'm on the phone."

"Oh, did I embarrass you, Mr. Hendrix, in all of your glory? Woohoo! Slow down, world! My big, bad, big brother is on tha phone! Everybody stop what y'ur doin' and bow down to the man of the hour, day, week, month and year!" The obnoxious, small-framed woman raised her hands high in the air, and did a dolphin clap. "The world don't revolve around you, sunshine. This is what you get for duckin' and dodging me all week."

"Life is a big disappointment, and you're now at the top of my fuckin' list… English, let me call you back, honey. If I don't, it means I'm wrestling my sister."

"Oh, Lord." She giggled. "Okay, I'll talk to you later."

"You sure will." He ended the call and looked at Dallas, who sported bleach blond messy hair and a fringed brown leather jacket, tight jeans, and cowboy boots.

"Damn. You don't have nothing to eat, Axel." She peered in the refrigerator as if looking for Waldo. "When's the last time you've been to the store?" She flung him a glance from over her shoulder. He shot her the bird and drank his Mountain Dew. "Must've been when Nickelback's 'Rockstar' hit the airwaves."

She slammed the refrigerator door closed, put her hands on her hips, and gawked at him.

"What are you doing here, Dallas?"

"Checkin' on my brother. You ain't called me or Mama back."

"I don't need no checkin' on. How many times do I have to tell you that?"

"Who was you on the phone with?"

"None of your business."

"It's a girl," she taunted, her blue eyes sparkling like a hunting cat's in the night. "You got that look about you again."

"What look?"

She pulled out a chair and flopped down in it, then crossed her arms. "When you get all enthralled with some new woman, you have this look about you. It's sickening. Googly eyes, a dumb ol' smile." She chortled.

He wiggled his fingers at her. "Come on and give me my key."

"No."

"I'm going to change the lock and the security code on my alarm system and not tell you what it is if you don't hand me over my keys. I've done it before, I'll do it again, so why don't you just save us both the time and aggravation?"

Her eyes narrowed on him, she dug in her hip pocket, pulled out the key, and slapped it in the palm of his hand.

"Stick that up your ass."

"I will when you drown in a lake. You talked to Tommy, didn't you?"

She sighed and stared out the kitchen window. "Daddy come callin' me talking about you're mad at him. I don't know why he calls me every time y'all get into it." She shrugged. "I don't care none. That's between you two."

"Why're you over here then?"

"'Cause you didn't call me or Mama back. Just like I said. I'm afraid someone is going to hurt my brother."

"Like when you hurt me by stuffing pieces of toilet paper in my nostrils and mouth while I was sleeping when we were kids? Almost killed me." His sister's face reddened, and her eyes were sheening over with mirth. *Sicko.* "Or that time you hurt me by calling my girlfriend, Holly, when I was in the ninth grade, telling her that I preferred her twin sister over her, and I was only comin' by to see her because her mama could cook good."

"It didn't break y'all up, so it didn't even work. I was telling the truth though; you *did* like Dolly better. I couldn't stand that stuck-up trick." Dallas rolled her eyes. "That didn't hurt you because you two stayed together long after that."

"It did hurt me when I broke up with her though, because she brought that up again. Saying I had flirted with Dolly in math class. I denied it, but her mama could really tear it up in the kitchen. I tried to come by a few weeks after we split up to see how she was doing. I guess she thought we were going to get back together. She realized I was full of shit when I asked what did Ms. Ellis fix for supper, and could I have some."

Dallas started laughing and rocking around in her chair.

"Remember that time Mama got mad when you painted your bedroom with black spray-paint?" He grimaced, hating this story. "You took some white fingernail polish of hers, both bottles, and speckled it all over, for the twilight effect. It looked God-awful. You said it was supposed to be like Star Wars… looked more like a bunch of spit wads on a Black bear's ass. Pigeon poop on tar. Picasso you are not."

"Well, let me paint you a shitty, but suitable, picture then. What about that time you tore up all that damn Styrofoam in the house from the boxes Mama had set up for her cosmetics sales job? Avon or something. She asked why the hell you did it, destroyed that filler like that, and you said because you wanted it to be snowing."

"Don't tell this story!" She cackled.

"Naw, I can't stop right before it gets *real* good. Mama beat the shit outta you, then you turned 'round and lied, and said I helped you do it. She got my ass, too!"

They were both laughing so hard now, their faces were hot and red.

"Mama said, 'You want snow? I'll give you two some damn snow!' She was singing Christmas carols as she whooped us! 'It's the moooost, wond-er-ful time… of the yeeear!'"

He could barely breathe now. When they finally calmed down, his belly no longer undulating with merriment, Dallas turned real serious.

"As much as I'd like to bash you in the face with a hot

skillet and bury your big burly ass in your own backyard some days, Axel, you're family. *My* family. You're my favorite person, besides Mama and Lucas, in this whole damn world. I love you big, brother…" She picked up his glass and drank from it. "Can't nobody do nothin' bad to you without hearing from me. I'm protective of you, even though you're the elder."

"I know… I appreciate it."

"So, I ain't gonna apologize for worrying about you and coming around. You like to do everything on your own. I know you. In and out."

"You want something to drink? I got more in the garage. Some beers and such."

"Yeah, I'll take a beer. I won't stay long, though. Gotta pick up Lucas from his daddy's house tonight, but stop by the grocery store first to get his cereal and such."

He retreated to the garage, opened up the small electric cooler he kept in there, then brought in two ice-cold Budweiser beers.

When he returned, Dallas had his phone in her hand, thumbing the screen with a look of deep concentration on her face. He set the beers down and snatched it out of her fingers.

"This is why Mama should have swallowed you."

She started laughing all over again.

"You were trying to guess my password, just to be annoying. Get me locked outta my own shit."

"I had one more try, then you would've been locked out." She laughed in some insane, high-pitched witchy tone. "That phone is new?"

"Yeah. Had it a couple of weeks."

"I bet the camera on it is good. Take a picture of me."

"No. I don't want to accidentally download a virus."

"You asshole." She cackled.

"Drink your beer and get out."

"I'm not leaving until I'm good and damn ready."

"If I throw a stick across the kitchen, will you leave then?"

"You're left-handed, awkward, and untalented. You can't throw straight no way, Axel."

"But I heard you were throwin' that ass in a circle down at the club last week. Gotta call that my sister was acting like a harlot. My nephew deserves better."

"A harlot? Who are you? Grandma Betty?" She ran her fingers through her hair and blushed with what he'd consider nothing short of pride.

"I see you're not embarrassed. Honestly, there's no need to be ashamed of yourself, Dallas. That's what Mama is for." Dallas laughed so hard, beer sprayed out of her mouth. They'd gone after each other hard since they were children. Simply for sport.

"I do need to take a nap soon, though. I gotta go in for a job tonight." He yawned as he opened his phone mailbox and checked to see if there were any pressing emails.

They talked a bit longer, finished their beers, and gave each other warm hugs. Then, he walked Dallas to the front door and opened it. It was a bit cooler outside now.

"I'm going to call you in a couple of days. Don't act like you don't see me ringing you up, as you usually do.

Make sure you answer the phone." She kissed him on the cheek and made her way down the steps toward her white Honda in his driveway.

"Give Lucas a hug from his Uncle Axel. Tell him I'll see him soon. As far as *you* are concerned, trust me. I see your calls. I just choose to ignore them. Anyone else you call should do the same for their own sanity. Drive safe."

Dallas gave him the bird, then got into her car and drove away.

Returning to the kitchen, he picked up his phone and called English back. He got her voicemail.

"Hey, Dr. Sexy. We were in the middle of a good conversation when my sister came by and impolitely interrupted us. Give me a call in the next hour or two. Otherwise, I'll be at work and unable to answer."

He disconnected the call, and as he was on his way to his bedroom to freshen up and take a quick snooze, his phone buzzed. It was a text message from English.

English: *Can't chat right now but want to see you soon. If your schedule is clear for Saturday night, let me know. I'd like to invite you over for dinner.*

Chapter Nine

ENGLISH SCANNED HER dining room to make sure she hadn't missed something. After all, it had been a long while since she'd had a man over for dinner. This was her sanctuary, her treasured private domain filled to the brim with Bath and Body Works scented oils and candles, garage-sale antique furniture blended with modern pieces, plush rugs, vases and linchpins from local thrift stores. She rested her gaze on her favorite centerpiece: a crystal basin from her trip to New Mexico, filled with shiny indigo, teal and violet globes.

She'd set up with cerulean square plates with hand-painted silver trim, wine glasses with white frost around the rims, and the most perfect sky-blue linens that she rarely used, given to her as a birthday gift from her grandmother many years ago. God rest her soul. She glanced at her watch and tapped her French manicured nail against the glass face. Not once had Axel been late for a date, and she safely assumed this evening would be no different. There were about seven minutes to spare before he ruined his record.

Walking away from the table, she entered the kitchen to check the fare: Heirloom tomatoes with fresh basil and mozzarella over a bed of bay leaves for decoration, dressed with olive oil and vinaigrette, for their first course. Lobster macaroni and cheese for the entrée, and a simple white cake for dessert, topped with fresh raspberries and a drizzle of melted chocolate. She caught her reflection in the kitchen sliding doors that led to the balcony, and ran her fingers through her hair to look a bit more 'effortless.'

Sporting a simple black V-neck, long-sleeved shirt and taupe slacks, she gave herself the once over, happy she'd decided to add a few chunky silver bangles to her outfit. Just the right touch. While she debated on changing her lipstick color from the deep berry she currently wore to a more neutral chestnut brown, the doorbell rang. She checked her watch and smiled. He was exactly one minute early.

Making her way out of the kitchen, past the dining room and through the foyer, she looked out the peephole, opened the door, and took in the gorgeous man before her. And to God be the glory … because He is good, all the time. *God made man, and with Axel, he was showin' out!*

From the top of this man's head to the bottom of his black-boot-covered feet, Axel looked like a walking dark and sexy fantasy. His beard was flawlessly trimmed, and long bone-straight hair had been knocked into submission. The strands held a healthy shine, no split ends, and flowed over his right shoulder. Button-down white shirt, the top open just enough for her to see his thin gold chain, a bit of chest hair, and a peek of a chest tattoo drawn in black ink.

"Good evenin'. These are for you." He handed her a bouquet of deep red roses, his cheeks taut from a handsome, yet slightly devilish, grin.

"Awww, thank you! They're beautiful, Axel." She stepped aside. "Come right in."

"You're welcome, 800."

That had been the bastard's thing, now. He at times called her '800,' the number on the label of some cheap, convenience store alcohol—Olde English 800 malt liquor. She initially thought she remembered the beverage from a Billy D. Williams television ad her grandmother loved long ago, but Axel had corrected her, saying that was Colt 45. How he knew such a thing was beyond her, but he seemed to be quite well-versed in many subjects, which made him more intriguing to her.

"Nice place."

She locked the door and caught him checking everything out.

"Thank you. Come on into the dining room and get comfortable. I'm going to set these in some water."

"Do I have to take off my shoes or somethin'?"

"No, baby. You're fine."

She walked ahead of him and could see him trailing his gaze all over her as they passed a series of wall mirrors. Now, his gaze was keenly fixed on her rear end. She shook her head and suppressed a smile, then pointed to a chair in the dining room.

"Go on and have a seat. I'll bring the food out." She

collected their serving platters from the table, then started to walk to the kitchen.

"Hold on. Let me help you."

"No, I've got it. Really. I'd prefer you just take a load off."

The sounds of 'Lazy Song,' by Bruno Mars, played as she placed the roses in a vase. She peeked in the dining room as she began to plate the food, seeing Axel sitting at the table, looking down at his phone. Plating everything in a pleasing arrangement, she then brought in their bounty. He looked up from his phone, stared at the plate she sat before him, then returned his attention to his phone as if it were nothing special at all. In fact, the son of a bitch yawned.

Rude ass. He could have said thank you, that it looked good or something. I don't know why I even care about this. Maybe I want to impress him? Now when have I ever given a damn about things like this? Ewww… I must really like him.

She laughed to herself as she walked off, grabbed their wine glasses from the kitchen, and returned. As she clutched the sides of her chair to take her seat, he casually placed his phone down on the table and rushed over to pull the chair out for her.

"Thank you."

A romantic jazzy tune serenaded them as he went back to his seat and placed the napkin over his lap. He began to serve himself the lobster macaroni and cheese, forgoing the appetizer that was perfectly displayed on the side of the plate.

I should have had them on separate plates, but then I saw that gorgeous picture in that cookbook for inspiration, and it looked better on one serving platter. Like an extraordinarily ornamental entree. Why in the hell was I even looking at cookbooks? To impress him, of course.

She sipped her wine, legs crossed. Song after song played and Axel was strangely silent, to the point it was getting pretty damned uncomfortable. Although not an extrovert by any stretch of the imagination, he usually knew how to keep a conversation going, and he was easy to talk to.

"Is everything okay?" she asked, unable to take it anymore. Conan Gray's, 'Disaster', started to play.

"Everything is okay, technically, but I'm a little perturbed is all, I 'spose you could say." He jammed a forkful of lobster in his mouth.

"What's on your mind?"

"Oh, just bullshit. On my way over here, I got a call for a job. I refused to go in and sent another guy I trust. One I trained myself. Chase. I know he can handle the particulars."

"Why is that a problem if you trust him?" Her body betrayed her as her nipples hardened beneath her blouse while she watched his lips moving. Real slow like…

"'Cause they wanted me to be there specifically, and the officer who called for the services threw a hissy fit when I said I wasn't comin', but he'd be in good hands. He couldn't understand it, and I found that mighty strange. Usually, when I can't do a job and send someone else, they're all just happy I can get someone over to wherever the location is in a timely manner. The hell with who. They just want somebody competent." She nodded in understanding and chewed on a forkful of salad. "I explained to him that I had important plans and I wasn't breaking them for nobody but Jesus." Her cheeks warmed at that. "Sometimes, these police officers can be a real piece of work, English."

"How so?"

"We help 'em look good. Most of 'em can't even keep their lunch down when they walk into these places, and then they have the nerve to act like they're better than the cleanin' crews. They act like we work for them sometimes. Being demanding and saying things that don't make a lick of sense or want to try and tell me how to do my job. I don't work for nobody but *me*. I'm my own boss, and that's how it'll always be. 'Nough of that, though. Can you pass the salt, please, baby?"

She reached to her left, grabbed the salt shaker, and handed it to him. That was when she noticed an apple tattoo along his pinky finger. *Odd. I hadn't noticed it before. That's not like me. I'm into details.*

"It's new."

"What's new?"

He sprinkled salt on practically everything.

"The bitten apple on my hand you were givin' a gander to."

"Too much sodium, my country rock star. You're going to have high blood pressure."

"I'm high off life, my blood is already tainted with self-inflicted venom, and the world is full of pressure. Pepper, please."

She grabbed it as well, and this time, his fingertips brushed against hers.

"You're either super sarcastic or a sourpuss." She sucked her teeth, swished her wine about in her glass, and shook her head.

He offered a limp shrug, then started stabbing his tomatoes as if they'd called him a bitch.

As she got ready to crack a joke, her phone buzzed on the coffee table in the adjacent living area. The vibrating device rattled her nerves. She could feel Axel's eyes on her. "Excuse me," she mumbled, then got to her feet. Tossing her napkin down on the table, she made her way to her phone and felt clammy all over when she saw the screen.

"Go ahead. Answer it. I don't mind," he called out around a mouthful of food.

She looked over her shoulder, seeing the back of him as he continued to eat. Something about the way he spoke made her feel as if he *knew* she was avoiding taking the call. As if he was aware she had a secret to hide, and he was onto her. *I hate this shit. It's not even in my nature to not be upfront with the men I date, but how can I explain this?! My whole damn night will be ruined if I answer that phone, or don't play it cool.* Her chest hurt as that thumping heart of hers started to work overtime.

"It's not important. I can call them back later." She returned to her chair, forcing a smile across her face as she picked up her fork and began to pick at her food. Appetite officially lost. "Do you like your dinner?" she asked. The answer didn't matter. She desperately needed the conversation to go in another direction.

"It's good. Did you cook this?" The man raised his brow, sporting an incredulous expression.

She cocked her head to the side, then burst out laughing.

"How insulting. Didn't I say I was inviting you over for dinner?"

"Yeah, but that doesn't mean you cooked it."

"So, you think I can't cook?" She crossed her arms and straightened her back.

He grabbed his glass of wine and sniffed it, wrinkling his nose as if fumes of white vinegar had just crawled into the depths of his nostrils.

"Well?" she pushed.

"I didn't say you can't cook, but even Martha Stewart I 'magine orders a pizza every blue moon."

"And you'd be right. I didn't cook any of this shit."

They were both laughing now.

"I knew it."

"It was a lucky guess. You didn't know a damn thing, Axel. I wanted the credit all the same." She smirked.

"So you were going to pretend you'd done this?" He pointed to the fare and took a taste of the wine, making the same bitter face as he swallowed.

"No, but I wasn't going to volunteer the information, either. If you'd asked, then I was going to tell the truth. I *can* cook, by the way, but I was short on time today, and wanted you to have something special," she explained.

"The quality of the food is good, but it's not seasoned enough. Glad you didn't cook it 'cause I would've wondered, where's the damn cayenne? The buttery flavor for the lobster? Why is there no salt on the noodles? Things like that." He worked his tongue in between his teeth in the most incongruous matter, then proceeded to gulp down more of his wine.

"I wish you would stop making that face, Axel."

"What face?"

"That sour expression you keep making… like you're drinking battery acid. If you don't like the wine, don't drink it. I have other things you can taste." *Shit. That came out wrong.*

She chanced a look at the man, and he was sitting there with a smile so greasy, it rivaled the face of a cat perched by a mouse hole.

"Well… what flavorsome liquid delicacies did you have in mind for me to taste, English?" He winked at her like some dirty old man in the club. And she liked it.

"I happen to think that—" She paused. Her phone buzzed again.

Axel set his empty wine glass down, folded his big hands with the long fingers she'd envisioned sliding against her thighs, and glared at her. Her blood ran cold. The man practically stared right through her, seeing her broken insides like shattered pieces of stained glass in a burning cathedral. Broken mirrors in a house of horrors.

"Who keeps calling you?"

It was obvious he didn't give a shit that it wasn't his place to ask. He wasn't her man. She wasn't his woman. His brows rutted, lines formed along his forehead, and the corners of his lips drooped.

I have three choices right now…

1. *Tell Axel the truth.*
2. *Lie my ass off.*
3. *Tell him the truth, but without the entire story so he doesn't run for the damn hills like in that episode of 'Everybody Loves Raymond,' where Robert Barone discovered the lady he liked was obsessed with frogs and had eaten a fly just like his brother, Raymond, had warned him about.*

Axel swiped the napkin across his mouth, tossed it on his plate, and stood up. He leaned over the table, wrists crossed, head cocked, and darkness in his eyes.

"I'm only asking you one more time, English. Who keeps calling you? If you have a man and lied to me about it, tell me. If you are back with your ex, tell me. If you have somethin' going on that you don't want to tell me, tell me anyway."

I don't like how he's speaking to me right now. That's not the point though. He's picked up on something, and that's not his fault. He's just perceptive, unlike most men. Shit.

"Axel…"

"No." He stood straight and waved his hand about. "I don't want to hear a lie. I can call my daddy for that. I don't want to hear no sugar coatin', either. I don't want to hear no excuses. So, before you do any of that beating around the bush, just know you've been warned. My food ain't got to come from your hands, but the truth damn better come from your mouth."

This fucker right here… Doesn't he understand this is hard enough already?! Well, of course he doesn't. He doesn't even know what's going on. I didn't want to do this tonight. I wanted to invite this man over for dinner and ride him like his first name is 'Disney' and his last name is 'World.' Everything is going to shit!

"I'm not doing this with you, English. I know that manipulative brain of yours is workin' overtime right now. You're looking calm, trying to make it seem like I'm acting silly or overreacting. All the while, your brain is just uh workin'… trying to come up with a story." She gulped. *Damn, he's good.* "That'll work on most folks. But not me. No games. Not tonight. Not ever."

"…I'm not playing games with you, Axel. That's not it at all. The phone calls. I'll tell you. It's just somebody from the past and they won't go away is all. It's not a big deal."

"It's a big deal. A very big deal. You're a strong woman. You can handle yourself, but even with all of that, I saw how you looked when the phone went off and when you came back to the table. Something is wrong and whatever it is, it has somethin' to do with who's callin' you. And before you even go there, I do have the right to know." He pointed at himself. "This is about respect, and I'm not comin' second fiddle to any fuckin' body."

"I'm not dating anyone else right now." She lowered her head.

"I'm supposed to be at work right now, but instead, I sent someone else 'cause I wanted to be here with *you*, knowin' damn well I might not even get a 'happy ending' tonight to make it worth my while. Every time I send someone else in my place, that's my reputation on the line. I'm a stickler when it comes to my business. My product. I believe in my heart of hearts that can't nobody do what I can do, as good as I can do it, and that goes for every damn thing I put my mind, heart, soul, and definitely my body to."

Did he really have to say it like that? It's strange to be terrified, mortified, and turned on all at once. And yet, here the hell I am. Feeling it.

"I'm here anyway because this is where the hell I want to be. Now, the least you could do is be ten toes down with me, be a woman about it, and tell me who in the hell has been blowin' up your phone and making you look like a vampire. Color just drained from your face."

Their eyes hooked and she sighed, closing her eyes.

If this is meant to be, you can tell him the truth. If it isn't, he will think you're crazy, and vanish. Either way, it has to be done.

She bit her lower lip, crossed her legs, and lifted her glass of wine to her lips. After a few seconds, she waved her hand at his chair, motioning him to sit down. He hesitated for a moment, as if he was not certain he wanted to comply, then, he yanked the chair from the table and slammed his body into it. He slowly unbuttoned his shirt, and she watched in disbelief, intrigue, and confusion. Moments later, he positioned it across the back of his chair. She was now faced with one of the most magnificent, muscular yet lean bodies she'd ever laid eyes on. Veins covered his arms and upper chest. That chest was covered in exquisitely drawn tattoos of Greek and Roman mythical beings, mortals and deities. Raising a hand to his gold chain, he rolled the jewelry to and fro between thumb and forefinger. His green eyes hooded and his jaw tightened.

"Start talking."

"I'm trying to figure out where to begin. It's a lot to unpack." She sighed and took another sip of wine, bracing to unburden her soul.

"…Let me help you. Let's imagine it's one of those old books of yours. The kind you work on for a living. Once upon a time, in a land far away, there lived a princess named English. Her phone rang, and on the other end of the line was a dragon."

Chills ran through her very soul! He knew! On some level, he sensed the heart of the story, without ever having read the words. Axel had inched into the depths of her internal shadows, the recesses of her brain, and pulled them out with a hard, hateful yank.

"…But English wasn't any princess. She was everything but. She'd met the wrong person, at the wrong time, and got caught up in a web of bullshit. It was no fairytale." Her hand shook as she took yet another sip of wine, then set the glass down. "This book doesn't need a curator. It doesn't need to be salvaged or saved. No operation of restoration can be performed. It's fit for the dumpster and was ready to be burned as soon as it was written. This story almost ruined the heroine's life." She blinked away angry tears. "Chapter One – The Master has spoken…"

Chapter Ten

WHEN AXEL RETURNED inside English's house after taking her trash out to the street curb, he found her curled up on her couch with a cup of tea in her hands, shoes off and a faraway look in her eyes. He braced himself to continue what they started. The conversation was necessary to shine a light on the elephant in the room. In spite of the impromptu break, he wasn't going to allow her any wiggle room to flee from the situation.

This seemed out of character for her, not opening up and exposing the truth. Her truth. Something was holding her back, making her a prisoner of her own mind. Of course, he'd only known her a couple of months, but still… something didn't feel right. This didn't match what he'd witnessed from her. She was usually fearless about expressing herself. Whatever was going on in her life, it seemed to almost paralyze her emotionally.

He scratched along his earlobe, curing an itch. He looked about the living room, and decided to sit across from her on a plush purple couch with sophisticated silver hardware. Her entire first floor, from what he could see, was decorated with pricy furniture and well-placed art. A crisp and clean space, smelling faintly of lemon Pine-Sol and Pledge. Her tastes were not his style by any stretch of the imagination, but it screamed intelligent, sexy, feminine…

"You didn't have to take out my trash, Axel, but thank you."

"It needed to be taken out. I saw it. I did it." He shrugged, then ran his hand over his hair and massaged a kink in his neck.

Her phone buzzed again. This time, a text message. He grabbed her phone before she could reach it.

BITCH, CALL ME.

That was all it said. But that was enough for him. Red-hot rage fermented inside of him. *Who was talking to her like this? And why would she allow it?* After reading that, instead of keeping his foot on her neck and demanding answers, he decided to take five. She was clearly distressed. Her eyes sheened over. Not one tear dropped, but she was visibly fighting her emotions.

He took that time to clear the table, refill her glass of wine, and tidy up the kitchen.

After all, that's what he did: clean up messes.

Removed the grime, stains and blemishes, reminders of what was now gone forever. Vile memories replaced good times so quickly… He made haste to solve an ongoing problem, all in an effort to assist the living. She was alive, yet something inside of her was rotting with shame.

So he dipped his cloth in the invisible solvent, and prepared to clean her hurt away.

"One of my daddy's favorite songs is 'Enter Sandman,' by Metallica," he began. His hands became lovers as they wrapped around one another. Rough skin gliding, fingers intertwined, warming to his own touch. "It's funny that sometimes, when I talk to him, even on the phone, I can hear him playing it. At first, I thought it was a coincidence, because he'd tell me he just turned on the radio and there it was, but then, I figured he was almost summoning that song."

English looked down briefly into her teacup, a sad smile on her face, then looked back up at him. She was the most beautiful thing he'd ever seen.

Eyes big, dark, and expressive. Cheekbones full and high. Lips thick and juicy, soft like an angel's.

"The lyrics of the song are about crib death… of all things."

Her gaze narrowed on him, interest obviously piqued.

"I never knew that."

"A lot of people don't. My daddy had a baby that died from crib death. A woman he was messing with while married to my mama. One of many women." He grimaced. "He didn't know the song was about that either until years later, but he claimed to be drawn to it. Metallica is one of his favorite bands. I like 'em just fine, too. I'm telling you about this, English, because sometimes, we are drawn to things or people, and we don't know why at first. But it all points back to something we felt we wanted or needed. Somethin' from our childhood we're trying to heal or run from, or something bad that happened long ago. An unexpected event."

"That's quite introspective and wise of you."

He wasn't certain if she was being serious or sarcastic, but it made no difference.

"Based on that text message, I'm guessing the person behind it is an old flame. Somebody who once had control over you." She didn't respond, and her expression was flat. Unreadable like gibberish written in white ink on white paper. "We choose certain people to date, and we don't look deep enough into why we're attracted to them. Hardly anyone does." He shrugged. "We think it's because he's handsome, or she's pretty, things like that. Sure, that plays a part in it, but they have something we want, and we think if we saddle up close enough to them, we can get it. We want to feel a certain way, and we think they can help us achieve that."

"Energy. It's their energy. We're attracted to souls, and don't even know it."

"Dallas, my sister, is into all that crazy shit."

"What crazy shit? Energy readings?"

"Yeah. You know, crystals, runes… but one thing she said to me about all of that stuff that I agree with is: we're all energy. So, I agree with you if that's what you were getting at."

"We're vim, covered in flesh and bone. I think we're also spiritual beings, too."

"Same thing. We're saying the same thing."

She nodded in understanding. "Energy attracts like a magnet, or it can repel, like a sonic boom."

"So, we either attract what we want or need, or we invite a lesson to be learned. Kind of like what you and I were talking about weeks ago. If our energy is not to someone's liking, English, then it repels them. One twist to that is, if they think they can get something out of us, good or bad, then we bring folks around us that we might not want there. People that feed off good energy like piranhas."

She placed her tea down on the coffee table and lounged back against the love seat.

"Axel, that's unfortunately true. Bad people see our light. It sounds a bit sophomoric the way I said it, I guess, but doesn't make it any less of a fact." Her voice trailed as she looked away.

"They see the light… or our darkness." She threw him a curious look as he spoke, then swallowed. "We become deaf to the truth if we've taken a liking to someone who means us no good. We hear no evil as they say, but sometimes, it ain't evil at all, English. It's just the plain truth, but usually one we don't want to hear, so we say the devil is tryna interfere in our love life, or break up a happy home, when it ain't got nothing to do with Satan, and that home was far from happy to begin with. Got folks in this world getting themselves in unhappy relationships for money, or they say, 'for the kids.' Bullshit.

"Most people get comfortable and are afraid to be alone because that's the biggest human fear of all. We're not okay by ourselves. We keep loyal to a bad choice we made a long ass time ago, and keep punishing ourselves by stayin' true to it. It's got to do with our own bad choices, not facing reality, and not wanting to get out of the mess we've made or allowed someone else to toss on us, day after fuckin' day. The bottom line is, we could save ourselves a lot of time if we'd just acknowledge things for what they are and move on. Stop making excuses for our situation. Friends are one backstab away from becoming an enemy, and lovers are one kiss away from walkin' out the door."

"This is another thing I love about you." She reached for her cup and took a sip of her tea.

"Yeah? And what's that?"

"You remember the things I say to you. I admit that I stereotyped you based on how you look, where you're from, and what you do for a living. You're a deep thinker. You're funny. You're… protective. If you weren't, you wouldn't care about what was going on with me." Her complexion deepened and she broke their eye contact by looking back down into that teacup of hers.

"I'm not easy to get along with sometimes. I told you what some of my problems are. The question becomes, will I address them for the right person? More than likely I would…"

"…All of this. These things you say to me puncture me deep inside, make me bleed and feel something for you. You were right when you told me you were different, boy." Her smile grew, and her eyes sheened over once again. "Or maybe you and that silver tongue of yours is just a way for you to look good in my eyes, to prove yourself, your resume as you call it—but either way, it's working, Axel. We both know it."

"I have a silver tongue. I'm a good salesman, I'll admit that. I'm a smooth talker when I need to be I suppose, but right now, I take this seriously because you're not okay. And I'm not playing any games with you, 800. Tryna get over. You've got a lot of trust issues. So do I—just different reasons as to why."

They were quiet for a bit.

"Axel, you have a funny way of putting some of those things we talk about in a different context. I like that. You're a good listener. No one is perfect, but uh, clearly, you're a good catch. *Very* attractive, with a spiritual foundation. You've got swag. You work hard. You're financially stable. Seems to love your mama. Good relationship with your sister and people in town look up to you. Admire you. The list is growing."

He leaned back against the couch and they sat listening to Al B. Sure's, 'Nite and Day'.

"I don't understand why you're single. You must be holding back some dark, ugly secret."

"I think the fact that I've killed two people in one year is dark and ugly enough."

She burst out laughing.

"Yeah… that's not all that great. Looks bad on paper, but I understand the context. If anything, once the details are understood, it makes you even sexier or more irresistible. Shows you can handle yourself."

"I'm single because I want to be. I told you that."

"But you don't act like it. You seem to want more than that, Axel. I'm not your woman, but you treat me like I am. Calling me. Texting me. Gifts. You're good to me…"

"I also told you that if I met the right person, I wouldn't want to be single anymore, and that I don't date casually. I date with intention. I am fine being single. I'm okay with it."

"How can you want to be single, but not date casually?"

"You're not listening."

"I am listening, Axel. You're contradicting yourself. Do you want some tea, honey? I'm sorry I didn't offer. I fixed it while you were outside with my trash."

"I'm not contradicting myself, and unless that tea has ice and a ton of sugar and lemon, no, I don't want any."

She scoffed, then laughed at him.

"So now you want diabetes *and* high blood pressure. Nice!" She giggled.

"Life is short. I want my food seasoned. My tea sweet. My gun loaded. My cigarettes by the carton. My beer cold, and my sex nasty. All I was saying is that all sorts of people can be good with being single. Meaning, it's no sweat off our noses. We're not sittin' at home looking mopey or tossing and turning in our beds because we aren't shacked up with some lady, or in a long-term relationship. I don't want another dysfunctional relationship just for the sake of sayin' I'm in one, or one that's not goin' anywhere.

"You could be with someone for twenty damn years and feel miserable as hell. I refuse to be that person, because I value each and every day the good Lord gives me, 800. I refuse for it to be wasted on someone who wouldn't spare a second on me if it inconvenienced them in any way. People show you who the hell they are pretty fast. You just have to know what to look for. When I get married, I want it to be for life. I don't want to have to do this shit over three, four, five times, or end up in someone's court squabbling over visitation and alimony. I'm not gettin' any younger, either. I want to get married and have a few kids one day, with just one woman," he held up his finger, "and still be young enough to outrun my children, play with them so much that they fall asleep hard. So, I'm just not into lost causes, while still dating with intention."

"You seem to have pretty high standards."

"I do. Everyone who is worth a damn should."

"Do you think you'll ever get married?"

"I have faith that I'll meet the right woman and settle down, English. The lady for me might live all the way in London, have an amazing British accent, and drive one of those crazy double decker buses, or she might be English in a different way… sippin' tea right now while lying on a purple couch, smelling like fresh lavender, vanilla and mint, and looking pretty as a daisy."

Her smile lit up that room…

"When I date, if I and that person are not meshing, I am okay with that and move on. If we're doing really good, I'm fine with taking it to the next level, because that's what I want. You can want something but be okay that you don't have it. That's where I'm at right now. I work long, crazy hours. I've got a jealous streak. I'm protective, like you said, and I think some things a man should do, and others a woman should do. Some might think that's sexist, and that's fine, but it's just who I am, and I'm stickin' to it. I'm not afraid of commitment. My future plans match my current plans, and that's by design. You got it now?"

She smiled, then nodded.

"Would you like a tour of my house? I'm quite proud of it." She hopped up like a rabbit, zeal in her eyes.

"Okay." *You're not off the hook, 800, but I'll let you have a few more minutes to get yourself together.*

She started by showing him various paintings and African and Egyptian style statues, then moved on to a book or two, explaining their history.

"…And this room has amazing brick arched doorways because it was once the school entryway."

"It's crazy how this used to be a small school, and someone turned it into a house. You got lucky finding this gem. I told you I dabble a bit in real estate. I own two rental properties right now, and I flip houses on occasion."

"Yes, you did tell me that! I understand you do some of your own electrical and carpentry, too."

"Yeah, I do. A little plumbing and other repairs, too. My father was at least useful in that way. He taught me how to fix a few things, and my mama taught me how to paint walls right, and hang pictures and shelves, things like that. Nothin' too complicated, but I figure if I can save money doing some things myself, then I will."

"That's smart because the cost of help and supplies is constantly rising. This place was a steal, too, because it needed a lot of work. So over here," she pointed to the kitchen as they drew closer to it, "There was a bit of plumbing for a small washroom. They updated that and created the kitchen and half bath."

Her kitchen was full of retro style baby blue and silver appliances. It reminded him of a 1950s diner and was pretty cool to look at. They completed the first-floor journey, then he followed her up the stairs.

"I had to have the staircase totally redone. The steps were steep and old."

"Looks like a new banister was added. It's decent, but it's a wood handrail, and they didn't varnish it evenly."

She paused, looking perplexed as she studied the banister.

"Yes, I recently got that replaced again. What's wrong with it?"

"See this? That is shiny, but right here, this tiny spot is matte. Here's another one, and another one. It's a patchy job. I can redo it for you, but I'd have to sand the whole thing down if you want to keep the same one instead of buying a whole new one."

"Oh my God, you're right. How'd you even see that?" She giggled. "It depends on how much you charge me if I feel it's worth it."

I don't want any cash, baby. The price is some pussy. I'll take care of it right after I plow your back out.

He kept his sleazy thoughts to himself, but as he walked behind her and watched her hips swing to and fro, her ass bouncing like a ball in her pants, his dick strained against his briefs, and it was hard to ignore his strong sexual desires for her. They kept moving about the house, and he listened to her talk, until at one point, he cleared his throat.

"I ain't forgot."

"...Neither have I." She tossed him a glance from over her shoulder and rolled her eyes. "And over here is a rug my old college roommate gave me. Over the years it became old and ratty, so I cut it down to this small section, to remember her by. She was from Nepal."

I. Don't. Give. A. Shit. Who the hell is calling my woman and harassing her? My woman? We haven't even fucked yet... I never commit without smashing first. I need to be sure she's good in bed, the added cherry on top. Right now, none of that matters. She'll be mine soon. I can feel it... Unless she tells me the person that's calling is some administrator from an insane asylum trying to get her to come back to the hospital. Knowing my luck lately, it probably is.

She opened the door to her bedroom, and they walked inside. The first thing he noticed was a posh sitting area with cream furniture: a small two-seater couch, two matching chairs to the left of it, and two side-by-side mirrored coffee tables with silver and muted gold embellishments. Atop it also sat decorative dark gray and white books, and two silver ottomans, trimmed in gold around the bottom, were positioned to the right of the couch. Purple and slate gray pillows with hints of silver and gold design adorned the couches and chairs, and a large abstract painting in shades of gray and purple hung on the wall.

He looked to his left and noticed her bed. It sat high on risers, covered in cream sheets and a thick duvet. A silver runner ran across the width of it, embellished with gold tassels.

The matching nightstands were mirrored and featured two oversized clear 1970's retro-style lamps.

"This is nice. Not my style, but nice."

"Thank you." She turned to him, something flashing in her eyes. Wrapping her soft, warm hand around his neck, she rose on her toes and pressed her sweet mouth against his. He returned the favor and savored her as their tongues glided against one another. "I've been wanting to kiss you all night," she said when she broke free, breathless. Lust filled her gaze. "It might be our last kiss, though."

"Why?"

"Please sit down." She pointed to one of the chairs. He obliged. "That way, I can dramatically call after you as you run out of my bedroom, down the steps, clutching the banister that needs work. I will then fall to my knees and start bawling when I hear your truck door slam, and your tire wheels squeal as you maneuver frantically out of my driveway. Hopefully, Alexa will choose a good sad song for me while I lick my wounds and discover minutes later that you've blocked my number."

"Would you stop all of this silly bullshit, and just get to it?"

She grimaced, then sat across from him, on the couch.

"Here we go… This is the part where I sit you down and spill my guts, but before that, I feel the ridiculous need to begin by explaining the context. Everything I'm about to tell you is true. You deserve that much." She took a deep breath. "Okay, here goes nothin'. I've never told anyone this except my parents and brother and sister, Axel, and not even they know every single thing that happened. None of my ex-boyfriends or close friends know about it, either. I didn't want to talk about it. Never had a reason to."

"Got it. Please, for the love of rice and gravy, just tell me what's goin' on without all of this filler. I don't need any side dishes. The main course alone will do."

She started picking at her cuticle. "Please let me explain this in my own way… Don't rush me. Don't be rude, Axel. I'm serious."

"I'm not, but damn! Okay, I'm sorry… that was… I just…" He sighed. "Please… just tell me what's going on."

She took a long, deep breath. "Anyway, years ago, when I was in college," she glanced his way, then went right back to that cuticle. "I got involved with someone I shouldn't have. I was exploring my beliefs at the time, as many people in their late teens and early twenties do, and I was also in a mental state where I was vulnerable."

"Why were you vulnerable? I was a hellion at that age. Wild and free."

"Well, instead of enjoying college parties and living it up, I was havin' some personal issues. I had just broken up with my high school boyfriend—nothing crazy happened, we'd just grown apart—and my parents weren't getting along. My brother was going through some stuff. He'd gotten in trouble at school, and my sister, who I had been pretty close to, had moved out of town.

"I was a freshman and felt a bit out of place, so on and

so on." She paused, got up, and walked over to a mini fridge. Upon her return, she handed him a bottle of Minute Maid lemonade and opened herself one, too. After taking a big gulp, she continued. "On campus, when I was in a study hall, a man approached me. He looked normal. He was nice looking, actually. Nothing over the top that would make you say, 'Damn, who is that?', but attractive enough. He was dressed nicely, too. The thing is though, he had a way about him… an aura. He introduced himself. Explained that he was between classes and had to stop and speak to me. He was an American history and African American studies major, so that got my interest because, as you know, that's my thing. Long story short, we started talking that day, got a coffee and some bagels at the café, and had a great conversation. He was extremely personable, laid back… and he made me feel comfortable speaking to him.

"Unfortunately, due to my lack of discernment at the time, I didn't realize he was priming me—trying to see if I'd be appropriate for grooming." She sighed and bit on her bottom lip before going on. "He had some rather unusual religious beliefs, but he explained that they were part of our culture, of our African ancestors, and that we'd been brainwashed by the White man's religion."

"What were *his* religious beliefs?"

She hesitated while she mulled the question. "It's complicated, but I would describe his convoluted version of spirituality as a mixture between Judaism, Bahá'í Faith, and Islam, if I had to put a title or description on it. In spite of his eccentric views, I believe most people would have regarded him as quite intelligent. He knew how to slick-talk folks, too. He used actual texts to prove his points, and that could trip some people up. He mixed all of this with African American culture, in order to pull on the pain and emotionalism of the atrocities that had occurred to Black people in this country, in the past, and to this day. Things like, Black people were the original people. I agree with that. The first humans were believed to have come from Africa. He also said, we were kings and queens.

"Not all of us were. That was a way to be manipulative. I mean truly, how many kings, queens, and princesses can you have?" She sucked her teeth. "Anyway, this was paired with positive affirmations to make a special bullshit brew. Then, the discussions turned to Black people being superior to other races, and that those other people should be basically worshiping us. Now, that I didn't believe at all. I do believe we're resilient people. I believe we're amazing, and wonderfully made from our various skin tones and hair textures to our culture in this country. We're inventors and originators.

"All that said, I don't believe God finds Black folk to be *more* special than any other race, and nobody more special than us. I don't think God plays a game like that and if we pretend He does, it could have serious consequences. High self-esteem doesn't need to be built on the back of puttin' others down, or seeing them as lowly. Beneath us. We're taking a page out of the oppressor's playbook. I believe we're important and gifted, and we've been treated badly in America and all over the world for that matter, but to go as far as to say we're superior is just not true. I believe in one God, and he didn't put one man over another. That's human frailty. A sickness of mankind."

Her voice cracked, and he imagined her heart ached, too.

"I rejected that notion, but he beat it in my head that I was wrong, and if I were to be friends with non-melanated people, then I would be tainted. Let alone date and have sex with a White man. This man's grandmother was White, for God's sake, because his mama was mixed, but whatever. My parents never told me no mess like that. I didn't grow up hearing such things. I was raised right. He explained this hierarchy that contradicted everything I was taught. I started to believe him when he said White people were inferior and evil. Now, please understand, he did this over the course of many years. Not days. Not weeks. Not months. He kept hammering at me a little bit at a time. He earned my trust first, and I thought we were in love."

"You don't have to explain. I understand how faith-based indoctrination works. Go on."

"He then began holding these classes and inviting more people in. He already had a small group of friends I'd met, but I thought they were just friends. Come to find out, they were what he called his devotees. He believed he was the second coming of Christ."

She looked at him, as if to check for his reaction. Sure, he believed whoever this man she was speaking about had to be a fucking lunatic, and he would've seen right through his façade, but he wasn't the one falling in love with a charlatan at the age of twenty-one. Under the right conditions, he might have become a victim of a batshit crazy lady, too. He had his share of close calls, that was for sure. There was no need for him to gasp or throw up jazz hands in hysteria. Shit happened.

"Crazy people are worth a dime a dozen. You've said nothin' that is worth my running away from you."

"I'm not finished."

He opened his drink and took a gulp.

"Do you mind if I smoke in here?"

"I do. I have some rare books in here, and cigarette smoke could damage them."

"Okay. I'll just wait until you're finished and go outside."

She nodded, took another sip of her lemonade, and continued.

"So… let me make something clear. I wasn't a virgin when I got with Master, but I wasn't what I would call experienced, either."

"Wait. This motherfucker is named Master?"

"He legally changed his name to that. His birth name was Lerone."

"You can't make this shit up. You just can't. Go on, go on." He took a huge gulp of lemonade and looked up at the ceiling in disbelief.

"So, I wasn't a virgin, but I had only been with two guys before him. My first, a boy I had grown up with, and that was just one time, and then my ex-boyfriend from high school. So, he knew this, and he and I started having sex. Again, I thought I was in love, and I was fine with that. Then, things got strange. He wanted me to have sex with some of his devotees."

He passed her around like a collection plate. Great. So much for what would Jesus do…

"I didn't want to. He reacted by telling me I didn't love him because I was not submitting and being obedient. He tried to show me scriptures that he had twisted up in his own head in order to confuse and manipulate me. Being stupid as hell, I let him convince me to sleep with a couple of them. It was one of the most humiliating experiences of my life, Axel. I felt so degraded and dirty. He'd stand there with his arms crossed, and watch."

Axel slowly got up, sat next to her, and wrapped his arm around her waist. He could feel her shaking.

"So, that went on for a while, and then, the physical abuse started. First, it was a push here and there. Then, twisting my arm. We'd get into arguments, and he'd berate me. Infuriated that I dared question or challenge him. Mind you, I was keeping this crap from my family. I didn't tell my friends, because by then, he'd alienated me from them, or turned them against me. I wasn't talking to my parents regularly anyway, especially my mother because she and I were going through a rough patch when she'd legally separated from my father at that point.

"So, Master smacked me so hard one afternoon during an argument, I blacked out. After that, he never hit me on my face again. He said he couldn't have me going around people looking like that, and I should be ashamed for making him do that to me. His cult, because that is what it was at this point, was growing, and he was feeling power hungry. He was speaking at various engagements, and people were just loving his narcissistic ass. I was finishing up grad school, and about to graduate. By the end of my senior year, despite being brainwashed, the abuse did somethin' to me. It changed me. Forever. I didn't want to be with him anymore. I didn't care how popular he now was, and him hitting me didn't make me fear him or silence me, like he'd hoped it would. Instead, it empowered me to leave.

"I had outgrown him, despite all of his programming and manipulative tactics. We were living in an apartment together at the time, so that made it harder for me to get a moment to myself, but I managed. So, as a last-ditch effort, once he realized I was slipping away from his mind games and control, he wanted to have a ceremony with me, in which we'd get married in front of the congregation. I agreed to it, but I knew I was going to leave anyway. He didn't want me to start my Master's program. That would mean more time away from him and his control, new friends, and people who might be able to persuade me to leave him. So, instead, he wanted us to lead his "church" together, and start a family."

Right then, the thought of her married and impregnated by anyone, *especially* someone as dreadful as the person she was describing, made his fists tense. He looked down at his hands, and they were balled up tight. He could feel his heart beating harder, too.

"Two nights before we were supposed to have this fake marriage ceremony, I put my escape plan into full gear. I got the courage to finally go to the police. I literally had to crawl out the second story window and drop down. Down below, I already had a small bag packed, hidden in the bushes of our apartment complex. I walked up the street, then called for a cab at a store. Once I got to the police station, I told them about the abuse, his financial schemes with which he'd been robbing and tricking people out of their money, and also about the sixteen-year-old girl he'd had an inappropriate relationship with that I had literally just found out about, four days before I left him. Well, here I was thinking I was spilling the beans, but Axel, they were onto him long before I had arrived. The police had Master on their radar for years! He'd been accused of *many* burglaries, had served time for theft which I knew nothing about, and lied about his age! He said he was twenty-two when we met, and he was actually thirty! He wasn't even a registered student anymore! He'd dropped out months before he met me.

"He had a daughter in another state, and was still legally married to someone back in Oklahoma, which is where he was from originally. He had several domestic violence charges from that relationship and was even accused of pimping someone. I was sick, Axel. So, not only was I dealing with a violent lunatic, he really believed he was Christ. I know that, deep in my soul, he believed this. A fact that made him even more dangerous. The police escorted me back to his apartment and stood by while I packed the rest of my things. The whole time, he was acting his ass off. A real Oscar-worthy performance, pretending to be a broken-hearted, dutiful boyfriend. Telling the police I could have left at any time, and that the stuff on his record was in the past. He kept saying he was not the same man he'd been, but when I turned around with my bags, and looked at him… I will never forget his face for as long as I live, Axel.

"It was pure evil. At first, when I had moved out, he kept calling me, asking for forgiveness. Once he realized it wasn't working, he then started threatening me. He said he'd hurt my parents, too. By this point, my parents were working out their differences and were involved in the situation. My father has a friend who's in law enforcement. He told him what was going on, and Master got a visit, so he backed off. Then, a year or so after that, he messaged me online. I wasn't using my real name on there, so I don't know how he found me, but he did. I blocked him, but right before I did, I noticed he was married to some woman, and it looked like he had a son now, too. A couple years passed, and he messaged me again, from a different profile.

"A real stalker."

"Yup. This time, I saw photos of him leading some church and wearing all of these strange, gaudy outfits. He had all of these women around him, too. Women he was calling his wives. It was peculiar and disturbing. In this message to me, he was talking about how I was the one he loved the most. That I should have been the 'head wife.' That he knows he messed up with me, because he didn't allow me to grow and have any breathing room, but he forgives me, too, for leaving the way I did. He was talking about how proud he was of me regarding my education, and that he'd been checking up on me. He knew some of my friends' names, and my boyfriend at the time, too. Axel, I felt sick to my stomach. I asked him to leave me alone. I told him I'd moved on and was in a committed relationship. He said it didn't matter because I belonged to him, and always would."

"Two words. Restraining order?"

"Several attempts. He didn't have an address at one point, and no job, so he couldn't be served. Finally, I got one served to him. Then, for many years, I didn't hear a word from him. For some reason, he has started contacting me again."

"Did you tell the police that he's back?"

"No, because at one point they weren't much help. It's like he basically has to kill me in order for them to do anything about this. I even spoke to his ex-wife a long time ago, and he harassed her for a long time too, but left her alone eventually. But me? No such luck. He is *still* running that cult, too, from my understanding. Master key devotees. He's had people over the years try to email me on his behalf. A bunch of lunatics. I used to block his various numbers but stopped because I wanted a paper trail. Proof of him calling and harassing me."

"Two more words. Smith and Wesson."

"Oh baby, you already know it. I have a gun now." She got up, walked across the room, and opened up her nightstand drawer. She removed a revolver, held it high so he could see, then placed it back inside the dresser.

When she returned to him, she was wringing her hands, and looked mentally exhausted.

Oh, he's going to get his. I promise you that.

"We're done with this conversation, baby. At least for now. I came over here to have a good time with you, and that's what we're going to do. Let's watch a movie. Something funny. I make some amazing popcorn. I know how to do it on the stove. I'll teach you if you don't know."

"But all I have here at the house is microwave popcorn. I don't have any kernels or—"

"I brought it over myself. It's in the truck. You weren't the only one thinking ahead." He went out of the house, pulled a backpack from his truck, and returned to her. She was standing in the middle of her bedroom, and he could tell she'd been crying those few minutes he was gone. He opened the backpack, pulled out a canister of popcorn oil, kernels, some cheesy DVD movies he figured she'd like, and two wine coolers.

"I told you, wasn't nobody but Jesus stopping me from getting to you tonight."

Her eyes lit up and she wrapped her arms around him, buried her face between his neck and shoulder, and squeezed tight.

He kissed the top of her head and squeezed her right back.

Just you wait and see, 800.

Chapter Eleven

...Several days later

MAMA PLACED THE silver gift-wrapped box in the middle of the dining room table, then sat down with a glass of ice water garnished with a slice of lime. The house was full of people there to celebrate Mama's birthday, and her sisters and brothers were making the most ruckus of all. Uncle Bruce sported a dated beige suit that was two sizes too small, while Aunt Tasha had her ample bosom on full display, and smelled like vintage Charlie perfume. Uncle Jerold wore a ridiculous gray handlebar mustache, Aunt Georgia looked demure and studious in thick-rimmed navy glasses, plain powder blue A-Line skirt, and button-up cardigan. Finally, great-aunt Beverly, who could barely hear but always pretended she could, was chastising anyone who suggested she get a hearing aid.

English leaned against the floral wall-papered partition in the home she'd grown up in and turned her attention back towards her mother. The lady of the day was sitting surrounded by those she loved most.

Mama's exhilaration was shiny and heavy. It packed the house like golden bricks stacked up to the heavens. The big smile on her face put her in her mind the image of a white rainbow lying on its back. Her slender legs crossed, the silver anklets gleamed under the lighting, she was clearly enjoying every moment as she smacked her lips before taking a great big gulp of water.

English committed this day to memory—this feeling—hearing the laughter yet to come, and seeing the tears of joy yet to fall. Mama must've heard something hilarious then, for her eyes grew large, and she burst out laughing. She sounded like a colorful song, and looked like gratitude and love. It had been a while since English had traveled home to Dry Ridge, Kentucky. It was nice to be here, even if only for a day.

"En." Roosevelt slipped close to her, clutching a beer in his beringed hand. "We're going to sing 'Happy Birthday' to Mama in a little bit. I looked in the kitchen, but didn't see anything. Where's a lighter?"

"I bet she and Daddy have one in their bedroom since she has all of those Diptyque candles and whatnot in there. I'll go check. Be right back."

She traveled down the long hallway, almost bumping into her cousin, Chloe, who was on her phone while exiting the bathroom. Chloe's pink and blonde weave was piled high atop her head, her hair-sprayed curls adorned with rhinestones and vibrant faux jewels in an up-do that rivaled Marge Simpson's. Chloe often worked as a model in hair shows, typically traveling to Detroit, Michigan and

Atlanta, Georgia with her stylist. When she smiled, her dark purple lipstick framed a mouth full of tightly packed teeth, the left front one shielded in gold with a diamond chip shaped like a tiny star.

That's probably the same star the three wise men followed to meet baby Jesus… Why did I think of that? Silly. I think I drank too much wine, and the night is still young.

"HEEEEY, ENGLISH! I ain't seen you in a minute, baby. Lookin' good. You still messin' with them old Negro Spiritual books in Po'land? Po'land, Kentucky, right? Not Po'land, Oregon. Did you move to Oregon or stay here in Kentucky, girl? Shiiiid. I can't remember, chile."

She barely slowed down to even wait for a reply, so English tried to respond quickly, before Chloe all but disappeared.

"They're not all Negro Spiritual books, Chloe, but yes, I'm still book curating at the Roots 101 museum in Portland. Still here in Kentucky."

"Mmm hmmm, that's nice! I'll come visit soon, baby!" Her cousin sauntered away, not really giving a damn, then began yelling something English couldn't understand as she finessed up the hallway toward the crowd, hips just a rockin'.

English shook her head and continued on to her parents' bedroom. As she entered, she half-expected to see her father sprawled out across the bed, asleep. She hadn't seen him for at least thirty minutes now that she thought about it. Daddy hated parties and wasn't a stranger to slipping away during some shindigs, taking cat naps here and there. But the room was empty, the neat queen-sized bed simply dressed in lilac and white sheets, surrounded by oak furniture and a large flat screen television mounted to the wall. As always, it smelled like fresh linens in here. To her left stood a curio holding family heirlooms and leather-bound photo albums, and to her right, Mama's vast collection of pretty perfumes, assorted purses, candles, nail polishes, and drugstore cosmetics. Her guilty pleasure.

She made her way over to the dresser and opened the top drawer to find a stash of old receipts. Daddy usually kept those as a record for business expenses. He'd recently retired from his position as manager of a large lawn care and gardening company, but still earned a bit of extra cash doing repairs on related equipment. After plundering through that drawer, she soon realized there were no lighters.

She opened another drawer, and hit the jackpot. Grabbing one of two options—a red, white and blue one with 'Texas' printed across it—she turned to leave, then paused when an envelope lying on the vanity, addressed to Mama, drew her attention. Her heart sank. She stepped closer, an agonizing sickness running roughshod over her. A slow sweat began in her core and oozed outward, leaving moisture along her brow. Her gut felt like a miniature roller coaster ride within her.

She shook her head in disbelief. Her eyes felt suddenly dry, and she blinked as if to wish the vision away. After a few moments of swimming in the deep end of trepidation and unrealistic expectations, she managed to pull herself together and snatch the pink envelope that was lying there, mocking her.

I know that handwriting.

She'd recognize it anywhere. The way the first letter of each word was oddly larger than the rest, and the peculiar mixture of cursive and block script that popped up every now and again. Hallmark brand, dark ink on the envelope, addressed to Mama. It looked as if it had already been opened.

The lighter slipped from her grip onto the dresser. Then, she glided the card out of the envelope which featured an artistic rendering of a Black woman standing by another woman, looking contemplative and content.

Happy Birthday.

I hope it is all that *you* wished for.

Every Day that passes is a new opportunity

that *you* create. Seize it.

It wasn't signed. But she knew.

Damned if she didn't know…

With envelope in hand, she raced out of her parents' room to ask her mother about this appalling discovery—an otherwise innocent piece of mail to those with an undiscerning eye. In the living room, she was met with a horde of people in tasseled party hats blowing birthday whistles. Some were dancing, others speaking loudly, their words blended together and clogging her thoughts like an ever-growing wad of gum.

Mama was not where she was sitting just moments

ago. In fact, it was as if she'd been swallowed in the middle of the mass. A birthday bash blackhole. Frantic, English searched all over, her head spinning. All she could see were shades of Earth all around her. The odors of mingling sweet and spicy fragrances, tobacco, strong cigars, sweat and fried foods assailed her. Abrupt nausea came on, her stomach clenching like a fist around one's last dollar.

The blasting sounds of Maze and Frankie Beverly's 'Happy Feelins' weaved its way from the speakers, while the merrymaking crawled into her ears and banged on the drums of her brain. She felt as if she were being seduced by a strange emotional sorcery that caused her to feel lightheaded, sluggish, and weak.

And then, she burned with anger. The rage built and built, and this was the brick that would make the whole thing tumble like a bad move in Jinga. The envelope in her hand twisted in her grasp. When she finally found Mama talking to one of her best friends, Alisha, she pushed her way past some man she didn't know, and screamed for her mother's attention. She was certain that she looked insane, but appearances be damned.

"Mama, where did you get this card from? Did it come with a gift or anything, too?"

"Card? What card, honey?"

"I was in your bedroom to get a lighter for the cake, and saw this." She held the pink envelope up high and followed Mama's line of vision.

Mama narrowed her gaze on the envelope, as if seeing it for the first time. Then, she relaxed and nodded with a smile.

"Oh! That came in the mail 'bout two days ago. It had an Italian food menu in it. Strange. A place I never heard of. I don't know who it was from, though," she said with a shrug. "I got so many cards and gifts this year, baby, I can't keep up." Mama's cheeks reddened with pride.

"Was the Italian restaurant outta Portland, Kentucky, Mama? Place called Vincenzo's?"

"Yes!" Mama's grin widened. "That's the name of the place… don't know where I put that menu, though. It was way over there in Louisville, so I knew I wouldn't be goin' anytime soon. What a blessing to know so many people were thinkin' about me. Wasn't no return address on it, though." Mama shrugged, then her smile faded and her eyes widened as she said, "Is something wrong, English?"

Vincenzo's was a place she often went on her lunch breaks. *He's been watching me…*

English swallowed. For a split second, one fleeting moment in time, she nearly blurted out the cold, unfortunate truth.

I'm not going to ruin her birthday. If Mama and Daddy know Master is harassing me, they'll start worrying all over again. It took years for them to stop babying me after what happened. This situation was supposed to be dead and gone. Buried. This is probably the only address he knows for me. It makes sense he'd try to go through her to get to me since I haven't responded to his messages. They tried so hard back then to encourage me to get out of that outlandish group and leave that monster, but instead, I caused them so much stress and sleepless nights while they were dealing with their own issues.

"No, Mama… I, uh, I just was told by a friend of mine that she sent you a card and didn't know if you got it."

Mama gave her an odd look. English was not an experienced deceiver and was typically pleased that she hadn't grasped the art of trickery, but in cases like these, being convincingly disingenuous would've been quite helpful. But no doubt, Mama knew she was hiding something. The woman was no fool. She could tell in the way her attractive mother peered at her over her thin-framed gold glasses, the slight cock of her head, and her hand on her hip.

English quickly turned away and placed the lighter and card on the counter by the cake and pulled herself together. She put on as convincing a smile as she could, and to seal the deal, she wrapped her arm around her mother's waist and kissed the top of her head, squeezing her tight. It wasn't long before they were all singing happy birthday to the woman of honor.

Mama's eyes lit up, reflecting the small flames all aglow on the cake. She cracked a joke that English barely heard, and thanked God for another year on planet Earth. When she finished blowing out the candles, the place boomed with applause and whistles. While everyone was busy eating and celebrating, English stared at the envelope, now smeared with white icing. She looked around, ensuring the coast was clear, then slipped it into her purse.

I feel sick having anything he touched near me, but I am taking this shit out of this house. Tonight.

…One day later

I could never be inducted into a cult…

She just was with a crazy guy. I woulda been done left…

Couldm't have been me.

Why would she stay so long?

She's gullible as hell.

She's too pretty to have gotten wrapped up in a cult.

How could she let him do those things to her?

He wouldn't have been able to fool me like that.

People who get into cults are followers, instead of leaders.

She must've had a messed-up childhood she was trying to escape…

She didn't pray for discernment.

His teachings were right, but he was the wrong messenger.

How can she be so smart, yet…

…SO DUMB?

English had heard all of these things during the worst time of her life, and following her escape from a mental Alcatraz. Still, now, she kept hearing them. When the crap had first hit the fan, some people believed she'd simply escaped a horrible ex-boyfriend, when in fact, she'd been stripped of her identity and dignity. Everything she loved and treasured, including her core values, had been snatched away, ripped to shreds, and tossed into a big bonfire. She was no longer a person. She was a thing.

English sat in the police department lobby, waiting. The strong scent of Folger's coffee and that odd odor old printers made, mingled and created a familiar, yet cold, feeling in the air. The heat of machines, ink, and paper climbed over the scent of ground beans turned into liquid. People chatted. Officers came and went. Phones rang.

English glanced down at her cellphone, where she was researching various addresses Master had resided at. Using a fake online profile, she browsed his social media. Not that she found much, but enough to see he was still up to his delusional ranting and raving. Nothing short of the calling card of a madman.

"Would you like some coffee while you wait?" A pair of blue eyes hooked on hers from behind gold-rimmed glasses.

"That's nice of you, but I'm fine. No, thank you."

The front desk receptionist had already offered her water before, and if she were to wait much longer, she might even propose lunch or dinner. The woman seemed nice enough, sitting behind a glass partition with her shoulder-length reddish brown hair and black cat eyeglasses. A light blue and white sleeveless polka dot dress complimented her 1950s look, made edgier by the tattoo of a mostly bald, wrinkled cat with a pink mohawk on her shoulder.

"English Price?" An officer approached her from the Louisville police department.

"Yes."

"Come with me, honey." The middle-aged police officer motioned to her.

Grabbing her purse from the empty seat next to her, she got to her feet and followed him into a small, sterile office. He left the door slightly ajar, then pointed at a chair for her to have a seat. The man grunted and cleared his throat as he sat down on an old chair across from her, with the sun, trees, and highway behind him. She looked out of his window as he shuffled some folders about, then typed on his computer.

"How are you doing today, Ms. Price?" he questioned. It sounded more like an afterthought, something to say to fill in the gaps.

"I'm okay."

"I reckon you could be better, based on what I see here."

She nodded. Outside, cars were whizzing by. Looking at the flying reds, whites, grays and blues kept her nerves a bit steadier.

"I see a PO here, for—"

"PO is a protection order, right?"

"Yes, ma'am. I see the PO here issued for a Mr. Master Whitefield, dated over nine years back."

"Yes, and when I tried to have the restraining order reinstated when it expired a year after issue, I was denied."

"What was that denial based on? Do you recall?" He folded his hands and leaned slightly forward.

"I was told by the magistrate that Mr. Whitefield was no longer a threat to me, based on the lack of contact and other particulars that were completely irrelevant."

"Well, Ms. Price, from my understandin', there's been no further contact."

"Well, Officer Niles, your understanding is wrong. Texting me, following me, sending mail to my mother—all of that's contact. Just because I haven't responded doesn't mean it is not. I have already explained in detail." She waved her hand at his computer. "I also submitted the greeting card that he sent my mother as proof of him potentially disturbing her peace with a veiled threat, while simultaneously letting me know that he is aware of what I do, and when I do it. Hence, the Italian restaurant menu I frequent often with my colleagues being enclosed."

"I took the liberty to look up Mr. Whitefield's criminal history."

"Then you already know that this man's felonious history is extensive. Theft. Burglaries. Stalking. Domestic Violence. To name a few. Y'all got papers on him that not only extend to his dealings with me, but several other women seeking assistance, one of which was underage at the time of the offenses. He beat her so badly, I found out after I left that she was in a coma."

Officer Niles cocked his head to the side and offered a faint smile.

"Ms. Price, that's awful, it really is, but to get back to your situation, sending an unsigned card that has no evidence of a threat in it, along with a restaurant menu, does not constitute stalking."

"It's unwanted contact."

"You have no way of proving it's him though from this alone. I want to help you, I do, but—"

"What about all the text messages I emailed you? I even had my cellphone provider turn over official records, so you could be sure it wasn't me fabricating the information with one of those text message apps."

"Yes, you did. You took the extra steps, but the problem is, those aren't real phone numbers the texts are originating from, Ms. Price. I checked before callin' you in here. They're throw-away numbers. You know, like from a burner phone."

"And you don't find that suspicious? By the way, Verizon told me it's not a burner phone, but they could not provide the phone number they originated from. Those numbers are being generated from an app he's using. One phone. Several numbers. What upstanding citizen disguises his phone number, sends messages that read, *"Call me back, bitch, or you'll wish you were dead,'* from an untraceable number, and means no harm?" She shrugged, feeling somewhat in disbelief by how nonchalantly he was treating this, but at the same time, somewhat expecting it. "Is that somethin' the paperboy, Nancy that runs the soup kitchen, or Jesus would do, Officer Niles? Does this remind you of choir boy behavior?"

"I understand what you're saying, Ms. Price, but the problem is, we have no way to prove that this is in fact Mr. Whitefield harassing and stalking you again."

"What will it take for y'all to do something? Do I have to be dead? Let me know so I can give you the obituary details right now in advance, or is that your newspaper department?"

"Oh, come on now, Ms. Price. That's not fair. I can't break the law based on a hunch. Now look, I've got a daughter of my own. I don't take what you're saying lightly at all. Not in the least bit. I would never want something like this to happen to her, or any other woman, and I sympathize with you. If it were up to me, I'd pay this guy a visit, but with no evidence I could be settin' myself and the entire department up for a lawsuit of epic proportions."

"Lawsuit? Let me tell you something. Master Whitefield should've been an attorney himself, because he knows the system better than anyone I know, and he plays it well. This demonic waste of flesh stayed away from me just long enough so I couldn't get any legal assistance, but I know that in the state of Kentucky, the classification for stalking in the first degree, which is deliberate trailing and tracking with explicit or implicit threat of physical or sexual contact, injury, or death is serious business, Officer Niles. It could be a Class A misdemeanor, depending on whether it included the use of a deadly weapon. Stalking in the first or second degree is a can of worms, whichever way you want to open it and slice your finger on the jagged edges. It's code 508.140, and regardless of whether he's using throw-away numbers or not, he can still be investigated because those numbers are being used on a cellphone that is completely traceable. All cellphones have an address, if you will. The postage service he used is traceable, too. He—"

"Ms. English, I mean, Ms. Price, I have no doubt in my mind that you're the cream of the crop as far as aptitude. I saw that you also have no criminal record, graduated at the top of your class, have several accolades and degrees, and are mentioned in quite a few scholastic articles."

"And why would you know that, and what does that matter?"

"When these cases are brought to our attention, we do a quick background check of all parties involved. It helps us figure out what we're dealing with. I looked up Master Whitefield, too, and between you and me, he's nuttier than a squirrel turd, and I see why you're concerned." She nodded in understanding. "Regardless, I appreciate that you've practically memorized the laws for stalking. Well spoken. Well put together." *Ain't you a good little Negro…* It took everything in her power to not utter her thoughts out loud. "I know I'm not dealing with some hysterical woman or a fool, and I understand you went through a traumatic ordeal with this rascal. But unless he's trying to get into your house, or callin' you and we know it's him, or God forbid, inflicts bodily harm, no one has the green light to exert the time, money, and energy to trace a cellphone that may or may not be his, for a crime he may or may not have committed."

"I bet if it was your own daughter though, the one you made sure to reference earlier, you and your friends here would be doing all of that and then some. Laws be damned."

His complexion deepened and his brows bunched. The man's lips drew tight, and he swallowed before taking a couple breaths.

"Ms. Price, it is also illegal to do such a thing without probable cause. So stop waving this birthday card around," he snatched it off the desk, "demanding that the post office pull cameras to see who dropped it off for delivery. I don't know if you've been watching too many crime shows, but that's not how this works. This is a stalking case from a decade ago."

"He's stalking me right now! It's not from a decade ago. You just said I seem to have my marbles in order, so why in the hell would I be sittin' here talking to you about someone who hasn't said a word to me in over a damn decade, unless he was back like a virus? He isn't some Johnny-Come-Lately, but this is an old hat for him. Out with the old, in with the new, then reverse it. Par for the course. What in the hell is wrong with you that you can't seem to grasp the most basic information right now? This isn't rocket science."

"There's no need to cuss and become belligerent. I've explained everything. I've made it clear as to why we can't just go and arrest him. Now, you have to be reasonable."

"I *am* being reasonable, and you're being dismissive and condescending, acting like I don't know the difference between a crime show and reality. This man is a clear and present danger." She tapped his desk with her fingernail, desperate and angry. "I know it's him. I believe you know it's him, too. I went through hell getting away from this man. I went through over ten months of therapy and deprogramming." She swallowed as the knot in her gut tightened. "I have anxiety attacks every now and again, things that remind me of him. A smell… the way someone says my name…"

The man gave a heavy sigh, and for a split second, he looked genuinely concerned.

"I believe you, Ms. Price. It's an awful thing. I wish I could do more… I really do."

"What about the message of him calling me the cult

name he gave me?" She could barely get the words out. "Can't you use that as evidence?"

"All he'd have to say is that someone is impersonating him, or that it's another member of his congregation, or anyone else in the world for that matter. He could also say it's not his number, and so on and so forth."

She huffed in frustration, shook her head and tapped her foot. *Mama always said hope for the best, but expect the worst. I did. But why does it still feel so bad?*

"If he calls you directly, leaves a message, a voicemail, anything like that, something where we can hear his voice, then that'll help. We need something tangible, Ms. Price. If he comes by your place of work or home, then you can call us right away, and we'll be over there faster than a tick on a hound dog's rear end. But you gotta give us something to work with… I'm sorry. I know this isn't what you wanted to hear."

"I already know how this works." Her jaw tightened, painfully so. The muscles practically locked as anxiety and fury soared. "If he comes by my job, he'll stand on the sidewalk. Y'all will say there's nothing you can do about it because there's no active restraining order, and that sidewalk is public property. If he drives past my house… same story…"

She shrugged. "If he leaves a voicemail threatening me or my family, you'll just say the numbers don't match, and he'll deny it was him. He's been real careful this time around, 'cause the jails never kept him long, and he learned from his mistakes. All y'all did was train him to be a better demon. He'll continue to beat the system because he knows it ain't made for folks like me. It's made to protect folks like him. And like you. And your daddies, uncles, and sons, 'cause God knows that men make these laws with all of these loopholes, and y'all gonna guard your own interests at all costs. I don't expect an elephant to tell me how to take his tusks."

"Now hold on, that's not true, Ms. Price. These laws are made for everyone. Sex and gender aside. Race, too."

She laughed at that, got to her feet, grabbed her purse, and headed toward the door.

She paused with her hand on the knob, and looked over her shoulder. "Officer Niles, I'm not going to end up on some program where people are using my death for a new law to be made, or an old one to finally be enforced. I'm not going to be in a coffin for my Mama and Daddy to bury and mourn."

"I don't think that you—"

"Y'all go on and wrap yourselves up with these lukewarm laws and half-cold regulations. Listen to me closely. You can take this as a warning, or whatever you wish, but I'm telling you right now: if he steps one raggedy foot in my general direction, it'll be the last step he takes."

"Now Ms. Price, you call us if—"

"No. I'm done callin' y'all. You just remember that you put me in this position, and many more women like me." She pointed at him, her blood boiling. "'Cause I don't do lukewarm nothin', Officer Niles. I'm either all in, or all out. I'm not that scared college student who'd fallen in love with the wrong man, joined his twisted cult based on racism and warped religion, and ended up brainwashed anymore. That girl is gone. She's dead. Now, I stand here in her place. I vowed, after that treatment and grueling deprogramming program I endured, I would never let him or anyone else do me like that again. I'll admit to you that when he first started texting me again after all of this time, I froze up, and that little girl in me tried to take over.

"All of that fear, as I'd felt when I was planning my escape at the risk of death and after all the abuse I'd endured, came rushing back. My heart was beating so fast, I thought I was going to shatter into a million pieces. That fear had me by the neck for several weeks, but then, I remembered who I am. The stock I come from, and how brilliant and wonderfully made I am. I had to shut that little scared college girl down…

"My name is English Price, and I'm about that life. Winter is comin', Officer Niles, and I got that heat, and as God is my witness, the flames of Hell will be waiting for ol' Master. I'm ready to send him back to his maker, and it sure ain't the good Lord above. He's going downstairs, to the ocean of flames, to drown in the hot ass river and lakes that he's used to."

With that, she walked out, closing the door behind her.

AXEL SPLASHED WATER on his face at the kitchen sink while his slices of bacon fried up crisp in the skillet. He'd had another dream, a visit from Ms. Florence, and though he wished to pretend he hadn't, he knew she'd slipped in his ear while he slept to remind him of the importance of the preservation of life.

Grabbing a carton of eggs from the refrigerator, he cracked four of them open into a bubbling pan with melted butter, then scrambled them fast as he replayed the dream in his mind.

Ms. Florence was once again sitting, this time dressed in various shades of green, and with peacock feathers all around her. Her wooden chair was old and not as elegant as the others, yet, she claimed it was her favorite.

Axel reached for the salt and pepper and seasoned the eggs, then took them off the hot eye before they cooked too hard. *Scrambled and soft. Just like most of the women in my life. Fuckin' crazy, but give the best hugs 'nd kisses…*

With a welling anger, he slammed a jug of orange juice onto the counter. As he reached for a glass from the cabinet, he noticed his damn hand shaking.

Ms. Florence told me new stuff ain't always as important as the old stuff, 'cause the new stuff didn't make us who we are. The old stuff stuck with us through thick 'nd thin. Made us stronger. Wiser. New stuff might be pretty, but it's not as tough. Not built to last. New stuff hasn't had time to prove its loyalty. She said that's why she was in that old, wooden rocking chair, and if I would just listen, I would get an answer. An answer from the past.

Just listen and I'd get an answer? I don't know what the hell that means…

He poured the glass of juice, put a couple of pieces of bread in the toaster, then sat down at his kitchen table with the television from the living room playing the morning news. Time ticked by, and his thoughts settled for a while, only to begin racing again. He glanced at his watch. He hadn't been home long. Earlier that morning, around 4:17 A.M. to be exact, he'd received a call about a motorcycle accident on 22nd street. The guy had run into a storefront, crashing headfirst into an automotive supply place, and died.

Pieces of him lay scattered inside the store. Once the body and the mangled bike were taken away, he and a few members of his crew began the tedious work of cleaning up the broken glass, blood, tissue, hair, torn clothing, and the like. Erasing the scene as if it never happened—to protect the citizens, the family from driving past and seeing a horrific vision of their loved one. It was just another fucking day of misery.

The man's last ride. He shoveled a forkful of eggs into his mouth, then paused. His heart thumped so damn hard, it reminded him of the shitty high school band rehearsing on the field. Out of tune, obnoxiously loud.

She said the old stuff… loyal… Just listen and I'd get an answer…

He got up from his chair and snatched his phone from the living room table where'd he left it when he got back home. *That's it. I ain't finished what she told me to do.* He immediately called Caspian. Voicemail again.

"Shit."

Axel rolled his eyes, then shut them tight. He paced the floor, clutching the phone to his ear.

"…Caspian, it's Axel. You've got the number. This is my second call. I don't know what's going on, but it would be good if you'd do me a solid and call back. I ain't callin' you again 'cause I just happen to miss the hell outta you. Fuck you. This isn't about you, but it is important."

He ended the call, then immediately dialed Legend.

He expected to leave a voicemail for this guy, too, but was surprised when the deep voice of his brother—not by blood, but by choice—greeted him on the other end.

"'Ello…"

"Legend. You motherfucker… I've been tryin' to reach you."

"Who is this?"

Axel could hear reggaetón music playing wherever Legend was. The half White, half Puerto Rican man loved that music, and yet Legend was as Southern as cornbread and fried chicken smothered in gravy.

"Don't play with me. I told y'ur sister to tell you to holler at me if she ever ran into you. She said you've been duckin' and dodgin' her, too."

"Who the fuck is this?" Legend repeated.

"You know who the hell it is! It's Axel."

"I know," Legend laughed in a lazy, almost taunting way. "What's up, Thor?" the bastard teased. "I ain't hard to find. Unless I *want* to be."

Legend sounded drunk out of his damn mind. It was early in the morning. Jesus.

"What do you want, Axel?"

"What do I want? We need to talk, that's what the fuck I want."

"Well, talk then, nigga."

"Where the hell are you? I need to see you face to face."

"Just tell me right now. I hate that shit… when people tell me, 'I got something important to tell you,' and then they say they'll talk about it later. Say that shit *now*, mothafucka."

"This isn't something you talk about over the phone." At that moment, he heard dogs barking. They were so loud, they had to be inside the house.

"Be quiet!" Legend yelled. "Today I'm busy. But you can come through tomorrow. I'm in Jacobs."

Jacobs was on the southside of Louisville, one of the most crime ridden areas of the city. Axel had had his fair share of calls there. Regardless, if anyone could handle themselves in that environment, it was definitely Legend.

"Address?" Axel grabbed a pen and pad.

The man rattled off the address of a house he was renting, and then abruptly got off the phone. Axel tossed the pen back down on the living room coffee table and stood there for a moment, soaking it all in.

One down. One to go.

Chapter Twelve

"I DIDN'T KNOW where else to go…"

She looked into Axel's eyes. Barely awake, the man opened his creaky front door, allowing her access into his home. It was eleven at night, and she herself hardly recalled getting into her car and making the ride. Things were becoming a blur. A series of washed out, foggy twists and slow turns. When the door closed behind her, she heard it lock twice, and he reset the alarm. She swallowed her reservations and second thoughts about showing up unannounced, and looked down at her rain splattered boots while his scent surrounded her. Clean. Masculine. Safe.

"Why didn't you call me before you came by?" he asked, crossing his arms.

"I didn't want to risk you turning me away."

He ran his hand across his mouth, but offered no reply.

"I've driven around for hours," she explained. "My mother's birthday just passed, like I told you, and I've barely slept because of it."

"I talked to you earlier tonight, English, and you said you were okay."

She shrugged and sat down on the couch.

"I thought I was."

"Are you afraid of him?"

"...Yes and no. Not for me. For my family." She slipped out of her boots, setting them neatly beside her legs. An occasional tremble from the cool air that still clung to her bones rattled her nerves.

Axel disappeared into his kitchen, and after some clanking around, he returned with two cups of hot coffee. They smelled strong. He handed her one, along with a couple of packets of sugar, then sat across from her, wearing only a pair of white boxer shorts that accentuated the bulging rattle snack ... er, um, rattle*snake* ... in his underwear. Tattoos covered his skin like a well-illustrated map. His hair was a bit messy, in a sexy sort of way, and so was his beard, but his volcanic voice was rib-rattling and clear as a bell.

"You sure the card was from him?" He took a sip from his coffee, then set it down on the table between them.

"Not a hundred percent certain, but close enough."

Tearing open one of the packets, she added the sugar to the beverage and stirred it with the small teaspoon he provided.

Axel leaned back into the couch, resting the crown of his head against a cushion, causing his hair to sprawl, like sun rays. It looked so strangely beautiful with him sitting below the stained glass windows in his home. He kept his eyes on her as he cracked his knuckles.

"What can I do to help you get some rest?" His eyes hooded, and for a brief moment, she forgot her troubles while allowing seedy thoughts to reenter her mind and wander free.

"I don't know. Just being here with you makes me feel better."

"I have to leave in a few hours." He looked up at a clock on the wall, then back at her. "I'm going to bed. Lie down next to me and try to get some shuteye."

He didn't ask. It was definitely a statement. Standing, he walked away and up the staircase, never pausing to see if she was following. She stood, ran her palms against her upper thighs, and made her way up the creaking stairs, one by one, taking deep breaths along the way.

Everything seemed louder than expected at that moment. She got to the top of the staircase and looked around. Axel's second floor was dim, but blue light seeped out from an ajar door, which she presumed was Axel's bedroom. She approached it, and heard music playing: Chris Brown's, 'WE.'

...Sexy music. Low lights. He must be crazier than a soup sandwich to think I don't know this is a thirst trap... and I'm crazier than him, because here I am anyway, taking a bite...

Wrapping her fingers around the door, she opened it further and entered. Axel lay on the bed, looking up at some abstract art program on the television. When she looked at him, her breath caught in her throat like a baseball in a catcher's mitt. His dark silhouette was impeccably chiseled. Incredibly long, muscular legs were slightly parted, and shadows with hints of light touched his form. Her eyes drifted and strained. It was too dark to make out the exact details, but he appeared to be completely butt ass naked. Something long and thick was resting against his thigh…

Her teeth sank into her lower lip, almost piercing it.

He patted the bed beside him, his attention on the television. She made her way over to him, pressing her knee into the mattress, then curling her body alongside his. He slowly turned towards her, and she could see his smile now.

Brushing her hair away from her face, he groaned, then leaned in close to press his lips against hers. She filled with liquid lust like an empty jug, waiting to be blessed with a drenched floral bounty right between her thighs. Slipping her fingers along his chest, the fine hairs flattened against her touch. Heat and strength emitted from his core, and entered hers. Their gazes locked as they tasted each other's lips. Wrapping her body around his, she felt the hardening flesh of a man who'd become her friend, her enigma, her love. He pressed himself against her, drawing wispy purrs from her and growing more demanding by the second.

Tems' 'Higher' regaled them and as she witnessed beautiful art in shades of ivory and blue flash across the large television screen. She blinked and turned away, her vision capturing the beauty of more stained-glass windows, beautiful and colorful, religious and spiritual, behind them. These were even larger and more vibrant than the ones in his living room.

Her eyes watered as his deep voice rasped close to her ear. Her temple was in the safety of an iron warrior covered in Greek and Roman art. Her needs poured out to him. Begging to be touched. To be wanted. Purely. She wasn't certain how it happened, but somehow, some way, Axel had gotten her shirt and bra off without her even noticing. Like some perverted yet beautiful magic trick. Heat and moisture bathed her neck as he breathed harshly against her, then kissed and gently sucked her throat. Her heart quickened when he raised her arms high over her head, securing their hands as he situated her flat on her back. Long locks of light hair drifted down her body like the willowy touch of a satin saint. His kisses were meaningful, not one of them unnoticed, hurried, or wasted.

Hard, powerful hands pulled at her jeans… then her panties. All she could see was art. All she could hear was art. All she could feel was art. Naked and cool. Exposed. A slow spinning fan on the ceiling rotated as if only a lazy breeze were pushing it forward. Back arched and an aching escape of oxygen caught in her chest when the first touch of a curled tongue traced her pussy. He moved like the wind. Crashed like the waves. He was Kentucky bourbon on ice.

"Oh, God…" Her eyes fluttered then clamped shut as the sounds of him eating her alive echoed all around them. Axel wrapped his arms tighter around her thighs, holding her down. She couldn't move even if she wished to. His licking and sucking of her petals and folds grew louder. More demanding. She snuck a glimpse of the Goliath that was devouring her love. He popped his finger in his mouth, then winded it slowly inside of her. Their eyes passionately locked on one another's, as if to blink would mean instant demise. Her clit was surrounded by soft warmth as he sucked it, then kissed… flicked. Repeat. He finger-fucked her, dips shallow and slow, while sucking on her clit fast and hard.

She cried out when her orgasm loomed, climbed fast, then burst free. Gripping the sheets, she fell apart, the art on the screen becoming blurry. Her hips rocked uncontrollably, and her feet couldn't lie still. He said not a word to her since she'd entered that room, and yet, somehow, she heard his demons and angels speaking in many languages, all of which she could fully understand.

He glided towards the top of the bed as she lay there, helplessly slammed by orgasmic aftershocks, and placed a soft kiss on her forehead.

Sounds amplified. The rattling of a drawer opening. Plastic tearing.

Her pussy throbbed with need and her heart throbbed with worry. She'd been falling for him hard. This was the final nail in the coffin. Nailed. Fucked. Screwed.

His back was now towards her, but out of the corner of her eye, she could see him sheathing himself. It wasn't long before his heavy weight consumed her, and they kissed each other all over. She buried her face against his neck, his shoulders… Caressing him. The hard muscles. The scars. The flesh of a man that had seen the ugliness of the world ten times over. He had pain on the inside that he dared to show. She saw that dark, gunky, hurtful shit flash in his eyes when he spoke of his father. Of his mother's resilience and her hardened heart. Whatever troubles the man had seen, he understood them as fact. Axel spoke in truths, but he refused to listen. Maybe for fear they'd be nothing more than self-trickery and lies.

"...I know so much about you, Axel, yet so little. Your heartbeat is telling me things you won't. I can hear it. Can you?"

He ran his tongue along her earlobe, and she seized up with another wave of desire.

"Shhh... Quiet now, darlin'. I want to put you to sleep so you can dream of me even when I'm not inside you. Be still now, and let me write my first and last name on your walls...read and study it in your wet little pocketbook."

Her pulsing organ quickened its beats—a response to what could not be verbally spoken.

She looked over his shoulder at the art now on the screen. No abstract paintings anymore. Vincent Van Gogh was now debuting. How ironic. How forlorn. How poetic. *Van Gogh went crazy and cut off his left ear. Axel refuses to hear. It hurts too much...*

"Shit!" A hard thrust rocked her as he entered her without warning. Instinctively wrapping her body tighter around his, he placed one hand on her head, crowning her, while drawing her in for a hard, manic kiss. His hips pumped fast then slowed to a crawl, teasing her. Driving her crazy. A man in full control. He slipped his other hand between her legs and stroked her tender center. Rising up on one elbow, he trailed his hand from her head down to her waist to caress her hip as he pumped faster. Harder.

Deeper. The bed began to make an odd noise each time he thrust, blending in with the sounds of 'Dark Red,' by Steve Lacy. She stared at the tattooed angel soaring above her…

Working limbs. Invisible wings made of old stained glass. Pronounced veins and thorns from the grapes of wrath. Eyes shut tight, inviting the darkness, and his neck stretched, swallowing his pride. Axel placed his hand against the headboard and groaned so deep, the tremor of his voice rattled her loins. Her bones. Her blood. Her brain. Her soul. She wrapped her thighs tighter around his waist, locking her heels in place at his lower back. Rocking to his rhythm, she rode that forceful groundswell with him, and then he slowly opened his eyes and looked down at her.

A deluge of warmth filled the condom as he rapidly pivoted his hips for the final round. He decelerated, then groaned with pleasure. He rested against her for such a short while, it barely registered, and she sighed with pleasure when he engulfed her nipple, sucking it hard as he massaged the other. He switched breasts, then slipped his hand under her ass cheek and gave it an ample squeeze.

Their breathing was in sync. One accord. The timing, mood, place felt so right. After a few moments, he stirred and rose from the bed, stumbling away into the bathroom and serenading her with the sounds of soft, running water. Chris Brown's, 'Call Me Every Day' played when he returned, rubbing his hands on a small white towel. The lavatory light streaming in the room now provided her a new chance to view his amazing physique. He'd put his hair in a ponytail now, and the strands flowed over one shoulder.

His sexy smile made her pussy pulse with the penchant of pending pleasure. Tossing the hand towel onto the nightstand, he opened the drawer and retrieved another condom from a black box.

"What are you lookin' at, 800?" he asked with a smile.

"You. Damn…" She licked her lips and pulled herself closer to the edge of the bed to get an even better view.

"I thought you was high falutin', but come to find out, you ain't got any home trainin'. It's rude to stare," he teased.

"It's even ruder not to invite me for a taste. You got to eat. Now's my turn."

He smirked, placed the box down, and stood before her.

"You can have *more* than a taste, baby… Lick and suck this dick all you like."

He stood flush against the side of the bed, arms resting at his sides. Lying on her stomach, she grasped his dick, loving the heavy feel of it in her hands. She wasted no time running her tongue along the tip. He sighed as she put more and more of him in her mouth—consumed it, sucking hungrily on the long, veiny delicacy. His grunts and groans blended with her gagging and pausing. Saliva and precum dripped down her chin as she devoured him whole. He grabbed a fistful of her hair, steering her into his rapid thrusts. She kept gobbling him up, loving the feel and taste of his fat cock pushing towards the back of her throat.

Slipping away from her oral grasp, he reached for the box once again, removed a fresh condom, and glided it down his massive dick. She stiffened when she felt him slide his arm around her body, then hoist her from the bed into his arms. As he carried her away, the art, the sounds of the music, and their breathing became an orchestra for the senses. Before she knew it, he'd cleared his desk of papers and bent her over it, right in front of a closet door mirror. He knocked her legs apart with a swift motion of his knee, placed one hand on her lower back, then gripped his dick, his attention drawn to their reflection.

"Ahhhh!"

"I wanna live deep inside you, baby…" he said, grasping her hips, and working her body as if he were playing a game of pinball. She watched her body lunging forward toward the mirror as he brutally fucked her. The sharp, deep thrusts felt more like subterranean nosedives into areas of her body she'd never known could be reached. She was screaming at the top of her lungs, cursing his name, and begging, too.

"Oh, shit! Don't stop, Axel! Fuck me just like that… just like that. Don't stop!"

He smacked her ass, and kept right on going. Fingers digging hard into her waist as he rode her to the moon and back. She clutched the edge of the desk, knocking over a container full of pens and mechanical pencils. They rolled all over the place, hitting the floor as he lunged inside of her, sweat dripping down his body like a waterfall. His thighs were slick, hot and wet, for she felt him each time he entered her, and the slapping noise of his hairy balls reminded her of the sounds of a drying machine on the fritz. They came at the same time, reaching for each other. He pulled her arm to him, and she grasped his wrist as he drained inside of her. She was soon met with soft kisses up her spine, and a proud look of satisfaction on his face when he pulled back and wiped the sweat from his forehead.

He picked her up in his arms, carried her to his bathroom, and ran a tub of warm water. Without much fanfare, he placed her inside, discarded the condom, then situated himself behind her in the bathtub. His long legs cocooned her, knees up. Her new favorite resting place. Relaxing her head against his chest, she listened to Justin Bieber's, 'Peaches,' featuring Daniel Caesar and Giveon. He slowly washed her back, neck, shoulders and arms, and she washed the parts of him she could reach. Limbs up. Kisses down. Dripping faucet. Trickling thoughts that made no sound.

She placed her arm along the edge of the tub, toying with sleep. The last thing she remembered was Axel intertwining their fingers, and him humming softly to the music…

Somehow, she'd drifted away to the point where there were no dreams. Just blackness. When she awoke, she was situated in his bed, a soft ache between her legs. She didn't recall leaving the bathroom and being placed under the covers. How strange. Now she was lying here dressed in a gray wrinkled t-shirt that read, 'Free breast exams.'

Chuckling at his choice of attire, she pushed the sheets down that he'd wrapped around her body. The television was off, the sun was ushering in.

She looked over to the other side of the bed, and saw no one. He was gone. She looked around, then noticed a glass of juice and what appeared to be a piece of toast on a small white plate, laid out on the desk where they'd fucked a short while ago.

She got to her feet, her pussy sore and happy, and made her way over. That was when she saw the note he'd written…

800. I could have sent you a text message, but this seemed better. I told you I had to go to work in a few hours. I'm at work. I didn't want to wake you. It looks like I did good on my promise and put you to sleep. I'll be back by 4.PM. If you want to stay in my house until then, that's fine with me.

Watch TV. Relax. Whatever. The WIFI password is: I-AM-THE-GOAT-1989. There's some fruit, juice, eggs, bread, ham, and leftover cheese and sausage pizza in the refrigerator. Cereal, pasta, beans and rice in the cabinet closest to the table. Help yourself to anything in the freezer, too. Feel free to make a fresh pot of coffee. If you need to leave, set the alarm. The code is 3212953. The front door will lock as soon as you close it behind you. If I come home and find you still there, then I take that as an invitation. I'll be putting you back to sleep. It's not up for discussion. I went easy on you today, but the next time, you may sleep for

3 days straight. The Sandman Cummeth...

Axel

She grinned as she folded the letter, then placed it aside. Staring at the stained-glass windows, she picked up the glass of juice and took a taste. Freshly squeezed.

I want to freeze this day in time. I want to pretend, for just a moment, that only the moment I arrived here, in the now, is all that has happened, and all that exists…

She continued to drink her homemade orange juice made just for her, swaying to the sounds of, 'Heartbreak Anniversary,' by Giveon.

He's mine. I'm his. I'll make him listen. Not by force, by design. I'll make him hear my heart, and memorize the lyrics word for word…

Chapter Thirteen

AXEL TURNED OFF his truck, and tossed his cigarette out the cracked truck window with a flick of the wrist. It was unusually hot that evening for an Autumn day. He'd been blasting the Nashvillains' 'Chickasaw Bayou,' as he pulled up and parked in front of the small gray house with missing shingles on the roof. When his truck went quiet, all he could hear was rap music playing from a nearby apartment building, dogs barking from various directions, and people yelling back and forth to one another.

He checked the time on his phone, slipped it in his jeans pocket, and got out of his vehicle. As he made his way up Legend's walkway, the concrete uneven and weeds taking it over, he realized the house was practically pitch black, as if empty. It was a big tombstone with its paint peeling, and surrounded by a front lawn that desperately needed care. Before he could ring the doorbell, he could hear aggressive barking from the inside.

He rang the bell and waited.

Knocked and waited.

No answer.

Suddenly, he saw a light turn on, and a tall, big shadow approaching from behind a curtain. Seconds later, the door was unlocked, and pulled open. Legend stood before him in a crisp wife-beater, two guns strapped across his heavily tattooed chest, and three big ass dogs at his side. A Rottweiler, a Doberman, and a German shepherd. The dogs began to bark, snarling and gnashing their teeth, going apeshit.

Axel slipped his hand against his holster, just in case.

"Quiet down!" Legend yelled as he gripped a beer bottle.

What a difference a few years make. The man was nothing but muscle now. He'd always been broad and built, but it was obvious his last stint in prison had been spent pushing massive weights. He'd been the runt of their group when they were kids in school. The small, skinny one. Those days were long gone. Now he was about the same height as Axel, and looked like a fucking fourth dog. A pit bull.

They stared at one another in silence for a long time. He noted the light freckles on Legend's cheeks and nose. As a kid, he'd hated them, but later on, they'd become some sort of girl magnet. Not too little. Not too much. Just right. Axel always felt that they gave him a more youthful appearance, an interesting contrast to his light beige skin. But his eyes didn't look lively and full of life. The hazel orbs appeared dull and tired, as if he'd seen and schemed far too much. His hair was cut in a low, jet-black fade, with natural waves going in a circle—a 360. His thick black beard was groomed almost to a point, and a diamond earring in his ear sparkled like a star.

"My man, Axel… Come on in, come on in." Legend finally cracked a smile. He opened the door further, and Axel stepped inside to be immediately hit with the smell of weed. They slapped hands and hugged. Axel looked around the pigsty of a house. Papers everywhere. A television was on, the sound muted, and the living room was occupied by old mix and match furniture. The black leather couch seemed to be falling apart. The foam oozed out where the fabric split and it had so many cracks, they looked like the veins of a collard green leaf.

"How are ya doing, Legend?"

"I'm okay," the guy replied before disappearing into a small, dingy kitchen, the dogs hot on his trail. "Go on and sit down, man. Make yourself comfortable."

Axel sat down in the living room. He noticed a couple of chewed up raw-hide dog bones, marijuana papers, lighters, empty beer bottles and cans, and something he hadn't seen in forever: a copy of Hustler magazine.

Something is seriously wrong. Legend used to be more of a clean freak than even me. He had that brief stint in the military… always kept his things tidy. He likes lavish shit. Expensive shit. He used to have maids, and live in nice ass apartments and big houses. He had a bunch of cars. Beautiful women. And he didn't drink so much that he was out of his mind. He could hold his liquor. Shit. He isn't the same… My brother is hurtin'…

Axel sighed and stared at the television screen. There was a commercial on about some medication for eczema.

Suddenly, the Rottweiler came barreling in, but instead of an attack he was braced for, it began sniffing him insistently. He pet the dog a little, letting her have her way. Legend approached with another bottle of beer in his hand.

"Here you go, man."

Axel reached for it. "Thank you." He took a gulp.

Legend sat across from him, set his beer down, and began to pick up shit off the table, frantically cleaning up as if he didn't know he was about to have company. *Hell, maybe he didn't even remember?*

"So, what is it that was so important that you couldn't tell me on the phone?" the man questioned as he tossed the junk in a big garbage bag.

"Before I get to that, I want you to tell me why you're living here… like *this*," Axel looked around, then back at him. "And not talking to your family."

"What's this? An episode of CSI?" He chortled mirthlessly. "Maybe you're Dr. Phil's ol' phony ass, huh?" He tied a knot in the garbage bag, then tossed it aside. He then opened the porn magazine, and began to roll himself a blunt between the pages. Between the ass cheeks, actually.

"You don't have to be defensive. It's a question." Axel threw up his hands. "That's all."

Legend kept working on his high, but his expression drew tighter.

"Axel, don't come over here wit' that big brother shit. You only like five months older than me, and always tried to toss your weight around. I don't have to answer to you, mothafucka. You come in *my* house and start up right away, huh? Demanding shit. Tryna force a mothafucka to do what the hell you want them to do. That's just like you. This is why I stopped fuckin' with you to begin with. You haven't changed a bit… The great inquisition." He laughed in a lazy sort of way. "Always think you runnin' some shit."

His words were angry, his voice was calm.

"You chose to stop speaking to the people who care about you, Legend, because you were in prison and angry about it. You were blaming the world, including your brothers. Me and Caspian. You lashed out at us, and I'll be damned if I'm somebody's punchin' bag, verbally or physically. We didn't have shit to do with the choices you made. Sounds like you have some pent-up resentment towards me even before all of that went down."

"Like you give a shit."

"If I didn't, I wouldn't be here. The liquor is talkin'… You never told me you felt this way about me. Not in all the years we have been down, man. Regardless of the raw deal you got in life, I thought we was better than this."

Legend shrugged as if he didn't give a shit. Axel knew better. The man was on the brink of falling apart. His dead eyes said it all.

"Legend, want to talk about blame? It goes both ways. I don't let anyone get close to me anymore, because of you and Caspian." Legend rolled his eyes. "I have no friends, just a bunch of employees and associates, and that's exactly how I like it. The way you acted was fucked up. We were all we had, and both of y'all flaked out on me. You kept going to prison and then wouldn't accept my calls, as if *I'd* put you there myself. You put your own self there."

"Shut up."

"Make me shut up, motherfucker." They glared at one another for a long while, until Legend turned away. "And Caspian put his career before everyone else, wanted to pretend like he was different from us. It broke my heart, man, but I didn't have a temper tantrum about it like some baby… like *you*! I realized the only one true friend I got in this world is myself. Nobody knows anything about loyalty anymore. Friends nowadays will shoot you dead, then hug your mama at the funeral. And furthermore, asshole, I didn't come over here to mess with you. I just—"

"Why *are* you here then?" Legend cut him off, his lips pursed and a hateful, dark rage in his eyes. "To judge me? To think you're better than me, then rub it in my face?"

"I'm here because you're my brother."

Legend shook his head, and averted his gaze. The other two dogs sounded like they were eating in a nearby room, while the Rottweiler lay down on a dirty rug, clearly tired.

"I'm not leaving you alone until you tell me why you're living in squalor, Legend. This ain't you. This ain't where you belong! You're one of the Brother Disciples, man! You, me, and Caspian. We were kings, if only in our own minds! Are you working? What's happening with you? Melanie said that—"

"Who the fuck is gonna hire someone wit' no college degree, no experience, a short-lived stint in the army that didn't give me no credentials or skills? I got a long ass record for sellin' drugs for the majority of my adult life. I got two felonies, man." He held up two fingers. "I'm a killa. They got me on paper for one, not the rest. I ain't no upstanding citizen. Rebellious and disorderly fuckin' conduct. Violent tendencies. No conscience. A problem. A half-breed that most people mistake as 100% White, so I get called a Wigger, and dumb shit like that because of how I dress and the music I listen to. I'm a misfit. A bad seed. A nightmare."

"Your mama loves you. Ms. Paula is worried sick about you, Legend."

"Aww, man!" He waved his hand at him and rolled his eyes. "My mama doesn't know what it's like for me out here in these streets, and she ain't never try to find out. She's just a White lady who is impracticable, unreliable, gullible, and silly. You know how messed up my relationship with her was, so don't even go there. And as far as Melanie, she don't know nothin', either. She's a woman."

"So what? What's that got to do with anything, Legend?"

"She can bat her eyes and pop her pussy to get what she needs, that's what the hell it has to do with it. Women can literally walk out of their house, man, stand on the corner, and give a quick blowjob for ten minutes, walk back in the gotdamn house, and pay their phone bill. I ain't gay, and female clients aren't runnin' amuck out here tryna buy dick or get their back blown out on a consistent basis. But every block, I bet you there's at least twenty guys who will pay to get their dick sucked. My sister has never had to put her neck on the line like me. Mel been fuckin' over boys with her feminine wiles since Kindergarten. Had sugar daddies since she was fifteen damn years old. Besides, I don't want no woman takin' care of me, no how. That's some bitch shit. We played by our own rules. Wasn't no man in the house. She knows the game. I can't roll like that."

"Melanie wishes that you—"

"Melanie can wish and dream all she wants. I live in reality. She has no fuckin' idea what it's like for a man like me in this world. Just like Mama. I had to cut them off because all they did was nag and tell me what I need to be doin', while neither one of them is doin' shit, either. Mama is still with that mothafucka that messed our lives up, and Mel ain't innocent, neither. She's done her dirt, and I never held that shit against her. That's my sister. My baby sister. She means the world to me, but I'll be damned if I'm going to let her and my mother try and tell me how to live my life, when only I can, and its mine to fuck up!"

His voice rose suddenly, and a darkness shone in his eyes. "I was the fuckin' man…" He brandished a sad smile. "I created a legion. People who worked for *me*. I didn't have to sell shit but a pipedream. I'm in charge of my own life, even if it ain't much to be in charge of…" He slipped his tongue along the edge of the blunt, and sealed it.

"Those days are gone. You have to start over."

"You can take the dealer out the streets, but you can't take the streets out the dealer, man. That's all I know."

"To me, you're not defined by that. I look at you, and

I see Legend. Forget your troubled past. I'm trying to talk to Legend. Not this puffed-up persona you wear to survive and get over. You ain't got to try and hustle me. Besides, it's a waste of your time. I know the game. I didn't have to play full time to understand the rules."

Legend cocked his head, lit the blunt, and smirked. "You know we only understand four things, man. It don't matter the race or age of the man, either. Those four things are…" He placed his blunt down in an ashtray, and began to count off his fingers. "Power. Paper. Pussy. Property. And depending on who you ask, the last two are one and the same. I am used to all four of those. I can't get them back because I fucked up, and now, things are the way they are. I've accepted it. I'm just survivin' at this point."

"Excuses. I hear a bunch of excuses. Legend, you are capable of some amazing shit. It doesn't have to be this way. You're a damn warrior, man! If someone won't give you a job, create your *own* job! If someone won't feed you, stop waitin' around like a dog for a scrap, and go grow you a fuckin' garden, and get a farm! You've always been hands on and take charge! You sittin' here, looking crazy, drinking your problems away—but that shit is still there in the morning!"

"Let me tell you something, mothafucka!" He pointed an accusatory finger at him. "I am here, in this shit hole, because I am protecting myself from becoming my own victim and worst enemy! To stay away from the people who cheered me on, when they shoulda been puttin' their foot in my ass! I lost my way… tryna get back on track, but you can think whatever you want."

"I ain't got to have a vivid imagination to come to this conclusion, man!" Axel jumped to his feet, his heart beating with anger. "I'm here listening to one of my best friends try to relive his felonious glory days, while in the same breath, feelin' sorry for himself, blaming other people for why he can't catch a break, and cussin' me out because I dare to show concern and not want him to fall into this pit of despair and bullshit!"

"I don't need your help or pseudo-psychological evaluations. Just tell me what the hell you want, and get the fuck out." He snatched the blunt back from the ashtray, lit it, and began to smoke it.

At least a minute passed. No one said a word. They barely moved.

Axel slowly lowered himself to his seat, and tried to calm himself down.

Me yelling at him isn't helping. I have to try and figure out what's going on with him though, before I tell him about the dream…

"Man… please." He placed his hands together as if saying a prayer. "Legend, I'm beggin' you. Just tell me why you're here and what your game plan is."

After a few seconds, Legend's eyes turned to slits, and he flopped back on the couch, looking lazily at the television as curls of smoke eddied from his mouth.

"I am trying to stay away from the old hood, where I did my dirt. I came with a plan, Axel, and it's not working out so well." He coughed, then settled. "You wanna hit this?" he offered.

"No, I'm good. Anything else going on?"

"My girlfriend was stealin' from me, the little bit I had, so I had to throw her ass the fuck out a couple months ago. She got on that shit."

"Fentanyl?"

"Yeah… and meth, 'cause it's cheap. Before that, she had a job 'nd shit. She had a degree and everything, but then she got caught up in that. Ironic, huh? Irony came and bit me in the ass." His complexion deepened, and a look of deep regret flashed across his face. "That left me holdin' the bag on half the rent. I need money, but I'm not selling my dogs—they'll just be used in dog fights—and I can't go back to sellin', because I can't afford to go back to prison, man. This last time was the worst."

"*Every* time should have been the worst."

"Not all of us can turn out like you, Mr. Wonderful!" Legend's eyes narrowed on him, but Axel didn't react. He'd seen this side of this man before, though it was rare. Hurt. Pain. Exposed and raw. The alcohol was making him tell the truth. Liquid truth. When he was sober, Legend wouldn't dare allow anyone to watch his secrets froth out of his mouth like vomit.

"Every time should have been the worst, Legend, because you're too good for prison. You weren't made for prison. Prison is not created for men like you. You are not to be tamed. Confined. Told when to go to bed like a damn toddler. Now, do you want to get out of here or not?"

"Just because I said I need some cash; doesn't mean I'm asking you for help. I don't want your money." He snatched his beer from the table, and began to chug it.

"I didn't offer you any money. I am offering you a job. Actually, two."

Legend finished his beer, smoking his blunt in the meantime.

"What kinda job?" he asked, looking at him out of the corner of his eye.

"First, I want you out of this neighborhood, and out of this house. You're going to end up in trouble out here. I know you left Portland to get away from the old crowd, but trust me, this is worse. Look, I got a couple rental properties. You can move into one of 'em, and pay rent to me. I'm going to have you trained in my company. You know what I do. If anyone can stomach it, it's you. That's job number one. You'd be workin' 'bout twenty-five to thirty hours a week, and always be on call. No drinking on the job. No coming in high, either."

"If you think I'mma do all of that, why even take a chance on me?"

"'Cause I know you. I know who you are deep inside. When you commit to something, make a promise to a friend, you stick to it. It might be years down the line, but you keep your word. You were always dependable, if nothin' else."

Legend stared at the television for a moment, puffing on his blunt.

"You're a death scene cleaner, right? We ain't spoke in a minute, but that's the business you're talking about?"

"Yeah. You'd make damn good money, too. It's hard work though. Mentally and sometimes physically. You'd earn your keep. Save up your money, cash to start over, then do whatever it is you really want to do in life. Just give it one year—you'll get trained and everything."

"I'll think about it. What's the second job?"

"The second job is a bit less conventional. I got a girlfriend that's run into a problem with a slippery, weird ass delusional son of a bitch. Stalker. He won't leave her alone. I need you to help me with a little project regarding him."

Legend stared right through him as if he were a pane of glass.

"The second job sounds better than the first…" He smiled mischievously. "You still ain't tell me why you're here. I know this wasn't it. To hire me to clean up guts, and help you handle your girl's problem."

"No, it wasn't." Just then, the Rottweiler got up, approached him, and he gave her a good rub on the head. "There's no easy way to say this, so I'm just going to let it all out." Axel took a deep breath, leaned forward, and clasped his hands. "I've been having some dreams. Ms. Florence has been visiting me… told me I made a promise to her long ago. And I had. I don't want to get into what the promise was, but I will tell you that I haven't fulfilled it, Legend. She said you made a promise to her, too, and so did Caspian. She's mad about this. She's disappointed in us. She wants us to do what we promised her, and if we don't, she said we ain't gonna ever have peace."

He expected Legend to burst out laughing, or call him crazy. Perhaps even accuse him of being on hard drugs like his ex-girlfriend. Instead, the man's color drained from his face.

"I thought I was trippin', man. I thought it was the late nights, some bad weed, and the alcohol… the stress I'm under."

"Shit. You saw her, too?"

Legend hesitated, then nodded.

"Yes. I dreamt about her one night, too. She was in a big pink chair, dressed in all these bright colors… looked just like she did when we was kids, and she told me, *'Legend, you aren't living very legendary.'* She said I ain't seeing the writing on the wall. She said I am blind, and refuse to see the truth, 'See no Evil,' and until I open my eyes and look at what is in front of me, really look at it, I'll always be walking around here sightless. She told me the next time my phone rings, I need to answer it. 'Bout 1 minute later, my cellphone rang, man. Guess who was on the other end?"

"Me."

"Fuckin' bingo…"

Chapter Fourteen

AXEL LOOKED IN his rear-view window and realized the black car with the tinted windows was still behind him. In an effort to test his hunch, he'd maneuvered many back roads, to try and see if the folks in the Buick would follow. As sure as shit stinks, the person driving that hunk of metal did, turn for turn. Only a local would have reasons for drifting up and down these back roads. Niko Moon's, 'Good Time' played through the speakers of his truck at loud volume. When he reached for his gun in the glove compartment, his phone flashed on the dash. Daddy was calling. *Perfect timing as usual. I'm being tailed by a jackass, and being called by one, too.* He ignored the call, looked back out his rear-view window, and realized there may be two men in the car. It was hard to see, with the dark windows and all, but two faint body outlines were clear as mud. One in the driver's seat, one in the back.

"Shit!"

Suddenly, the car swerved, and got on the side of him. He hit the brakes hard, forcing them to skid on the dirt road. Then, he kicked his truck in reverse and gunned it, dust and debris forming a cloud behind him as he shot like an arrow in the opposite direction. Neck strained and eyes tingling with sweat trained on the road, he kept going until he heard the sound of gunfire. He slammed on the brakes once again, grabbed his gun from his waist, as well as the one from the glove compartment, rolled his window down halfway, and pulled that trigger a few good times. The Buick veered, almost flipping down into a gulley before the driver got a hold of the wheel.

Another car approached as Axel hit his vehicle in reverse once again, so he hit the brakes to avoid a collision, then gassed it, zooming forward and turning onto several sideroads. Zigzagging in the brush. It didn't take long before the black car was again behind him. He could practically hear the bullets zooming past, some pelleting his truck. A hot adrenaline rush flowed through his blood, muscles, down to the damn bones, and it happened so fast, his face felt tight and about to burst, his skull throbbing beneath sweaty skin.

3…

2…

1…

He hit the sunroof and sat up a little, just enough to raise the gun through the opening.

POP! POP POP!

The car spun as he shot out both front tires, going around and around in a circle until it ended up flipped on its side. Closing the sunroof, he rolled real slow towards the carnage he'd left behind. He pulled up to the car and hopped out, his long hair in his eyes as he barreled closer. Sure enough, there were two men in the car, bloodied and bruised, staring up at him with life and death in the balance. The driver had a busted lip and nose, and was wrapped up tight, a tangled mess, in his seatbelt, while the one in the back attempted to exit the vehicle, crawling over broken glass to reach for his gun that now lay on the dirty path.

"Oh, you want the gun? I can give you a gun, but it just won't be yours."

BOOM!

"Ahhhh!"

The one in the back screamed when Axel shot him in the back. He then turned his attention to the driver.

"Why do y'all keep comin' for me, huh? I sure as hell didn't send for ya! Who gave you orders?!"

Violent coughing ensued. The one he'd shot was bleeding out badly, hacking something awful. He returned his gaze to the driver, a White guy in a denim jacket, jeans, and cowboy boots.

"I asked you a question, motherfucker." Axel snatched the gun from the ground and slid it in his jacket, then cocked his own gun.

"Something is in my leg… My leg is messed up!"

Axel peered a bit closer, and noticed the guy's leg was in fact covered in blood.

"Well, ain't that too bad? You'll probably lose that leg if ya don't get help soon. Guess the folks back home will call you 'Hip Hop,' if you survive tonight, huh?"

"Please just get us to the hospital… just…" The guy

stopped speaking, as if it required more energy than he could muster.

"I'll leave you here to die a slow and painful death, and shoot your friend in the head, put him down like a sick dog, if you don't get to singin' purty like a bird named Taylor Swift. Now you answer my damn question."

"...You're going on the witness stand. They don't want that," the driver blurted, his eyes wide and red. Seemed he'd gotten a second wind. Perhaps staring into the barrel of a gun so close to his face made him perk right up. Like a cup of coffee.

At that moment, Axel realized this wasn't simply about some revenge plot. He'd been at the wrong place at the wrong time, walking in on some big timer trying to cover evidence of a murder he'd committed, then Axel had the unmitigated gall to wipe him off the face of the map. No one in their squalid organization cared if it was self-defense. In their eyes, he should have taken that bullet. He'd compromised whatever was going on, but most of all, he'd seen too much and because of that, the case was ruled a homicide, rather than an accident.

"Witness? Who thinks I'm going to court?"

The driver stared at him. The guy in the back kept coughing. A dying cough. The kind that didn't last too long, for the end was near.

"Seems to me you've got two choices. Talk, or death. I want a name, and if you don't tell me, I'll light a cigarette and toss it down on you fuckers and have my own bonfire. Smores galore."

The driver's face went from expressionless, to sheer

panic. Axel walked around the other side of the car, pulled out a knife he always kept in his boot, and sliced into the gas tank.

"No! Nooooo!!!!"

"Yeah… You smell that? That's time tickin' away. It'll make things easier for me. I'm tired of havin' to explain myself to the police. If I shoot you motherfuckers, I have to go down to the station and clear my name. Again. Not this time. I want no part of this. Mmmm… that gasoline sure smells good though, doesn't it? I always wanted to try Texas Barbecue."

"They don't tell us names! We're just runners, man! Small fish!"

"Lies. I fucking *hate* liars! And let me tell ya right now," he leaned against the car and peered down at them, "I'm going to make you keep talking until you tell me the truth, and to make sure of that, just so you know, I'm going to make a call to check 'nd see if all that information you tell me pans out. I have connections, too. I know people, and someone that high up, who can have me tailed and harassed for months on end from states away, has some power. He wouldn't send tiny fish out here to get rid of me. He'd send people he trusts now that I keep icing his people. Naw, you're special to him. People he thinks can do the job. Now, that type of guy has made a name for himself, for sure. Folks in the life would know. Tell me his name, and if you're lyin' to me, the discussion is over. Won't be no call to the EMT. Won't be no more chances. It'll be just you and 'Backseat Bullet in the spine Betty' here, burnt to a crisp."

"Okay… I'll tell you! His name is… Thunder."

"I want his *real* name. Not that street cred shit!" He slipped a cigarette out of his jacket pocket and then a lighter.

"OKAY! OKAY! His name… his name is Clyde Martin! Parker Davis, the guy you killed at that house, the one you were cleanin' up, worked directly under him. They don't want you talkin' to the police and district attorney, man. They need you gone."

He in fact had been contacted by the Houston District Attorney regarding this drug-dealing group from H-Town. The murder he'd accidentally uncovered led to an FBI investigation, who already had the ring under surveillance. There was a slew of charges which included kidnappings, extortions, drug trafficking, larceny, sex trafficking, witness tampering, and countless homicides. Considering what happened, he was asked to be one of the eyewitnesses, but hadn't made up his mind yet.

Looks like they want to make it up for me.

Axel took a few steps back, placed the cigarette and lighter in the grass nearby, and slipped his phone out of his pants pocket. He didn't miss how the driver strained to turn his head and listen in.

"Look, it's Thor again. Don't you have Jane Foster to go fuck or somethin', Axel?"

"Maybe after I finish with your mother. Look, I've got—"

"I'll be down that way in a week. Comin' a few days early, Axel. Is the apartment ready, man? Room for my dogs?"

"Yup. You know I got you covered. Just like I said I would."

"Cool."

"Question for you. Ever heard of Clyde Martin? Nickname Thunder?"

Legend drew quiet as if wracking his brain. "Naw, who's that?"

Legend had been in prison multiple times, and the majority of those charges were linked to his nefarious activity and affiliations in the Louisville drug trade. One of the bonuses of that, he'd explained many years ago, was traveling to exotic places and meeting others in his "profession." Besides, knowing who was who was important. *Keep your friends close, your enemies closer, and your friends who become enemies, the closest.*

"I don't have time to get all into the details. I've got a situation I am trying to handle right now, so please don't interrupt me and ask me any questions. Just let me speak."

"Bet. What's up?" He could hear the man blowing smoke.

Axel proceeded to give a very brief version of what had been happening to him, and what led up to his current circumstances. "…and now I am bein' told their boss is Clyde Martin, out of Houston."

"Clyde Martin?" Legend laughed in a lazy sort of way. Blew more smoke. "Nah, man… don't know no Clyde Martin… funny name… Now, I ain't been in the game for a minute, tryin' to keep my nose clean as you know, but to make it that high up the ranks, if he's what you *say* he is, you have to have some skin in the game. You can't just pop up out the blue, either. You *earn* that position. Guy outta Houston, you say?"

"Yes. Runs the operation. Things have gotten messy." *And I'm about to clean all of this shit up…*

Legend drew quiet for a spell, mulling his words. He did have an amazing memory—one of his best qualities. Somewhere in that rolodex mind of his, he had the information Axel needed. He was certain of it.

"Clyde. Thunder. Nah, there's a… Oh, wait. You know what, man? There *is* this mothafucka named Cymone Louis, spelled with a 'C'. C.Y.M.O.N.E. Black dude. Never met him, but heard about him. I bet that's who it is. He definitely runs a big operation there and some of his product is made here in Louisville, and Columbus, Ohio, too, so it makes sense that he or some of his guys would be here from time to time. He mainly deals with Fentanyl, from my understanding. If you give me an hour or two, I can make sure for you."

He heard the guy in the backseat coughing again, and shot his gaze to the driver. The truth was written all over his face. Busted.

"I gotta run."

"Bet. Whatever you got goin' on right now, handle that shit."

"You know I will."

Axel disconnected the call and marched back up the car.

He'd overheard the conversation, no doubt about it. Surely, he knew this was the end of the line…

"Ain't it funny how you think you can know somebody, and you don't know a thing about them at all? Y'all mistook me for some hillbilly idiot. Thought I just clean up blood, power-washed sidewalks after shootings and suicides from tall buildings in a single bound, and filled out papers all fuckin' day. Let me make somethin' crystal cock-suckin' clear to y'all." He dropped down on one knee and glared at the guy in the backseat, who looked passed out now, then back at the driver. "I try to be a man of my word." He turned and spit, then narrowed his eyes on the man. "But you weren't a man of yours. I warned you. I told you I hate liars."

"Man, you got it all wrong!"

"I have a disgust for folks that look me dead in the eye and tell a big ass tale, just like you've done tonight, even though your life was on the line. You know what type of motherfucker I am by now. Now when have any of y'all came here and I played with you? Notta once. My time is too precious for this. Y'all are getting on my fucking nerves. You gambled and lost."

"I didn't lie, man… I didn't lie!!! I got kids, man! Come on!"

"And my mama has an only son. My employees a boss. I'm key to their livelihood, and most of them got kids, too, that they need to raise and take care of, but you didn't care nothin' 'bout that. I am a brother to my friends. My sister's only brother. My nephew's favorite uncle. I am the mate, the partner of a woman you could only dream of. I guarantee you if I was gone from her life on account of you, she'd cry a river, and I'd do the same for her, so don't talk to me about having any compassion! I'm finished with emotional charity work. I'm doing the Lord's work, and those children of yours a service, you rotten bastard, because their father is a horrible piece of chicken shit!"

"We were just following orders! It was never personal. Please… just think…about this!! YOU'RE MAKING A MISTAKE!"

"Naw, the only folks that made a mistake tonight, was you and your friend there, when you decided to come after the King of Portland. We don't play here in the 'Ville. Ain't no Clyde pullin' your puppet strings. The man who sent you is named Cymone. I saw your face when I said his name aloud. Your eyes told the truth, while your mouth bought you and your friend here some front-row tickets to the pyro-inferno show. That's another word for firestarter in case you're slow on the drawl."

"I don't know a Cymone! God! PLEASE!"

"Chestnuuuuts roasting on an open fire… Jack Frost nippin' at your nose," he sang. "Well, it's been real nice chattin' with you tonight, sir. May the flames hit you, where the devil split you."

Axel took a few steps back, lit his cigarette, and puffed on it good. The man was yelling and pleading now, his voice carrying, but they were in the middle of nowhere. There would be no help for him or his friend dying in the back. Not now. Not ever.

"Okay! Okay! I lied! I'm sorry! His name is Cymone Louis! He woulda killed me, man! You have to understand! … AHHHH! AHHHH!!!"

Axel flicked his cigarette and enjoyed how the flames shot up like an orange rocket, bursting and crackling. The blood curdling screams went on for quite a while, and then… they subsided. Quiet. He watched for a spell as the men practically melted like candlewax. Smelling the commencement stench of burning flesh, he turned and walked away. He got in his truck, and made his way off the dark back road, heading to the main drag that was dimly lit from one street light post.

"Siri, call Donnie at the body auto shop."

Donnie was a friend of his who worked on all of his trucks, cars, and motorcycles. King of the Dings.

"Calling… Donnie's Auto Repair and Bodyshop…"

"Yello… This is Donnie."

"Donnie, it's Axel. I know you close in 'bout ten minutes, but my truck got all shot up from some damn kids shootin' bottles nearby. Can you take care of it for me in the next day or two? I can drop it off tonight."

"Damn you, Axel. Why would you wait until I'm almost out the door? How far away are ya?"

"'Bout twenty-five minutes. I'll pay you a bit extra if you stay and take her in out of the cold. I don't want her parked on the street. She's too pretty."

"You son of a bitch. Donna made lasagna tonight. She's going to think I'm foolin' around on her again on account of you… All right, man. Bring 'er in."

"Comin' through…"

He ended the call, turned on the radio, and tapped his fingers along the steering wheel to the sounds of 'Fall In Love,' by Bailey Zimmerman.

Chapter Fifteen

"YOU AIN'T EVER been out to a holler before? Really? Not even when you traveled to Tennessee or Virginia?"

"Not that I remember. It's remote. I'm not really a nature person. It's pretty though. Why is this lane so narrow?"

All he could do was laugh at that. English was sitting with her hands pressed against her body like a baby Tyrannosaurus Rex. Totally uptight. At least, she was *trying* to relax and live in the moment.

"They're designed that way. This was coal mining land. A holler, or cove as the stuck-up folks call it, ain't nothin' but a narrow creek valley 'tween hills or mountains."

"I know what a holler is, Axel." She rolled her eyes, as if annoyed. "I'm from here, too. I'm not from L.A. or Paris. Just as country as you."

"Then why did you ask why the road was so narrow? Did you expect it to be a six-lane highway with a roundabout in the middle of a bustling metropolis? Ask stupid questions, get simpleton answers."

"You make me so sick!" She cackled.

"Way back then, people lived around here. Some still do, but the population has thinned a lot since the mines shut down."

"Axel, slow down. You're taking these curves too fast."

"Is it me behind the wheel or you?" he asked sarcastically. "You got a big ass, but it ain't big enough to sit in both of these seats."

"Don't sit there gettin' smart."

"You prefer I stand up? 'Cause either way, you know by now this is how I am, and this is the response you're going to get. Now settle down, Miss Daisy. I'm doing the driving."

"You about to find yourself tossed out that motha-fuckin' window like a used tissue, talkin' to me like that! Then we'll hear a *real* holler!"

He burst out laughing, despite her now looking mad as hell.

"All I'm saying is ants don't tell bees how to make honey. I've been comin' 'round here my whole life. I could drive these roads in the dark. No headlights. Blindfolded."

"Boy, these hills and mountains are big. They've got me awestruck." English pointed at one of the mountains on the right, its peak so high, it could barely be seen through the veil of thin clouds. It was a cool autumn day, beautiful albeit overcast. Most of the radio stations, except one somewhat, had stopped coming in clear some time ago. Dolly Parton crooned 'Jolene,' the static filling in the apertures as if they belonged there. A part of him felt as if he'd stepped back in time. He loved coming out this way, and hadn't been in years.

They went over a big bump in the road, causing their bodies to bounce. He didn't miss how English's breasts sprung up and down in her tight green t-shirt with each dip in the road. He hoped they'd come across even larger bumps up ahead, forcing her to really put on a show.

"I needed this…. To get away. Thank you." Taking a deep breath, she stared out the window.

It had been a couple of weeks since he'd had to have his truck restored after the "black car incident," and the nonsense that followed had to be kept under wraps. In the interim, he'd driven his other truck, an older black F-150 he used mainly for hauling lumber, paints, and whatnot for house flipping projects.

Other things were going as planned. Legend had moved into one of his apartment buildings, much to his happiness. He knew it wasn't easy for his good friend to relinquish control and accept a helping hand. As part of their negotiations of sorts, he'd asked him a favor—to find someone discreet who could keep an eye on his woman. Legend knew practically every damn body in the city, and if the person was into something illegal and ugly, he knew them two times over.

Axel regarded English out of the corner of his eye. He fell in love with her smile, right then and there, as if he'd never seen it before. He cleared his throat and turned away… feeling those emotions creeping up inside him, burning him within. It was happening. He was in big trouble. Things were getting complicated, and he was going to become annoying as hell. Jealous. Overprotective. They were going to argue because English's personality was loud, and he refused to back down. What did he expect from such an amazingly beautiful and intelligent lady? There was a price to pay when you were a fool for sexy nerds.

Smart or not, this Master Whitefield bastard isn't taking her seriously. He won't back the fuck off. I'm not going to just sit here and let it happen to her. Of all things, she had some lunatic harassing her and that set his gears in motion. Now, he was a runaway train. *Choo, choo, motherfucker…*

He just hoped English would be okay with who he was because there was no changing this part of him. He'd always been this way, even as a child. He didn't want this thing between them to be short-lived, then fade away like smoke.

He snuck another glance at her, and smiled. She was definitely enjoying the scenery. Taking in the moment. Regardless of his philosophy of honesty being the best policy, Axel damn sure wasn't going to tell her she had a bodyguard in the wings, so to speak. She'd resist, tell him it was unnecessary, and insist she was handling it. *It hasn't been handled all of these years. Time for someone else to step in and take the reins.*

The latest suspicions were that someone was watching her when she traveled back and forth to work, and when she was at home. He hated it had come to this, but while English spent an obsessive amount of time online gathering information about this fucker, making sure her pepper spray, gun, and knife were on her at all times, and calling the police with updates just to leave a paper trail if nothing else, she was wearing herself thin. Just the other night, he'd had to wake her up from a nightmare about that fanatic monster. He was impressed, however, with her tenacity in protecting herself, especially after the police all but told her to jump in a lake. She wasn't going down without a fight, and he found that extremely sexy.

"I wonder how many people live around here?" she asked, jerking him out of his thoughts. "Seems practically empty."

"Oh, there's some folks… but you can't see all of their houses 'cause some of 'em live farther back from the main road. Some of the newer construction is up front. Still a lotta space between the land and houses, now. You'll find big trailers here and there, too. Everyone knows each other. Most of the folks don't work here no more. They got jobs right outside Van Lear and Prestonsburg. Most of the old timers were either sharecroppers or coal miners, like I mentioned."

"Any stores or anything here?"

"Well, it ain't bigger than a stone's throw when you compare it to other parts of Kentucky, but they've got four or five spots, even a little museum, I believe. There's a small grocery store down the way. Webb's, I think it's called."

"Is somebody going to try 'nd do something to me if they see me, Axel?" She turned to him fast, as if the thought just came over her and grabbed her by the gut.

"What do you mean? Because you're Black?"

"Yes. You know some of these people out in these isolated areas probably haven't seen a Black person in their entire lives, unless you include when their great grandpa was in the coal mine and came home covered in soot!" They were both laughing now. "I'm serious, though."

"Ain't nobody gonna do nothing to you, girl, and you know if somethin' strange goes down, I'll handle it. They may not uh seen many Black people in their lifetimes, but they damn sure know they exist."

"How you figure? They could think we're some myth, like the Loch Ness monster… or be cross burning racists, thinking they can redo the Civil War. They might be some of those mountain people that haven't stepped outside their own town ever, and just regurgitate what their racist mamas and papas taught them. The generational curse."

"First of all, this is the birthplace of Loretta Lynn."

"Bad example, buddy. She's the same woman who during one of her concerts told the crowd that if they wanted to know what coal looked like, to look at the Black security guard, and the light shined down on him. This place ain't produced no woke folks, Axel. You act as if you just said the man that stopped Apartheid or cured Sickle Cell was born here. Something beneficial for Black people."

"I didn't know anything about her saying that, so if it's true, and that really happened, just forget I brought it up. Secondly, they're—"

"Ain't no 'if it's true, and if that really happened.' You

know I read and research periodicals, books, and legal information regarding racism and race relations incessantly for a living, right? I think you need to be reminded. She did this in front of hundreds of people, while on stage, and admitted it. Sayin' she was just trying to put on a good show. Fuck Loretta Lynn and the broken one string banjo she sailed out this place on. Now what's your next excuse for me to feel safe out here with these people that are probably hand-washing their KKK white sheets as we speak?"

"Why would you bring this up just now, when we're here, English? A three-hour drive?!"

She shrugged, looking at him as if to say, *"That's a damn good question."*

He'd driven the three hours from Louisville to the Butcher holler, planning to camp out with her in the truck and enjoy their night. But here she went, bringing all of this up.

"We can still turn around and go back, Axel. This isn't Gilligan's Island. Three-hour drive, not a three-hour tour. We're not stranded."

He could tell she was trying to keep from laughing. *She grates my nerves so damn bad... And yet, I can't leave her alone. She's like a bad itch.*

"Stop it. They're Appalachian, not brain-dead, ravenous monkeys. Not everybody from out here is racist. You're acting like they don't have any TVs 'round here. Like it's just an old 1940s radio that fifty people crowd around to listen to reruns of, 'The Adventures of Ozzie and Harriet,' and they communicate by making grunting noises and tongue clicks. Stop being paranoid and silly."

That landed them both in ribbons again, laughing their asses off. It was truly beautiful, this time they were sharing, and the sky and land they passed on their drive. This was a true getaway—a bit of one-on-one time together after a couple of weeks of working himself to death. There'd been a terrible fire from an electric heater at an old man's house, and multiple car accidents—including one where he knew the victims—a couple of messy natural deaths, and a shoot up at an apartment building. It was call after call after call. The money was good, but there was little time for much else. He'd missed his baby.

"This is a good spot to take that walk in the woods." He pulled his truck into a small clearing, and they got out. "We should go up this way," he pointed up ahead, "so we won't accidentally be on nobody's land, and we can finish and be back 'fore dark. There's a restaurant not far from here, so after the hike, we can go get a bite to eat. That sound good, baby?"

"That sounds fine." English put her jacket on and zipped it up. Tossing her hood over her head, she tucked her ponytail inside. "You believe in Bigfoot? You sure look like him," she teased, poking at him as they often did to each other for sport. In that respect, she reminded him of his sister, which gave him a sense of comfort. A sense of trust.

"Is that so? When you put that hood on, it makes your head look real long. Like an eggplant. Naw, more like an alien."

"Good. Then maybe the locals will leave me alone," she said in a husky voice. 'I saw an alien without no dern flyin' saucer, Hank! It was walkin' upright, wearing humanoid clothes, and speakin' the same words we do! They've been watching us again, preparing to take over Earth! Oh Lord, hurry to Otis' cornfield 'fore it's too late!"

He chuckled as he gathered a few things, bear spray and what not, and tucked them in his outdoorsmen vest. After he put a couple of water bottles in his backpack, they started on their way.

The grass was so green and lush, he had to pause and run the tips of his fingers over it. The air was sweet, and a nice breeze caressed their faces. It was cool outside, but not so much that he was cold. He took English's hand, and they engaged in a bit of small talk, following a path probably made by animals or hunters over the years. Every ten minutes or so, the trees became a bit denser. Some stood so high, he couldn't see the tops of them. They passed wild mushrooms and flowers, and all manner of foliage.

Then, he heard it. And so did she. She squeezed his hand hard.

"What's that noise?!" she whispered. "Sounds like a cat."

"Fox."

Her mouth dropped open.

"Shhh..." He stepped back with her, leaning against a tree. "We don't want to scare it away..."

"The hell we don't!"

"Shhh! Don't you want to see it? I hear it coming." They crouched down, and sure enough, a fox began approaching.

"Do foxes jump on people?" she whispered.

"Jump on people? It's not a kangaroo or toad. Oww!" She hit his shoulder, and he quickly covered his mouth. The fox suddenly looked up, visibly sniffing the air. "...They generally leave folks alone," he said in a low voice. "If you want to get 'em to leave, just make a lot of noise. They're more scaredy cats than anything else." She nodded and they watched as the fox slowly walked away.

"That fox was beautiful. I am so tired of using that word today, but nothing else can describe it. I have never seen one that up-close before."

They got to their feet and resumed their walk. From the sound of water, he figured there was a creek up ahead. Sure enough, after a few more minutes, they came upon it. The faint sunlight was now a little lower in the sky, and the water practically sparkled.

"Oh, my goodness." English grinned as she walked ahead of him, bouncing towards the water. "It looks so clean and clear. I can see the rocks... there's fish!" Standing behind her, he wrapped his arm around her waist, drawing her in for a gentle kiss. The sounds of the stream blended in with the chirping of birds. Everything sounded louder, yet fine-tuned. Rich. Clean.

"We've got a whole natural orchestra out here." She wrapped her arms snugly over his.

"We sure do. This kind of peace is priceless. No cars. No big buildings blocking everything out. No political signs all over the place. Just trees galore, plants, insects, animals, water… love." She turned around and they pressed their foreheads together. Stayed that way for a while, but not nearly long enough—because long enough would've been forever. "Axel, do you know how to climb a tree?"

"What kind of weird question is that?"

"It's not weird. Do you know how to climb a tree?" She repeated smugly, putting one hand on her hip.

"I've been climbing trees since I was born! I'm a climbing aficionado!"

"Typical. Can't ever get just a straight answer… always has to turn into a brag-a-thon, and probably none of it's true, Sasquatch Bill."

"E.T., let me call Sigourney Weaver to come get your alien ass! How 'bout that?"

"You go ahead and call her. I'll be waiting by the mothership. You're hairy like a Sasquatch, too, just so you know. I've been meaning to tell you. I could start my own wig store by shaving just your legs and chest tonight!"

Now he was chasing her around, pretending he couldn't catch her just yet.

"Speaking of head gear, make sure you put a section in that wig store for snacks for the customers. Loaves of bread and such, or just take the one off your shoulders, because your head looks just like a footlong sandwich under that hood. Subway, eat fresh!"

Now they were laughing their asses off again, and play fighting. Swatting at one another. He tackled her to the ground, and they rolled about, amongst the pebbles and all. The giggling subsided when he had her on her back, and he got on top of her, looking deep into her eyes. Pressing his lips against hers, he damn near exploded from the lust building inside of him. She squirmed beneath him.

"Remember what I said earlier? Well, guess what? I bet you I can climb that tree." She pointed to a cluster of trees in the near distance, stood up on her black sneakers, then dusted the dirt and grass from her jeans.

"Okay. Let's see." He was mighty surprised about this turn of events. "The girl who isn't into nature all of a sudden wants to climb a tree. You're a strange woman, English."

"I know I am… and you like it." She winked at him before sauntering away. He crossed his arms and watched her sashay to the base of the tree, then stand there for a good long while.

"Are you going to climb it or try to slow dance with it? What's the hold up?" he barked.

"Shush!" A few moments later, she got her footing, and began to make her way up. Slowly, but surely.

"Well, I'll be damned! You *can* climb a tree!"

"My brother taught me and my sister how!" she called out.

"Don't go too far up, English. The branches might start thinnin' out up there, unable to carry your weight."

"I know… I just wanted to show you. Almost where I want to be." After another minute or so, she paused, leaned against the tree, and looked around. "I wish I had binoculars! You should see the sky from here, baby."

"I've got some. I'm coming up." He slipped his backpack off his shoulder.

"You just don't want to be outdone!" she screamed.

She had to know that was a challenge he couldn't refuse.

"You aren't a better climber than me, Dr. Zoidberg, and you just don't want the competition."

"Seeing is believing!"

He took the binoculars out of his bag, placed it on the ground, and jogged to the tree. In half the time she'd done it, he got up that thing, pleased with himself. She rolled her eyes, then laughed as he gave himself a pat on the back. He was huffing a bit and his palms burned something awful, but it was worth the aggravation. Pulling up behind her, he pulled her close and they rested against each other, cheek to cheek. Her light perfume drifted to his nostrils.

"I can smell you. Very nice, but I told you not to wear nothin' out here. Attracts bugs."

"I forgot." She yawned. "It's just a little body spray."

"…And it'll be a lot of body *bites* later on. They've got their own troop waiting for you now. Mosquitoesfor-English.org."

As she laughed at his joke, he felt her giggles vibrating through his body, too.

"Here." He removed the binoculars from his neck and placed them in her hand.

She held onto the tree with one arm and looked out of them, with the other. He listened to her talk about the birds, the dead branches of some nearby trees, a nest, and she even spotted a few squirrels below. He threw in a few "hmm hmms," here and there, only half aware of what she was saying. For having her close messed with his head … and other places. His nature began to rise, and he found himself grinding his groin against her ass.

"…Axel. What the hell are you doing?"

He ignored her, pulled her hoodie down, and began kissing on the back of her neck. He could hear her breathing accelerate as she held onto the binoculars with a slightly shaky hand. Gripping the trunk with one hand, he reached around to the front of her pants and undid the button, then yanked at the zipper.

"Stop! Are you crazy?!" This was followed by a nervous giggle. "We're in a tree!"

"Then call me the Keebler Elf. I'm tryna play with your cookies. Shit, I know where we are… I climbed up it, after you, remember?"

"But we're in a tree," she said again.

"And so are the birds and the bees. Fittin', wouldn't you say?"

He snatched her zipper the rest of the way down, and slid his hand in her panties. The soft pubic hair flattened against his palm, and now, he was upon the best creek in the entire forest—the sweet one between her legs. She began to purr like a panther, rotating her hips against his dry humps and finger acrobatics. He stroked her clit nice and slow, kissing all over her cheek and shoulder as they held onto that tree. He took the binoculars from her hand, draped them around his neck, then continued to play with her, his dick hard as concrete.

"Sweetheart, you're so wet… wetter than that there

creek… wetter than the ocean. You make me so fucking happy, baby…"

She sighed, and he knew it wouldn't be long. Her head bowed as she lulled against his chest, her stomach rising and falling… eyes closed… panting… The purrs turned to all out guttural moans, and he held her all the tighter.

"Fall back. I've got you, honey…"

She released the tree, practically convulsing as her orgasm broke free. Before she'd even settled, he locked one leg around her and pulled her panties and pants down past her ass, exposing soft brown ass cheeks that looked good enough to eat.

"…Are you going to really fuck me up in this tree, Axel?" she said breathlessly.

He unzipped his jeans and slipped his dick out from the slit of his boxers. Carefully repositioning himself, he grabbed his shaft and…

"Ahhh… SHIT!"

They groaned at the same time as he pumped his hips, thrusting in fast and short lunges. The wind blew through his hair, carrying her perfume, and his hand burned as he gripped the tree for purchase. He managed to hoist himself higher, locked his ankles around her body to ensure she stayed put, and let her have it…

"AXEL! OH, GOD! SHIT! That feels so good." He slipped his hand down from her waist to her clit, where he strummed his thumb over it, feeling it swell. Her snug walls swallowed him in, driving him crazy.

Then, she made a noise he'd never heard her make before. One of the branches right above their heads shook violently as he had his way with her, and birds flew away from nearby trees. Their grunts, sighs, and moans of pure ecstasy echoed in the air.

"You wanted to see the sky. Figured I'd give you a little slice of heaven…"

She came again as he kissed the side of her face, her once neat ponytail now sloppy, the scrunchie holding on for dear life. She trembled against him and yelled his name right before he came deep inside of her, chasing the end of his climax with a few fast pumps, draining himself completely.

They went quiet for a moment. Hearts beating fast.

"I made you holler in the holler," he joked.

She laughed lazily, panting, eyes closed. "I bet you couldn't wait to say that."

Moments later, they managed to get back down to Earth. His muscles felt like rubber bands after such an unusual workout, and all he really wanted to do was curl up next to her in the truck and go to sleep, but he figured he'd catch his second wind soon enough. Besides, he was hungry, too. So off they went past the creek, taking pictures along the way. When the sun went down a little more, they trekked back to the truck. After they got settled inside, he grabbed a root beer from the cooler, and handed her one.

"Awww! You remembered when I told you that me and my daddy used to always pick up root beer when I'd accompany him to remote areas in the woods for his job when I was kid. He'd help with the lawn services. I can't believe you recalled that."

"Yeah. I remembered." He could feel himself blushing, and hated it. Starting up the engine, she suddenly leaned over to him and planted a big, fat kiss on his mouth.

"I ain't never screwed in a tree before. That was a first."

"There's more where that came from," he promised.

She grinned from ear to ear, then plopped back in her seat, clicking her seatbelt in place.

"Got me out here feeling like Jane with Tarzan." She popped the lid, and slurped loud and happily.

He pulled away from their makeshift parking space, and gained speed on the road. After a few minutes, he turned on the radio.

The staticky sounds of 'Captain of her Heart,' by Double, greeted them.

He took her hand and held it for the rest of the way up that old bumpy road…

Chapter Sixteen

ONE PRETTY DAY, I was sitting outside, in Central Park, New York. I was in the bustling city for a convention. I hadn't attended one before, but always up to travel, I jumped at the chance to meet and speak with other book conservators, curators, and periodical preservers. Our jobs are sometimes monotonous. Although often thankless, this is also the most rewarding occupation I've ever had, and I wouldn't trade it for the world. On this particular day, I had a few hours of downtime before our group was to meet for dinner, so I decided to go to the Metropolitan Museum, then head across the street to Central Park.

I walked around for a while, checking out the sprawling greenery, dogs catching balls and frisbees, couples holding hands and talking as they strolled past. There were children and adults of all races and sizes—such a diverse landscape of folks, making it the kind of place you imagine Heaven might be like. The air smelled like smog and hot pretzels covered in salt. Finding an unoccupied park bench, I sat down, placed my favorite black and white striped canvas tote bag on my side, and pulled out a book to read—for pleasure.

Strange how after all of these years I don't remember the name of that book, or the author for that matter. If you know me well, then you are aware that is almost unheard of for me. What I do recall is that it was a biography, an obscure literary nugget nestled between the reads about the great civil rights leaders of the 1960's, and Black inventors of the 20th century. If my memory serves me right, it had something to do with a Black male dancer in the 1930s, who was hiding his true identity, including his sexuality. It's all a bit murky. I didn't enjoy or not enjoy the book. It was just something to look at, something different for the day. I like different. I do remember something that was written in it though that I felt I should keep in my mental back pocket until the next sunrise when God would request my RSVP for a hard lesson in my life…

"Sometimes people disappear, in order to be found…"

Now isn't that wild? Maybe this is the day I pull it out of my back pocket, and give it a recall in pure clarity, and understanding…

English sat naked in her bedroom chair, curled up next to Axel's T-Shirt as the scent of strong incense and Bath and Body vanilla and patchouli candles did its thing. She took a sip of her green tea, and mustered a smile.

My sunrise is here…

I knew this day would eventually come. I've gotten weary of looking over my shoulder. Calling my mama to see if anything has come in the mail, all while my heart is beating crazy inside this body of mine, and my mouth has run dry from the stress of it all. I'm tired of the nightmares. Tired of being with my man, and sitting there beside him in movie theaters, restaurants, bars, plays and events I've dragged him to, smelling his intoxicating scent that makes me die and come back to life with just a whiff… the sun drifting in those stained-glass windows as I lie next to him in his big ol' bed, and looking him in the eye…pretending I am okay.

'ACHE,' by Emawk played from her Alexa speaker. She sat up, placed her teacup down on her nightstand, and picked up her phone. There were many text messages. Messages full of dried blood. Old scars. Crusted-over cowardice. The serrated knife rantings of a lunatic.

3:56 A.M. - Stupid ass bitch.

4:19 A.M. - I saw you.

5:02 A.M. - Who is that White boy you are with? Is that your man?

5:57 A.M. - You fuck cavemen? Foreal?

…The next day

7:12 P.M. - You're a nasty ass bedwench.

7:20 A.M. - You will always be mine.

7:43 P.M. - Bitch, you have turned your back on everything I taught you. You're broken. I have to fix you.

…and so it went.

She'd never answered her phone when she suspected it was him. Never texted back. Never acknowledged she'd seen the birthday card he'd sent to her mother, or that she knew without a shadow of a doubt that he was following her whenever she returned home to visit her family, and at least a few times when she was at work or leaving for lunch with her friends. Axel too had come to her job and taken her to lunch a couple of times. It was now evident he'd seen them together—perhaps witnessed them holding hands, laughing, smiling at one another, and kissing the way lovers do.

She ran her thumb along her phone, dialed a number, then, closed her eyes. Her heart was beating faster, though she tried to assure it that all was well…

"It's about time you called me back. Listen. We've got a lot to talk about. The first thing, Shira, is arranging for us to get together and speak in person, but—"

"Mister Confused, I'm not goin' no damn where with you. I'm not meeting you *NO*where, either. I'm not trying to hear you, see you, talk to you. You do not exist to me. You are the shadow of a shadow. The dirt beneath the mud pit. The sludge at the bottom of the swamp. This isn't no pleasure call. This isn't no, "How do you do?" situation. I'm not sure who you believe you've been texting and harassing, but she doesn't live here anymore… This is a warning. DO NOT. UNDER ANY CIRCUMSTANCES. CALL ME AGAIN."

"Who the fuck do you think you're talking to, Shira, and who are you calling Mister? My mothafuckin' name is Master, bitch! And—"

"My name is English, not Shira. I'm not calling *you* Master. Your name is Mister 'Confused' Whitefield. I also need you to increase your vocabulary because the B word insult is getting old. The only bitch on this phone is *you*. You'd have to be, to keep calling someone who clearly wants nothing to do with you, and I want to thank you for this time together, because now I have proof for the police that you're back to your old tricks. This phone call has been recorded."

The bastard burst out laughing, then began to yell and scream into the phone. So much so, she could barely make heads or tails of what he was saying.

"Mmmm hmmm… You have a blessed and prosperous day."

She quickly disconnected the call, placed the phone down, grabbed her tea, and finished the cup. The music kept playing while her stomach somersaulted. Forcing herself to calm down, she dialed another number.

"Mama?"

"Hi, baby." The woman yawned.

"Did I wake you, Mama?" English glanced at the clock on her bedroom desk. It was only 8 at night, but her mother wasn't a stranger to falling asleep in front of the television after dinner.

"I'm up, baby. How are you doing?"

"I'm doing just fine. Is daddy there?"

"Mmm hmmm. You wanna speak to him?"

"Yes, please put him on speaker so you both can hear this."

"Okay. Hold on. Anthony!" She heard her mother muffle the phone, "English is on the phone. Wants to speak to us."

Daddy must've been sleeping, too. A smile crept across English's face as she imagined their foreheads leaning together as they slept. They'd been close to divorce at one time in their marriage, but now, they were more in love than ever. Their love story always encouraged her. True love always returned to you if it was meant to be. You didn't have to beg, plead, or force it.

"Okay, baby, we're both here. You got some good news? A promotion?" Mama asked. She could hear the smile in her mother's words. "Or maybe you're finally bringing your boyfriend over here so me and your Daddy can meet him."

"Not yet to any of that, but I'm sure that's on the horizon. Axel's work schedule and mine don't always jive, but we're working it out."

"Well, good, 'cause you haven't been serious about nobody since Willis, and—"

"Yes, I know… Thankfully, I learn from my mistakes, and Axel is a good man. He's got a good head on his shoulders. He's independent, resourceful, funny, good to me and just… a good person. I think y'all will like him."

"Axel? Sound like a rock band name. Oh, wait a minute… is it that White boy you told me she seein', Lacey?"

"Yeah."

"…I hope thangs don't get too serious. Maybe I should go on ahead and introduce her to Bishop Blue's son. He been divorced for over three years now, got a good job, and always said how pretty English is," her father murmured.

English shook her head. Dad could never whisper well.

"Shhh! Uh… hold on a minute, baby." Mama muffled the phone, but English could still hear the muted words.

"You ain't gonna do no such thing!, Bishop's son is one pebble away from bein' a full-blown crackhead. I wouldn't set that boy up wit' my Toy Poodle, let alone my baby! And yes, her boyfriend is White, but that don't matter as long as he's good to her. You hush up, ya hear me?! Don't say that again... What if she overheard you?!"

"Well, I hope she did..."

"Just foolish. That's what you are. You gonna make her 'fraid to be honest with us, Anthony. Be quiet! I mean it! Okay, baby..." Mama took her hand off the receiver. "English, you sound a little funny. Tired maybe? Is everything okay?"

"Not really." English picked up her teacup to take another drink, but had forgotten it was empty. She was certain her look of disappointment was clearly written all over her face. "I'm just going to get right into the nitty gritty. I am calling you to let you know that Master has been trying to contact me again."

Not to her surprise, she was firstly met with reticence. That silence meant her mother was brewing... changing quickly into a boiling hot madness. That silence meant Daddy felt horrible, as if once more, he couldn't keep his baby girl protected. This feeling had reared its head during a family counseling session they'd undergone as part of her deprogramming treatment. Time ticked, demented little seconds jumping off a cliff and landing face first into a sea of awkwardness.

Then, at last silence was broken like a rock slamming into a glass window.

"That son of a bitch!" Mama yelled, her words ringing

in English's ear. Mama's cool was lost, never to be seen again. "I told him if I *eva* saw his face again, English, I'd rip it off with my bare hands! WHERE IS THAT CRAZY CULT LEADIN' MOON FACED BACKWARDS HOTEP MOTHAFUCKA?! Call the poe-lease, Ant! CALL 'EM!"

"Lacey! Come on, now!" Daddy barked. "Calm down. Let's hear what English has to say."

"Mama, it's okay. I've contacted the police already. It didn't go well. They said I needed proof. Well, I got the proof they need now, and I'm going to file a restraining order first thing tomorrow. I told you that I refuse to live in fear. I mean it. He is trying to steal my peace. He can't have it. It's not for sale."

"How long he been sniffin' around you, En? How long he been back on the scene?"

Mama now seemed at the brink of tears. Rage and despair met and merged. It was a heartbreaking thing.

"For a while now, Mama."

English debated telling her about the birthday card being from Master. Her mother ranted and raved, bringing up all the treacherous mess from the past. How she'd lost her baby to a nutjob. How she was never the same after hearing about some of the things she endured while under Master's control… and nobody but English knew that was just the tip of the iceberg. Some stuff was going with her to the grave. It would kill Mama to know such details, and besides, they couldn't be changed. History had already been written. There would be no eraser big or strong enough to make it disappear. And even if one were able to delete the words, the emotions would still be left behind—imprinted in white ink, on white pages. Nobody but your heart could read it.

"Mama, please calm down. He hasn't done anything to me, and I'm not going to let it get to that level. My friends at work know now, too."

"You told them folks at work?" Once again, she could hear the worry in Mama's tone. English had explained for years that she wouldn't discuss the issue with anyone, unless absolutely necessary.

"Yes, I did. I didn't have a choice as far as I was concerned. I had to break down and tell them, Mama. Just in case."

"…In case he pops up around there," Daddy said. "That way, they'll be in the know and can report it if they see something suspicious."

"Yes. That's right. All of my business is out there now." She sighed. "And though it wasn't something I wished to talk about at work, of all places, I was relieved to find that not only was my boss understanding, but he also genuinely cared about my safety and thanked me for being honest."

They spoke for a while longer, and though the conversation had shifted, and she promised to contact the police again to request yet another restraining order, she knew deep down they'd be worried sick from here on out. As long as Master was walking the Earth free as a bird, or more accurately, the vulture that he was, there was really no peace that could be obtained and sustained.

That's what he wants… to rock my family. The people who love me. To keep me up at night. To cause me to not enjoy myself while out and about, for fear he'll show up. He didn't expect me to call back and not sound afraid. He didn't expect me to do a lot of things I'm more than willing to do now.

"I love you, Mama and Daddy. Talk to you soon." The call ended with laughs and declarations of love, just as she'd hoped for. After all, she'd put on the performance of her life.

As she got to her feet to fix another cup of coffee, her phone buzzed. A text message from Axel: *I love you.*

Just three simple words. No fanfare. Nothing crazy and over the top, poetic and flowery, and that made it all the more special. He said it with his actions. He said it with his care of her… but now, he'd confirmed what she already knew to be true.

She smiled down at her phone, then typed back:

I love you more…

…Two weeks later

"THAT'S HIS LICENSE plate number. No address yet. She'll get it though. Chànney said he hasn't approached her or anything like that, but the description matched him. I showed her the photo you found online and she's 99.9 % sure it's Master."

"Okay." Axel stepped out on his mother's porch, phone in hand. He was unapologetically having English followed from a safe distance. He refused to just let her be some sitting duck, especially while he tried to get his hands around this thing. In his ideal scenario, he'd be watching out for her himself. He needed to be in two places at one time, but since that was against the laws of physics, he came up with a plan B. Legend in turn called up one of his people to do the gig. His homegirl, a Puerto Rican lesbian named Channey.

Legend had made it clear she wasn't the type of person you wanted to fuck over. She'd done some amateur boxing, and she had bigger balls than some of the dudes he knew. Besides, she'd do what he asked. Axel spoke to her on the phone before she began her special assignment, and felt good about it. She seemed to know her shit. Legend vouched for her. 'Nuff said.

"I just got a job request before you called me. You want to come in with us tonight, Legend? I could use another pair of hands."

"I'm up for it." He could hear the man blowing smoke.

"Is that weed? Do you really have the audacity to do that while on the phone with me?"

"You Matt Riddle lookin' mothafucka, what I do on my off time is none of your business." Legend cackled.

"What I'd like to do, right about now, is shove a closed can of dog food down your throat, and make you shit it out. I told you I can't have you showing up high, Legend. I worked too hard to build my company from the ground up. You're not even finished with your training, and you—"

"Nobody ever knows when I'm high…"

"That's not the point. You know what? Quiet as kept, I've been wantin' to kick your ass since I reconnected with you, Legend. All the times you hung up on me when you were in prison. That slick ass mouth of yours… Let's go on ahead and brawl and get this shit out of the way because you—"

"I ain't smoking weed. Damn! It's a cigarette…"

"I should make you take a pee test."

"Give me the test, I don't give uh fuuuuck! Hey, where the bitches at?" Axel rolled his eyes. Legend still had the attention span of a gnat when he was forced to be sober. "I remember there being more nice-looking women here in Portland before I got locked up last time. Now all I see is flat booties and missin' teeth. Where are they hiding, man? I'm trying to fuck."

"Maybe if you stopped calling women bitches, you'd find someone."

"Look, Bret Michaels, you think just because you're in a relationship you can poke your chest out now, huh?"

"No, I'm just saying a little courtesy goes a long way. Be what you want to attract."

"Fuck that, and fuck that relationship guru shit. I'm not getting serious about anyone for a long ass time, and you said the same thing. Now here yo' ass is, all boo'ed up." Axel smirked and swallowed a big gulp of his beer.

"I said that a long time ago, man. Things change, Legend…"

"I remember how you used to run through them hos, Axel, like water down a drain, so you can miss me with the Mr. Goody-Two-Shoes act. So, what time you need me to come in tonight?"

"Uh, let's see," He looked at his watch. "I know you

worked this morning, so I appreciate this. 'Round ten would be good. I told you it's like this sometimes." He kicked a pebble across his mama's porch, and it skidded. "We either go a day or two without anything happening, or boom, we're getting back-to-back calls, nonstop."

"What happened with this one? I need to figure out if I can eat first. Todd was in the middle of training me and then he threw up all over my fuckin' jumpsuit this morning."

"Yeah. I heard. That lady had been in there for three weeks before anyone found her. Not exactly the best situation for you to cut your teeth on. Todd flaked out I see."

"That smell.... Fuck, man. It's crazy. Her boyfriend put her in the basement, wrapped in a carpet, then fled. That's some sick shit."

"I know. The one tonight isn't like that. Natural death. The police said it's over there near Josh's place."

After ending the call, Axel went back inside to find his mother eating a hamburger and watching some game show.

"An E!" she yelled around a mouthful.

Just then, his phone rang. Legend again.

"Who's that? You've been on the phone more than you've been here visiting me. You could have taken phone calls at home." She sucked her teeth, her gaze fixed on the television.

"It's Legend. He probably just butt dialed me. Hold on."

"What's up? You change your mind about tonight?"

"Channey just called and said Master attacked English! She had—"

"WHAT?!!! Where is she?! Is English Okay?!"

"She's in front of her job, and I think so, but—"

He ended the call, grabbed his keys, and raced to the front door.

"Axel, what's wrong, honey? Axel?" He heard his mother saying his name, but he was afraid that if he slowed down to listen, to *truly* listen, he'd explode. There were no words to describe how he felt at that moment—panicked came nowhere close. "Axel!"

He sped down the steps, to his truck, his heart slamming against his ribs.

"AXEL! What's going on?"

"MAMA, I'LL CALL YOU LATER!" he managed to say, then hauled ass out of her driveway…

Chapter Seventeen

THEY CALL IT intuition…

I felt different. Something was off. Askew. Wrong.

I felt like the sun was melting, and the moon was freezing, and the once happy celestial couple were arguing over the fall and winter. Two out of four of their children who were always competing with one another, at odds.

There was confusion in the air and the music of my soul kept skippin' like a scratched record. The song hurt my ears with its strange, uneven rhythm and bizarre guitar riffs. I put one foot in front of the other as I left work, the museum closing for the day. There was that feeling again. Invisible fingers along the hairs on the back of my neck. I turned around, but saw nothing. I kept on heading to my car, while thinking about how I'd left my coffee cup in there, and how its contents would need to be tossed out as soon as I got home.

I looked up at the sky, where the sun hadn't set. She was sitting low, but not yet finished shining. It had been a great morning, followed by a fine afternoon… but now, all that remained was an unseen terror. The early evening felt tight and twisted. A forewarn-

ing.

English looked at her car, about forty feet away from her work building. The hairs on the back of her neck stood on end as a black Land Rover slowly meandered around the parking lot, then parked in a spot it wasn't supposed to be. Her boss' space. He was gone for the day.

She walked a bit faster, her gut protesting. Out of the corner of her eye, she spotted a man approaching… no, a woman. Her features held a softness about them, framed by buzzed black hair. Flat chested and tall, she had tattoos all over neck and hands. *Who is that?* The woman suddenly pulled a black mask down over her face.

No, no, no!!!

"HEY!" the woman screamed out.

English sprinted across the lot, her briefcase, backpack, and body swinging as she gasped for air with each dash. Air whizzed past her ears, mingling with the sounds of Juice Newton's, 'Angel of the Morning,' from a passing truck.

"Hey, baby! Stop walkin'!" someone called out. She didn't slow down to find out who.

Of all of the days for me to purposefully park far in order to get some more steps in! God, please let me survive this! I know I don't go to church anymore, but I am begging you!

Something told her to turn around—a voice without words, yet she knew what it meant. Slowing down, she looked back to see the woman pull out a gun and aim it somewhere to her right. Everything seemed to happen in slow motion. Instincts and adrenaline kicked in, heart pumping hard, silent prayers and loud screams taking over. A few people also screamed as they watched the scene unfold. Her chest throbbed with a pain that wouldn't settle. *I'm almost to my car… almost there…*

Then, a man stepped out from the back seat of the vehicle, someone she didn't recognize. He started to run in the direction of her car…

Oh, God. He's going to make it there before I do!

English dropped to the ground as gunfire rang out. Scrambling about on the concrete, she dug into her bag, her trembling hand grasping cold metal. She checked the chamber and wrapped her finger around the trigger, then rose up just a little to see if anyone was coming.

"STAY DOWN!" the woman yelled as she thundered right past her.

Shrieking. Shouting. More gunfire. Car doors opening and closing. The squeal of tires peeling out…

Footsteps came fast towards her.

"BY GOD I WILL BLOW A MOTHERFUCKIN' HOLE IN YOU!" English jumped to her feet, covered in sweat, shakily holding her gun in front of her. She aimed it at the woman who was now standing there before her, her mask still on, her chest rising and falling hard with exertion.

She ran past me. Told me to stay down.

English looked beyond the woman and noticed a smattering of broken glass ahead. The Land Rover was gone.

"English, hey, I'm Channey Hernandez. First of all, the police have already been notified about this situation. Thankfully, no one was hurt. They are looking for the vehicle that man exited from. I've taken care of that. Now, I know you want to know why I'm here and what this is about. Do you know Legend Vidal?"

"No… but I know his sister, Melanie."

The woman nodded in understanding. She slipped her gun back into her side holster and slid her mask off, jamming it in her back pocket.

"Axel Hendrix asked Legend to hire me. I'm not cheap."

English couldn't believe her ears. *But on second thought…*

"Axel sent you? Why?"

"The police didn't do anything to help you, from my understanding, so here I am." The woman threw her hands in the air, then ran her hand over her buzzcut hair. "I work for a protection agency. That's just a fancy way to say bodyguards, so Axel figured I'd be good for the job."

"Channey, you said your name was?"

"Mmm hmm." The woman put her hands on her waist.

"What is going on here? Job? What job? First, you are running towards me with a ski mask and gun. Then, some weirdo gets out of a car and races towards mine. I hear gunshots and yelling all around me, and when I get back on my feet, you're standin' there with a smoking gun, telling me you were hired by my boyfriend's best friend."

"Lady, the small details mean nothin' right now. Do you know that your ex-boyfriend killed someone before?" The woman's brow shot up, an almost smug certainty on her face.

"…No."

"He's responsible for this situation. I'm sure you already figured that out though. Master Whitefield. Cult leader. Many aliases such as Master Lord. Black Jesus. Sampson." She laughed mirthlessly. "He wasn't charged or convicted, but he did it. Some woman from his little group. The streets talk, English. You're not safe until he's gone because he wants you. Dead or alive."

A burning sensation filled her. "But why would—"

"Axel wanted someone to make sure you stayed alive," she cut her off.

"Do you work for the police?"

"Nah. I report to the police when things like this happen, but I don't work for them. I've been to prison. I'm a reformed criminal, if you will. The police know who I am, and they know the company I work for. They knew me when I was out in the streets sellin', and they know me now."

Her horror and trepidation turned into an inferno of anger.

"Let me ask you something. Why would Axel do this and not tell me, though? We keep no secrets! Who was in that car? I don't know that man. None of this makes sense!"

"You mind putting that away?"

English had no idea she'd been waving her gun around the entire time she was speaking to the woman. She quickly slipped it into her bag.

"Sorry."

"Look, I know it's a lot at once, okay? It's coming at you fast. I want to commend you though for doing what you needed to do. I've been tailing you for several days now, and you pay attention to what's going on around you. That's a good thing."

"Obviously not good enough," English rolled her eyes and crossed her arms, "because I never noticed *you*." She bent down and picked up her spewed belongings.

"I don't count. I'm trained to not be noticed if it suits me or the assignment. I wear the mask so that I'm harder for my targets to identify. I wasn't supposed to encroach your personal space. I only activate if I see something suspicious. I've spent the majority of my adult life tryna blend in. I was in a male dominated profession when I was a drug dealer, and I'm still in a male dominated profession, workin' security—only now, I don't give a shit about what anyone thinks of me. As far as your boyfriend, maybe he didn't tell you because he knew you wouldn't understand, or try to fight him about it. His mind was made up. He wanted you safe, and if you were mad about it afterwards, that was the risk he was willing to take."

English allowed the words to marinate within her. "On one hand, I appreciate his concerns, but on the other, he still should have said something. Regardless, thank you for intervening in what could have been a disastrous situation. A kidnapping. Murder. Who knows what was planned for me?" She exhaled a ragged breath.

"Come on, let's walk you to your car."

They walked side by side to the vehicle.

"Unlock it for me."

English waited while the woman checked various areas of her Lexus, including the trunk, and underneath it.

When she was finished, she dusted herself off.

"This is completely insane."

"Look, I don't know Axel. Legend has told me about him over the years, though. They're like brothers. Better than brothers. They bump heads, they fight, but they love one another. Legend didn't have time to trail you, or I'm sure he would have done it himself. The other problem with that is, eventually you'll see Legend because he and Axel are hangin' out again. Working together, too." English nodded in understanding. "So, they didn't want to take that chance of you spotting him. I say all of this to say that this was done out of love and concern for you. Legend doesn't know you, but he asked me to do this because he loves Axel. Period. So, the next steps are that you will need to fill out a police report."

The woman's phone buzzed. She took it out of her pocket and checked the screen.

"Give me a second, English. I have to call Legend and let him know what just happened."

"Should I call Axel?"

"Not yet."

Channey made the phone call, while English stood there with her blood boiling, threatening eruption. Her anger towards Axel was fleeting. It came and went. Now, her ire was directed to the main culprit: Master.

I should have killed him when I had the chance!

One night, he'd smacked her clear across the room after accusing her of flirting with a minister from another group. Her lip had split, and her right eye was practically swollen shut. It had all been a figment of his twisted imagination. Later that evening, he'd fallen asleep as if nothing had happened, his gun on the nightstand beside him. She'd stood there for a long time, in her white nightgown splattered with blood, wishing she'd had the strength to grab it and blow his brains out. The next morning, he'd told her over breakfast, her mouth swollen to three times its normal size, that she was an idiot. *"Shira, next time you think I'm asleep and you want to stand over me and think about killing me, make sure the gun has bullets. You must think I'm stupid. Like you…"*

She overheard Channey mentioning a license plate number, and describing Master sitting in the back seat of a car. In all of the hoopla, English hadn't seen his face; however, she knew some other man had been driving.

This isn't the end. It is only the beginning.

A chill ran down her spine.

"I want him gone!" The woman shot her a glance, her phone still to her ear. "I know it won't change anything, but I need to feel safe. I don't feel safe. The police aren't going to help me, Channey. I can write down all the reasons why they should, show them a mountain of evidence, but they will still brush me off. I have him on tape, submitted it, and they said they'd look into it. Look into it?! People have gotten killed while we waited around for the police to look into shit!"

Channey nodded, and got off the phone.

"I understand. That's why I'm my own police. Some cops are okay. Half the time, they're full of shit. 'Specially towards Black and brown folk, like you and me."

"Something ain't right with you either, Channey."

"What do you mean?" The lady looked at her curiously, as if insulted.

"I know you're getting paid, but you're still at risk. On top of it, you just admitted you don't even like working with the police, so why would you do all of this for a stranger?"

"The police haven't protected you up until this point, according to what Axel told Legend. Legend and I go way back. I'm not going to go into what happened, but that man saved my life. We used to be colleagues, if you will. He asked me for a favor. I obliged. On top of that, I take your situation personal."

"Why? You had a stalker, too?"

Channey shook her head. "No. My big sister got hooked on drugs after bein' in an abusive marriage with her husband. For six years, he beat her ass, told her he was going to kill her. I believed him. Our mother believed him. She didn't. He'd apologize. Buy her things. Then it would start up all over again. A vicious cycle. He made her family out to be the enemy. My mother was called a bitch, and nosy. I was called a dyke. Our brother was called retarded… he has a learning disability. He said we were all failures, and she was nothin' without him. I'm Puerto Rican, and in our culture, the man is the head of the household. Divorce is frowned upon. We're Roman Catholic.

"Even my mother, though she hated him, was tryna tell me and my brother to butt out, and let them work it out. Religious beliefs sometimes override common sense. I hate to say it, but it's true. I begged her to leave him,

English. She wouldn't. Said it wouldn't be fair to the kids… said he was a good dad, just needed help with his anger. But one day, he put her in the hospital, and we didn't think she'd pull through. Knocked out several teeth. Her brain was swelling. Broken bones. The police asked who did it to her, and after years of lyin' and covering for him, she finally told the truth. Instead of protecting her, the police left her out there like a sitting duck."

English pressed her purse to her chest. "What happened?"

"He went AWOL. They tried to find him. Couldn't. Four days later, he broke into her house, tried to get her to drop the charges. She said no. He ran into the kids' room, grabbed my niece and strangled her… killed their daughter right in front of her." English's eyes watered. Channey stood there, stone-faced. Her jaw tightened, and she swallowed, but she remained stiff. Cold. "To hurt her. To hurt *us*. The people who loved her. My niece was dead. Three days after that, my sister, Juanita, my beautiful big sister, overdosed. On purpose."

Channey readjusted her belt, then shook her head. "So, now you know why I'm here, and why I do what I do. You understand why Axel deserves a medal for thinking ahead. You see why I commend you for bein' strapped, and being aware. You got away once, English. He's not going to let you get away again." She knew that to be true. Damn, was it true… "You can't go it alone. In these cases, nobody escapes without help. He can't take a child away from you, but he'll find the equivalent. He'll kill something or someone you love, even if it is your sense of peace. And when he does, he'll stomp on it with all that is within him—right in front of you. That's how these deranged cowards operate. They hate their mamas. They hate women, period. They hate themselves. He don't have shit to lose. You were the one who got away… and baby, he's not planning to lose twice."

Chapter Eighteen

CIGARETTE SMOKE PURLED out of the cracked window. A cold rain fell from the sky as 'Blue Monday,' by New Order, played on the oldies radio station. He wasn't much in the mood for his typical headbanger music. He wasn't much in the mood for anything. Axel sat behind the wheel, shirt off, muscles tense, breathing slow and easy. He didn't care about anything at that moment, except English. When he arrived at the parking lot of her job, apparently surprising both her and Channey, he was amazed she didn't launch into a verbal attack now that the cat was out of the bag.

Rather, she appeared shaken up, but grateful. She'd leapt into his arms, wrapped her limbs around him, and squeezed him so damn tight, they had no choice but to share their next breath.

Everything after that was kind of a blur. Movement. Cursing. Irritation and frustration. Thank goodness he'd had her followed.

The three of them headed to the police station and he

spent the majority of that time being elbowed by English, who didn't want him to say anything. Every time she or Channey tried to discuss the events, it was almost like they were being interrogated—not believed.

Getting to his feet, he proceeded to demand justice. The laws were ass-backwards. There was no justice for some folks. Plain and simple. The police were walking on eggshells after some recent police brutality charges, the limelight was on them, so now, everyone was a sitting duck. Talks of defunding the police had resurfaced, and soon after, people complained that their calls to the districts garnered slow reaction times. 911 sometimes didn't dispatch an officer until folks were dead, and the perpetrator long gone. This was the climate they lived in—where the police were afraid of the criminals, and the criminals were encouraged. Roaming free. Untouchable.

The officer said they were still on the lookout for the vehicle, and gave her further information, including some relating to a court date. Deep down, they all knew it wouldn't lead anywhere. They left the station, devised the next steps, and Channey parted ways with them. Axel had it from here. He hated this for her. English now sat in the passenger seat of his truck, her police paperwork in hand. A vacant look on her face. The lights were on, but no one was home.

Michael Jackson's 'Chicago' played on the radio as he winded down the back roads on his way to taking her home. He didn't want her driving. She was far too upset. English had given Channey the keys, and she said she'd bring her car over later that evening.

"Sorry for being so quiet."

"You don't have to say nothin'. I know you're upset. I know you're scared."

"I'm not scared. I'm angry, Axel. Angry that he has once again gotten away with this. He's emboldened by now. I was ready to kill him dead if he came towards me… sick of this shit!" Her voice rattled. She nervously chewed on her nails while staring out the window. He looked at her reflection. Her eyes were trained on the bursts of vibrant green tree leaves, falling rain, dense foliage flashing in fast motion providing snapshots of nature as he drove past.

"Nothing wrong with being scared, English." He jammed his cigarette in the ashtray, killing the flame. "As long as you don't let the fear stop you from what you need to do, being afraid sometimes is just part of life."

English had to be fearing for both her family and her sanity. By the time they'd finished with the police, he'd heard the story three times, and it never got easier to understand how such a thing could happen in public, in broad daylight, and they were gone without a trace. The police were looking for the car in question. Footage was being pulled from a nearby camera. One problem did exist, however. The license plate came back fake. Big damn surprise.

Master was slick about his shit—an expert at staying right under the radar and having others do his dirty work. A regular ol' modern day Charles Manson. Master manipulator, and crazy as fuck.

He made sure he wasn't the one driving, or the person who

slipped out of the car to try and circumvent English getting away. This motherfucker…

Channey was an eyewitness and she'd seen him, but despite her training and credibility, it would still be her word against his. He imagined if things got hairy, her criminal background would be tossed into the ring to discredit her. The odds were stacked against English.

I'm going to level the playing field…

"Pull over."

"Huh? Why?"

"Just pull over, Axel. I need to get out of the car."

"English, you're almost home and it's rainin'."

"Just do it! Pull over!" Her eyes sheened over as 'Time' by Culture Club came on the radio station. He jerked his truck over to the side, careful to not slip into a nearby embankment. Before he could barely get it in park, the passenger's side door flew open, and English was outside. He rushed out to grab her, to force her back into the truck, only to stop in his tracks. She spun around and around, her arms outstretched, dancing in the rain—in her work attire—as cars zoomed past on the road. Her face beamed, her eyes raised towards the sky, arms extended like a bird's, spinning around and around like a flower being twirled between a child's fingers.

He made his way back to his truck to turn the music up at high volume. 'Eyes Without a Face,' by Billy Idol, was now on. Returning to her, he wrapped his arms around her waist and lifted her into the air. She opened her mouth, gulping raindrops as if they were candy. Her body trembled as if she were silently sobbing, releasing her frustration. Angry tears disguised by the rain. But more than that, she might be forcing herself to forget her troubles. To live in the moment. He couldn't be sure. That was the thing about English. Every now and again, he wasn't certain why she did what she did, or said some of the things she'd said, but in the end, he seemed to always know how to respond.

He lowered her to her feet, then rested his chin on top of her wet waves as they slow danced. His hair was heavy and slick with rain, and she was soaked to the bone. It was cold. Wet. Miserable. Yet, somehow, they were suspended in time, unbothered. When the song ended, he helped her back into the truck, and soon, they made it in front of her house. No words were exchanged as he followed her inside, and watched her close and lock the door. She walked past him, disrobing along the way. A wet jacket here. Saturated sweater there. The sopping garments hit the wooden floor in thuds, until all that was left were a pair of sheer ankle-high stockings on her feet. Pausing by her kitchen, she leaned against the counter, rolled them off, and placed them neatly on a barstool before making her way to the refrigerator.

Bottle of white wine in hand, two wine glasses, they settled together, nude, under a large blanket in front of the television, a candle burning and the electric fireplace roaring in her living room. He glanced at his wet clothing set in a pile off to the side, then sipped the wine, as she gulped hers. She leaned against his shoulder, remote control in her hand, and channel surfed. She was still so damn quiet. That wasn't like her at all…

She was tormented. Angry beyond words. All he wanted to do was love her. He hoped it was enough. His version of love included things she may have fantasized about, but was too good-hearted to do. He heard her dark wishes. She wanted that man dead. He certainly deserved it.

Ms. Florence, I know you're watching me right now, and you know what I'm thinking. I reckon you don't approve. You know what I'm up to. You always knew what I, Legend, and Caspian were up to, and for a lady who had no children of her own, you sure had a strong motherly intuition. I dreamt about you last night again, so I knew something was going to happen today. You warned me, in your own way. You ain't say nothing, but I could feel it. I want to tell you, as I sit here holding my sweetheart who in many ways reminds me of you, that I'm no killer.

Is that a lie? I try to be as truthful with you as possible. At least, that's what I used to tell myself. I've seen so much death in my life, Ms. Florence, from the time I was a little boy. Death has always danced around me like rattling skeletons and brain-hungry zombies, huntin' me in the afterlife.

My dog gettin' hit by a car right in front of me when I was just a lil' boy set it off. A few years later, my daddy shot 'nd killed his friend right in front of me, too. Found out that friend pulled a gun out on him and tried to steal over $5000 he'd saved up to get a new trailer. Mama didn't kill nobody, but she shot some man she was dating in the face. He thought he could jump on her, put his hands on her, but Mama wasn't havin' it. I liked that man up until that point… funny how I can't even remember his name right now. Strange how all of this viciousness became normal to me, so early on. Made me hurt somethin' terrible. I didn't want to hear that pain no *more.*

Grandpa and Grandma died. Other folks in the family passed away—cousins, uncles, friends of the family… and then you died on me, too. I think that was the final straw, the one that broke the camel's back, Ms. Florence. How'd you get bone cancer? I wanted to fight the whole world. We ain't know you were sick. How could you keep a secret like that from us? I was messed up over you. I almost didn't make it to your funeral, but Mama dragged me out the house with my wrinkled suit and tie on. I slept in it all night. My heart broke each time I thought about you in that casket. Cold. Alone.

I made you a promise. You made me promise to take care of my problem, but I never did. I just turned off the sound is all. I made sure I didn't hear no evil… You found out about my troubles at home, and you talked to me about it. Nobody had ever asked me how I felt, not even my own mama, and I know she loves me something fierce. If I was sad or upset about thangs at home, it was just too damn bad. We were just expected to buck up, and shut up. You gave me a voice, and eyes to see. But most of all, you gave me an ear to listen, so I could hear things I hadn't heard before. Excruciating, cutting, terrible things I had blocked out.

I slipped back into my old ways… I don't like listening to pain. I turn it off like I would a dial. Hearing it does something to me. Makes me feel enfeebled. The sound of tears fallin' from the woman I love. She ain't crying on the outside right now, but I know she is on the inside. She feels helpless and enraged. She's afraid to even admit she's afraid… What a shame.

I hated the sound of my mama sobbing because she didn't know how she was going to pay the rent, or explain to us that our daddy wasn't coming to pick us up and take us out to eat, like he promised. Instead, he was drunk somewhere, with a woman, taking care of her kids instead.

I hated the sound of my sister yellin' and screamin' that don't nothing ever go right in her life because she don't know how to love nobody, and when she takes a chance, it always blows up in her face. Those are cutting things to hear. Soul drainers.

Ms. Florence, I have been forced to become someone I never wanted to be. A disregarder of life. Now, I have to hear that truth, too. I have to hear myself break souls, stop breaths. I stole the breath of four men… made it so they'd never inhale or exhale again.

Life is precious. That's what you told me. That's what I believe. Despite how many dead bodies I've seen over my career and life as a whole, I know this to be true, but I must be deaf or dead, and don't even know it. I don't feel nothing when death comes whispering in my ear. I don't feel a damn thing when I walk into a place, my uniform on, ready to work in the bloody muck and guts that the recently deceased left behind. Maybe everything that's happened to me over my lifetime, my own pain and resentments, my detachment from death, helped fashion me into some type of monster. While people are throwing up at a crime scene, I'm humming a song…

Or perhaps I'm looking at this wrong… maybe my respect for life is what compels me to make sure Master never bothers her again. Maybe my respect for life made me not think twice 'bout killin' that first man, then the second, and the third and fourth? I needed to preserve my OWN life first, and respect for life needs to start at home. It don't even phase me now. I've done four of 'em. What's one more?

I can try to rationalize it, to tell myself those were bad people who deserved it. I'd be right about that. Maybe I'm justifying it right now, but I just don't feel no ill way about it.

I sit here next to my baby, and she's lying on me, looking at the

TV. Her hair is soaking wet, and I hope she don't catch cold. She's curled up in a ball, a million thoughts racing through her mind, I'm sure… I 'magine she's gonna finish the rest of that bottle of wine by herself, then grab another. I 'magine she's going to want me to fuck her until she goes deaf, dumb, and blind. I'll do it. I'll turn the music on, touch her all over, and fuck her clean out of her mind, and I'll give her peace of mind, too. I'll kill for this woman, Ms. Florence, and won't think twice about it. That's why I imagine you're not too pleased with me. I can't change that, though. I am who I am. I can sit here and pontificate about how I became this way until the cows come home. It won't change a damn thing. You and I both know it.

I've fallen for her hard. We don't have to say it to each other all day—we just know how we feel about one another. It's real. It's for grown up folks, and I'm here for the long haul. She's fallen in love with a cold-hearted, deaf-to-pain killer…

I don't want my baby to have to live that way though. Once you kill someone, you ain't never the same, Ms. Florence. You can't ever go back. Legend refuses to tell anyone how many folks he put down like sick dogs, but I know the number is something out of this world. We killed for different reasons, but there's more than one way to do it, and sometimes, it don't involve no gun, no knife, no weapon—except the mind.

Sometimes, all you gotta do to kill somebody is set their world on fire with obsessions, lies, neglect, mind games and manipulation. Then, once they're good and burning, you sit back, laugh, and refuse to let them dance in the rain…

Chapter Nineteen

"IT'S BURNT, HONEY, but if you put enough butter on it, you won't be able to tell."

English could do nothing but burst out laughing as Axel's mother placed a jet-black biscuit on her plate, patted her shoulder as if to say, 'best of luck,' and kept it moving. Axel had disappeared to the restroom, leaving her alone with his family. His mother was a thin, tall woman with blond hair, a bit of gray at the temples and brow, bright blue eyes surrounded by crow's feet, and fingers that looked as if she'd been a dishwasher her entire life.

"Mama, nobody's eatin' that. The chicken is good though," Dallas said, tearing into a piece of baked chicken. Her young son, Lucas, sat beside her, head down, playing on his handheld gaming system. English didn't expect this sort of introduction to Axel's family. One minute, she was at work, and the next, he told her he was going to swing by when she got off work. *"You're coming by for supper, and to meet my mother."*

New Order's 1980's classic, 'Bizarre Love Triangle,'

played from a radio in the dining room, which sat wedged between assorted knickknacks and artificial plants covered in layers of dust. In spite of the clutter here and there, Axel's mother's home was nice, and appeared clean where it counted.

A wave of embarrassment washed over English as she felt herself secretly judging others. *I've just been around too many White women who see me as some sort of anomaly or trinket. Here I am, this Black woman, dating her White son, who I know was a highly sought-after bachelor around these parts. Kentucky has all kinds of people… Lord, I hope she's the right kind. I don't even know if Axel told her I was Black before bringing me over here. She doesn't seem terribly surprised or phased though.*

Axel had always spoken highly of his mother, and realistically, too. For one, he'd told her how overprotective the woman was, always trying to tell him what to do. The nerve of the man—wasn't that the pot calling the kettle black? But she kept that thought to herself. He also said she was stubborn and had a temper. Another hypocrisy. Axel didn't seem to realize he was so much like his mother, it was almost comical.

Suddenly, she heard police sirens in the far distance—perhaps a street or two over. Flashes of her recent visit to the police station came to mind, making her feel heavy inside. To make matters worse, the police had contacted her that afternoon and said they pulled the video camera footage, but it was fuzzy due to the camera's age and poor quality. There was no audio, either, all due to budget cuts and the city not keeping up with such things. Someone could have said Master had pulled up in a magic pink and blue polka dot school bus, then shot an arrow out of the window, and no one would've been the wiser.

"Everything all right, Axel?" his mother asked, jerking her out of her thoughts.

Axel made his way back to the table and sat down. "Yeah. Why wouldn't it be?" He grabbed his beer and took a swig.

"Well, you were gone a while." she explained while piling mashed potatoes on her plate.

"Probably was in the bathroom playin' with himself like he used to when we was kids."

"Dallas! You stop that!" The older woman's face flushed, then she and Dallas burst out laughing. Axel played it cool, as if his sister had said nothing at all, and started to eat his chicken. *Choke the chicken…*

"I'm so happy you're home, Axel! I mean, not home, but here," the woman beamed so proudly at him, and he simply nodded. "I so rarely get to spend time with you. Last time you had to fly out of here. Not sure what that was all about. Anyway, I couldn't believe it when I called you this morning, told you I was cooking and wanted you to come by, and you said yes. You never say yes to dinner!" she squealed.

Her exuberance made English tingle and feel good all over. She could feel the woman was genuine, and over the moon with happiness that Axel was there with her.

"Mama, I say yes sometimes, and we talk on the phone all the time."

"Talkin' on the phone and lookin' you in the eye ain't the same. I need to touch you, wrap my arms around you, every now and again. If you ever have children, you'll understand. English, do you want some more mashed potatoes, hon?"

"No, ma'am. I'm fine. Thank you."

"So, English," his mother smiled big as she picked up a big glass of Mountain Dew, "Axel explained that you're a book curator. I think he was surprised that I knew what that was!" She chortled.

"Yes, ma'am. I am."

"I used to love to read! I don't have much time now, and stopped doing it regularly once I got married and started havin' kids, but it was one of my favorite pastimes."

"What's one of your favorite books?" English reached for her glass of iced tea.

"Oh, I had so many, but I was a big 'Flowers in the Attic' fan! VC Andrews. I liked mysteries and scary books best. So what are you workin' on now?"

"Well, usually, I deal with historical texts, but I am helping out with a new project right now. It's going well."

"Oh, really? What project?"

"A project regarding racial microaggressions."

Great. A dinner discussion to totally derail the 'good time' mood. Well, I wasn't going to lie. Nothing says smiles, joy, and laughter like discussing unintentional racial discrimination. Yippee! Goooo, English!

"Microaggressions? What's that?" Dallas and the mother asked at the same time. She shot a glance at Axel, but he was too busy playing on his phone while simultaneously wolfing down a spoonful of mashed potatoes.

"Microaggressions, when discussing racism, are essentially incidental, indirect, or unpremeditated bias or discrimination against members of a marginalized group."

...Both of them are looking at me like I'm crazy. They probably have no damn idea what I'm talking about, even after an explanation.

"Mama, another way to explain it is, well... let me give you an example. It's like tellin' an Asian person you bet they can beat someone's ass at Karate, or tellin' a Black person they sure speak nice and proper, and are a credit to their race." Axel's gaze remained fixed on his phone as he spoke around a spoonful of food. "Do you understand now, or do you need further explanation?"

"I know what the hell it means, Axel! Condescending twit. I understood her explanation just fine without your Professor Dolittle input. I may not be high falutin', and no Bill Gates or Einstein, but I ain't the dullest knife in the drawer." Axel sighed as if bored, still looking at his phone. He clearly didn't give a damn that his mother might be insulted or embarrassed. That made it all the funnier.

"Well, you're the one sittin' there looking at her as if she has two heads... like you didn't understand. I was just tryna help."

"How would you know how I'm looking when you've got your nose in that there phone? You act like I only finished the second grade, and my teacher was a damn bed bug!" his mother barked. Dallas burst out laughing, while English barely controlled herself, almost losing the battle.

"Back on topic now, English." The woman rolled her eyes at Axel, then turned back in her direction. "So, is the project a book about micro… micro—"

"Microaggressions."

"Yes. So, there's a book about microaggressions? Is it like Axel said, or something else?" she questioned, looking genuinely interested.

"Actually, it's a screenplay based on the true life of a Black actress who endured racism, while working her way up to local stardom. It happened right here in Louisville. I was asked to take a look at it, and offer some historical insights."

"Well, isn't that something! They're gonna make it into a movie, huh?"

"Yes, ma'am. You know what? On second thought, I *will* have some more mashed potatoes."

"Oh, you don't have to pretend you like 'em, English. Mama made them from a box. She added enough salt in 'em to swell up a creek and turn it right into an ocean," Dallas teased.

"Oh, shut up, Dallas! Nothin' is wrong with those 'taters, and they're homemade, I beg your pardon! But something is wrong with *you*… I must've dropped you on *my* head because you became my instant headache."

Dallas and Axel snickered.

"Oh, and for the record, I didn't understand what the hell microaggressions meant, English, even after you explained it, as I'm sure you already guessed, bein' as smart as you are and all, but I just didn't appreciate my son tryna make me look stupid is all."

"Make you look stupid? Oh, for God's sake. Just say, 'I still don't understand what you're saying.'" He laughed before gulping down some tea.

"I'm surprised you didn't cut in and tell me what a screenplay was, too! Or ask me, what's two plus two! My handsome, intelligent, yet also impolite, obstinate, and hard-headed son here thinks he knows better than everyone else." Axel rolled his eyes, and looked back down at his phone. "English, Axel is crazy. Since he wanna learn everybody today, act like some college dean! Did he school you on that? Crazier than a two-dicked rooster trapped in a hen house!"

"No, ma'am." English was about to burst as the woman was now yelling, a big, greasy smile on her face. "He didn't tell me he was crazy. Should I be concerned?" English goaded.

"Yeah, because Axel is a loon. The cheese slid right off his cracker. Started when he was seven or eight. That's when I noticed he got his father's lunatic genes. He's two bricks short of a load."

Everyone was laughing now.

"…He's a good man though." Her smile slowly faded, and a sweetness shone in the older woman's eyes. Pure love. "Axel and Dallas mean the world to me. They'll tell everyone that I'm too clingy, but I'm not—I just look out for 'em. The world ain't always kind." English nodded in agreement. "They're all I got." She shrugged. "I work part time now at the Dollar General, just to keep busy more than anything else. Axel don't really talk much about his dating life, and I don't ask very often, but I'm glad he brought you here tonight. You're so interesting! And pretty, too."

"I'm glad to be here. It's my pleasure, and you've given me such a warm welcome."

"You're different…" The woman tapped her chin thoughtfully. "I don't know much 'bout race stuff. I don't know much about historical books, either. But I do know 'bout my boy. Whoever makes *him* happy makes *me* happy. I stay outta his private life," she reiterated, then waved her hand emphatically in his direction. Axel's facial expression read: 'Untrue. False. Lies.' "As far as women, things like that, especially, and it's been a minute since I've had the pleasure to meet someone my son took a likin' to. You seem like a real sweet girl. This was such a treat!"

"Well, thank you so much, Ms. Hendrix. I really appreciate that. I hope we can continue to spend more time together, and get to know one another better. He's spoken so much about you and Dallas, I feel like I'd already met you before I even came through the door."

"Axel and I are real close." Dallas had a heavy energy about her. In one way, she seemed fun-loving, sociable, and silly even, but in the next, she always seemed to be observing. Sizing her up. "Do you have any brothers and sisters?"

The Cure's, 'Just Like Heaven,' started to play now.

"Yeah, I have an older sister and a younger brother. We're all one year and three months apart."

"Middle child. Your parents together?" Dallas asked.

"Yes, they are. Maybe one day you can meet my family too, Dallas." English winked at her, and Dallas winked right back. *Curious woman…*

"Boy, you ain't gonna talk to ya Uncle Axel?" Dallas

nudged her son, who seemed totally engrossed in his game. The little boy with dirty blond hair lifted his head, showing big blue eyes and a snaggle-toothed grin.

"Hi, Axel," Lucas said in a soft tone, with a slight rasp. "You comin' to Mom's barbecue?"

"I sure am. I wouldn't miss my sister's party for nothin'. In fact, I—" Just then, Axel's phone lit up and buzzed on the table. His eyes turned to slits. "Hold on a second," he mumbled as he snatched it from the table, got to his feet, and walked off.

"Probably work." Axel's mother rolled her eyes, then sucked her teeth. "They call him all hours of the day 'nd night. He's gonna be right there in the grave with 'em, with the way those people work him to death. You'd think he was the only cleanin' crew service in town! English, what do you think of my son's job? Don't it give you the creeps?"

"Oh, Mama, don't start! Be supportive!"

"I *am* supportive."

"Turn this old music off. I wanna hear something else. At least he's workin' though, Mama. Hell, half of these guys won't keep no job or they're on that shit, and couldn't keep one if they tried."

"Was Daddy on that shit, Mom?" the boy questioned.

English slowly ate her food, but kept her eye on the drama unfolding at the table. Dallas got up, yanked the radio station dial, and 'Problem With It,' by Plains drifted from the speakers.

"Yup. Your daddy was a piece of shit before *and* after the drugs. He got sober, but he's still an asshole."

"Dallas, don't talk like that in front of my grandchild! We know Lucas' father wasn't worth a damn, but you don't have to tell him so."

"Why not? We knew our own daddy wasn't shit before we could even talk or walk, Mama."

"Not on account of me. I tried to keep that sort of thing 'way from y'all. I kept my mouth shut."

"Oh, please, Mama! You can't be serious? Daddy was every bitch, bastard, and asshole known to man 'round this place. If I hadn't known any better, I woulda thought my daddy's first name was Son, middle name Of-a, and last name, Bitch."

The conversation went on and on, only halting once the front door slammed. The talking stopped immediately, and everyone looked towards the dining room entryway. Axel stood there like a foreboding brick wall. He sucked all of the air out of the room with his mere presence. His nostrils flared and his chest heaved.

"Axel, what's wrong?" Dallas asked, breaking the awkward silence, her voice a bit quaky.

"Daddy done got himself locked up."

Well, speak of the devil…

"That was Tammy callin' me, talkin' 'bout they got into a fight. He was drunk and pushed her, and she fell. Hurt herself. Now she's tryna drop the charges, and wants me to bail him out. That motherfucker." He glanced at his watch. "Now I gotta go get him."

"Oh, like hell you do!" Axel's mother tossed down her napkin from her lap, and began massaging her forehead as if a headache was brewing. "It's just like him to have his drama spread everywhere like a disease! We're sittin' here having a nice dinner, and now look! I never get to see ya! Spend time with you! I say let his ass rot in there!"

"Mama, Axel can't do that," Dallas stated meekly as she stroked her son's hair.

"And just why not?"

"Daddy's sickly. You know that. He won't last in jail."

"He got himself sick from all that drinkin'! Pickled his damn liver. He's in remission, but instead of being thankful, he's drinking again. You think if the shoe was on the other foot, that piece of shit would come and help either one of y'all? I called him when Axel broke his arm when he was nine, messin' around playin' baseball with Robbie and them. I didn't see a dime for that hospital bill, and he didn't even come visit his child in the hospital!"

Axel slowly closed his eyes as his mother and sister went on and on, bringing up the mess of yesteryear. He looked utterly drained. Disgusted. Livid. English slowly rose from her seat, walked up to him, and hugged him tight.

"Can he be bailed out tonight?" Dallas asked.

"Yeah."

"Do you want me to go with you? I can ride with you," English offered.

She stared at her man, framing his face with her hands. Looking into his eyes. She saw him torn in two. It was as if he had one foot planted in his mama's house, and the other already outside, stepping on the gas.

"Mama, I hate to cut this visit short, but I gotta go."

"Unbelievable!" she yelled so loud, it rattled English's

core. "He don't deserve a son like you. I barely get to see my son 'cause you work all the time, and I get on your nerves so you avoid me, then this evening I get to sit down with you, finally break bread, burnt 'nd all, even meet your pretty girlfriend here, and then here comes Tommy! Crashin' the party like a wreckin' ball. Everything he touches, he fucks up! He's only done two things right in his whole, miserable, pathetic life, and that was give me you 'nd Dallas."

"Mama, come on. Calm down." Dallas got up from her seat now too, speaking calmly. The jokes and silliness were well over, and now agony submerged the room.

"That man wouldn't offer you a match if you were cold! He won the lottery with y'all. I tell you that much. Dallas drives him around town when his car is broken down, and Axel checks up on him, gives him money, and works on his house. He's an ogre walking the earth! I should've choked the shit out of him when I had the chance."

...I know the feeling.

"Mama, come on, now! That's terrible. He was an awful father and husband, but none of this is helping right now. He's still our father. You're sounding bitter, when we both know you don't want nothing to do with Daddy and moved on a long time ago, so just cut it out." Dallas was now all red in the face.

"I'm not bitter. I'm just reminding y'all of what went on. Seems you've got selective memory. I don't want my babies being used."

"Mama, I'm only doing this because Tammy is distraught. If I don't do it, she'll just find someone else, but that person might charge them a bunch of interest and what not. It could be financially devastating for them, 'cause Daddy don't have much savings, and Tammy is the only one working. I just want to see what's going on, talk to the bail bondsman, and—"

"You're crazy, Axel, if you think he didn't put 'er up to that phone call. He knows you got the money to spring him. He belongs exactly where he is. Behind bars. All he does is lie. Drink. Blame everyone for his problems. Use others like toilet tissue. All of my life I worked!" The woman pressed her finger into her chest, beating her point in. "I never asked neither one of you for a dime, or anyone else for that matter, even when I could have used it." Her voice quaked. "Got on food stamps a few times… worked under-the-table jobs to help ends meet, and that man did nothin' but act like y'all didn't exist, until he found you convenient. My children are not an inconvenience!"

"I know that, Mama, but this isn't about—"

"You both take care of your mama… take real good care of me, but I earned every hug I get from my children, English!" She turned towards her, her eyes watery, pink graves of anguish. "Earned every kiss! Each diploma! Axel went to college so he could run his business right, and I was the loudest in the crowd on the day of his graduation. I was there for my children, and I still am. They can call me day or night, and I'll answer. I earned every birthday and Christmas present, too. I ain't perfect, honey, made some mistakes as a single mother 'long the way, but I was and *am* a damn good mother. Tommy never cared about these kids!"

The woman wiped a tear away from her cheek. English's mouth twitched. She wanted to respond, to say something, to make people feel better, but there was no point. She didn't know these women, or this child in the room. She only knew Axel. She couldn't say she understood their pain, because she didn't. She had a good father. Her mother never had to struggle to pay bills. They were far from rich, but didn't live in hardship, either.

"Ms. Hendrix, I'm ignorant of the circumstances right now, but it's obvious that Axel and Dallas love you. I need no convincing. I think Axel is currently in a tight spot. All I can say is that I'm sorry this situation brought up some bad memories for you."

The woman smiled sadly, then nodded. Ms. Hendrix walked slowly around the dining room table, looking at nothing in particular. She held onto the chairs as she approached each one, tiredness in her eyes.

"I ain't one to brag, but I'd like to think Dallas got her strength and care for Lucas on account of me."

Dallas dropped her gaze and shook her head. "I did, Mama…Now, you gotta trust Axel and I to do the right thing. You're done raising us, even if whatever that thing is involves Tommy. We're not kids anymore."

"You'll always be my babies. Being a mother is a lifetime commitment. Not droppin' in here and there, when you get good and damn ready. Even when he was in the home, he was a million miles away. He didn't do anything with y'all." She stopped pacing, took a deep breath, then sighed. "He was an awful, neglectful, and downright evil husband. I got rid of him, because I had to set an example for my kids, English. No daughter of mine was going to pick a man like 'er daddy, and no son of mine was going to grow up and act just like him. I wanted to break the cycle. My mama was married to a bastard. Her mama was married to a bastard, too. My sisters married bastards. I turned around, and did the same dumb mistake. But I got away… I realized my worth and refused to have my children sucked down a drain.

"I understood the assignment, as the young folks say. That lowlife sits there in jail, after puttin' his hands on that lady, knowing she has low self-esteem. English, Tammy is a sweet and caring woman from what I gather, but she's big as a house, and Tommy makes fun of 'er because of that. He picks on her because it's easy. Like some bully. He treats 'er like trash, and now he gets to skip off into the sunset. It ain't right!"

"Mama, please…" Dallas wrapped her arms around her mother and squeezed her.

Axel leaned against the wall, his expression blank. He was there, but he was gone…

Just like she'd been during the ride home from the police station. They took turns being shades of gray.

"It may seem like I'm overacting, like this is just a phone call… just one of those things, but it's not. It's an omen. A sign." The woman's voice grew steely, and uneasiness hung in the air like smoke.

"Mama, it's not. Daddy did what Daddy does. That's all. Don't make this out to be more than it is."

"That man ain't done using you, Axel. He's going to push you too hard, and then, you'll be on him, like some animal. I know my boy… One day, Axel, you're gonna blow up on him like a great, big volcano. All of that pent up rage you got deep inside of you on account of him—it's going to come on out when you least expect it. Like hot lava. You and he get into it all the time according to Dallas, but he really ain't seen nothing yet." She shook her head, an angry grin on her face. "He don't know his son like I do. When Axel blows his top, won't nobody be able to save Tommy. Not even God." The woman's eyes turned to slits as she looked all around the room at each and every one of them.

"English, I'm sorry you had to hear all of this." She blew her nose into her napkin. "I'm sorry that our night together was ruined. That man has a way of doing that. An uncanny ability to steal joy."

"It wasn't ruined. I still had a good time, despite the fact Axel has to tend to this issue." English stepped to the woman and extended her hand to her. Ms. Hendrix smiled at her once again, then brought her close, enveloping her in a hug. When she let go, she looked at her closely. Ms. Hendrix smelled like pleasant soft perfume, cigarettes, and baked chicken.

"I suppose I've made quite the impression… me and my temper. All of my yelling didn't help. I probably spooked you. Made sure you'll never come 'round again."

"Not true," English reassured her. "I'll be back."

"Anyway, I'll try to make it up to you soon, if you'll let me. At least make you some rolls that ain't burnt." She laughed mirthlessly. Before English could respond, the woman stormed off.

Chapter Twenty

I WANTED HER shades of gray. I wanted her angelic wings, and evil horns—dull, scorched, and black. I wanted her broken glass and twisted vines. Her bitter wine, and melted chocolate. All of that darkness and disaster was mine. *She* was mine. Including the rest of her, all of her wrapped in layers of gold, from the inside out. The bits of her that were wild, vast and free, which she only showed to a select few. She was a free spirit, with a conservative soul. A complicated woman with beautifully simplistic approaches to life.

I wanted her crunchy, dried leaves, and deadly black ice. I wanted her venomous snake bites, wasp stings, and excruciating shark attacks. I am not just here for the summers and springs. I don't sit here only for the glow of a new day, and the rainbows that color the sky. I wrap myself around her stratums of gold, and cover her in my tainted, splintered wood. I protect the valuable parts of her, with the ugly parts of me. I let her enemies toss their stones at me instead. I protect her at all costs. Because her love has protected me from myself—now, things are reversed…

I don't like being wrapped in her warm gold, beamed on by the early dawn, and then told more vibrance is to come after the storm. I don't believe in fairytales, happy endings, knights on horses, or damsels in castles who sing melodies or spin thread into gold. I am used to blocking out the light by turning off the sounds, but how can that continue when I've fallen in love with the blazing sun herself, and her rays are so damn loud?

"Axel… do you hear me? Are you listening?"

English's voice dragged him from his thoughts as he gripped the steering wheel, headed to the Department of Corrections. He reached for his pack of cigarettes, but she snatched them from his hand.

"Nuh uh… I've been speaking to you for like thirty seconds straight, and you've said nothing in response. Now listen, I don't know what's going on in that head of yours right now, but you have to talk to me."

"Talk to you about what?"

"Axel." She sucked her teeth, leaned back in her seat, and crossed her arms. "You and your father have a complicated relationship. You've told me about how he wasn't around, cheated on your mother, neglected you and Dallas. Your mother gave even more details today, to let me know just how messed up it all was, but you are going to have to address this. This may be the best time, now that he's at your mercy."

"Address *what*? Nothin' can be done about any of that, English. He is who he is, and he's done what he's done."

"Did you hear what your mother said?"

"Which part? She said a lot."

"See… you're actin' up. Don't do this. She said one day he's going to push you too hard, and you're going to do like Tammy and fall, only you're going to fall right on top of him."

"That's not exactly what she said."

"Stop playing these games with me. They won't work. You're going to blow up on him if you don't have the tough conversations, Axel! What are you afraid of?"

"English, stay the hell out of this."

"What did you just say?!"

"You're not deaf. You heard me. I am sick and tired of you, Dallas, and my mother trying to pretend to know what's best for me. You don't! This was a bad idea, bringing you along."

"I don't believe this. I can't believe you are talking to me like this!"

"You just kept going on and on! I tried to ignore you and be polite, but you insisted on havin' your say in something that doesn't concern you. I can drop you off at home because I'm not in the mood to sit on your couch and get counseling like you're some headshrinker. You've got your own problems—seems you'd be more concerned about making sure Master leaves you alone instead of fixating on my deadbeat father."

"You raggedy piece of shit… listen here, boy. I'm not stayin' outta *nothin'*! Not a damn thing, motherfucka!" She pointed her finger at his face. "Did you stay out of it when you sicced Channey's Miami Vice ass on me? Had her babysit me without my knowledge? Did you stay out of it when you told your homeboy all of my personal business?"

"What are you talking about?"

"Legend's felonious, crazy behind with his 200 AK-47s, wicked right hook, and killa dogs—and that's according to you and Melanie—is runnin' around here loose, knowin' *all* my trauma, which was none of his damn business in the first place, since you want to sit there and act all righteous and indignant. I don't know that man from a can of paint! Did you stay out of it when you called the police behind my back, and told them that if they don't find that car Master was riding in, there's going to be trouble? You out here threatenin' police officers and shit, sportin' your White man privilege on account of me, making things worse! Let my Black ass say some shit like that to them… You'd be bailing me out too, right along with Tommy, for threatening a police officer. Don't you sit there and tell me to mind my business again, sir, when this right here," she pushed her finger into the side of his head, "as it pertains to me and mine, and you're mine, ALL MINE, *IS* my business!"

She didn't stop there. The verbal lashing and bashing continued… She was speaking as if she didn't have a PhD, and was damn near feral. She sounded like someone off the corner who was lambasting the world, all decorum and class lost. He turned up the music, trying to drown her out. Gnarls Barkley's, 'Crazy,' played at top volume. How fitting. His entire truck rocked from the loud music. He could see her out of the corner of his eye, but could hear no evil… All he could see was the vein in her neck jutting out, her finger winding around and around, close to his face, and her head bobbing back and forth in the way Black women sometimes did.

Yeah, he couldn't hear her… not a single word. She was drowned out, like an awful song playing deep underwater. His head throbbed, his heart sobbed. Anger rose to the top of his mind like cream.

She began pushing the radio buttons then. Static… commercials… more songs…

He was surprised she didn't just turn the damn thing off. Instead, she became crazy right along with him. Matching his insanity, turn for turn. They began to fight over the radio. He'd turn it off, she'd turn it on, then start changing stations over and over again.

"Stop it!" she yelled after acting as if she were going to bite his fingers. And then she growled, like some animal. He burst out laughing. Partially amused, partially in shock.

"You're crazy! You're *really* crazy, English! Like bat shit bonkers!"

'I Can't Go for That,' by Daryl Hall & John Oates was now on the air, and she didn't change the station. He looked at the radio, read the artist's name and song title, and froze—then snapped out of his trance and twisted the knob.

"TURN IT OFF!"

She turned it back on…

Hall and Oates were right back at it.

"LEAVE IT OFF, ENGLISH! I'm serious!"

She turned it back on, this time, leaving it at a lower

volume.

"This song reminds you of someone. Axel, talk to me. What is going on?"

He took several deep breaths.

"I don't know why I'm surprised. I shouldn't be surprised! FUCK!" He beat the steering wheel with his fist.

English adjusted her seatbelt, crossed her legs, and just stared at him. He quickly averted his gaze, for looking at her would kill him. He'd be exposed, once and for all. She'd see through him—but he had no doubt it was too late now.

She knows me too well... Just tell her. It'll be easier that way.

"I told you about my teacher, Ms. Florence."

"Yes. You said I remind you of her. What else?"

"This exact song was playing on the radio when I went to see her at the hospital... Like I told you, nobody knew she was sick. She kept it to herself. I went into that room, while Caspian and Legend waited outside. We all took turns talking to her in private. She was on a lot of pain medication. She took my hand, and she... she made me promise something..."

"Promise what, Axel?"

He drove a little faster, for his pain came a little harder. He was hearing a little more evil. And it hurt...

"Promise what, Axel?" she repeated, placing her hand around his neck and lightly massaging.

"Promise that I'd tell my father the truth 'bout how he hurt me. Promise to listen, and not block him out. I promised her that I would talk to him. But I never did..."

"And now she's in your dreams."

He nodded.

The music kept playing, and he was thankful when the song changed to something by Culture Club. It was strange how they kept ending up on this radio station, one he seldom listened to on his own. At last, they arrived, and he pulled into a parking spot.

"I want to warn you about something before we walk into this building, 800."

"What?" She unsnapped her seatbelt.

"My father is a bigot. He wasn't like Klan status or anything, but it was clear what he thought about non-White people. So, he might say somethin' stupid, maybe even insulting. He probably won't mean nothin' by it, or maybe he will, and I will deal with it immediately should it happen, but I just wanted you to be on alert."

English said nothing, but her grip tightened on her purse. He turned the truck off and helped her out of the passenger's side. Once inside, they went through the detectors, then headed to the bail bondsman's office.

"Hey, my name is Axel Hendrix, and I'm the son of Tommy Hendrix, a detainee here. He was arrested and booked yesterday. DV charge. I'm here to try and bail him out." He pulled his wallet out of his back pocket to show his ID.

A guy behind the desk walked him through the process, and explained what papers he needed to fill out.

"Make sure you put Jefferson County right there at the top, too, and I need you to give his full name, and date of birth," the man instructed.

Axel sat down next to English in the waiting area.

"I'm sure you'll never forget this night, baby. Burnt biscuits. My crazy mother and sister screaming at each other, then at me. You and me arguin' in the truck, and now this." He flipped the page attached to the clipboard, and started to fill it out.

"I'm going to remember it all right, but not for the reasons you think. There's nothing wrong with your mother. She's just clear about how she feels, and isn't ashamed to expresses it. Your sister is hard to read, the jury is still out on that, but I think I like her."

"She's just protective of me is all."

"Yeah, I figured. She's been through a lot. Tries to come off stronger than she actually is. *Wants* to be stronger, like your mama. Your nephew is sweet and innocent. As for you?" She shrugged. "You're crazy as hell, just like your mother said, but I love you."

"…And I found out tonight that you're crazy, too. Did you *really* growl at me? Cujo and The Hound of the Baskervilles, up in this bitch!"

They both burst out laughing.

"I don't know why I did that. It just happened." She laughed. "I was just in shock about us going at each other like that… There was a lot of tension, but it really had nothing to do with us. Too much is going on, we're both incredibly stressed out, and things just blew up." He nodded in agreement. "Anyway, your mother was right about another thing, too."

"What's that?" He crossed out a wrong number, and corrected it.

"You're a damn good man. From the top of your

head, down to your feet. You're hard on the inside, not just the outside, but there's a part of you that actually gives a damn about other people. Not just yourself. I love that about you. Empathy. Compassion. You've got good sense, and almost like a sixth sense. Case in point: You seem to know what I need without me telling you. That's dangerous. Men aren't supposed to be mind readers."

They smiled at one another. He wanted to kiss her right then and there, but resisted. *Stay focused.*

"I think you can just tap into folks real well, Axel. See behind the bullshit. Maybe that's why Ms. Florence came to you in your dreams. She knew you'd get the message loud and clear, and alert your friends. You don't know if Caspian has had any dreams of her, since he's yet to return your calls, but something tells me even if he has, he wasn't the first. She chose you to roll out her red carpet for, with good reason."

He kept on quietly filling the paperwork, chatting at intervals with soft music in the background—right then, a country song he'd never heard before. It wasn't long before he was back on his feet at that window by the bail bondman's desk, speaking to that same man, who took his paperwork and said he'd put it in the system. He went back to his seat beside English, and they waited, holding hands.

About an hour later, Daddy appeared at a door in the back of the room, an officer by his side. The man had a paper sack in his cuffed hands, possibly containing his jacket and cigarettes, and as he approached, his eyes lit up. Axel gave him the once over. *Daddy is looking as skinny as ever.* Face drawn as though a vacuum hose had been stuck down his throat. Unshaven, with white and dark stubble all over his face. Arms long, scraggy, and dangling, with no muscle tone. His thin brown hair was brushed back into a weak ponytail, showing his widow's peak and broad forehead.

Daddy's lips curled when they laid eyes on one another. And soon enough, he was nothing but teeth. "Axel! I'm so glad to see you!" He shot a glance at English. "Howdy," he offered, looking a bit confused.

"Hello, Mr. Hendrix," English replied dryly. It was more than evident what he'd told her about his father was at the forefront of her mind. He hated that for her.

Daddy looked even more perplexed now, but said not a word so far. Axel signed another form as the handcuffs were removed from his father's wrist. The man behind the desk gave a couple more bits of information, and off they went.

"Come on. Let's go," Axel said. Nobody said a word as they went down the steps, and out the door of that big brick building with all of those windows. Once they were settled in the truck, Axel lit a cigarette and offered his father one. Daddy took it, then made himself comfortable in the back, stretching and grunting and such.

"I sure am thirsty. You got any beer, son?"

"No, Daddy, I don't. Just a bottle of water. You want that?"

"No."

"Then you ain't thirsty. This lady here is English."

"Hi again, English. That's an unusual name." He

laughed lightly, as if he'd said something original, and she'd never heard such a thing before.

"Yes, I suppose it is. My father named me. He saw it in a magazine," she murmured.

"You look awfully well put together… speakin' like that and such." He laughed once again, and the sound turned Axel's stomach. *Isn't that great? That micro-aggression shit is at play, right before our eyes.* "You an attorney or somethin'?" Daddy questioned. "Axel hire you for my case?"

"No. I'm a book curator."

"Book curator? What in the hell is that?"

"Daddy, English ain't doing any interviews tonight, and she ain't here for you, all right? She's here for me. She's my girlfriend." He tapped his ashes in the tray, and blew smoke out the side of his mouth.

Daddy didn't say anything else after that. He could only imagine the thoughts racing through the old bastard's head, and he was sure they were nothing short of ridiculous. Axel got a glimpse of his father sitting back there in the shadows. He was hunched down, cradling his cigarette like a precious baby, smelling like fresh mud and old sweat.

English cracked a window for a minute or two, in spite of it being chilly outside. He knew why. Daddy's nerves must've been all torn up like a puppy that had gotten a hold of a newspaper. He sat there in his own mental slop, perspiring like a pig.

"Tammy wants to drop the charges, but the prosecutors are tryna make trouble for us. Probably use me as an example. It's an election year 'nd all. Headline news."

Axel rolled his eyes. "Daddy, I doubt anyone gives a crap about your case. They have bigger fish to fry. Like murderers and big drug ring stings." Axel turned on the radio. That damn Hall and Oates was playing again. He turned the station… and there it was again. A flush of heat came over him. He turned off the radio altogether, but not before catching English looking at him, her eyes wide as saucers.

"You can just drop me off when we get to the house, son. Don't worry about visiting or nothing like that. I need to get some sleep." The old man yawned. "Sure as hell couldn't get any in there, I tell ya that much. Bunch of fools hoopin' and hollerin'. Crazy bastards."

"Well, I'm sure you'll get plenty of rest tonight. It's 'spose to rain, Daddy. That's good sleeping weather."

"Mmm hmm… can you hurry up? I'm thirsty, and you ain't got shit in this truck for me. So much for a greeting!" He laughed, though Axel knew he meant every word. English's grip around her purse tightened again… "Not tryna rush you, son, but you seem to be driving a little slow is all. If I had a big ol' truck like this, I'd be flooring it just for fun! I used to have a rare Ford Mustang that went—"

"Do you know how much it cost me to bail you out?"

"Tammy told me. I 'spose you want to be paid back? You know I'm on a fixed income, and you've got that company and all, so—"

"Naw, I don't expect you to pay me back, Daddy. I just expect a little appreciation is all. You're talking pretty slick right now, especially to someone who just shelled out thousands of dollars on your behalf. I was busy tonight, too."

"Busy doin' what? Being a butt?" The old man cackled, slapping his knee.

"No, Tommy, I was busy at dinner tonight with Mama. We were kinda having a family gathering of sorts, a little shindig, and had the night all planned out. Mama even spent two hours looking for her deck of cards to play some games, and she went out and bought that good popcorn for us to sit 'round the TV and watch a little something after we ate dessert, her famous apple pie with the flaky crust."

"Your mother always tries to show off and impress folks. She cares too much about what other people think." The old man made a show of clearing his throat.

"You're one to talk. I don't even know who the hell you are, you lie so damn much."

"Axel… don't," English said in almost a whisper.

"What the hell is that supposed to mean?! Look, if you just bailed me out to get a slap on the back and for me to kiss your ass, then you can turn right on 'round and take my ass back to jail, you son of a bitch!"

"I'm a son of a bitch, all right, but that bitch ain't Mama, motherfucker. I'm sure you can do the math."

"Axel, please."

"Tommy, you messed up everything, as usual. Just like mama said. She was mad as hell tonight, and rightfully so."

"Your mama is always mad about something! What's

new?"

"I didn't get no dessert or movie, no extra time with my nephew, your grandson who you never ask about. All I got was yelled at, 'cause she's sick of you."

"Well," the old man snickered, "I'm sick of her ass, too. She was ungrateful and tried to wear the pants all the time. She wanna be a man? That's on her."

"She didn't want to be a man. She did what she did because you weren't pulling your weight. If we'd only relied on you, me and Dallas wouldn't have had nothin' to eat, or a roof over our heads. You need to be thanking her."

"I paid that woman from every one of my checks! Diapers, baby food, you name it! You want to listen to only her side of things—you was too young to remember the truth."

"I'm surprised that every time you say the word 'truth,' lightning doesn't strike. It's a foreign word to you, ain't it? Doesn't roll easily off the tongue."

"I don't need this shit right now, Axel."

"And I do?" It began to sprinkle, so he turned on the windshield wipers. "You think I wanted to be at the Department of fuckin' Corrections today, all because you like to put your hands on women?"

"I didn't put my hands on her!"

"You did! Tammy defends you all the time. She wouldn't lie about this. My question is, why in the hell would you push her in the first place? She's a woman!"

"She weighs three times as much as me, and could pound me into the ground! Her being a woman don't have a damn thing to do with it!"

"I don't give a shit if she weighed as much as five elephants stacked on top of one another. She's *still* a woman, someone you say you love. What really makes this outrageous is that this isn't your first rodeo. It was just the first time the police were called about it because she was in the hospital and got confronted. Tammy practically licks your boots when you walk past. Maybe that's why you did it, because you don't respect 'er and it's easier to terrorize someone you see as weak. Poor excuse for a man!"

"I didn't hit her first!"

"Oh, so it went from 'I didn't hit her' to 'I didn't hit her first." Liar. Every time you open your mouth, liquor goes in and lies come out."

"She smacked me. I instinctively pushed her, Axel, and she fell back. It was an accident! I never hit your mama, and I ain't never hit no lady I've been with on purpose, so stop tryna paint me out to be the bad guy!"

"You knew if you hit mama, she would have shot you faster than a narcoleptic falls asleep. You got drunk again last night, and went crazy. As usual."

"Just shut your mouth and take me home. I'll make sure you get your fuckin' money back, so I don't have to hear shit else about this! You make me sorry I had Tammy call!"

"Good! All you want to do is get in this house and get sloshed anyway, even after all that happened." He made the wipers go faster, as the rain was now coming down harder. "You don't have a relationship with your grandson, Dad. Dallas avoids you half the time because you're nothin' but a big pit of festering negativity. You only call me when you need something, or think you can get some type recognition off my name, and you treat your ol' lady like crap." *I hate you…*

"Axel, if you want to talk to me about this, we ain't doing it in front of mixed company. You're showing off because this lady is here. That's what is going on."

"Bull. I always talk to you like this, and you complain about it. Each time, I hope and pray that my outrage will mean something to you—just one time—but it never does."

"WHAT THE HELL DO YOU WANT FROM ME THEN, AXEL?!"

"Honesty! I JUST WANT THE TRUTH!" he exploded. Something was happening, and he no longer had control over himself. His heart was beating so fast, it hurt, and his anger soared so high even heaven looked far away.

"The truth about what, Axel?! What is so damn important that if you don't hear it, your entire world will crumble?"

"I want to know who you really are! I'm thirty-four years old, and I *still* couldn't tell you what you like to do for fun besides drink. I have no idea what type of childhood you had because you only told me lies. I don't know what foods you enjoyed growing up—simple things like that! And the things you did tell me, well, so much for that! I found out a lot of what you said to me when I was a kid wasn't even true. Do you know how that made me feel?!"

He slapped his chest hard, so much it stung. Burned. But nothing hurt worse than what Tommy had taken him through. The abysmal void that was never filled, only grew wider, deeper, and darker. "I felt like a damn fool, tellin' kids at school that my father had been a famous baseball player."

"All fathers make stuff up like that, Axel. It was just a joke." The man offered a choppy, stilted laugh.

"It wasn't a joke to me, Tommy. You told me that with a straight face. You told me I wasn't throwin' the ball right, and that you could teach me because you were a professional. Then came the long, elaborate story—a bunch of bull. You didn't even get in the minor leagues. You can barely hold a catcher's mitt right. The kids were makin' fun of me at school 'cause Danny's papi came over, tellin' the truth about it all. They said you were a high school dropout, trailer trash, and a loser. My friends and peers accused me of lying, but all I was doing was repeating what you told me. I believed you! For five seconds, I was proud of you! Not because of the lie you told about being famous, but because that was something I thought we could bond over. You teaching me how to play baseball. You never said another word about it, and you never tried to help me get better at it, either. That's when I realized the kids at school were right. You'd lied…"

"All right, Axel! So you want me to admit I was a bad father? Okay, fine! I was a horrible father! Ya happy now?! Does that change anything?"

"…You never came to any of my games. You'd lie and

say you were sick or had to work, and come to find out, you was at the damn bar by eleven in the mornin', or on top of some woman that wasn't my mama. Your wife at the time."

He glanced over at English, who was looking down at her phone. She'd removed herself from their space. Somehow, someway, she'd drifted away, allowing him to feel as if she was close, but not in the midst of it all. She looked undisturbed—at peace, even. It was unnerving, yet comforting.

"You believe everything your mama told you, as usual. Your mother lied on me, Axel. I am not trying to say I was perfect, but neither are you! And neither was she!"

"Mama never outright, deliberately lied to me, Tommy. I can trust her."

"Whoop dee fuckin' doo!" Daddy cracked up laughing, rolled down his window part way, and let the ashes fly out. "Is the air bothering you, sweetheart? Is it too cold in here now?" he asked English.

"No, sir. I'm fine. Thank you," English responded, not looking up from her phone.

"Go on, Axel. Go off and yell at me, 'cause you best believe, I won't be speaking to you for a long while after this shit! I have had it with you!"

"Do ya promise you won't be speaking to me again, or is this just one of your many thousands of lies? If you never opened your lyin' mouth again, that would be the best damn gift yet!"

"Axel, baby, come on. Let's try to—"

"Come on nothin', English. He doesn't want to speak

to me once I get him home and he's done using me. It'll be only a few weeks before he's ringing me up again, pretending like none of this happened, asking for some money so he can buy a bunch of scratch off tickets, or booze. And let me make something clear," he went back to addressing his sorry excuse for a father, "you can bash mama all you want. She never tried to pretend to be someone she wasn't."

"Here you go again…"

"You're damn straight here I go again, because we're not going to talk ever again after this, remember? So I'm going to have my say. Mama isn't perfect, but she's honest, and she tried to be a good mother. No, she *is* a good mother, despite the hard times we had, some of them on account of you. I know who she is! Mama's favorite color is green. She had a mutt dog named Furball that she loved to death. Her mother, my grandma Maybelle, had eleven children, and five of them died before the age of twenty-five, due to workin' in the coal mines.

"Mama went to college three times but didn't finish because she was raising two children and had no money. She's good with numbers, and wanted to get an accounting degree. She's never been farther than Ohio, but would like to go see Las Vegas one day, just for fun. She thinks it looks pretty on TV. I know a lot about mama, and barely anything about you, and that's the whole problem."

"Are you finished talking about your mother being some sort of saint, boy? Because if I wanted to see some bullshit, I would just go to a cow pasture. Why are we even talking about her?"

"You brought her up, trying to discredit her, when I was explaining to you that I was at her house for an early dinner with my girlfriend, but had to leave on account of you. I didn't bail mama out of jail. I bailed you. It's *you* in this truck. Focus on YOURSELF. The million-dollar question remains. WHY DO YOU DO THE THINGS YOU DO?! Why are you always making up stories? Do you think I'm not worthy of knowin' who my father is?" Daddy slumped even further in his seat. He looked out the window, looking thoroughly unconcerned. "I always wanted to connect with you when I was a kid, but couldn't. You'd shut me out by making up things. That was your wall. You never turned away—you'd just make up a story, one that always made you look the smartest. The biggest. The baddest.

"I JUST WANTED MY FATHER! I didn't care if you were White trash or the president of the United States. You were the one who put on airs! I never could get close to you because you weren't your authentic self. And then you'd use your lies, compare them to me, to put me down. You tried to destroy me with lies. Your own son!"

He felt the wetness on his face, and hated it. There was no turning back. The promise was having its way… the promise was being fulfilled…

"Everything was a tall tale! LIES on top of LIES on top of LIES!" Hot, angry tears blurred his vision. "I promised Ms. Florence I'd tell you what I felt, and listen to you… but I can't listen to any more lies, Tommy! I just can't! Lies didn't break me. It's the reason you told them that did."

English took his hand and squeezed it. His bones felt heavy, his body weighed down with the mass of the whole world.

Everyone was really quiet for a long while. Axel hoped it would stay that way. However, his hopes were soon dashed.

"You know what, Axel?"

"What?" He looked in his rearview window and saw his father absorbed in a cloud of smoke, his features barely discernible.

"When you get like this, boy, I wish I would've put your ass in foster care and forgotten 'bout you."

"*Fuck* you!" The truck swerved to the side of the road and he kicked it in park.

"Axel!" English placed her hand on his shoulder. He turned and looked at her. "Drive him home. We're almost there."

"He can crawl the rest of the way for all I care!"

"Axel, baby… don't stoop low. You be the man that you are, the bigger person. It's going to be okay…" She spoke in a matter-of-fact sort of way, and it helped him refocus, get back on the road, and drive.

There were only about five more minutes to go. Maybe this wasn't a good day for a discussion, after all. Maybe dad's forced sobriety caused him headaches and physical pain, which made him even more malicious and revolting than ever. Mixed emotions wracked Axel after unburdening his soul like that. In one way, it felt good. Like a relief. In another way, it opened up old wounds.

It seemed to take forever, but he was comforted when they finally arrived at the house. Axel pulled into the gravelly makeshift driveway, and could see several lights were on inside the house. *Tammy must be home.* The back door of the truck slowly opened, and dad slid out like hot bird shit. The old man tossed his cigarette onto the lawn without so much as a word, and smooshed it with his boot. Bag tucked under his arm, he got to the front of the truck, and paused. Axel looked straight ahead, refusing to give him eye contact. The bastard rested against the driver's side door and peered through the window.

"Okay, English. You take care now."

She nodded, gave a wave, and he turned and walked to the house. Once Daddy was on the steps, the old man paused, and just stood there. His back turned towards them. Axel started the truck again, getting ready to put it in reverse to ride out of there like his life depended on it.

"Hold on… do you see him?"

"Yeah. He's standing there on the steps. So what?"

"Don't drive off."

"Why not?"

"Axel, you've already exploded on him, just like your mother anticipated you would, though I doubt she realized it would come this soon. You may as well finish the job."

"What job? I've said all I need to say."

"Trust me, that's not it. I was sitting here on pins on needles! I didn't want either of you to say another word, but it was important that you did. You finally told him how you felt! You let it all out! Now, you have to listen…

you have to give him a chance to talk to you. Not with me, or with Tammy around. Just the two of you."

"I did give him a chance to talk, English. Even before you were around. Countless times. I asked him over and over to tell me—"

"No, Axel. You'd make a statement, and ask a question, but it was obvious no answer would have been good enough for you in the heat of that moment. Because you're hurting. You talk about his wall. Well, he taught you how to build walls too, baby, because now that this is all exposed, he can't get over yours. You built it too high! You have to give him a chance to climb over. Throw him a rope. Not to hang himself, but to meet you halfway."

He hung his head. It was all he could do. Look down at his boots. He didn't want to feel this anymore… He didn't want it to continue. It took all he had in him—more upsetting than having to shoot a man dead. Worse than Ms. Florence's funeral. This pain gnawed at him from the inside. It was an old pain, one determined to be a part of him. English grabbed his hand once again and squeezed.

"When you see him, you see lies, despair, and evil. You have to listen to his lies, to get to the truth, Axel. I know that sounds crazy, but just listen. I gave a good look at your father. I know he is everything you and your mother said he was, but I also saw how he looked at you when we first got to that jail. When we picked him up, he was so happy to see you! It was a genuine smile."

"That's just because he was happy to be out of that cell. He don't care about me."

"I don't believe that, Axel. I think your father is a

frightened little man. Little in character, not stature. When people lie all the time, especially to those they love, it means they are trying to hide something. Something they may be ashamed of. I was lyin' to my parents about Master all the time. I never did that before. I was ashamed of the truth, so I hid it from them. I think before you drive off, you need to toss him a lifeline, and listen. You need to *hear* him…"

Chills ran down his spine. That was exactly what Ms. Florence had said. He looked at the radio, and wondered if that song was on again. He swallowed, turned it on, and something else was playing. He sighed with relief.

"Just because Hall and Oates isn't playing, baby, doesn't mean you're off the hook." There she was, reading his mind again. Just like he often read hers. "If Ms. Florence did that song business that happened earlier, mess with the radio, then she already said her peace. She doesn't need to repeat it and play that song again, like a broken record. YOU HEARD HER JUST FINE THE FIRST TIME…"

Axel's father was now sitting on the steps, looking down. Looking broken, like an old toy.

"I don't know what's going on here, Axel, regarding this whole Ms. Florence business, but to dismiss it I believe would be more foolish than not believing it. There are things in this world and beyond that we can't explain. To some folks, it's a miracle that you and I even met. To other folks, we shouldn't even be together. What matters is only what you and I think." She pointed at him, then herself. "Now, you go on and talk to that man, and you do so with an open mind. I'm going to sit right here in this truck and read, send an email or two. He probably will do what he always does and not tell the truth, for whatever reason," she lifted both hands and shrugged, "but this is actually not about him, baby. It's about you. And if I believe in you, which I do with all of my heart and soul, then I believe in your peace and healing, too."

She wrapped her arms around him and hugged him tight. When she pulled away, there were tears in her eyes. The sight tore him apart.

"The promise you made to Ms. Florence wasn't for her, baby. She had you make that promise for *you*." She leaned forward and pressed her soft lips against his.

Wrapping his hand around her neck, he drew her impossibly closer to deepen their kiss. Then, he reluctantly pulled away, opened the driver's door, and stepped out onto the driveway. When he closed the door, his father slowly lifted his head. Father and son were looking at one another. The eyes were the windows to their torn apart souls.

Chapter Twenty-One

THE FRONT SCREEN door creaked open like a slowly opening mouth. Tammy stood in the doorway, her brown hair in a plastic clip and a bandage on her arm. An oversized denim dress flowed down to her swollen ankles and puffy bare feet. In the background, the sounds of Christopher Cross', 'Ride Like the Wind' could be heard.

"Hi, Axel," she said timidly. "Tommy, what are you doin' out here in the rain? Come on in 'fore you catch cold. Axel, you come on in, too." Her forehead wrinkled and she motioned for them to enter.

Dad sighed, shook his head as if beside himself with grief, then stood up. He dusted off his pants with the back of his hands, then started to walk up. Axel stood at the bottom of the steps, watching his father make his way to the front door. Rigid appendages moved like a spasmodic android in need of emollient along the hinges.

"Tammy," Axel called out, taking a step forward.

"Yeah?" She held the door open for his father, who entered the house and soon disappeared.

"I'll come in, but I need to speak to Tommy alone." He came up the steps, and looked at her, eye to eye. She cocked her head to the side. "He's had a long day. I 'magine he's going to go lie down upstairs. I can talk to him there."

"Axel, you don't look so well. Have you eaten, son?" She placed her hand on his shoulder. "I've got some food put away. It ain't much, but it'll do." He looked at Tammy's arm all bandaged up, and his core seared with distress and indignation.

"Tammy, I've already eaten at my mama's house. Thanks for the offer, though. Can you do me a favor?"

"Yes."

"Would you mind stayin' down here on the first floor for a few minutes? Don't come up at all. Don't talk to him. Don't say nothin'. Me and that man need to have a word."

She clasped her hands, and her face flushed with shades of red. He wasn't sure what to make of it. Perhaps she was worried for Tommy, though he'd tried to sound as calm as possible. "I was going to straighten up down here anyway." She suddenly turned away as if seeing a burst of light and looked out the front door, towards his truck. Axel followed her line of sight, and took notice of English sitting there, the glow of her phone on her face. The headlights were still on as he'd kept heat running, so his baby would stay warm.

"Who's that in your truck?"

"My girlfriend."

Tammy rocked back on her heels, coughed, then

placed her good hand on her hip.

"You thank she'd wanna come in here? It's awfully miserable out there. Rainin' and all."

"I've got the heat on. I didn't plan on stayin' long, but I can ask her."

Tammy's cheeks warmed to a pretty pink shade as they plumped like baking bread. He made a mad dash to his truck, returning moments later with English in tow.

"Hi, there. I'm Tammy. I liken myself to Axel's step-mother, though I know that's not accurate. Tommy and I ain't married, technically. We may as well be though. Just something I tell myself." Tammy chortled as she extended her good hand to shake English's.

"Hi, Tammy. I'm English. It's nice to meet you."

"Baby, I won't be long." He wrapped his arm around English's waist. "I'm going upstairs to speak with Tommy." English nodded and followed Tammy into the living room, where she took a seat on the floral printed couch.

As he went up the steps, he heard Tammy offering English a drink and a slice of chocolate cake. The steps squeaked under his weight, and he took deep breaths as he climbed. Once he reached the second floor, he noted how dull it was, especially on such a dreary night. It was an old house, rich with history, smells, and strange sounds. The walls were a peculiar shade of blue, and looked as if they were made of wood. They weren't. It was wallpaper that had splintered and torn over the years.

Framed photos of famous baseball players and mostly relatives of Tammy's hung on the wall. The area smelled like cinnamon air spray, mildly of mildew, and strong bleach. He tapped on the closed master bedroom door, and heard his father moan. Taking that as an invitation, he turned the knob and entered the room.

The radio was on, and the television, too, but on mute. Joe Jackson's, 'Steppin Out,' played at that moment. His dad lay down with a can of beer in his hand. It was unopened. Axel sat down on the edge of the bed.

Neither said a word for a long while. Axel looked around the room, noticing Tammy's make-up and perfumes neatly displayed on a mirrored tray, atop a vanity with matching chair. The windows were covered in pink and white floral curtains, and it smelled like baby powder and cigarettes. The sound of the can opening broke the silence, followed by hard gulps.

"Why'd you bail me outta jail?"

"Because Tammy asked me to." Axel stretched his legs and leaned back.

"If I had called you, you wouldn't have come?"

Axel thought about that for a moment. "…I don't know. Probably not."

Another minute or two passed.

"I don't expect you to finally open up and tell me the truth about your life, or take any accountability for the shit you've done over the course of my entire life. Takin' accountability would mean being responsible, and we both know how you feel about responsibility. If anything, what happened today might make you dig your heels in even more. All I know, Dad, is that before you die, it would be nice to know who I come from. The REAL man behind the curtain. Not the stories. Not the deceits. The real story of Tommy Hendrix the second."

Daddy sat up, then closed his eyes. He took a big gulp of beer, then set it down on a coaster on the nightstand.

"I was born in Albany, Kentucky."

"You already told me that."

"I know I told you that, but it bears repeatin' in case you forgot. My mother, Gayle, was a homemaker. My father worked here and there. Odd jobs. He only had a third-grade education, but was a self-taught electrician. He ain't have no license or schoolin', but he did a good job, I 'spose. He made enough to keep us from starving. I had two brothers, yer uncles—Theodore, who we called Ted, and Barry. Ted went off to war and never came back. Barry is still kickin', but he has a bunch of health problems last I heard. I saw him 'bout fifteen years ago, pure coincidence. We had one sister, Bethany. She was a flight attendant. Moved away to Virginia, married a teacher. She's dead now. Somethin' about her heart."

"Are your parents dead, too? I never met my paternal grandparents."

Dad took another swig of beer, then placed it back down.

"Yeah. They're gone. I left home, moved to Portland a long time ago, but I know they're dead. Family news always gets back to me, no matter where I run off to."

"What about my grandfather? How'd he pass away?"

"Story I heard was that he had a huntin' accident." He shrugged. "I don't know. Mama got dementia. Passed on in a nursin' home."

"How old were you when you moved away?"

"Fifteen."

"Why so young?"

Daddy's shoulders went up and down. "Just ready to start my life, I 'spose."

Axel turned away, and took a deep breath. The old man was closing down again. Feeding him bits and pieces of information, the bits he felt okay with. The bits that were less stained and tattered.

Ms. Florence, I tried. I told him how I felt, and he isn't doing his part. I knew it wouldn't make any difference. He ain't gonna change. The lies are more important to him than me. The lies are a comfortable tomb, and he'd rather die than live his truth.

"All right." Axel stood, refusing to sit there like some idiot and be force-fed substandard revelations. *I'm done practically begging for a miracle.* "I'm gonna head on out now."

Daddy's eyes widened, and his forehead wrinkled.

"Why?"

Axel didn't respond. *I'm not playing these games with him. He knows damn well why.* He slid his phone out of his pocket, checked the time, then put it back.

"Okay… I get it. I figured if *I* knew the truth, that's all that mattered." Axel turned to his father. The man swallowed and looked away towards the window. "I ain't one of these folks that believes my own stories though, Axel. I know the truth from fiction. Life is a bitch, and then you die. I disappointed myself, too. Not just you and Dallas. Son, what was the sense of us both being disappointed?" The old man turned back towards him, then pointed to the bed for him to sit back down.

Axel slowly sat down, but was mentally prepared to get

right back up.

"I left home when I was fifteen 'cause my daddy was strict and ruthless. I went back at sixteen, and stayed until I was seventeen. When I left the second time around, it was for good. I know there ain't nothing wrong with discipline. Spare the rod, spoil the child, but he… he was beatin' us real bad." Daddy's voice trailed and he looked towards the television, as if it had called his name. He ran his hand along his jaw bones. Over and over, petting himself.

"He was drinkin', and kickin' us. Using closed fists. Smackin' us around. All of us. If he was workin', he'd spend the check up at bars. Get drunk. Beat us worse. I was the oldest. I got it the worst as far as I'm concerned. I'm not sure why, but I did. He used to call me stupid all the time. Hit me in the head, over and over again. He fractured my leg one time, too. Wailed on it with a bat because he said I wasn't doing my chores.

"Mama took me to the doctor after a couple of days. It swole up and hurt so bad, I couldn't walk."

"He had a hunting accident, you say?"

Daddy sported a decidedly peculiar expression. His eyes grew larger, then shrank, and tightened as if he were trying to peer into a dark room.

"Axel, I don't think he had no huntin' accident. I think my brother lured him out yonder, and killed him." A strange silence spread between them as his father looked at him, darkness in his eyes. *I wonder if that the truth or a lie?* He had a funny feeling he'd never know for certain. It just felt off. Not quite right.

It wasn't his brother. It was him. That's why he left the last time. English said, 'Sometimes you have to listen to the lies, to get to the truth.'

A chill went up his spine.

"How'd you get along with your mother? I've only seen pictures of 'er. When I'd ask you about her as a kid, you never said much."

"Mama… Well, I found out from Daddy when he was drunk one day, she was pregnant wit' me 'fore they got married. It was a shotgun weddin'. I never knew that. I found out when I was about twelve or so. I ain't no psychologist, but I reckon Daddy resented her and all of us kids. Axel, my father wasn't any good. I ain't, either. Sometimes, I tried, but still fell short. It's just how it goes." He laughed mirthlessly. "Guess I got it honest. I did the best I could with what I had."

"You must not think you have much at all, then."

"Depends on what you want from me. I ain't got no big talents. Nothing anyone can hang their hat on." He tossed up his hands. "I can't sing, or play no instrument. Not good at sports. Play some decent baseball, but nothin' special. I always wanted to be real good at baseball. *You* were pretty good at it." Dad's eyes hooded. "It was a dream of mine. Didn't want to be no lawman, and wasn't interested in much, career wise, at all. I ain't got no money to live fancy free. Don't have no use for a college education." He shrank down, pushing his body against the pillow.

"Everybody has a talent. We're all born with something we can do better than the average Joe. You drove trucks at one point in time. Believe it or not, drivin' isn't just a skill. It's a talent, too. Just ask Austin Dillon."

A big smile creased Daddy's face.

"I was happiest when I was a truck driver, but then, I lost that job on account of that DUI I got." The smile quickly vanished.

"I know you had a couple DUIs in the last few years, but I never knew you had to stop drivin' because of a DUI back then."

"Yeah." Daddy ran his finger along the top of his ear, and he folded into himself. "I told everybody that the company was layin' off folks. Didn't want your mother to get wind of the truth. If she knew, she would've kicked me out. Axel, I just ain't worth shit, and ain't good at shit, all right?" He huffed. "I could get women though. They say I'm charmin' when I want to be, and clean up well." He shrugged. "People used to say I was good lookin' back in the day. I had that going for me. Got married to a lady before I met your mama. She cheated. I cheated back. We were young. Nineteen." Axel never knew of that, either. "She filed for divorce. Met your mama a few years after that, and we hit it off. I fell in love with her. More than even my first wife, Evelyn."

"What caused the problems between you and Mama when I was a baby, in your opinion?"

"She says it was my drinking. I got into drugs for a little while there, too. Cocaine, Crack and Quaaludes. Things like that." Daddy hung his head. "Guess I didn't love 'er enough after all." He paused and scratched under his arm, by his ribcage, then leaned over and lit a cigarette.

The flicked lighter illuminated his face, making his eyes glow like a cat's.

"Is this truthful enough for you, Axel?" Daddy smirked in an almost obscene way as he blew out smoke rings.

"There's no barometer for the truth. It either is, or it isn't. The truth is not arguable. It's a fact. This isn't a test."

"Sure as hell feels like it. How is me telling you all of this bad shit helpful? I'm doing it to prove to you that I can. You talked about accountability, being responsible, but that doesn't have anything to do with it. Life is just shitty, and there is nothing I can do about it."

"Nothin' you could do about it? You say your family life was screwed up. You were estranged from them. You started a new life here in Portland, and in all of that time, you never learned a trade or tried to figure out who you really were, being out from your father's thumb. You blame other people for crap that you personally could change or control. I understand." Axel threw up his hands. "A child is not a man. Everything in your childhood was what it was, but when you became a man, you *still* behaved as a child, Tommy. That was on *you.* You were beaten by your father. That wasn't your fault. You tried to beat me down with your words when I was a youngin. That IS your fault. I'm trying to understand. No more disguises. Costumes. Excuses. We're done."

"…Are you wearin' a disguise, boy?" Daddy flicked his ashes into a chipped, wooden bowl. "Everyone lies. It's survival. Not everyone needs to know the truth, no matter how much they beg and plead. The truth don't set everybody free. I learned early on that lies slowed down the beatings. Lies make women love ya, and want you to stay. Lies garner trust, and can give you talent and admiration, even for just one damn day. That's better than nothin' at all. You've killed two men."

"And? You know the circumstances around that."

"What kind of man can walk around feeling okay with blood on his hands? Even if it was self-defense? You know I had to kill someone when you were a boy. A so-called friend of mine. I've never forgotten it. It changed me."

"That was the second time you killed someone... We can leave it at that."

Daddy looked at him and swallowed. Averting his gaze, he brought his cigarette to his mouth.

"Axel, you're strong." He puffed deeper, exhaling slowly. "You've always been strong. Born just seeming to know who you were in life. Smart. Capable. You're good with your hands. I ain't beat you down with words, as you say, 'cause I hated you, was ashamed of you, or didn't want you. I did it because I loved you."

He reached for his beer, and took a big gulp. "I talked to you somethin' awful when you was a kid. I know it. I did it, Axel, 'cause I didn't want you to end up like *me*..." Dad's eyes washed over with a fine sheen. "I'd say I succeeded. You ain't nothin' like me!" His voice shook then. "That makes you special. I wasn't special. I'm never going to be special, either. I wasn't nobody back then, and I'm nobody today. Just a dirt-poor country boy whose daddy wished he was dead, and whose mama wished he'd disappear. I gave both of them their wish. I guess I'm good at something after all…"

Chapter Twenty-Two

"YOU KNOW, A coochie board," Melanie repeated. "That's what I need."

"Mel, I have no idea what a coochie board is. I think you're making this up." English walked away and sat down in her friend's apartment, shaking her head. The couch was ivory and plush. Melanie had invited her over on her day off, wanting to catch up, but English found her surroundings suspicious. The expensive 'fast fashion' furniture and decorative accents weren't something one could afford on a bartender's salary. All of this was brand new gear. *What has Mel been betting on?*

"What are you watching?" she asked, pointing to the television.

"One of them court tv shows. I DVR'ed it. I forgot what this judge's name is, but she's pretty cool. English, come on, help me remember the name of it. I need to order one for my birthday party. I could just order it online, but I want it pre-loaded."

"Preloaded? With what? Yeast infection cream?"

"Stop playin' with me. I'm probably saying it wrong, but close enough. You know those boards!" Melanie started clapping her hands and growing annoyed, as if English were to blame. "I know you know what I'm talking about."

"No, I don't, and I'm tired of talking about this, because it's just silly at this point." Melanie was looking pitiful now, putting up bowls in the kitchen cabinets. "What does it look like, Mel?"

"They have olives, and some come with grapes or little tomatoes. They're supposed to have cheese, pepperoni slices, and crackers. Things like that. You know, coochie boards!"

English sighed long and hard, then burst out laughing. "You have got to be kidding me. How have you survived this long in the world?!"

"Bitch, just tell me what it's called!" Melanie cackled.

"Call the grocery store and order a coochie board, Melanie. Wait and see what happens. Ask for a dick tray while you're at it. You're a crazy nut! That's a charcuterie board! Not coochie! Lord have mercy."

"Sounds the same to me. That's a stupid name. How am I supposed to pronounce that?"

"You taught yourself to speak fluent Spanish. I am sure you can figure this out, too. By the way, charcuterie is French."

Melanie shrugged and poured them both a glass of wine. The woman sat beside her, then rolled herself a joint. Knowing English didn't smoke, she no longer offered. English sipped her wine and looked at the television for a bit.

"Yes, your Honor. I signed a contract with Ms. Hopkins on the 8th." The plaintiff handed paperwork to the bailiff, who then approached the judge with the forms. "I gave my deposit of five hundred dollars for her to supply all of the desserts for my bachelorette party. Ms. Hopkins assured me that she knew how to make a banana pudding cake."

"…And I do."

"Ms. Hopkins, please stop interrupting Mrs. Dantley."

"Sorry, your Honor."

"I ordered three of these banana pudding cakes to accommodate my guests. Instead of usin' sugar and real bananas, like normal people, Judge, Ms. Hopkins here bought a bunch of those vanilla flavored Snack Pack pudding cups from the Dollar Tree, and some—"

"You don't know where I bought the ingredients from, hussy! And it sure wasn't no Dollar Tree!"

"We all saw the wrappers in the trashcan, Brittany! You're ratchet!"

"Liar. It was Aldi's and I got the proof! The only thing that came from the Dollar Tree was that bubble gum machine wedding ring you got on! It looks like a Barbie Disco ball. 'I love the nightlife! I like to boogie! On the Disco roooound! Oh yeah!' Be mad about THAT!"

GAVEL BANGING LOUDLY

"Ms. Hopkins! This is your final warning! Please continue, Mrs. Dantley."

At this point, English and Melanie were dying laughing. It felt so good to not think of anything but relaxing and giggling with her friend. It was long overdue.

"Thank you, your Honor. She definitely went to the Dollar Tree, because I have the receipt for that too, and this person," the plaintiff rolled her eyes at the defendant, "bought store brand vanilla wafers for the crust. There were no graham crackers like she said she'd mix with it, and she used brown slices of banana which were all throughout the dessert. Mushy. That dessert alone, for three trays of it, came up to six hundred dollars. I then had to pay an additional four hundred for two store-bought box cakes that I could've made myself for about ten dollars each. It was barely worth five bucks for all of it, and nothing was from scratch!"

"Don't matter! It still tasted good, and it took me a long time to make them."

"Ms. Hopkins, please tell the court why you are not willing to refund Mrs. Dantley's money?"

"Your Honor, I object. This isn't fair, and it isn't right. This lady's guests ate the desserts all up—no one complained at all. In fact, several people asked for my business card. I have been baking desserts for all kinds of events for over eight years, your Honor, and I have a 4.8 rating on my social media pages. How is she going to have the nerve to ask me for a refund after the food is gone? Make it make sense. On top of that, she paid the rest of the invoice. Now it's three months later, and she wants to complain. I heard she's fallen on hard times. I heard her husband lost his job, and that's probably what this is about."

"That don't have anything to do with this!"

"Like hell it don't! You're looking in the seat cushions of couches trying to find a dime or two, aren't you? You're not about to ruin my reputation and shake me down, sweetheart!"

"And you're not about to stand here in court, lie, and pass off some smooshed twinkies, stale cookies, and ninety-nine cent puddin' cups for a pack of four as wedding party cakes! Bootleg, ghetto Betty Crooker! Run me my money, honey!"

"Why do you watch this mess? You know most of these cases are staged." English giggled, tickled with the broadcast regardless.

"It's entertaining, and not all of them are fake."

"How do you know?" English reached for a bowl of popcorn Melanie had set before her earlier.

"Because my friend Kyla was on one for a paternity test, and it was real. He was the father, just like she said, but from what I know, he still hasn't paid child support… I'm so damn glad I don't have kids." Melanie slipped her tongue along the edge of the joint, sealing it, then flicked a lighter. "English, when were you going to tell me about this shit you're going through? The stalking?"

English pursed her lips, then made a conscious effort to relax her muscles.

I knew this would eventually get back to her.

"Melanie, it wasn't a situation I was telling anyone at the time. It happened a long time ago, and that's where I wanted it to stay. It was traumatic for me, and," she shrugged her shoulders, "even though there's a fair share of embarrassment and upset attached to it, I've gotten through it. It only had to be discussed because the son of a bitch resurfaced, just like a characteristic psychopathic narcissist. I tried to handle it, but the police wouldn't help me."

"Why not?"

"They said there wasn't enough evidence. By the time they started taking me seriously, I was in the middle of gunfire, in the parking lot of my job."

"Yeah, I heard."

"Who told you about this?" She popped some popcorn into her mouth, then set the bowl back down.

"It doesn't matter who told me. It only matters that I finally know. No wonder you've been acting a little withdrawn lately. Comin' to see me less at the bar. I figured maybe it was because you were hanging out with Axel, but then I'd see him and Legend, and some of his other friends, everyone except you. You're usually outgoing and lively. So what's going on with the situation right now?"

"Well, the police finally found him and questioned him just a few days ago. Of course, Master denied everything, and was cocky about it."

"That's really his name? Master?"

English nodded. Melanie rolled her eyes and shook her head. "Go on."

"So, you know the deal. He even had his fake alibis in order, but Axel already knew he'd do that. Regardless, the police told him to stay away from me and he was served with a Protective Order, which stipulates no contact of any kind, electronic or physical. I went to the court date, he didn't show up, so it worked out in my favor. Things have calmed down. No more calls or text messages after that, but I don't know… I still feel like he's not finished. The calm before the storm. He's a sore loser."

Melanie brought the joint to her mouth, and puffed.

"If you had told me, I could have helped you," she said in a groggy pitch as her eyes turned to slits.

"How?"

Melanie's cheeks compressed as she took another hit and exhaled.

"I've got guns so you can protect yourself. I keep 'em all around my apartment. Whatever you needed, I could've helped you get it. I would have lent you one in a heartbeat, honey."

"Oh, baby, don't let my suits fool you. I've got one, too. Her name is Henrietta, and she don't play."

Melanie laughed lazily, and nodded. "Cool. Good. Weapons sometimes can be taken away, fall, or jam. Do you know how to fight? With your prissy self." She sucked her teeth.

"Like, throw a punch? Yes."

"You weren't raised in the hood like me, where fightin' wasn't an option but a necessity. I need to see what you got. Get up." Melanie set her joint down.

"Oh, come on, Mel! I'm not trying to do this with you."

"It's for your own good. Now rise up." Melanie stood, straightened out her light gray leggings that clung to her shapely thighs, tugged at her crop top, then ran her hands along her thin arms, one covered in a tattoo sleeve. Her long, wavy dark brown hair was tucked behind her ears, and her stiletto shaped dark pink nails glistened under the recessed lights.

"You invited me over tonight, said you were free, and now this has turned into this mess. I just want to chill, Ms. Coochie Board!"

"Get up. For real. I'm not even asking you anymore. I have to make sure, in my heart, that you can take this guy on if he catches you by surprise," Melanie stated sternly before going behind her couch. Moments later, English was standing a couple of feet away from her. Both in their socks, they looked silly.

"Put your arm up like this. No… higher…" This went on for several minutes, with Melanie showing her how to stand, and land a solid punch.

"I told you I already know how!" English kept thrusting her arm in the air, landing most of her blows.

"You aren't that bad, I'll give you some credit, but you could hit harder, English. You have to put more power behind those punches. Legend taught me how to hit. My brother hits *hard*. Now, I'm going to show you how to do the same."

"I have a brother, too, I'll have you know. My sister is the one who taught me to fight though. I can hit way harder than this. Did you stop and think because you and I are just practicing, and you're my friend, that I'm not putting my all into it? I'm not trying to break your nose."

"Show me. I can take it. What you need to do is—"

Suddenly, her friend's phone rang. "Hold on. Stay right there." Melanie went back into the kitchen and grabbed it.

"Hey you, what's up? … Uh huh… yeah, you can drop it off… Huh? Oh, English is over here … Uh huh … Just like we talked about … No. That's not fair, you could have called him and told him that yourself… I don't give a shit, that still didn't… I said no! Why would I lie about that? … You've got me messed up. What sense does that make? Boy, bye… I will see you when you get here…"

English wondered who Melanie was speaking with. Whoever it was knew about her. A feeling of dread filled her. Making her way back to the couch, she put back on her shoes and grabbed her purse.

"English, where are you goin'?"

"I remembered I had to take care of something," she mumbled as she made her way to the front door. Her body became hot, her head throbbed—the start of a panic attack. She prayed she could get to her car before it took full effect.

"English!" Melanie raced after her and grabbed her arms, standing in her way. English began swinging on her, fighting for her life. The practice drills were all over. This was the real McCoy. She could feel the woman trying desperately to block her blows. "English, stop! YOU'RE HURTING ME! What the fuck is wrong with you?!"

English pushed Melanie off her, and they both landed on their asses, breathing hard, panting, and glaring at one another.

"Who were you on the phone with, huh?! You know Master! I KNOW HE'S GOTTEN TO YOU! He's coming right now, isn't he?!"

When she saw the look on Melanie's face, she knew she'd lost complete control. She'd made a serious mistake.

"You actually think… you actually think I'd do something like that to you?" Tears welled in Melanie's eyes. "No, I don't know no man named Master! That was Legend on the fuckin' phone, English! My brother! He is the one who told me about everything that happened to you. He didn't even know you and I were friends when he finally started speakin' to me a few weeks ago! We've been estranged. I told you that. I had asked him what he was up to, and he said he was moving back to Portland. I wondered why, since last I heard, he swore up and down he'd never live here again.

"He said Axel came to see him and convinced him to return, that it would be better than where he was at. He then told me he had a job lined up, a place to stay, and that Axel's girlfriend is being messed with by some weirdo, and he was helpin' him keep you protected while Axel was at work. Said he was going to reach out to a friend of his who could help. That's when I told him that, *'Hey, I know English. I introduced them. She's one of my best friends.'* That's all! That's it!"

English scooted away into a corner, brought her knees to her chest, and started to pound the floor. Too much had happened, far too fast, and it didn't stop. Pure torture. The son of a bitch had even sent a photo he'd taken of her when she was entering her job the week prior. She didn't tell Axel for he would have gone apeshit. The showdown in her work parking lot was the last straw. Channey was still watching her, and now she was grateful for the extra set of eyes, despite holding resentment about the matter, too.

"Melanie, I'm sorry! Sis, my life isn't mine anymore, and I'm losing my mind. One time, Master got into a friend of mine's ear and turned her against me. All of that started coming back to me when I heard you on the phone. I know it sounds crazy, but it was like I was havin' a PTSD episode. Not only do I have this weighing on me, but you know Axel had that trouble with those guys, whoever they are, bothering him because he saw that man trying to destroy evidence. I'm worried about him. He said everything is fine now, but you know him. He's probably not telling me what's really going on. If something happens to him, that will hurt me so badly, Mel. I love him so much. I don't want him going to jail or worse, on account of me."

"I know you love him, English, and despite you getting mad at me initially about betting on you two that night at the bar, I knew you'd be good together. I hadn't seen Axel in forever. It was like a miracle."

She smiled at her friend, and wiped her tears of anger away with the back of her hand. "Girl, it's been rough." Melanie scooted closer and wrapped her arm around her, squeezing. "Your brother's friend babysits me. That's sad. Pathetic."

"No it's not. Just be glad you got someone that'll do that for you."

"You're right, but it still sucks. I can't go to the store without being paranoid… wondering who's around." She sniffed and shook her head. "All this time has passed, and this monster is still thinking about me, Mel. I was afraid to leave him, not only because of what he'd do to me if I got caught, but what he'd do to the people I loved. He isn't done. Protection Order or not. I just want my life back."

Melanie kissed her cheek and squeezed her once again.

"English, I know what kind of woman you are. You like to be in control. I wouldn't say you give a damn about controlling other people, but as far as your life is concerned, yeah, you want to run that, and run it well. I admire how you set goals and meet them. You're the lady that's calm and always has the answers. I call you about so many things, and if you don't know, you always help me find out. I ain't never have somebody stalk me like this, so I'm not going to even pretend I know what you're going through. Hell, even when I was a dancer and the occasional crazy guy would try to do some weird shit, it never got to this level. You're my girl, and I wish you would've told me. I know I already said that, but… I could've been there for you is all, just like you've been there for me."

The two just sat there hugging one another tight. They were two different women. Totally different lives, backgrounds and interests. What drew them together was their strength. Melanie's buzzer rang. They both got to their feet, then Melanie made her way over to the camera.

"It's Legend. He borrowed some video game equipment from me. Damn, he got here fast." She laughed as she pushed the button. English returned to the couch and plopped down. "Come on up." Moments later, English was staring at a doppelgänger for Roman Reigns, only with freckles, 365 natural jet black waves, and piercing light hazel eyes.

"You look like Roman Reigns." She blurted out her thoughts.

"People tell him that all the time, but he doesn't see it," Melanie said with a laugh. "I think he does, too."

Sporting motorcycle gloves, he went to place a cardboard box he was carrying down on the floor by the door, and stared at her.

"Why are you looking at English like that?!"

"She's cute. Why else?!"

"That's Axel's girlfriend, the one you've been helping behind the scenes, so don't do no disrespectful shit and try to hit on her." Melanie pushed him, but he barely budged. "He's a damn pervert, English. Watch out."

"This is my first time seeing her," the big man said, and then, he burst out laughing so hard, he turned red in the face. English mustered a smile amid her confusion.

"What's so funny?" she asked with a smile.

Legend grabbed his phone from his pocket, keeping his eye on her as he dialed someone, putting them on speakerphone.

"AXEL!"

"What?" she heard her boyfriend reply on the other end.

"Maaaan! You ain't tell me English was a lil' chocolate drop!" Now he was laughing hysterically, almost toppling over. English grimaced, though the man's laugh was actually quite funny within itself. "You've crossed over again to the dark side. Does yo' racist, Skeletor, Crypt Keeper, White Walker lookin' ass daddy know about this shit?!" he teased. "I remember old man Tommy told me to turn my jungle music off, called me a nigger lovin' wigger, then offered me a beer. You cussed his ass out. Good times, man!"

"Legend, I'm busy. Do you actually *want* something, asshole?"

"You just can't leave the sistas alone, huh? I keep catching you with 'em, man! You're out of control, but at least you have good taste. English over here at my sister's spot lookin' like a snack." The man winked at her, and she scowled.

"I know she's there, and sadly I see she had to meet you today, too."

"You should have told me, man. This is good shit."

"I didn't realize I had to run my datin' life past you first. Are you the interracial courting police? You're mixed your damn self. You're not even Black. You're half White and half Puerto Rican, so why you feel the need to—"

"Man, I done told you a million times that Puerto Rican is not a race. I get so damn tired of tellin' people this." Legend's brows rutted. "And besides, I have a little African in me, on my father's side. My half-brother, Sutani, you remember him, he took one of those DNA ancestry tests. He has like seven percent African, so that means I probably do, too."

"A lot of Puerto Ricans have African blood, Axel." Melanie called out from the kitchen. "Even those of us who look White—it doesn't mean we are. Our father calls himself White, but his great-grandmother was Sudanese."

"Legend, thank you for the ancestry lesson, and for

letting me know you approve of my Black girlfriend… like I give a shit what you think. If I find out you were flirting with her, I'm gonna rip your tongue out of your mouth. I gotta go. You know I'm working. Make sure you're on time tomorrow. You were fourteen minutes late yesterday."

"Is this the part where you call me Toby, and tell me Toby is a good name?"

"Legend, shut up."

They both laughed.

"OKAY! YES, SUH! I will be quiet! I promise I will be right there early in duh mornin', boss! I was late 'cause I had to feed the hogs and tha dogs! Hey Master Thor, prominent God in Germanic paganism, you 1960's-Jesus-on-the wall-with-flaxen-hair lookin' mothafucka, want me tuh schuck 'nd jive for ya on FaceTime? I got my tap shoes on, just for you!"

"Legend, you're an idiot." Axel laughed, a stifled, somewhat uncomfortable sound.

"I shore promise it won't happen again! Meeze bein' late 'nd all! You just too good to me, suh! Got any cotton you want me to pick? Commercial say, it's the fabric of our lives!"

Axel hung up on him, causing Melanie and Legend to burst out laughing again. It was obvious they had the same warped sense of humor.

"Don't mind Legend, English. He's just silly," she stated, as if she weren't part of the problem. She returned with a couple beers, and the three sat down. After a few moments of small talk, Legend turned serious. He grabbed the remote control and turned off the television, then turned to English. The seriousness of his expression grabbed her soul and squeezed. Meanwhile, Melanie continued to smoke.

"Let me explain something to you. I'm not Axel. I don't love you, so I don't have to spare your feelings. You're bad. Ain't no denying that. Nice to look at, I can see why he noticed you, but this is no minor league shit. You fuck around with Axel, you've entered the big leagues. My brother ain't no punk. Love is a battlefield, and we fight tooth and nail for ours."

"What in the hell are you talking about?" she asked calmly, taking a leisurely sip of her wine. *This man is bonafide crazy. He's gorgeous—but crazy.*

"Baby girl, don't play stupid with me."

"I'm not. You can call me English."

"Lil' English Baby Girl." She rolled her eyes. "You're attracted to his lifestyle. You know damn well he's not just some rock 'nd roll lookin' type of mothafucka who loves his trucks 'nd shit. His profession is just the tip of the iceberg. Axel is about that life. You *know* who he is, and what he's about. So with that bein' said, you do realize he's going to handle that mothafucka, right? Point blank, period."

English shot Melanie a glance, but she didn't seem the least bit phased from the conversation. "Don't go lookin' at my sister to try and see if I'm for real. I'm talkin' directly to *YOU*." He pointed in her face.

"First of all, sir, you are entirely too intense. You need to take it down a notch or two, and keep your finger out of my face. Secondly, just because you sound like a Black man doesn't mean you are. Just thought you needed a wakeup call. Thirdly, I do not know you, or where that finger has been. Lastly, though the idea of him pushing up daisies appeals to me, I'll be honest, I know God would want me to rise above that."

"God? The same dude that sent a flood to wipe out ninety percent of people off the face of the Earth?" The man burst out laughing. "Oh, that's funny! God IS the creator of justice, baby! Sometimes, with justice comes violence. It's just that simple. We can't always compromise or talk shit out. Some things are beyond negotiations of any sort. That's not how the real world operates. God gave us fists."

He snatched off his gloves and shook his tattooed hands in the air. "These hands can make knives, grenades, bombs, airplane missiles, submarines, pirate ships, drones, swords, bows and arrows, razors, and of course guns. Rulers are not soft. God is the *ultimate* ruler, and He broke the mold when He made mothafuckas like me and Axel. I don't know why some people think God is like this old White dude in heaven preachin' peace. Nahhh… peace comes at a price. Ain't shit in this life for free. REAL TALK. Church."

"I wouldn't mind getting into a philosophical discussion about God with you, but I also don't want anyone, except Master Whitefield, going to prison if it can be avoided."

"That's why when we move by logic, and not emotion, things get taken care of smoothly. You see the ducks being put in a row—that's all by design. This isn't the first time we've had to send a message."

"Why are you so involved in this? I know Axel asked for your help, and you care about him, but you are risking—"

"You ain't alive if you aren't willing to take risks, baby. The difference now in my life, English, is that I make *calculated* risks. This isn't a small issue. You could literally die if this guy got a hold of you, and Axel doesn't play around when it comes to his friends, let alone his woman. I'm the same way. Axel helped me, and now, I'm helping him. This guy that's messing with you has gotten in way over his head and doesn't even know it. He's about to find out though…"

Melanie was quiet as hell, unnervingly so. It almost seemed as if she hadn't heard a word, but English knew better than that.

"Speaking of which, thank you for introducing me to your friend, Channey. She and I really clicked, and I'm glad she was there."

"Of course… of course… She knows what she's doing. This Master Harasser wants to stalk people? Well, we're now stalking *his* ass…" Her heart began to beat all the faster. "This isn't a game." His tone rose sharply, and the deep huskiness of his voice saturated the words. "So, don't you worry about a thing, okay? We're not going to let a damn thing happen to you. And that's on God." She nodded, not sure what to say. "My boy got this under control."

He ran the pad of his thumb against the corner of her eye, as if wiping away a tear.

"Hey, Melanie, I can't smoke due to Axel's rules—slave drivin' ass—but I do want a cigar. You got any left?"

"Yup. I got you." Melanie got up and walked off to

her bedroom.

English didn't say a word. She hated him already. He was loud and intimidating on purpose. Kind of like Axel, but less polished, and seemed to have less self-control. Still, she struggled with this first impression. He was abrupt, uncouth, abhorrent. And yet, somewhere beyond the iron fortress, he had a dark charisma—and a good heart. He cared a hell of a lot about Axel. It was actually touching. He cared about his sister, too. She didn't know their complete history, but the bit she was aware of made her understand that these two men had been through the fire and back.

In that moment, she felt more blessed than ever to have met and fallen in love with Axel and wondered if meeting Melanie first, so long ago, was already written in the stars? Maybe Ms. Florence didn't speak to Axel first, after all. Maybe, she got to her, years ago, putting her in the right place at the right time to meet Melanie, so everything could flow as it should. On top of it, Axel said that Ms. Florence was a history teacher. She understood the importance of the past, and how it shaped the future. Turned it into three promises…

She took another sip of her wine and blinked away tears—this time, ones of joy.

Maybe this was the hand of God, after all? A divine intervention of epic proportions…

Chapter Twenty-Three

THE SOUNDS OF 'Blue Moon of Kentucky,' by Patsy Cline, reverberated throughout Axel's house. A bad rainstorm had knocked the power out in much of Portland, and the moon was bright and high in the atmosphere, affording much needed light.

English slipped out of her black rain jacket and boots. The ritualistic weekend date she'd grown dependent upon was now underway, but a heaviness hung in the air, like the big raindrops that fell from the sky. It had been a few days since they'd had time together, and in typical Axel fashion, picking up some fast food, scarfing it down to the beat of rock and roll, then off to his house to screw was in his eyes the ideal formula for a romantic good time. *Those fries were good though…*

She could still taste the salty fries on her pallet. She slipped her tongue along the edge of her mouth to taste a bit more. Standing at the bottom of the steps, daydreaming, her thoughts turned into clouds—fluffy nothingness. When she went to lick her fingers for another taste of salt, he grabbed her hand and licked her fingertips for her. She screamed giddily when he suddenly plucked her from the floor like a flower, and carried her up his staircase, pausing only to kiss her. *He's been so quiet…*

That week, Axel called and texted, per usual, but they were far less expressive and specific. Her mind was working overtime, wondering what trouble he may have immersed himself in. She questioned him about the police updates regarding his own case, and he pretty much shuffled her inquiries under the rug, assuring her things were fine, and he was not worried. Well, at least that made one of them. She wanted to know more, and though she hadn't brought it up to him, Legend's words from the other day haunted her: *"He's got this."*

What was Axel planning? What did Legend know?

If I had asked, I might have regretted it.

So, she let it go.

"You comfortable, baby?" he asked after he deposited her on his bed.

"Mmm hmm."

Plop plop… plop… plop. Plip… plop…

"What's that?" She rose onto her elbows and looked across the room.

Axel casually glanced over his shoulder as he unbuttoned his shirt.

"Gotta leak I have to fix is all. A bucket is catchin' the rain. Roof problem there by the gutter."

She strained to see, but it was useless in the dim room. The sound of the leaky roof blended in with Apalachee Don's 'Eagles' in a strong, off-beat way. As Axel moved about the room, the floors creaked under his gait. He lit two white candles, placing them on either side of the bed. The small flames danced, creating monsters and angels that scaled the walls, big and tall.

"Power should be back on soon. Don't usually take that long," he assured as he undid the button of his jeans, jerked down his zipper, and discarded his clothes. Soon, he stood before her completely nude, dick hard. He gathered his threads and put them in a hamper. After lighting a fire, he fiddled with his phone, turning up the volume to make the music louder.

"I'll use my phone for a little ambiance. It's got a ninety percent charge. This should do."

The bed sighed from his weight as he reached for her arms, one at a time, and outstretched them like a bird's wings. Then, he placed earbuds in her ears, and the music from his phone played for her, in a private show. After disappearing for a spell, he returned with a small bowl of ice cubes. A lungful of air tethered within her as he placed the bowl on the nightstand, then proceeded to kiss her up and down her body… real slow.

Her eyes darted around the room, then, she focused on him solely, watching his every move, and her heart quickened when he grabbed one of the ice cubes, raised it high above her body, and let it drip all over her. The coolness sent chills through her soul, the room growing colder from the lack of electric heat, and he chased each drop with a swirl of his tongue, licking it up with the delight of a warm mouth. Cool air entered her mouth when her lips parted.

She watched him tasting every inch of her, traveling up and down her body like a tour guide of the carnal kind. The candlelight illuminated the hairs on his arms, making them appear almost translucent. He stopped to pick another chunk of ice. Placing it between his lips, he stared into her eyes as he traveled down her sternum, her stomach, the dip of her navel, and the valley nestled between her legs. Hips writhing, rising and falling, she screamed beneath him as he used the half-melted cube to tease her clit, creating intense sensations that blended with the heat of his mouth…

Plip… Plop…

Securing the cube in his mouth, he dipped low between her thighs and sucked her clover, his beard brushing roughly against her pussy lips with each hard suck and tongue fuck. She grabbed his hair, twisting the long strands between her fingers and yanking as he deposited a slither of ice inside of her. Slurping, pulling and licking her clit, he consumed her, his sighs and moans now loud enough to hear over the music. Djo's, 'Roddy' played so smoothly around his motions. He crawled up her body, his finger now on her pulse, a fast butterfly of movement… eyes rolling back as he sent her to the land of ecstasy, playing with her snatch like a pro. Seizing one bud out of her ear, he whispered in it…

"You taste like heaven, baby. When I'm without you, it feels like hell. I'm going to fuck you like a demon, and make you float away like an angel…"

"Ahhh…"

Back arching, chin up, eyes closed… *He can see me…*

He can taste me… He can touch me… He can hear me…

She exploded like a grenade as, 'I Only Have Eyes for You,' by The Flamingos came on. Gliding his tongue all over her inner thighs, he sealed his love with a kiss, then lay on his back. Positioning her over him in a reverse cowgirl position, he grabbed his dick and helped lower her down on the thick, long, addictive love muscle she couldn't resist. She fell back onto him, rotating her hips, gyrating and inching up and down his thrusting rod as he lavished her neck with kisses. She came again, and again, drizzling like the rain… her inner thighs streaming with her balm.

Crisscrossing his arms around her breasts, he held her to him as he fucked her hard and with due diligence from beneath her. The bed shook under their bodies as he kissed all over her shoulder, and the side of her face. Tommy James and the Shondell's, 'Crystal Blue Persuasion' played as another orgasm rose and took her down. Long, thick fingers reached between her legs and gently massaged her clit. Around and around he went, pumping her hard, making her so weak, she could barely speak.

Slipping from beneath her, he removed the earbuds from her, and allowed them both to hear the music at the same time. He slid his arms beneath hers, wrapped his hands around her face, and roughly kissed her. His hard, hot body moved up and down between her legs to the rhythm of the music.

"Give me that pussy, baby…"

He wasted no time pushing inside of her, full speed ahead. She looked into his eyes and fell in love a million times over. When he'd had his fill, he tossed her roughly onto her stomach, yanked her ass backward to meet his hot and sweaty groin, and fucked her from behind, his balls smacking loudly against her pussy. His animalistic grunts turned her on, as did his swaying hair that swept across her flesh like soft kisses with each thrust.

The lights flickered, as if they were coming back on… but it was only a tease. They remained in the dark, the candles still bouncing light, sweat dripping down and onto her body as he ravished her. She shuddered when he slipped his thumb into her ass, pounding her pussy simultaneously. The room began to spin, and song after song played until he'd broken her down to the point she was beyond gratified, and sexually delirious. Then, he suddenly yanked out of her, and she felt his velvety release.

"Uhhh! Uhhh!" The bed shook as he jerked his dick, draining his seed in fast spurts all over her ass cheeks and lower back.

Like a phantom with a big cape, he removed himself from her presence. The room was cloaked in shadows, and on his way to the restroom, he blew out one of the candles. She lay on the bed, using the little strength she had to roll over onto her back. Her pussy ached and pulsed from his beautiful intrusion. Thighs flopping open, she looked up at the ceiling, then at the big stained-glass windows. In the distance, she heard the water of his bathroom pouring, the plip plop of the rain filling the bucket, and the sounds of 'Crimson and Clover,' from Tommy James. Somewhere between the blue moon of

Kentucky and the 'keep on uh risin',' she fell asleep.

When she awoke, her sense of time was distorted, like a Salvador Dalí painting. Her body was weak yet satisfied, her mouth dry and her eyes weary. She was floating in a dream. Dense cigarette smoke filled the room, and she realized she was being watched from afar. Sitting up, she made out the outline of her beloved in the dark. Axel sat across the room, naked. His long, muscular limbs hung loosely as he sat in a chair, the moment Mazzy Star's, 'Fade into You' started to play. She could hear him singing along to the lyrics, and bobbing his head to the beat.

Plip plop… plip plop…

"Aren't you going to ask that I make you a sandwich since you laid it down on me so good?" she said between two yawns, a big smile on her face that she couldn't erase even if she tried.

He grinned, tapped his cigarette in the ashtray, and shook his head. "If you can get up to walk your ass down the steps and over to the kitchen to make a sandwich, then I didn't lay it down at all. You should be incapable of walkin' right about now, and if by chance you *still* can, I'll make sure to fix that."

She stretched, grinning wide now.

"800, I gotta question for you."

"Yeah?" She tucked her hair behind her ears and yawned again. "What is it?"

He took a drag of his cigarette, flopped back in his chair, then ran his hand through his hair, raking it away from his face. "What are you doing around this time, next year? Is your schedule open?"

She cocked her head to the side, not certain what to make of his question.

"What? Next year?" She shrugged. "I don't know."

He picked up a glass from a small table next to him, brought it to his lips, and swallowed whatever brown liquor was in it. Placing his cigarette in the ashtray, he casually stood up, stretched, and made his way over to the bed. He slid beside her, and she braced herself. If he was going for another round, she hoped her body could withstand it. She was sore all over, and it hurt so good.

Gliding his hand beneath her pillow, he pulled out a small burgundy box. Before she could process what was happening, he opened it, exposing a large diamond ring. Her heart throbbed.

Plip… Plop… plip… plop…

"I was hoping you'd be coming down the aisle toward me a year from now. So, is your calendar open or not?"

Wrapping his hand around the back of her neck, he brought her in for a kiss. Her body grew hot all over, and she fought tears of joy. Stomach knotted, she was riding a high of excitement and shock.

"Oh my God, Axel…"

"So, can I pencil you in for next year? Will you marry me, 800?" he whispered close to her ear. *Good God…*

"Yes! I'll marry you!"

They brought their lips together, relishing the wetness of tongues while eager fingers roamed each other's forms. He paused just long enough to slide the engagement ring on her finger. She barely had time to look at it before he snatched her, bent her over the bed, and knocked her knees apart. Grasping the sheets while the sun peeked through the stained-glass windows, she let loose her screams of elation and lust…

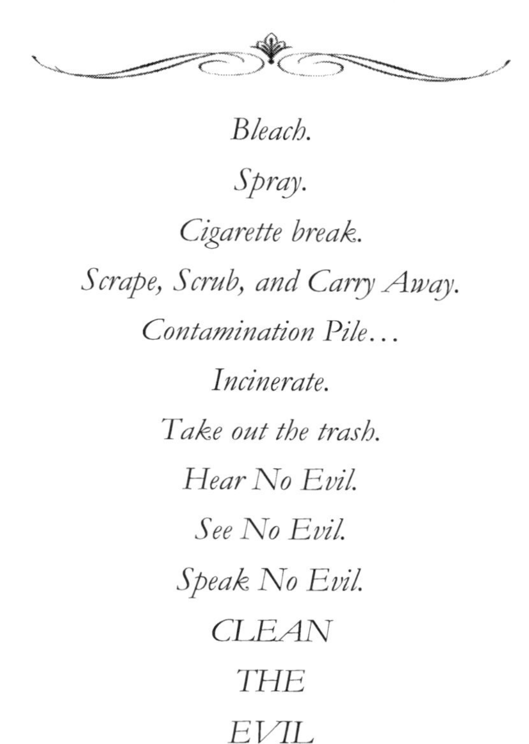

Bleach.

Spray.

Cigarette break.

Scrape, Scrub, and Carry Away.

Contamination Pile…

Incinerate.

Take out the trash.

Hear No Evil.

See No Evil.

Speak No Evil.

CLEAN

THE

EVIL

AWAY…

REPEAT…

A man cannot serve two masters…

Axel got in his work truck, exhausted from the day, but the night was just getting started. It crept in with tiny steps, sneaky and quiet, threatening to pilfer peace, and exchange it with catastrophe.

He seized his phone from the dashboard, and made an important call.

"Okay, it's time. I need to confirm for the final time. Are you certain he's there? It's really him?"

"Yes," Legend explained. "He fell for the bait, and said he's coming by himself, but we know that probably isn't true. This man trusts no one."

"As he shouldn't. He's crazy, not stupid." He disconnected the call.

He put his white, unmarked business truck in drive, then entered the flow of evening traffic.

'Night Crawling,' by John Cale played from his stereo, and he lit a cigarette as he headed over to the old, abandoned cathedral. Visions of broken stained-glass windows, Ms. Florence bowing her head to pray, and smokey images of his father cutting his wrist real slow while in his bed when he was just a little boy edged their way into his mind like maggots. After he and Tommy had that powwow and spoke hard truths, it was strange how even some of the shit Axel had buried and tried to forget re-entered his brain and forced him to rewatch the old movies of his past. The black, sticky tar of trauma came dripping down, shrouding everything in despair—but he stood his ground. Snatching himself out of his thoughts, he focused on the issue at hand. Using the Bluetooth, he commanded his phone to call his mother.

"Oh, my Lord, Axel. Now you know I'm old and asleep. I can't stay up past nine PM it seems!" Mama laughed. He could hear her television faintly in the background.

"Hi, Mama. Sorry to wake you. Just wanted to tell you that I love you is all."

"Oh… well… I love you too, Axel. More than you'll ever know." She yawned. "I spoke to English yesterday. We're going to meet up for lunch soon. I'm excited about the weddin'. I am so happy for y'all."

He smiled at her words. "Yeah, she told me y'all were getting together soon. She's excited about it, too. Look, uh," he ran his hand down the side of his face, then slowed as he approached a red light. "I just got off work, and I'm dog tired. Not going to hold you. I just wanted to hear your voice, Mama, and tell you how much I appreciate you. Even when I was givin' you trouble when I was a youngin, I knew how hard you worked so Dallas and I could have a decent shot at life. You're one in a million, Mama."

"…Are you high?"

He burst out laughing, then she followed suit.

"No, Mama, I'm not high."

"You don't normally talk to me like this. It's a pleasant surprise, but I 'preciate it all the same. I'll see you next week. Call me tomorrow, ya hear?"

"Okay. Goodnight."

"Goodnight, honey."

He ended the call, took a few puffs of his cigarette, then made another call.

CALL… TOMMY…

He didn't expect the old man to answer. Tammy said he'd been drinking himself into a stupor the last few weeks, far worse than before. That truth serum knocked him off of his feet, and Axel was certain he still hadn't heard even half of his old man's true tales. The truth was

Tommy's kryptonite, and he'd OD'd on it.

"Hello?" He knew from the tone alone, the old man was pissy drunk. Instead of it making him angry, he felt all the sorrier for him.

"Daddy, you probably won't even remember this because you're wasted, but I just want to tell you that I love you. That's it."

"…I… I love you too, son… I hi-dirk-fed…" The phone began to break up.

"Daddy, I can't hear you. You're breakin' up on me."

"Oh… I fell on my ass." The old man burst out laughing. "Can you hear me now?"

Axel smiled sadly, and tapped his hand against the steering wheel.

"Yeah, I can hear you now, Daddy… I hear your evil, and I hear your goodness, too. I gotta go. Be careful."

He disconnected the call and kept on driving. When he arrived at the old Catholic church with its boarded-up windows and dark smudges from a fire that had taken place in the 1990s, he looked around the parking lot and spotted a black Land Rover parked by itself. Tossing his cigarette out of the window, he cleared his throat and cracked his neck. He kept on driving until he was past the church, but kept it in his line of sight. It wasn't long before another car pulled up next to it.

His heart beat like a snare drum…

"He's got company."

His next breath, his will to live in the flesh, stepped out of a black van. English was wearing all white from head to toe, and her black hair was brushed away from her face. No makeup. A glum expression. Two women stood near English, and one had her by the arm, practically dragging her in front of a guy he knew by name and reputation. English appeared calm, despite the situation, but he was fast losing his grip on self-control.

A light complexioned Black man in shades and a gray suit stepped out of the passenger's side of the Land Rover, a wide smile on his face. Three other men got out of the car, standing all around him like a protective fortress. He spoke arrogantly to her, calling her Shira…

"My bride is here!" He threw up his hands, then embraced her. The men and women around him clapped and began to speak in a language he couldn't understand. "Shira is a Hebrew name. שירה … a Hebrew name of significance that means "poetry," "singing," or "music". I named you that because of your beautiful voice when you spoke, Shira. It was like music. The way you speak is like poetry. It was the first thing I loved about you, apart from your beauty. Your heart. Your intelligence. Your faithfulness. Your voice is unique, and captivating.

"The way you speak draws people to you. It always has. People get captivated by the way you express yourself… A beautiful Black woman who speaks with such elegance and is in the know. I'm glad you called me today, came to your senses, and realized where you belong. You still have to prove yourself to me. I can tell extensive damage was done to you." He looked her up and down, disgusted. "You being called English is an insult. I told you that when I first allowed you next to me. No Black woman should be called a name like that. It's an abomination, just like you. That name is below you! Do you hear me?"

"Yes, Master." She clasped her hands together and lowered her head.

"I forgive you for the trouble you've caused me, Shira, but it will take a long time for you to redeem yourself in my eyes. You're going to go through some trials and tribulations. Look how much I love you, all of the things I endured, to get you back. Traveling from city to city, following you. Watching over you to make sure you were safe, and what did I get in return? You runnin' to the White man! You went to the police, knowing they don't give a shit about us as a people. You were dating a White man, too. You're filthy! Disgusting! Contaminated! Like some animal! I bet you let that stringy haired beast nut in you. How revolting! You lay down with dogs, and are bound to have fleas. I will have to put so much time and energy into getting you back on track, it may not even be worth my while, after all, whore!"

He then lifted his arm and smacked her so hard, she fell to the ground.

Axel's fingers itched and his head began to throb. Rage bubbled within his core like a pot of water on the stove, getting hotter by the second. The fucker took a cloth, wiped her blood off his hand, then helped her to her feet.

"What do you have to say for yourself, you dirty ass bitch?"

"…I'm sorry, Master." English's voice cracked.

"Say it again."

"I'm sorry, Master."

"Sorry for *what*, Shira?!"

"For leaving you. Betraying you. Losing your trust. And disobeying the commandments."

"Get this slutty, white dick lovin' bitch out of my face! I'll deal with you tonight." He chuckled as he adjusted his pants.

The man seemed to turn on and off like hot and cold water, on a dime. Two women took hold of her and started to get her back into the back of the black van.

...And go!

Axel sped to one end of the parking lot, blocking the exit, while Legend watched for his cue, and blocked the second outlet. Jumping out, they ran towards the small crowd, guns blazing...

"DRIVE OFF IN THAT VAN, AND I WILL FUCK YOU UP!" Axel screamed.

Tires screeched and yelling ensued. Before he knew it, he was practically airborne, shooting into the night as the black van barreled towards him.

"TAKE HIM DOWN, NOW!" Legend yelled in the distance as he blasted his AK-47 into the Range Rover, killing the driver before he could even get out of park.

Blood splatter painted the concrete as cracks of light rent the sky, gunfire ablaze. Smolder from the weapons quickly filled the air. Limbs fell upon the pavement, and groans of pain and pleas came from all directions. Axel shot directly into the windshield several times, causing the black van to run into the side of the church. The front of it crushed like a tin can. Racing to the van, he opened the back door where English had been shoved.

"Baby..." he said when he saw her.

Her head was bloodied, but otherwise, she looked okay. He shot into the vehicle a few more times after seeing a couple of the bodies twitch, then picked her up in his arms and walked away. After he was a good distance from the vehicle, he released her, allowing her to stand on her own two feet—just as she wished to do. English stood there shaking like a leaf, grasping her gun tight, eyes wide. The damn thing was smoking.

"I shot him... I... got him..." She smiled sadly, tears rolling down her cheeks. "I SHOT THAT FUCK BOY!!! YOU DIABOLIC MOTHAFUCKA!!! ROT IN HELL!" She ran over to his dead body, and spit on it.

Damn...English, I didn't want this. You put me in a bad spot. You confronted me... you asked me what I was going to do, and I told you it didn't matter because you couldn't stop me. I didn't want to lie to you. You said since I couldn't stop you, then we had to do this together, you wanted to see that he was really gone, once and for all, with your own eyes.

He shot a brief glance around the parking lot. Blood and broken glass everywhere. "I never wanted you to be tainted like me. But now you are."

She'd shot the man in the head as soon as Axel began racing towards them. He'd seen the entire thing.

Arm up.

Finger on the trigger.

BOOM!

"I never wanted you involved, baby. I never wanted you to have blood on your hands, English. I didn't want your goodness ruined. I didn't want you to have to suffer anymore… just be free."

A tear streamed her cheek, and she smiled at him.

"Axel, I was involved the moment he re-entered my life uninvited. There was no turning back."

He leaned in close and kissed her.

"Stay right here," he commanded. She nodded as she got into the passenger's seat of his truck, and began the process of removing her blood-splattered attire, and the bullet proof vest she'd been given.

"You and English good, man?!" Legend yelled out; his guns strapped to his shoulders.

"Yeah! Get out of here, man, before the cops come. I got it from here!"

Legend threw up the deuces, jumped in his truck he'd driven over in, and peeled out of the parking lot blasting Nipsey Hustle's, 'Rap Niggas,' at high volume.

Bleach.

Spray.

No time for a cigarette break.

Scrape, Scrub, and Carry Away.

Contamination Pile…

Incinerate.

They'd chosen this place because it was deserted, and there were no cameras.

He stood over Master's dead body, and resisted the urge to pull out his dick and piss on it. Instead, he reached into his pocket, pulled out a disinfectant wipe, and cleaned up the saliva his baby hawked on his face. No DNA would be left behind.

"You fucked around and found out, didn't you? You sick motherfucker…" He kicked the body. Hard.

Axel made quick work cleaning up the crime scene—dead bodies all around, the smell of fresh blood blended with the night air. He picked up the shell casings, ensuring all evidence that he, Legend and English were even there, was gone. Their alibis were in place, just in case.

Everything will be sterilized.

I'm going to make it seem like it never happened. I am the cleaner. I am the one that washes all the discomfort and devastation away. Clean water. Suds. The smell of a fresh start.

"I am Axel Hendrix. Jack of all trades, MASTER of them all…"

Chapter Twenty-Four

...A few weeks later

"HE AIN'T GOTTA to tell me shit." Legend took a swig of beer and glanced at his cellphone. "It is what it is, man."

Axel sat beside him at the Wright Place, a local biker's bar. Live music was playing, and the vibe was chill.

"It's not that I'm upset about it. I'm concerned. This isn't like him. Caspian should've called me back by now. I'm gettin' married, man. Y'all both are supposed to be my best men. We talked about this when we were kids. We'd always be down for one another. The three Disciples. Just like Ms. Florence called us. Unless one of us dies, it's *always* supposed to be us three against the world."

Legend shook his head, then brought his hands together to give the band a round of applause.

"Legend, I've been meaning to talk to you about a few things." Axel lit a cigarette and hooked gazes with the man.

"Yeah? What's that?"

"First thing is, did you and Caspian have some sort of beef? Usually it was me and you gettin' into it, and he'd be the referee. But now it's like, whenever I bring him up, you seem agitated."

Legend grabbed his beer this time with both hands, and turned his back to the mass of people.

"Nah. We don't have no beef. I just feel like he thinks he's better than us. I feel like that's why he's been ignoring you. I called him too. Same thing happened. Straight to voicemail. The older I've gotten," he paused to scratch his beard, "the more it irks me, you know?" Axel nodded in understanding. "He came from the same dust and dirt as us. He had problems at home, just like we did. He had to be in detention in school, just like we were, and he was mentored by Ms. Florence, just like us, since all three of us were deemed 'at risk teenagers.'" He made air quotes with his fingers.

"Legend, I made a promise to Ms. Florence. I told you mine was to confront my father, and actually listen to what he had to say. To try and work on my relationship with him. She said I'd never be able to listen to him when he was ready to talk, because I was too busy being angry, and that my anger was louder than my healing. So, it couldn't happen because I was comfortable in my anger. I knew my anger was the truth, when really, it was a lie, too. It represented disappointment, hurt, pain.

"She was right. It sounded like some psychobabble at the time, but now I know she was dead on. She said I was going to repeat Tommy's same patterns if I didn't address this, and she wanted better for me. I did go through a brief period when I was drinkin' too much. I didn't have any kids to neglect and lie to, so there's that, but good thing I didn't." He shrugged his shoulders and brought his beer to his lips for a taste. "So, what was your promise to Ms. Florence?"

The band began to play again, this time a cover of 'Pistol Packin' Mama,' by Willie Nelson.

Legend slipped a cigar from his coat, snatched Axel's lighter from the bar counter, and lit it. He puffed on it a few good times, until he was framed by a halo of haze.

"I'm not conversing about this. I'm not talkin' about this shit. Not today. Not tomorrow. Ms. Florence knew what my problem was, and I made that promise to her under duress. My favorite teacher was dyin'… the only adult at the time in this whole fuckin' town who gave a damn about me. Now that I'm an adult, I'd rather be haunted by her for the rest of my life than go back there and talk about things I can't change. It's over. I'm done with it. Drop it."

The man meant every word, and as they sat together in silence, Axel realized that whatever Legend was holding in had to be so overwhelming, he couldn't admit it to his best friend, even if he wanted to. This thing had the power to destroy him. Perhaps it already was.

As the band began to play "Ring of Fire,' by Johnny Cash, he thought about how they hadn't discussed the 'clean up' job of Master. These things happened, and were not to be talked about afterwards. They had an understanding. Their brotherhood renewed. Legend's promise to Ms. Florence, however, would not go away easily. He, too, tried to ignore the nagging feelings, the bad dreams, and paranormal experiences.

I imagine, Ms. Florence, Legend will be a special case. If I knew you well, he thinks he can just walk away from this, but you won't let it happen. Promises were just that to you. You never broke a promise to us. You meant what you said.

"They're playin' Johnny Cash," Legend stated as he bobbed his head. "My grandfather loved Johnny Cash."

"Did you know his first wife was Black? That was illegal back then."

"Nah, I didn't know that." He took another gulp of his beer.

Guess who told me that?" Axel chuckled.

"Little Ms. Know-It-All, the book lady… my future sister-in-law," Legend snorted. "Mmmm, that's good. I wonder how he pulled that shit off?" He drew on his cigar.

"He claimed her as White, even went on record sayin' it. Maybe he thought she was," he shrugged, "But when I saw a picture of the lady English showed me, it was obvious she had some Black in her. I'm no expert, but I could just tell. Her features, you know? He got into it with the KKK about it and everything."

"Ain't that some shit? I'm not into music like that, but I can appreciate the talent, you know?" Axel nodded. "Cash was gifted, no doubt. They couldn't let the man just live his life. Messin' with him about his ol' lady." He tapped his fingers against the bar, and shook his head. "My mama only dated Puerto Ricans, Cubans, and Mexicans. Basically, if you were Hispanic, you were on her radar, but Black and White dudes need not apply." He shrugged. "She is White as hell, blonde and blue-eyed, got my freckles from her, but that's what she wanted. That was her thing," He blew out a ring of smoke. "People like what they like, and that's their business."

"Life is too short to worry about who other people love." He waved the bartender over for another round of beers. "Legend, one more thing before you get so intoxicated, I have to haul you out of here in a wheelbarrow." Axel grinned.

"What is it *now*?"

Axel dragged his phone out of his pocket, and pulled up an article dated two days prior.

"Read that."

He handed Legend the phone, and the man's eyes scanned the lines, showing no reaction. He casually handed the phone back, and polished off his beer.

"Well? You want to explain this?"

Legend was quiet for a bit, then began drinking from his new, ice-cold bottle.

"Explain what?" he finally asked.

"Don't fuck around with me. What the article says, motherfucker, is that the head guy is dead. Cymone Louis. The head honcho. You know when I called you that day, after I ran into a couple of his friends…" He narrowed his eyes on the man. "All of a sudden, the drive-bys past my house have stopped. The strange calls. People askin' about me that I don't know. It's all done. I've been dealing with bullshit from that for a minute now. I've had to become calculated and colder than ever, they forced my hand, but

I just figured I'd be fightin' for a while, watching my back until the big chief came to try and take me out himself."

Legend cocked his head to the side and smoke purled from his mouth.

"That's why you asked English to marry you, didn't you? You didn't know how much time you had left?"

"I asked her to marry me because I love her, man. I want her to be my wife. I want a family. I want the shit I never saw growin' up. The American dream."

Legend rolled his eyes.

"We're all on borrowed time," Axel continued. "I go to work and remember that. I have no choice but for it to be stained on my brain, as though written in blood. The message is loud and clear. I see death every day." He pointed to his eye. "It speaks to me when the family members race in, get in the way, and cry to me, beside themselves with grief. They just start talking, and won't stop." He pointed to his mouth. "I hear death every time I open my eyes, and especially when I close them…" He pointed to his ears. "I hear the evil. The agony. The hurt.

"I need some normalcy, Legend. Ain't nothin' normal about having to take a slew of motherfuckers out. But it was either them or me. I chose life. Mine. Normalcy is peace." He placed his hand over his heart. "English is my peace, man. She's the first note and last lyric of my favorite song. She's my sunrise when it's raining on the *inside* of me. Nah, man… I didn't want to marry her because I'm afraid time will run out. I asked her to marry me because time without her is just not worth livin', and I need every day, from this moment forward, to count."

"That's some beautiful, poetic bullshit, Thor," Legend's eyes grew dark and jaded as he cocked a half smile. "I like it though. You should write corny ass greeting cards on the side, or some shit."

He wasn't certain if Legend had ever been in love since their high school days. Or if he even knew how to love someone anymore. If that was true, he hoped he'd learn again. Love was the only thing that made life worth living, and he wanted him to have a piece of what he had—someone to center him, make him feel alright when the world got too dark.

"This article," Axel held up his phone and waved it, "the man running the show, who wanted me gone, is gone himself now. I imagine there's chaos in his circle. Things must be volatile. I don't know these people, but you did, at least through conversation and association. You used to be a big player in the dope game." Legend looked off into the distance, as if he didn't hear him talking. "I know all about it. Your reputation proceeds you, bro."

All he got was a smirk from his friend.

"You haven't been out of town, man. You've been right here with me. These bastards are in Texas. You've got some serious influence, even after all of this time, to be able to pull this off. I want to know how you did it? I know you're behind it, Legend. I can see it in your eyes."

Legend casually drank from his beer once again, then gave a big applause and whistle as another song ended. Removed the ball cap from his head, he placed it gingerly on the bar counter, exposing jet black waves.

"As honest as you are, Axel, and I admire that about

you, even *you* have secrets. Things only *you* know. You don't need to know how I got them off your back, man." He took another puff of his cigar. "None of that matters. Just be grateful." He turned away.

"It matters to *me*." Axel yanked his shoulder, forcing him to face him again. "I want to thank you for helping me not be in a position where I have to keep—"

"I don't want praise. I don't even care about acknowledgement. I don't want any money, no more charity… all I want, Axel, is your friendship. Your time, man. You're my brother. At the end of the day, if the roles were reversed, you would have done the same thing for me. I *had* to do something. You know how that story would end. You would have had to keep takin' them out, and things would have gotten worse and worse for you. They didn't know you or understand who they were dealin' with at first. They mistook you for a pussy. A lame. A square. Nobody thought a guy like you, who looks so pristine on paper, would be out here murkin' mothafuckas. You surprised the hell out of them. It pissed them off. They wasn't ready… But even mothafuckas like us end up meeting our match eventually, man. Prison or death. Bars or caskets. You know that. I know that."

"I 'spose I do know that Legend, but I was prepared to fight until the bitter end."

"Ultimately, the men who wanted to rush your expiration date, could have done one of two things, Axel. Let the shit go, because something far more serious is at their doorstep and you're no longer seen as a threat, or they up the ante. These weren't the type of mothafuckas to let shit go. I can promise you that." Smolder curled from both sides of his mouth. "They would've kept at you, picking and picking, until you were dead. They would have eventually caught you slippin'. It may not have been this year, next year, or even five years from now, but it would have happened, because now, your guard is down. You've fucked around and fell in love." He smiled at him faintly.

"What does that have to do with anything?"

"That makes us weak, man. Being in love with a woman weakens our defenses. Love makes us less cautious because we're too busy tryna make a woman happy, put her on a pedestal, satisfy her in every way possible, so we can't see the forest for the trees. We're distracted." He chuckled. "The sweet smell along her neck… the soft titties… the wet pussy… the round ass… the curves… the feminine voice… the nurturing… the tender kisses… the warm hugs… just her entire persona can ruin a mothafucka. She's our rib, man. Ain't no escaping that. You ever had a broken rib, man? That shit hurts! English, by no fault of her own, would have been your blessin' and your downfall, if this continued. I like her, don't get me wrong. It's nothing personal. I think she's good for you, but she has that power over you now. It's hers for the taking."

"This isn't about her."

"Yes it is, man. Women make us vulnerable. It starts with our mamas." He held up one finger. "No matter how close we are to our fathers, our mothers have this strange hold over us, and you know it. Even if we hate that bitch who brought us into the world, we still love her on some level, and want her approval. It's insane. Even killas who kill their own mothers, these psycho mothafuckas you see on these crime shows, wished that their mothers would have been different, man. Loved 'em harder…

"They *always* bring up their moms. Women make us feel shit that we ain't ever felt before. They make us less hard. They manipulate us just with a glance. Pussy is our demise, and you need to own that fact, but nobody, including me, is willing to give it up. It's a drug. These women in this world will make us open up and spill our guts. It's not safe to be the hunter *and* the prey, man, when you're in love."

"You sound fuckin' ridiculous, Legend. I don't care who I'm with, I'd never let my guard down when I know some folks around me ain't movin' right. I didn't before I met her, and I wouldn't *now*."

"Really?" Legend smiled real slick like, and laughed. "You let your guard down when you flushed our original plan to get rid of Master down the toilet, and let her come into the game to play. She was *never* supposed to be involved. You let your guard down when you buckled under the pressure, man, and told her what was up—something you'd never do. You gave her the blueprint to something she had no right to even build."

"That's bullshit! That wasn't me letting my guard down. I was—"

"You were listening to your dick and your heart, instead of your brain. That's what the fuck you were doing, all because you wanted her to feel okay about it." He sucked his teeth. "This isn't a judgment, chill man, it's just the truth! You allowed her to play a role, a game, with a deranged mothafucka, knowin' that if she didn't pull that trigger right then and there, she'd be forced to witness you pump lead in him like it was for sport." He pointed at his face. "I saw you, mothafucka… that look in your eyes, and your gun aimed right at the back of his head. One second of hesitation on her part, you would've wasted his ass. Both of us knew he wasn't getting out of this alive. He'd crossed the line years ago. Why do you think I yelled for her to do it right then? To shoot him? I knew in my heart it would've been easier for her to kill that mothafucka than live with the knowledge that *you* did it for her. I knew you were strugglin' with this shit, man. You didn't want her to be like us! To end up with that on her conscience. She's not from our world. Our way of life."

"You're damn straight she's not, but she's not no delicate little flower, either. I am the one who watched her when she had nightmares about him! The way she screamed and scratched at the air, as though she was tearing his eyes outta his skull. I am the one that stopped her from shootin' all of her windows out because she was certain he was right outside of her house. Once English makes up her mind about something, that's it, and if you're lucky enough to find a woman half as good as her, then I think you'll understand why there was a change of plans, you son of a bitch! You don't know the half of it. This is MY woman, I took her feelings into consideration, and I did what was best!"

"EXACTLY! You did that shit for love, and it could have cost you everything!"

They were in each other's faces now, nostrils flared, darkened eyes. Legend took a deep breath, and settled down first. "Everyone knows you're a straight shooter, Axel, in more ways than one. Even in all of that commotion, you would have hit your target blindfolded. We risked our lives unnecessarily, just because you wanted to make English happy. She endangered us by just being there! Our original plan was airtight. Man, I'm on your side. I'm just trying to make you see that love changes people!" Axel sighed and turned away. "She said she wanted in on this, and to do it herself, and you let her do it. You couldn't say no to her. Once our heart is involved, it's a wrap. Don't get mad at me for speaking honestly." He chuckled mirthlessly. "It's happened to the best of us. LOVE'S GONNA GET YOU! AND IT *GOT* YOU! Church!"

"That's it. Stop fucking talking about her. My question to you had nothin' to do with her. All I wanted to do, Legend, was acknowledge what you did. You saved me some time and—"

"Cool. You've acknowledged it. Anyway, you testifying would have destroyed these guys. You already knew that. They had to get you out of the way. This White man of upstanding character… career man… owns property… real estate… clean record… takes care of his mama, and now, has a pretty little thing on his arm." Legend said the words with a tinge of animosity and resentment. "They didn't stand a chance. On paper, you look like a pillar of society. They would have been servin' life behind bars because of you. That threat was real. You're a shark, man, but you don't swim in my ocean. The murky, dark, nasty body of water, filled with blood."

His eyes sheened. "You clean them oceans instead by eating everything in sight. You piss bleach and peroxide. Sparkling, like a diamond…" He jammed his cigar in the ashtray, extinguishing the flame. "No worries, brother." He shrugged. "I did what had to be done. Just consider it an early wedding gift, and drop this shit. *All* of it. Let's both move on. Next round of beers is on me…"

…One year later

THE OLD FARMHOUSE was decorated in white lights, and people were gathered from all over the state of Kentucky to witness their special day. Axel stood in his black tuxedo, his hair pulled and braided all the way down his back. A Black hairstylist English had hired had done it for him, as well as threaded his braid with white and black ribbons. He'd been staunchly against the idea initially as it seemed womanlike, especially when the stylist started trying to give him these little hair swoop things called baby hairs. He quickly made her undo them, but now, as he looked in the mirror at himself, he could see she'd done a mighty fine job.

He stood beside an open barn door, one of three being used as a changing room, while English was on the other side of the property, out of sight. He was surrounded by friends and family, employees and the like, and people he hadn't seen in a mighty long time—thanks to Dallas and Mama inviting everyone they knew and exploding their guest list. He reached for his cellphone when it buzzed in his pocket.

"Yeah?"

"Today's yer weddin' day?"

"You know it is. And you're not here. Tammy is, though. I guess she can pretend to be you if I shove a beer can in her hand, she starts cursin' out the reverend, then blacks out. Won't make a damn bit of difference."

"I'm on my way. I drank too much last night, son. I was sick is all. You know my health has been failin'. I wouldn't not show up for your weddin', Axel. Come on… please don't think that."

"Don't drive. I'll call you an Uber or something." He got ready to hang up.

"Naw, I ain't been drinkin' this mornin', boy. I pushed through, promised Tammy I'd stay dry. I don't want to ruin your day. I know you think I don't approve of you marrying that girl, but—"

"Tommy, I really don't give a shit about your approv-al."

"Now you don't have to go gettin' all upset and your briefs all in a bunch!"

"I'm not upset. I'm not angry with you anymore. We've gotten past that. This is who you are. I accept you for who you are and expect little, but appreciate any positive things you do or say, all the same. I love ya, Daddy, as God is my witness, but your approval is the last thing I search for, all right? And just in case you're confused about how serious I am, as much as I love Mama, even *her* disapproval wouldn't have mattered, or stopped me from making this woman my wife. Ya hear me?"

"I hear you, but that ain't the reason I—"

"You've got some nerve. It cuts both ways. English's parents, especially her father, wasn't too keen on me at first, either, though he didn't say it. He was polite when we first met, but had some reservations. I could read between the lines. English didn't care about that, just like I didn't. It was because of the color of my skin. You see how ridiculous that sounds? Someone was judging *your* son for the *same* unfair reason you judge others. Me and her father are fine now, though. We're fishin' buddies when I head out that way, and we have a good ol' time. He treats me like his flesh 'nd blood son now.

"It's a hurdle. Racism and prejudice don't happen in no bubble. I had some of it too growin' up around you and others… just regurgitating what I was hearing around me from you and your friends. The evil of it all. I didn't know no better, but Mama corrected me right fast and in a hurry once she heard me say something awful that she didn't approve of. I was only like six or seven, talkin' like that. Daddy, you have to build a relationship with folks, and stop judging books by their cover. It's sickening how we are in modern times, and folks are *still* carrying on about mess like this! It's fuckin' stupid."

"I've been around longer than you, Axel. You're still young. I've seen some things that Black folks do. Not all of 'em… but enough of 'em."

"And you've seen White folks do some fucked up shit, too, and yet you keep extending the olive branch. Don't matter the color of the person. There's people of every race that ain't shit. It ain't got nothin' to do with race. It has to do with character."

"Well, I agree with you 'bout that. I'm sure there's some mighty fine folks that are Black."

"One day, you'll have more grandkids, Daddy. I 'magine Dallas will get married and have another baby or two, and I plan to have some, too. The ones from me and your daughter-in-law won't be lily white. They'll be half Black. And they'll know it. And they'll be proud about it. They'll know *both* sides of their family, with or without you. They'll be content. Well fed. Clothed, and most importantly, loved. Their father will be in their life, 'cause ain't nothin' or nobody gonna stand between me and my children. Not no drugs. No alcohol. No job. Not a motherfuckin' thing. Tellin' them the truth is how I'll show love, too… being my authentic fucked up self, in all my glory!"

"But a child should stay in a child's place."

"And an adult should train up their child in the way in which he should go."

His father was quiet on the other end for a spell.

"I didn't call you to put a damper on your day, son. I ain't callin' to guilt you, or make you do somethin' you don't want to do, either. I wasn't raised around that sort of thing is all. It's different to me. I'm old school, but I'm tryin', son." Axel took a deep breath. "Dallas told me English is a real nice lady, and they get along plenty. I'm trying… be patient with me…"

Axel sighed, closed his eyes, and ran his hand down

his face in frustration.

"I'm pitiful, I know." Dad laughed sadly. "I know I disappoint you often. I want you happy, son, and if this gal makes you happy, then I'm going to show up, sober, and be there for you and her. You asked me to come to yer weddin', and come hell or high water, I'm comin'. Tammy told me it's never too late to try 'nd be a good dad to you and Dallas. I reckon she's right. I got a bit of the shakes, not used to not drinkin' first thing in the morning, but I'll be okay. I'll be there soon, ya hear? Don't you fret. I love you." Daddy's voice cracked, and he could tell the old man was crying when the phone call suddenly ended.

Axel stared at his phone for a moment, then slipped it into his dress pant pocket. Legend and a few of his employees were walking about in the near distance, all of them dressed in black tuxedos and camouflage printed ties, just like him.

Alan Jackson's, 'Country Boy' played through large speakers. He stepped out of the small barn and spotted his mother sitting with Dallas and his nephew, and several of their cousins. On the other side sat English's family—a whole slew of them. Some lady with pink and yellow hair stuck out like a sore thumb, waving a fan in her face. As he was taking it all in, he heard something. The snap of a branch. He turned fast and caught English with her dress hiked up, running to another barn.

"Oh no you don't! Get back here! I see you!"

No one seemed to notice as he made a mad dash towards her, catching up fast.

"Busted! You were lookin' at me!" He laughed as he

held her close and lavished her with kisses.

"You weren't supposed to be outside either until they called!" She laughed. "Oh, God…" She looked at him with tears in her eyes. "You look so handsome, Axel."

"Don't get to cryin'. I clean up nice is all." *I'm a hypocrite. I'm the one about to start ballin'…* "800, shit… you look so beautiful, baby. Like a princess." He looked around, then pressed her against the barn wall, crushing her lips in a kiss.

"You've messed up my lipstick, Axel! Now I've got to reapply it." She said the words like she was angry, but sported a big smile. Grabbing her wrist, he pushed the old barn door open. Nothing was inside but a few bales of hay. *Perfect.* He dragged her in. "What are you doing?!"

Hoisting her high, he set her down on a bale of hay and yanked her dress up to around her waist.

"Axel! No! Axel! AXEL!"

"Come on, now, girl! It won't take long. Don't lie and tell me you don't want me. Don't tell me you didn't think about me fucking you all night… making you cum all over my dick. Did you hump your pillow and pretend it was me? I know you missed this mouth and this dick, baby."

"Shit! I did! But we can't do this right now, baby. We don't have time for this. I've got on Spanx! This hourglass shape took me twenty minutes to form!"

"What does a damn girdle have to do with me? It's not blockin' your cookie, so I don't care!"

She began to play fight and struggle with him. He blocked her blows.

"I'm gettin' some of this pussy *right* now, so stop it.

You're wasting time! Come on and let me get up in that peach!"

Just then, he noticed something peculiar. Something handy…

"What are you doing, Axel?"

Ignoring the question, he grasped a short pole, a tool probably used to flip hay around. Both ends were dull, with rubber stoppers. He smirked at her.

"You're going to keep your legs open for me right now, and all night long after we say our 'I dos'. I'm gonna make sure of it, 800. Spread 'em!"

Ripping her panties down her legs, he tossed them aside, then jammed the pole horizontally between her knees, right behind where he stood, using it as a spreader to keep her legs wide open, just where he wanted them. Undoing his belt and unzipping his pants, he yanked his rock hard, ravenous dick out the slit of his black boxers. It was already dripping with precum. Her thigh high white stockings and the helpless look in her eyes as he roughed her up sent him over the edge.

"Look at that soppin' wet poon." He bit his lower lip, salivating at the sight. "All open, pink and warm, and drippin' wet, just for me. This is going to be fast and furious… I offer my sincerest apologies to your pussy in advance."

"Oh my God! Ahhh!" She bit into his shoulder as he drove himself deep inside of her, pumping hard and fast within her wet valley with all the strength he had. They held onto one another tight, foreheads pressed together, moaning and sighing, as he rocked in and out of her.

"Ahhh! Ahhh!" They came quickly at the same time, falling apart against one another. The next few moments were spent with them racing against the clock, trying to get dressed and look presentable.

"Do I have any more hay on my gown, Axel? Check!" she asked frantically as she spun around.

He brushed his hand against her ass, removing one tiny piece that was missed.

"All gone." He gave her a quick peck on the lips before hurrying towards the barn door to leave. "I love you," he whispered before heading out, fixing his pants as he hightailed it back to the other barn, prepared to pretend he hadn't just gotten a pre-wedding sample. He was still a little hard, and hoped it didn't show too much in his pants. When he arrived at the barn he was supposed to be waiting at, he stopped dead in his tracks. There, by the door, stood Legend… right next to Caspian. Transfixed, he struggled to complete the task of fixing his belt.

"Your fiancée called me," Caspian offered with a faint smile. He was dressed in a tuxedo and camouflage tie, just like the rest of them, looking tall, dapper and well put together. "She wanted it to be a surprise. Axel. We need to talk." He exhaled, looking forlorn. "I wasn't ignoring you. There was—"

"Let's talk about this later," Legend interrupted. "They need us in place."

"I'm just glad you're here, brother." Axel grabbed him, wrapped his arms around him tight, and squeezed. As the three of them began to walk, Legend pulled his shoulder back, making Axel halt while Caspian kept going for a bit, then waited for them.

"Here, take this tissue. You've got lipstick on your mouth," he whispered to him.

"Oh." Axel quickly took the Kleenex and patted his lips.

"And you smell a little bit like sex. You were just fuckin', huh? Tell English I'm down for a threesome, or we can just leave yo' ass outside for a few minutes if she'd prefer."

Axel, without thought, punched him in the shoulder with brute force. Legend rocked off his feet, howled, then laughed loudly, all while holding his arm as if he'd been shot.

"Damn, man! Don't shoot the messenger. Ain't shit we can do about that right now, playa. I was just kidding about the threesome."

"Sure you were…"

"Seems you were a busy beaver today. Literally."

They both burst out laughing as they made their way towards the minister, and the ceremony finally began.

After a few words from the minister, the bridal party came down. English's sister was her matron of honor, and Melanie her maid of honor. All of the women, some Black, some White, some Hispanic and Asian, a rainbow of ladies, were dressed in purple and white satin gowns.

Then, everyone stood as English walked down the aisle with her father to the sounds of Avant's 'You & I,' featuring KeKe Wyatt. English's hair was curled to look like jet black roses in a bouquet—it was the damnedest thing he'd ever seen, matching her beauty to a 'T'. Out of the corner of his eye, he noticed his father finally arrive, and take his seat.

English floated towards him like some angel in a dream, just like she had once he realized he had fallen so hard for her, there was no turning back.

Traditional, Christian vows… Tears and applause… He kept his words short, but his heart was beating damn near out of his chest every time he had to open his mouth. The intensity of his emotions at times failed him. He had to dab at his eyes a couple of times, just to make it through. People kept staring at English. She was breathtaking. He knew then that Legend had been half right. English weakened him—she did have a hold on him—but she gave him strength, too.

"You may kiss the bride!" the minister announced when all was said and done.

Axel stared at her, his lips quivering and tears stinging his eyes once again. He died a little with embarrassment when he heard people saying, 'Awww,' at his reaction. But that was okay, in the scheme of things. Wrapping his arms around her waist, he drew her close and gave her their first kiss as husband and wife…

Epilogue

...One year later

"HUH, BABY?" AXEL made his way inside the house, looking forward to watching a bit of baseball. The Cincinnati Reds were playing. He hoped he wouldn't get a work call in the middle of the game. That had been happening a lot lately.

"I said I'm going to lie down. I'm not feeling too well."

"What's wrong?" He locked the side door, then found her in the kitchen with a bottle of Pepto Bismol, and a woeful frown on her face. She ran her hand over her stomach and shook her head.

"I just keep feeling queasy today. I stayed home and worked from here instead."

"I'm sorry, baby." He kissed the top of her head. "I wish there was something I could do. As far as you working from home today, I told you that it's too close to your delivery date to be goin' to work full time right now anyway. The baby is making you sick again. My mama said

I did the same to her, even after birth. In fact, she said I made her sick just yesterday."

English burst out laughing.

"I'm going to lie down, Axel." She kissed his lips, and he smacked her rear end as she turned to head up the steps.

They were enjoying their new house in Lexington, not terribly far from where they were before. It was spacious, fairly new, had good bones and curb appeal. After washing his hands, he opened the refrigerator and pulled out a beer, then made his way to the living room, sighing with relief. It felt good to be home after working for over twelve hours straight.

Reaching for the remote, he switched on the television to watch the game. A commercial was on. His mind wandered, so he set down his beer and reached for some paperwork English had asked him to fill out for the hospital maternity ward that he'd been putting off. Just then, a white feather fell to the wooden floor, as if it had been stuck to the papers. He stared at it for the longest, his heart beating faster, then put the paperwork down beside him, picked it up, and twirled the thing between his fingers.

The dreams of Ms. Florence had stopped. He didn't want them, but once they disappeared, he wished he still had them. There was something comforting about her presence. About the promise, too.

Ms. Florence, I'd like a word with you… I thanked you after I had that fight with my father, the one that opened the door for communication. I thanked you on the first day of my honeymoon, with my bride. Watchin' the sunrise from our cruise ship. I've told English more than once that I believe in my heart of hearts, you brought us together. I couldn't have fulfilled my promise without her… I needed that encouragement. I needed someone to help steer me back on the right path. I think you knew that. If you're still around, and something tells me you are, despite the dreams no longer comin', I know you understand I have a child 'bout to come into the world. We found out a few months ago that it's a boy.

It's the scariest, yet most exciting thing I've ever experienced. This is the first baby for both of us, and we were taken by surprise. We sure didn't plan this, but we know that was God's plan all the same, and we're so happy. Thank you, Ms. Florence, for coming into my life again, in your own special way. Thank you for believing in me. My father and I are still workin' on our relationship. It's difficult, but much better. I wish he'd go to a detox program, and he said he just might, but seeing is believing. Dallas met a guy from Frankfort that seems to have his wits about him. I hope it goes well. Lucas needs more good male role models. It's been a rough and strange last few years, but I survived with help from my family, my wife, and my brothers, Legend and Caspian…

Legend is struggling emotionally. He's doing fine vocationally, and I gave him a promotion. Honestly, he could probably start his own company now doing the same thing, but this isn't his passion. He's an amazing man, my best friend, but he's shut down on the inside. He keeps me at arm's length if the conversation starts getting too personal or serious. I love my brother, and I hate how he is being right now, but I know I was the same way. It'll take some time. I haven't asked him in a long while if he's dreamt of you again, but I believe he has. He's haunted, and will continue to be until he does what he promised you. I know how this works. The journey continues until the job is complete.

Caspian is struggling too, and I don't know exactly with what. He calls now, but the conversations are meaningful, but brief. I brought you and your promises up to him, and he acted like he didn't know what I was talking about. I don't believe him. I know that man like the back of my hand, and no time and distance can erase that. Just because my part in this is over, that doesn't mean you're finished with me. You came to me first, with a mission. You knew I'd get everyone together. That I'd lead by example. English got Caspian for me—she's an extension of me. We're truly one. That lady is my heart and soul, but this next part, she can't do. It's up to me. Please help me help my brothers, Ms. Florence. I'm ready. I can handle it…

He looked out a large floor to ceiling window, and smiled when he saw his neighbors' horses frolicking about.

There's beauty in the simple things of life. Sometimes you can hold your blessings, like a new baby, but sometimes you can't, like an invisible visitor that shakes up your dream world, in order to make your life stable again. I've struggled most of my life with one thing or another. It's been an uphill battle for me, but that's just it. It was a battle, and I made it. Only the strong survive. I have to be that leader, that foundation, that strength. For my mama. My wife. My sister. My nephew. My father. My employees. And now, my son…

A new life is comin' into the world. One that me and my sweetheart created, out of love. In a way, I was reborn, too. Legend and Caspian will have to endure the same. Pain is what brought me and my brothers together– but love is what reunited us. It was a promise…one of three…

One made during death, to give us a new life.

Here I was, battling men that just kept coming after me, one after another… just like my problems with my father. You said I had to cut the problem off at the head. You said you stop a train by slamming on the brakes, not trying to wrangle the caboose off the track. Legend cut the head off the cobra on my behalf, and I slammed on the brakes, and listened to my father. I finally heard him, the truth this time around, once and for all.

Master tried to shut out the world around English… tried to make her not hear the reality of his manipulations and abuse. But she woke up and heard the truth. Mama heard the cries of her children, and did what she needed to do to protect us, including kicking out a man she loved to the bottom of her soul. Daddy didn't listen to good advice, and instead tried to force others, including me, to hear what he wanted us to hear… Lies that hurt. Lies that destroyed.

I heard no evil for a long time, but that didn't stop it from talkin'. It caught up with me, and made me listen all the same. The evil was dripping in alcohol. Covered in cigarette ashes. It was laced with drugs I didn't deal, money I didn't steal, but plenty of people I did in fact kill… But the evil wasn't just inside of my enemies, and my daddy. It was in me, too. It's been a part of me all along.

Legend sees no evil, but he'll be forced to remove his blinders, just like the horses out there runnin' around, to finally see his pain for what it is. Something he saw must've spooked him for life, and as tough and rough as he is, he'll have to face his fears eventually, and look them dead in the eye if he ever wants to be free. Legend will be ready to see whatever is distressing him in due time. The good, the bad, and the ugly.

Caspian speaks no evil—he barely talks to us, even after the wedding. He was friendly enough, hung out and acted jovial, and we've kept in contact, but something is bothering him. Something is on his mind. Something has him by the tongue, but he must fight it, and let his words finally be heard.

I'm ready to listen. To hear his pain.

That's who we are, the Brothers' Disciples. Three of the worst kids in school, who found solidarity in one another. We promised to always be there for one another, because at one point in time, we were all we had.

Now, the tribe is back together, and I'll be damned if we don't fulfill our promises. I'm leading the charge. No man will be left behind…

Axel reached for the Bible on the table, shoving his pack of Nicotine patches out of the way, and flipped to the scripture he read at least once a month…

> *Psalm 23:1–6 4 Yea, though I walk through the valley of the shadow of death, I will fear no evil: for thou art with me; thy rod and thy staff they comfort me.*

And that's on everything, Ms. Florence…

As Legend always says when he thinks somethin' is mighty true… CHURCH!

Love is a battlefield…

I'm in my armor, and prepared for war.

Free my brethren with two more promises fulfilled!

LET'S GO!

~The End~

MUSIC PLAYLIST

1. Mention of artist, Yelawolf
2. mndsgn – Rare Pleasure
3. Moneybagg Yo' – See Wat I'm Sayin'
4. Machine Gun Kelly – Bloody Valentine
5. Jack Harlow – Churchill Downs
6. Jack Harlow – Like A Blade Of Grass
7. Juvenile – Rodeo
8. Queen – Another One Bites the Dust
9. Paul McCartney – Let 'Em In
10. The Hollies – Long Cool Woman
11. Temple Of The Dog – Hunger Strike
12. Weezer's version of Metallica – Enter Sandman
13. Crew – Goldlink
14. Aesop Rock – Long Legged Larry
15. Mac Miller – Good News
16. Cool Heat – Bad Dream
17. Joan Jett – I Love Rock and Roll
18. Mention of, Nickelback's 'Rockstar'
19. Bruno Mars – Lazy Song
20. Conan Gray – Disaster
21. Al B. Sure – Nite and Day

22. Maze and Frankie Beverly – Happy Feelins
23. Chris Brown – WE
24. TEMS – Higher
25. Steve Lacy – Dark Red
26. Chris Brown – Call Me Every Day
27. Justin Bieber – Peaches (featuring Daniel Caesar and Giveon)
28. Giveon – Heartbreak Anniversary
29. Nashvillains – Chickasaw Bayou
30. Niko Moon – Good Time
31. Bailey Zimmerman – Fall In Love
32. Dolly Parton – Jolene
33. Double – Captain of her Heart
34. Emawk – ACHE
35. Juice Newton – Angel of the Morning
36. New Order – Blue Monday
37. Michael Jackson – Chicago
38. Culture Club – Time
39. Billy Idol – Eyes Without a Face
40. New Order – Bizarre Love Triangle
41. The Cure – Just Like Heaven
42. Plains – Problem With It
43. Gnarls Barkley – Crazy
44. Daryl Hall & John Oates – I Can't Go for That
45. Christopher Cross – Ride Like the Wind
46. Joe Jackson – Steppin' Out
47. Patsy Cline – Blue Moon of Kentucky

48. Apalachee Don – Eagles
49. Djo – Roddy
50. The Flamingos – I Only Have Eyes for You
51. Tommy James and the Shondell's – Crystal Blue Persuasion
52. Tommy James – Crimson and Clover
53. Mazzy Star – Fade into You
54. John Cale – Night Crawling
55. Nipsey Hustle – Rap Niggas
56. Willie Nelson – Pistol Packin' Mama
57. Johnny Cash – Ring of Fire
58. Alan Jackson – Country Boy
59. Avant – You & I (featuring KeKe Wyatt)

ABOUT THE AUTHOR

USA Today bestselling author Tiana Laveen writes resilient yet loving heroines and the alpha heroes that fall for them in unlikely happy-ever-afters. An author of over 60 novels to date, Tiana creates characters from all walks of life that leap straight from the pages into your heart.

Married with two children, she enjoys a fulfilling life that includes writing books, drawing, and spending quality time with loved ones.

If you wish to communicate with Tiana Laveen and stay up-to-date with her releases, please follow her on social media platforms as well as visit her website.

Tiana Laveen website

www.tianalaveen.com

OTHER BOOKS ALSO BY TIANA LAVEEN

https://www.tianalaveen.com/books.html

1. The Saint Series
2. The Zodiac Series (Capricorn – Sagittarius) 12 stand-alone books
3. The Race to Redemption Series: The 'N Word and Word of Honor
4. Black Ice
5. Fire and Rain
6. Here Comes the Judge
7. The Viper and His Majesty
8. Gumbo
9. Savage
10. The Fight Within

AND MANY MORE!

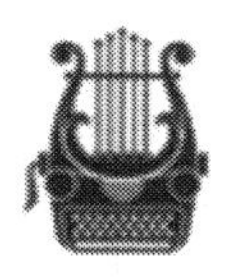

Made in United States
Orlando, FL
06 September 2022

22057437R00262